A drunk, an addict, a murderer, a mercenary, a psychopath, a tycoon, and a desparate young archaeologist walk into a mysteriously abandoned seaside manor...

THE
ACCURSED
HUNTSMAN

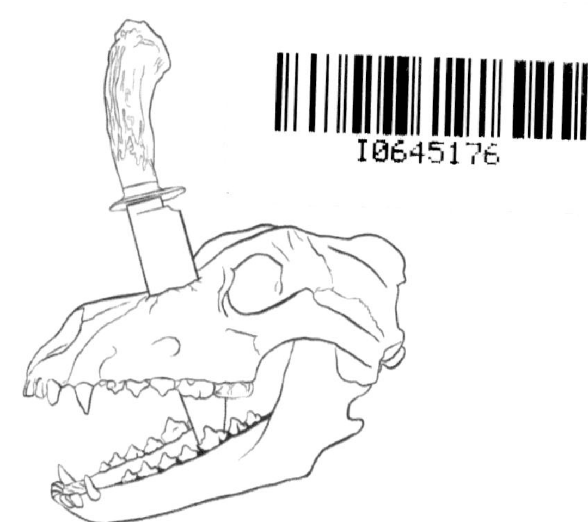

Douglass Hoover

www.blackpitpublishing.com

Published by
BlackPit Publishing Group
BlackPitPublishing.com

ISBN 978-0-9994074-9-3

Printed in the USA

*"What you seek you shall never find.
For when the Gods made man,
They kept immortality to themselves."*
— *Epic of Gilgamesh*

"Personally, I would not care for immortality in the least. There is nothing better than oblivion, since in oblivion there is no wish unfulfilled. We had it before we were born yet did not complain. Shall we whine because we know it will return? It is Elysium enough for me, at any rate."
— *H.P. Lovecraft*

PROLOGUE

Somewhere in Montana

THE DARKNESS was coming fast.

The sun had already dipped beyond the horizon of mountain peaks that crowned the valley. They stood jagged and half melted against the bruised sky. Through the haze of the drizzling snow, the distant stone behemoths glared down on him — obscure sentries of hell watching in apathetic silence as he fought to make his escape.

Jack Steward ignored their piercing gaze, thrusting a numb foot forward, then the other. There was no pain in them anymore. All feeling below his knees had melted away hours before. The only pain he felt now was the burning muscles of his upper thighs and the acute aching that erupted from beneath the rope tied across his chest. He didn't have to look to know that the skin under his jacket bore a bloodied stripe where the tight paracord harness rubbed.

It didn't matter, he thought. Soon enough, that would all be numb too.

His foot came down awkwardly, skittering along one of the ice-coated stones that littered the mountainside, and he stumbled.

"No, Sam, no, I'm alright," he mumbled to the mound of cheap winter layers and frozen flesh behind him.

But he knew Sam hadn't said anything. Perhaps some repressed part of him suspected Sam was already dead. The pathetic whimpers that had emanated from the makeshift stretcher had grown faint miles back. Now, besides the howl of the wind and the scrape of the stretcher against the frozen pass, there was silence.

"I gotcha, bud," Jack went on through chattering teeth, righting himself and struggling forward against the weight of the harness. "We're gonna get you home, don't you worry…"

He pushed forward, the narrowing channel of his sanity focusing entirely on maintaining his shambling march.

Time began to lose its grip on the world. The concept of hours and minutes and seconds dissolved into the frozen air, replaced only by the rhythmic crunch of boots in snow and rasping, desperate breaths.

He didn't register the shift in light as the dark blue glow of evening froze over into a blackened, star-speckled sky. Soon it was only the crescent moon and its eerie reflection off the icy snow that illuminated his staggering path.

But the obscurity of his route didn't matter to what little sense of reason he had left; he had no idea where he was going anymore. South had been their initial target. According to the map, there was a ranger station to the south… but they had used the map — along with the last handful of dollars and receipts in their wallets — as tinder the night before.

All he could do now was keep moving.

The cold sliver of moon rose higher and higher in the sky, watching Jack struggle onward, waiting patiently for him to succumb to the frozen wind.

But the moon wasn't the only thing watching him.

Waiting.

The first howl was distant. Distant, yet terrifying clear.

The wolf's unearthly song floated through the night. It cut through Jack's trudging footsteps, through the thick parka's hood, and echoed through his half-awake mind for a moment before it pierced the fog.

"Shit." The frozen skin tore from his lips as he cracked them apart for the first time in hours. "Sam, Sam! They're back!" The words burned his throat as he spun around to the dark mass he'd been towing. "Sam, the rifle!"

He clumsily fumbled in the dark for the .308 Ruger that he'd strapped to the sled alongside Sam. The rifle was gone, and he didn't have to think hard to realize it must have slipped off some time ago along the trail.

Another howl, this one closer.

Much closer.

Jack tried to yell, but the frozen air caught in his throat, drawing only a gagging cough. Sam lay stiff and silent in the moonlight.

"Sam!" Jack tried again, this time getting out a hoarse shout.

A rolling growl filtered through the tree line a dozen yards away.

"Sam, we need to run!" Jack begged, shaking the body violently. "Get up, damnit, get up!"

There was no response, and for the first time since the night before, Jack peeled back the fur-lined hood that covered Sam's eyes. The face that stared back at him glistened with a waxy sheen. Its once vibrant eyes now vacant and glassed over by a thin crust of ice.

Jack fell back and heaved, vomiting a burning line of bile. He had only a second before the throaty growl from the surrounding darkness forced his eyes back up to meet Sam's. The lifeless orbs stared straight through his soul.

A bitter gust of wind swept through the valley. It stung his face and dusted Sam's face with a powdering of fine snow. The white specs didn't melt, instead clinging to the dead flesh of his best friend's cheeks.

Deep inside of Jack, something snapped. The last dam of hope that had once stood in his mind had now reached its breaking point. Now, the thousands of thin cracks that spiderwebbed across the dam's surface began to rupture, and the horrifying waves of reality began to leak through.

Some ancient chemical mechanism in his brain raced to patch the growing tear in his sanity — this corpse wasn't Sam. It couldn't be. Sam was fine. He was still alive and they'd be back at school, back at their dorm room drinking beer and talking about girls and…

The dead eyes stared through him, screaming the truth.

No.

It couldn't be true.

This *thing* wasn't Sam. It was something else, some horrible wax effigy bearing Sam's semblance—

The growl came louder, stealing Jack's thoughts.

He grasped what had been their last hope — a road flare they had saved to signal for help — and struggled to uncap its striker with his numb fingers. A shadow darted through the moonlight in his peripherals, and he struck furiously at the ignitor. The explosion of light and heat blinded him, and the encroaching growls gave way to receding yips. But he knew the flare wouldn't last long, and the wolves wouldn't retreat far.

As his eyes adjusted to the radiant orange glow, he looked down at his best friend one last time. "I'm sorry," he whispered, feeling a hot tear cut down his frozen cheek. "I'm sorry, Sam, for all of this. I'm so, so sorry."

7 YEARS LATER

I

Jack

A THICK mid-summer fog crept lazily through the trees, blanketing hundreds of acres of dense woodlands. The air was damp and warm and held the muted stillness of pre-dawn. For a few fleeting minutes, the expanse of pine-shrouded wilderness existed as a reef submerged in a sea of opaque blue, its foliage gently swaying in the calm waves of mountain breeze. Then the darkness gave way. The orange glow of morning spilled over the horizon and enveloped the forest. The sun's radiant beams wove through the leaves and branches, the soft blues washing away into an earthy pallet of greens and browns. Warm light glanced off of pools of morning dew and glinted against the paper white trunks of birch trees, finally penetrating the rolling sea of mist that hung low over the forest floor.

From its discreet den nestled in the crumbling remains of a stump, a wary chipmunk emerged and sniffed at the fresh morning air. Then it was off. It bounded over the sunken piles of rotting timber and languid ferns before cutting across one of the many abandoned logging roads that ran through the forest — thin, winding scars left from wounds cut into the forest's heart half a century before. It paused for a moment atop the ancient remnants of a stone wall, then bounced away across the exposed forest floor toward the scattering of acorns that surrounded the base of an old oak.

Jack Steward sat motionlessly against the oak's roots. He knew that his perfectly assembled camouflage outfit allowed him to disappear into the other clumps of mixed vegetation and fallen branches that surrounded him. Still, he watched the chipmunk's approach with an air of trepidation. He'd spent the entire night stationed at the tree's base, blending in and letting the forest around him forget his existence. Now, as morning broke, came the moment he had invested the last twelve hours into. Sunrise was his best chance at his prey. The last thing he needed was for this seemingly innocuous little rodent to realize that the lump of brush and forest debris before it was more than it appeared. There was no alarm system in the forest quite as effective as the furious chittering of a frightened chipmunk.

The chipmunk darted closer to Jack's foot, frantically shoving whole acorns into the bulging pouches of its mouth. Jack slacked his breath and issued a silent command, willing the small creature to move on. It ignored his subconscious ushering, continuing to inch closer and closer until it finally came to the decision that the motionless rubber mound before it would make a perfect perch upon which to tally its spoils. It climbed atop the rubber tip of Jack's boot and set about shifting the acorns in its pouches.

The chipmunk froze.

Its head snapped up, sniffing intensely at the breeze. The stretch of fur along its back rose and shivered.

Jack followed its stare with his only his eyes, exceedingly careful not to move his head. As he did, the wind shifted, pulling south down the labyrinth of overgrown logging roads. It carried with it the faint *crack* of a breaking branch.

The chipmunk bolted, crashing haphazardly through the brush in a desperate retreat.

Jack sat up slowly, using the fluttering of the leaves in the wind to cover his movement. He retrieved the prosthetic lower leg stationed at his side and balanced it upright in front of him. Then he leaned back and balanced the barrel of his rifle atop its rounded socket.

He eased the scope to his eye and sighted in on an orange bucket he'd placed the night before. It stood at almost exactly one hundred-and-fifty-yard's distance and was visible only through a thin break in the otherwise dense brush. Despite the relatively small opening, it made for an easy enough shot.

Something moved through the brush beyond the bucket. By the time Jack focused on it, it was gone. Just like with the chipmunk, he silently willed the creature to do his bidding, this time to reveal itself. Once again, his mental volley was worthless. Several tense minutes passed before his chest began to cramp and he was forced to gently lower the rifle.

Even at just twenty-nine-years-old, Jack's body was starting to rebel against the unforgiving lifestyle he'd taken on. Whether it was from sitting among the roots of a tree for a dozen hours at a time or hiking for miles upon miles a day with a pack on his back while sporting a worn-out prosthetic, Jack knew his body wasn't going to be able to take much more of it. But he didn't care.

Jack was a wilderness guide. A professional hunter. According to a number of Maine wardens and a Yelp review page that he had never seen, Jack was one of the best guides on the east coast. At least he had been until recently. The minute he'd managed to pay off his humble cabin in the middle of nowhere, Maine, he'd retired from chaperoning emasculated suburbanites in their attempts at landing a trophy bear or buck in order to prove their manhood. These days, Jack hunted for meat, not for money. His paid work was almost entirely in conservation — tracking, tagging, and occasionally culling. And he only culled when there was no other choice.

This morning was no other choice. A week prior, the local warden had contracted him for help with a very wily black bear that had not only outgrown its range, but also seemed to have outgrown its fear of man. In the past month alone there had been three attacks on local livestock, bringing the total up to eight since spring. The warden had offered Jack a cool grand to cull the increasingly aggressive animal before the farmers got fed up and took action themselves. Jack had taken the job, but not entirely because of the money. Angry farmers in a shit economy were not the type of people to take lightly. If this bear was not taken cleanly and the threat extinguished, Jack feared that it would likely end with far more cruelty than necessary. Perhaps even with a vengeance-driven overkill of the local bear population.

The foliage beyond the bucket shifted again. Jack raised his rifle and flipped the safety off. The worn mechanism fell into place silently, and he slid his finger over the trigger.

Something dark slinked beyond the shrubbery, then a small triangular head birthed from the leaves. It cautiously eyed the clearing before skulking forward and closing on the stinking bucket of old beef trim. Jack eased his finger off of the trigger and sighed.

The coyote yanked a hunk of meat from the bucket and spat it on the ground. It sniffed the green-tinted mound for a moment, then proceeded to ravenously devour it. Like a herd of ghosts, four more coyotes materialized from the surrounding ferns.

Jack lowered his rifle and let defeat wash over him as the pack destroyed the last twelve hours' work. He'd figured there was a good chance of the coyotes finding the bait bucket in the night, but as the sun had risen, he'd figured he was in the clear. While bears fed at dawn, it was rare to see coyotes out in the light. All the cramped muscles and exhaustion had been for naught.

The brush parted once more, and something larger glided between the ferns. It was a smoky gray, standing a full head taller than the coyotes and at least one-and-a-half times as long. Jack's chest seized. Without considering his actions, the scope was once again to his eye.

The newcomer snarled at a subordinate member of the pack. The smaller animal cowered and dropped its mouthful of rotting beef in penance. The coywolf accepted the coyote's sacrifice — its hybrid nature made clear by the unmissable lupine slope of its shoulders as it hunched to consume the meat.

A terrifyingly familiar feeling strummed furiously against the frayed strings of Jack's psyche. Deep in the repressed recesses of his mind, the slope-backed shadows from that hellish mountain manifested. They darted around him, encircling him in the darkness — yipping, snarling, snapping, taunting. They hounded him, just as they had in every nightmare for the past seven years. Haunting, yellow eyes glaring at him over gnashing fangs. They nipped at his heels and thirsted after his blood as they ripped away the frozen flesh of his best friend's lifeless corpse...

Jack was not in control when the crosshairs fell over the coywolf's chest. Nor did he feel the recoil when the rifle went off.

Had he been in control, he would have considered the same truth that he had always acknowledged in those few moments of hateful confrontation with nature: that this was just an animal. An animal undeserving of the bubbling malice he held in his soul. This creature hadn't killed Sam. It hadn't caused the frostbite that took everything below his left knee. It hadn't driven him to the depths of despair and sent him spiraling down a near decade-long hole of endless drinking and regret.

It was just an animal.

An animal that didn't deserve to die because of one pathetic man's fear.

Jack *knew* that truth.

He lived by that truth.

But in that moment, Jack lost control. He gave in to the panic and the hatred that had been boiling deep in his belly for the past seven years.

A violent ripple of fur and flesh exploded outward from the bullet's point of impact. The coywolf stumbled, then collapsed. By the time the body hit the earth, the rest of the pack had evaporated back into the ferns. Jack watched the lifeless mound through the crosshairs, stunned at what he had just done. Slowly the image blurred, then melted away as tears filled his eyes. The rifle slid from his grasp, and Jack silently collapsed into himself.

He had committed a crime that, to others, might be considered little more than a lapse in judgement. But to Jack, it was an act of evil. One final selfish mistake that nudged him just beyond the brink of his own forgiveness.

THE DUST-COATED clock on the old Ford Ranger's dash showed noon as Jack pulled down the quarter mile driveway that led to his cabin. It had been a three-hour drive from the reserve to the rural township he called home. He'd spent the hours in silence, soaking in his misery and guilt.

Now the coywolf's body was packed in a cooler that bounced in the truck bed as he drove down the ever-eroding dirt driveway. He would throw it on ice for the local university biologists, hoping that maybe some good could come of his misdeeds. Perhaps they could find some value in studying the rare hybrid.

By the time the quaint log cabin he called home became visible through the wall of low-hanging branches, so too did the shiny new Audi parked in his spot.

Jack pulled the old truck up beside it. He ignored the uninvited guest as he retrieved the cooler and his rifle case, and he had made it up the front steps and onto the stubby porch before a nasally voice managed to call after him.

"Mr. Steward, wait!"

Jack slowly turned. The man who climbed out of the Audi was precisely the type that Jack had expected to come calling after his services. Short, doughy, pale, and painfully clean cut. The exact type to offer a small fortune for the bragging rights of bagging a trophy animal. It was, however, rare for them to show up sporting a business suit, as this one had. Most of the time they would be adorned in an ensemble from the most recent L.L. Bean catalogue, overpriced tags still fluttering from the collars and sleeves.

No matter. It didn't matter what this stranger wore. Jack was through with that type of work.

"If you'll just give me a moment of your time—" the man began.

"I only do work for the state these days." Jack cut him off. "Regardless of what you heard or who it was from, I don't guide hunts anymore."

"I understand, Mr. Steward, but that's not why I'm here," the man insisted, shuffling up to the porch and handing Jack a card. "My name is Thomas Meyers. I'm an attorney."

"A lawyer, huh?" Jack muttered after giving the card a quick once-over before handing it back. "Who's suing me?"

Meyers laughed. It was a disingenuous laugh, a pandering attempt to signify the absurdity of the question. To Jack, it might as well have been fingernails on a chalkboard.

"No one's suing you, sir. At least not to my knowledge. No, I've come here on behalf of the Emery Foundation to proposition you for a job."

Jack grunted dismissively and returned to unlocking his front door.

"Please, Mr. Steward, you come highly recommended and—"

Jack managed to rotate the stubborn lock and shoulder the door open, then slid the cooler and rifle case onto the scratched wooden floor inside. "I told you, I don't guide anymore."

"Two hundred thousand dollars for only six weeks of work. Maybe even as few as four," Meyers said.

Jack stopped in his tracks. He once again turned to regard the lawyer, this time searching the man's face for some sign that he was joking.

Meyers saw the look for what it was. "I promise you that I am extremely serious."

"Oh yeah? And what the hell does this foundation of yours want me to hunt? *People*?" Jack scoffed. "Listen, if this is one of those prank shows—"

It was Meyers' turn to interrupt. "No, nothing like that at all. My employer, Mr. Bill Emery, is recruiting a team for an expedition in Nova Scotia. An expedition of an archaeological nature, and one that requires an extreme amount of discretion. I can't tell you much, but I can tell you that the location of the project is *quite* rural. Thus, Mr. Emery has sought you out as a professional woodsman capable of both ensuring the safety *and* security of said expedition. I have to say, you've come *very* highly recommended by our contacts. I'm afraid I cannot give you many specifics at the moment, but should you choose to accept the position and sign a non-disclosure agreement—"

"Stop talking," Jack said.

Meyers came to a stuttering halt.

Jack searched the man's expression. Either this lawyer had an extremely good poker face, or he was being serious. It didn't much matter either way.

"Pass," Jack said, stepping into the cabin and closing the door.

Meyers stood in silence. After finally digesting the sudden end to the conversation, his muffled voice called through the door. "But, Mr. Steward, this is the job of a lifetime. Surely a man in your position can't pass this up!"

"My position?" Jack called back. "I'm exactly where I need to be, bud."

"This is a once in a lifetime opportunity. Don't be a fool!"

Jack glanced out one of the ever-dirty windows at the stunned lawyer. "There ain't nothing dangerous in Nova Scotia. That group of yours will be fine."

The lawyer came back with a series of stuttered arguments, all of which fell on deaf ears. After a few minutes, Meyers gave a resigned shrug and departed, but not before Jack saw him slip his business card under an empty beer bottle on the porch's railing.

Jack watched the glistening black Audi roll out of sight and tried to imagine what sort of absurd ordeal he'd just passed on. Whatever it was, it was no doubt illegal — or at least something that *should* be illegal if someone was willing to throw down that kind of cash.

Pushing the thoughts from his mind, he stripped out of the filthy camouflage attire and shed his prosthetic. Well past the point of even imagining using the long-abandoned crutches hidden somewhere in the back of the closet, he hopped the half dozen steps from the bedroom into the shower. Fifteen minutes later he emerged, soaked and exhausted, and observed himself in the fogged mirror.

Even after a shower Jack was a haggard mess. His chestnut hair was longer than usual — he hadn't bothered with his bi-annual cut yet this summer — and it blended in with an equally unkempt beard. In years past, his regular diet of fresh meat and homegrown vegetables had afforded him a healthy amount of muscle to match his six-foot frame. However, over the last half decade, that diet had devolved into mostly liquor, and while a life of hard labor still left him with his strength, his frame had lost a good portion of its bulk. Now he was sinewy and square. Lean like a fighter, his father would have said.

"Lean like a fighter, drunk like a skunk," he muttered, manifesting his father's face in his mind. The battered old 'Nam vet grinned back at him approvingly.

Jack gave a dry chuckle. How appropriate that the old man and he would meet the same lonely fate.

He slid on a pair of shorts, one small consideration for whoever ended up finding him, and ventured out into the kitchen where he plucked a bottle of scotch from one of the shelves. It was an eighteen-year vintage that he'd been saving for whenever he finally worked up the courage. He peeled away the paper that secured the cork. As he splashed a hefty serving over ice in his favorite tumbler, the blinking red light of the answering machine caught his attention. His mind working on autopilot, he pressed play.

There were three new messages.

The first was from his alma mater in Montana asking for donations.

The second was a political spam bot droning on about voting YES on some local prop.

The third started with a pause, then the soft voice of an older woman spoke:

"Hey, Jack. It's Catherine," Sam's mother began. "I just… I wanted to check in on you. I know you say you're doing alright, but I know it's tough. Trust me, I know." There was another pause. "We're having a get-together in Boise later this month, a little family thing trying to plan out some fundraisers for Olivia's cancer. You wouldn't believe what they charge for the treatments here— I'm sorry, that's not why I'm calling. I just wanted to see if you would come. We all miss you, and we all care about you, and we'd love to see you. That's all. I hope you're taking care of yourself. We love you, Jack. Oh, and say hi to Chewbacca for me. I hope you're not letting him get too fat up there."

The message clicked off. Jack found himself staring forlornly at the empty dog bowl across the room. Olivia, Sam's sister, had scrawled Chewie's name across it in permanent marker when he'd adopted the pit bull mix in college a decade before. Now the writing was little more than a faded black smear, and Chewie was at peace in a deep grave in the middle of his favorite grove out back. But Catherine didn't know this, just as Jack hadn't known about Olivia's cancer until just this moment.

He drained the tumbler in one long swig, then refilled it.

Catherine had been like a mother to him in that far away state. She'd taken him in the minute he and Sam had become dormmates freshman year. For the next four years, the lonely orphan boy from Maine had been to every family party and every holiday. He'd found out from the nurses later that she'd sat by his hospital bed every day during his three-week coma following the rescue.

She never asked him what had happened out there in those frozen mountain passes. All she knew was that they had gone hunting and gotten lost. She didn't know about Jack's bad shot, or the days they'd spent tracking while Sam begged to go back. He'd never told her about the wolves or the terror her son had faced in his final days.

Now it seemed she was poised to lose the only child she had left. Olivia. And no doubt go broke in the process.

How much more fucked could the world get?

Jack finished the tumbler a second time, grimacing at the liquor's burn. In a burst of anger, he hurled the glass across the room. It shattered against the log wall, fragments of glass clinking down into Chewie's deserted bowl.

What the hell had she done to deserve that much pain?

What the hell had *he* done to deserve all of this misery?

But he knew what *he* had done. It was his fault, after all. Every bit of the misfortune that dominated both of their lives could be traced right back to that singular decision on that hellish mountain...

He drank straight from the bottle next, and just when he knew he couldn't stomach anymore, he threw that too. He didn't need more liquor. He knew what had to be done. He couldn't give himself time to think. There wasn't a reason to think — he'd already made his decision. It was time to follow through.

Jack stalked out the front door, not bothering to close it behind him. His revolver was still nestled in the pack that sat in the truck's passenger seat. He yanked at the door handle, but it stuck.

"You're kidding me," he mumbled, trying to remember where he'd tossed the keys.

Fuck it.

He picked up a large rock from the grass surrounding the driveway and hurled it. It punched through the window with a crash, leaving a splintered hole just large enough for him to reach through. A moment later, he was leaning drunkenly on the hood, double checking the chambers to make sure the pistol was loaded.

A gust of wind swooped in from the mountains. It pushed the disheveled mess of hair from his eyes just as he raised the pistol. Even through the blur of drunken tears, a small white square caught his hunter's eye. The business card had come loose of its glass anchor and now fluttered along the ground at Jack's feet. His finger paused on the trigger just long enough to consider the note written in pen on the back.

$200k pls call

He slowly lowered the gun.

Two hundred thousand dollars could pay for a hell of a cancer treatment.

DAY 1

*"Men are more easily governed through their vices
than through their virtues."*
– Napoleon Bonaparte

II

Greg

ARJUN BANDI jerked violently awake in his seat, the tail end of the train's whistle still floating through the stale air around him. His hands, cramped and sore, grasped the nub ends of the armrests in a death grip and his entire body prickled with a fine wave of chills. His eyes darted around the passenger car, searching desperately for the source of the danger.

But there was no danger. No visible danger, at least. No one was staring at him, comparing him to the images on their phones or trying to recall just where exactly they had seen his face before. Hell, no one seemed to notice him at all.

Thank God.

Arjun sucked in a long, quavering breath and turned to the window. The reflection of his face was barely visible against the deep green-and-brown blur of pine trees that flew by, yet he could still make out the stippled beads of sweat that dotted his brow. Thick, dark bags hung under bloodshot eyes, and his lower lip was swollen and ragged where he'd been incessantly chewing it. Despite his run-down appearance, he still looked more like a teenager than a grown man. Unsurprising, since he technically still *was* a teenager, albeit only six months short of twenty.

He felt so much older these days. Exhausted. Burnt out. Turns out the old saying was true: life on the run really is no life at all.

Plus, he wasn't nineteen, at least not according to the passport he'd used to cross the border. The date of birth printed beside his little polaroid put him at twenty-one — an age matching the fake internet profile he'd used to secure the job that had brought him here.

Twenty-one. That was his new age, and he needed to remember it.

You are not Arjun Bandi. You have never met or even heard of Arjun Bandi. He closed his eyes and repeated the words in his head for the ten thousandth time. *You are Greg Gupta, you are twenty-one-years-old, you are a mechanical engineer from New Jersey, and you have never killed anyone.*

The train whistled again, and a voice crackled over the speakers. "We're about ten minutes out from Halifax, folks. We'd like to remind you to remain seated until the train comes to a complete halt. Thank you very much for riding with us today, and welcome to Nova Scotia!"

"Greg," he breathed, solidifying the persona in his mind. "Greg Gupta."

Greg.

Greg.

Arju— *Greg* pulled his laptop from the backpack that was tucked between his legs. He opened it with shaking hands and powered it on. This would likely be his last chance to review his carefully planned backstory before meeting his new employer. Despite being able to recite his own notes by heart, he still felt the need to do so up until the last possible moment. As he waited for the computer to boot up, he reached into the backpack's front pocket and pulled out a pair of pill bottles. One for anxiety, one for ADD. He filled his palm with a double dose of each then dry swallowed them one at a time.

When he moved to re-zip the worn backpack, his eyes caught on the envelope tucked just inside the pack's flap. He pulled it free and dug the letter out from within. A crimson and gray emblem of a chimera stood out boldly alongside old-English font reading *The Emery Foundation*.

It had been hand delivered by a courier two weeks earlier, brought to an address Greg had only been pretending to live at. Greg had been lucky that he'd caught the courier just as he'd arrived, otherwise the family that actually resided in the humble suburban home might have been in for a rather perplexing delivery.

Greg's eyes darted over the letter for the umpteenth time:

Dear Mr. Gupta,

I am extremely pleased to tell you that you have been selected to participate in the Emery Foundation's latest expedition. After reviewing the numerous applicants who applied for the position, you should be proud to know that your outstanding academic background placed you as the most capable candidate for the job. While I cannot be forthcoming with the specifics of this expedition quite yet, I can assure you that should you fulfill the terms outlined in the contract, you shall receive a one-time payment of no less than $200,000 at either the terminus of the expedition or the end of the next six-week period. If you would sign and return the attached contract via certified mail, then we can confirm you travel arrangements over email (your preference to avoid air travel has been taken into account). Do not hesitate to reach out if there are any issues. I look forward to meeting you soon.

Bill Emery

CEO, Founder — Emery Foundation for Archaeology and Cryptozoology

Greg shoved the letter back into the backpack and pinned his eyes shut. The butterflies in his stomach clung to each other and mutated into a writhing ball of pythons. When he finally opened his eyes again, the green and brown blur of the forest outside gave way to shades of gray. Seconds later, the trees were almost entirely gone as they passed through the outskirts of the city.

He focused on his chest, on his hammering heart and seizing lungs. This wasn't the time for an episode — not that there was ever a *good* time for a panic attack. He focused on sucking in deep, soothing breaths, quietly humming a nursery rhyme from his childhood as he waited for the pharmaceutical cocktail to kick in.

As his heart rate gradually slowed, so did the train, until it finally gave a small jolt as it came to a halt. Greg didn't rush to exit. Instead, he slowly gathered his things and surveyed the quaint station through the window. After a few minutes, he decided it was safe. Well, safe *enough*. He hadn't spotted any police, but he doubted he'd be able to pick whatever plainclothes officers there were out of the crowd if they really were waiting to ambush him. He pulled his baseball cap down low and quickly departed.

As soon as he stepped off the platform, he began searching for his new name among the scattered handful of sign-holding drivers that stood in a cluster at the exit. Near the rear of the group, he spotted a thin, hatchet-faced man in a chauffeur uniform with a sign that read:

JACK STEWARD
GREG GUPTA

Beside the driver stood a scraggly-looking man sporting a worn-out combo of jeans and a plaid button-up. Greg recognized him as one of the other passengers who had boarded in Montreal the day before. He was tall and broad, with wild hair and an unkempt beard. Despite having the aura of a textbook fur trapper, the relative youth of the face beneath the bramble patch beard told Greg he probably couldn't have been older than thirty.

Greg crossed the station casually, doing his best not to draw attention from the small crowd that meandered around him without *looking* like he was trying not to draw attention. As his eyes darted over the passing faces, his foot caught on another passenger's luggage. He wobbled for a moment, trying to catch himself, then toppled, sprawling across the tiled floor with a pained yelp.

For one heart stopping moment, all eyes were on him. The dozens of curious stares locked onto his face, absorbing the detail he'd worked so hard to keep obscure. He was found out. He was screwed.

His heart rate doubled, and an invisible hand yanked his guts up toward his mouth, spilling a trail of tingling adrenaline through his chest on the way.

Then, just as fast as they had latched onto him, the crowd of strangers was back to their bustling ways. No looks of recognition. No surprised *Aha!* Hell, not even so much as an expression of concern among the horde of indifferent faces.

Greg managed a deep, settling breath as he climbed to his feet. He swallowed the lump in his throat, then continued on to the two men who stood waiting for him across the station.

"Gentlemen, I'm G-Greg." He stuttered over the name, convinced for a micro-second that he'd said Arjun.

The driver nodded and went about meticulously folding his sign. Meanwhile, the bearded man held out his hand. "Jack. Jack Steward. It's nice to meet you, Greg."

"Thanks. You too." Greg gave a nervous smile and shook the out-stretched hand. It was rough with callouses, and Greg imagined his own sweat-wrinkled hand as a limp fish in comparison.

Together they followed the driver out of the station and into the warm summer air where the driver loaded Jack's luggage — a beat up old duffel bag and a double-wide rifle case — into the trunk of a waiting limousine. Greg couldn't help but notice that Jack's gait was slightly off kilter, and as they climbed into the vehicle and Jack's jeans pulled up ever so slightly, the glint of a metal bar rather than an ankle revealed why.

Minutes later, Greg found himself sitting across from the one-legged lumberjack of a stranger, once again watching the serene farmlands and pine forests of eastern Canada slip by outside.

A part of him wanted to say something. To start a conversation like a normal person and built on some kind of repartee. But Greg wasn't a normal person. He was *far* from normal, and, from the look of this stranger, it seemed they both shared that distinction.

Jack looked rough and gritty in a way that scared the hell out of Greg. Jack reminded him of backcountry corner stores and fishing catalogues. Of sports and the outdoors and all the strong, masculine types that enjoyed that sort of thing — of the type of men who loved to mock a little Indian boy with his face buried in a computer. Of the type of people who had made *Arjun's* life a living hell.

Greg shuffled awkwardly. He breathed in the dense silence that filled the car as long minutes came and went in slow succession. Only when he was sure that this Jack person was content to stare out the window in silence did Greg manage to fall inward, once more mentally reciting his latest backstory.

It wasn't a particularly hard one to remember. Not as hard as the last one, at least. His last backstory had been that of a poor chemistry student who hailed from California and was willing to work as a night janitor in exchange for minimum wage to pay off school debt. But that had led to too many questions that he hadn't had answers for. At least *this* backstory was similar enough to his true past that he wouldn't have trouble adlibbing answers. Arjun and Greg were both gifted engineers. Both had a handful of lifelong social issues which they combated with prescription medication. Both of them had attended prestigious universities, both at a freakishly young age. But Greg had actually graduated from his university, where Arjun had fled shortly before the end of his senior year.

"Hey."

Something small and heavy impacted Greg's stomach. He flinched hard and grasped at it, his fingers closing around cold metal. It was a dented steel flask.

He looked across the car. Jack was chuckling.

At first Greg imagined this strange man was mocking him, throwing things at him to gauge his reaction. Perhaps preparing some demeaning comment regarding Greg's awareness. But the laugh was warm, and Jack smiled apologetically.

"Sorry, bud. You just looked like you could use a drink."

Greg felt the tingle on the back of his neck. He didn't drink — well, *Arjun* didn't drink. Maybe Greg ought to. Afterall, why wouldn't he? Perhaps Greg's parents hadn't been as overbearing. Perhaps he had grown up in an environment a fraction more welcoming of inebriation. He cautiously unscrewed the metal cap and took a sip.

The liquor, which Greg could only rightfully define as smoke-flavored demon piss, burned a path all the way down to his stomach. He coughed violently enough that he almost vomited. When he didn't, Jack laughed and patted his arm reassuringly.

"You'll be alright, bud, you'll be alright."

Greg gasped in air, stifling another bout of coughing with his arm and handing the flask back. Jack took a long swig without so much as a grimace.

"Do you, uh… Do you happen to know where we're going?" Greg fought to keep the anxiety out of his voice.

Jack shook his head. "No. I'd guess somewhere on the southern part of the peninsula, though, judging by our route and the sun. But that's all I've got."

Greg nodded, a small part of him glad that he wasn't the only one out of the loop.

"I take it you've never worked for this Emery guy either?" Jack asked.

"No," Greg answered.

"Great." Jack leaned back and sighed. "Something tells me we both just jumped into a whole river of weird."

Greg eyed the relaxed composure of his companion for a minute, then wrestled to allow some tiny bit of his own nerves to deflate. "Yeah, real weird based on this guy's reputation."

"Reputation?" Jack perked up.

"Yeah, erm…" Greg glanced back at the divider that separated them from the driver. He knew from movies that the thin glass wall was supposed to be soundproof. But he also had the common sense to know that most of the things he'd learned from movies weren't true.

Jack must have understood his concern. He leaned forward on his knees and motioned for Greg to continue.

"I mean," Greg leaned in and muttered. "From what I've read, he's, well, he's known to be… odd."

"How so?"

Greg struggled to find a diplomatic way to say what he had to say, but after a moment he gave up. "There's a lot of people on the internet who like to make fun of him. He inherited a lot of money — a *lot* of money — then decided to spend it by…"

Jack sat still, waiting patiently for him to continue. It was nice to actually have someone listen, something that Greg had to admit he wasn't used to.

"He started a non-profit to have adventures, more or less," he went on. "Nobody knows whether he takes it seriously or not, since most of the things they pursue are pretty ridiculous."

"Like what?"

"Like Atlantis type stuff. Lost treasures. Cryptozoology — you know, animals that shouldn't exist, or ancient mythological artifacts you'd see in a movie. Things that have earned him a pretty bad reputation in the scientific community."

"So he's like an archaeologist?" Jack asked.

"No," Greg quickly corrected. "No, he's far from an *actual* archaeologist; the forums make that super clear. In fact, most of the stuff I found out about him online came from real archaeologists griping about him. He's more of a… well, I guess I'd call him a thrill seeker with deep pockets."

"Jesus Christ. Let me guess, he's never found anything he's looked for."

"Yeah, I mean, as far as I can tell, not a single one of his expeditions has ever led to anything of genuine scientific value."

"Of course," Jack groaned, leaning back once more. "Please tell me his reputation at least includes paying in time and in full."

"It does," Greg said with a sheepish smile. "That's why I'm here."

III

Margaret

MARGARET SIMMONS hunched over the cracked porcelain sink of the second-floor bathroom of Clayborn Manor and milled through the contents of her toiletry bag. She had packed minimally for the six-week job in Canada, with the only exception being the four extra sticks of deodorant that were jammed deep into the corner of the small leather kit.

She pulled out the "Desert Flower"-scented tube first, rotating the plastic wheel on the bottom until the entire stick of grimy white chalk was exposed. She carefully eased a small razorblade through the center of the soapy brick of deodorant until the pressure gave. After a good three minutes, she managed to meticulously cut a rectangular door in the hollowed-out stick. She could have been quicker, but time didn't seem to be much of an issue at the moment. Plus, she had no desire to pierce the thin baggie hidden within and taint the little pills with the bitter, flower-scented antiperspirant.

By the time she had successfully retrieved the baggy of pills from its hidden compartment, she figured that she'd been in the bathroom for about eight minutes. Nothing too crazy, she thought, taking her time to grind one of the pills down into a fine powder between the sink and the butt of an old soap dish.

"Dr. Simmons, are ya in there?"

Her heart leapt into her throat. She instinctively swiped the powder into the drain and spun to place her body between the door and the paraphernalia that now littered the sink.

But no one entered. The door remained shut since, of course, it was locked. More importantly, Margaret thought with an inward jab, the little ginger bimbo on the other side probably had the common sense not to waltz into a bathroom that was clearly in use.

"What do you want?" Margaret demanded, her voice holding an edge that was a fraction too sharp.

"Sorry to bother ya. It's just that the last two members of the team have arrived. Mr. Emery is about prepared to launch into dinner and the briefing." The girl's words rang with such a thick Irish accent that, coupled with the muffling of the closed door, Margaret had to focus hard to make out their meaning.

"Yeah, fine. I'll be down in a minute," Margaret snapped.

"Alright. Thank you, Dr. Simmons," the girl said politely. Margaret listened to her footsteps echo away down the long hall.

"You bitter old bitch," Margaret muttered, massaging the bridge of her nose before eyeing the mirror. The woman who stared back at her was ugly, old, and mean. Three things she'd sworn she'd never become. Hard creases wove a series of jagged spiderwebs out from tired eyes and thin lips. Her nose, once so cute and petite with its upturned end, now sat blemished and sunken between two baggy, rosacea-marked jowls like a piggish little beak.

She'd been embroiled in a bitter war against old age since the first gray hair had glinted in her reflection fifteen long years before. Now the close-cropped forest of salt and pepper stood as a vehement reminder that she had not only lost that war, but been captured, beaten, tortured, and dragged through the streets by Father Time. What he'd left her with was little more than a humiliated shell of what once was.

One of her friends — at least one of the ones that she'd had before the divorce and the treatments and the breakdowns and the pills — had always claimed that fifty was the new thirty. At fifty-seven, Margaret was tempted to find that lying bitch and slash her tires.

She glanced down at the sparse streak of powder that was left behind on the counter, then over to the baggy of oxycodone that sat atop her toiletries bag. It was a waste, for sure. One that she was not sure she could afford. It had taken a lot of work — not to mention nerve — to smuggle the drugs past TSA and Canadian customs, and she had a feeling that there wouldn't be any opportunity to resupply over the next six weeks. Not out here in the middle of nowhere.

"Waste not, want not…" she whispered to herself, licking a finger and using it to gather as much of the remaining powder as she could.

In the end, there was maybe a quarter of a dose — not enough to get her to where she needed to be, but maybe enough to stave off the shakes that she could already feel approaching. The powder tasted chalky and bitter as she rubbed it over her gums, and the last of it formed it a grimy ridge on the back of her teeth when she scraped her finger clean.

She braced herself for a high, but it didn't come. Instead, when she opened her eyes, she found that the woman staring back at her was just a tiny bit less mean. Maybe a bit less old and ugly too, and a little more like the hot young brainiac that had been featured on *Archaeology Monthly*'s cover twice in the late 90's.

A tantalizing thought entered her mind: with just a little more of that magic powder she could *feel* like that girl had. Maybe even better…

She eyed the bag of pills and felt the conflict between her reasoning and her craving well up in her chest. Another pill would hit the spot, sure. But it might also put her over the edge. It might turn her into a drooling, giggling idiot for this rich moron Emery's little brief. She couldn't risk that, not for the amount she was getting paid. She stuffed the baggie into a discreet pocket in the toiletries kit, zipped it up, and left the bathroom.

She had arrived at Halifax airport that morning. At the terminal, a limousine had picked up her and a bald, pudgy little Italian man who had referred to himself as doctor something-or-other. The driver hadn't spoken much (Margaret suspected that he'd done so on orders), and she'd sat in silence for the entirety of the several hour drive. Eventually the landscape had gone from rural farmlands to deep, untouched forest. For the last hour of the trip, she'd seen little more traces of civilization than the occasional sign for a nearby First Nations reservation. By midafternoon, they had pulled down an exceedingly long dirt drive and arrived at a cliffside Victorian mansion with a half-rotted placard reading "Clayborn Manor."

She'd almost gasped outright at the building's ugliness as she stepped out of the vehicle. It was massive, with a pair of decrepit turrets jutting from the roof like stubby horns. At least half of the salt-stained shingles that coated the exterior walls were either broken or missing, and the structure itself had an almost imperceptible sag, as if the soul of the old house had departed long ago. Far above the wrap-around porch on the second and third stories, loose shutters clapped in the wind. Their incessant clatter filled the air with an eerie cadence that only enhanced the feeling that she'd stepped right onto the set of some black and white horror film from a time before subtlety had been introduced to cinema.

The property surrounding the manor was largely bare. A dilapidated carriage house stood nearby, its bay doors open and displaying a pair of UTVs and a small truck with New York plates. A hundred or so yards beyond that the earth gave way to jagged seaside cliffs. The sprawling acres were overgrown, and the grass rippled in the strong breeze. A long dirt driveway bisected the front lawn and disappeared into a thick and seemingly impenetrable forest that surrounded the entire property. Overall, between the three walls of trees and cliffs opening up to nothing but blue sky and glinting ocean views, Margaret had to fight off the unsettling feeling that she had stumbled into a trap.

The inside of the house itself was little more than a poorly refurbished relic; the bowed porch gave way to a grand foyer still speckled with what appeared to be the original wingback chairs and antique tables. A dramatically embellished (though a bit cobwebbed) dining room and attached kitchen made up the northern wing of the first floor, while the southern wing was devoted to a handful of small studies, servants' quarters, and storage areas. Of the bedrooms that made up the second and third floors, only a few had been cleaned up and outfitted with new mattresses and accoutrements. The empty ones were dark and filthy and made Margaret wonder just how long the house had remained uninhabited before her new employer had so recently acquired it.

Now, as she made her way down the hazardously steep servants' stairwell that led into the kitchen, she couldn't help but appreciate how well the old building had held up against the ceaseless onslaught of time and weather. Despite the occasional creak in the floorboards or an ill-fitting door, the structural integrity of the century-old manor seemed intact.

In the kitchen she found the Irish girl busy darting between a handful of dishes as she made the final dinner preparations.

"Hey," Margaret said, carefully measuring her voice to be a degree warmer than earlier. "Sorry about being snappy up there. I'm used to living alone, so, you know…"

"Oh, ya don't need to apologize, Dr. Simmons. I'm sure this whole operation will take some getting used to for us all," the twenty-something-year-old insisted with a smile.

She was cute with her bouncing red curls and bright smile. Margaret suddenly felt a tiny pang of shame for having labeled the girl a bimbo solely due to her looks. This young woman would catch enough shit in the coming years, especially once those looks went away.

"It's Sophie, right?" Margaret asked, relatively sure she had remembered correctly.

"Yes." The young woman nodded and smiled warmly. "Sophie Kensington."

"Well, Sophie, if I'm a bitch in the future, please feel free to call me out on it." Margaret gave an awkward nod, then marched quickly out of the kitchen before Sophie could respond.

The adjoining dining room was long and dark. The walls were coated in wallpaper that seemed to be equal parts water stains and a terribly ugly maroon pattern. An aged brass chandelier served as the singular light source. Its dull yellow light flickered directly over a beautiful antique dining table. Centering the table and veiled dramatically in black cloth was a rectangular object the size and shape of a shoebox.

The doctor Margaret had shared the limousine with was already seated, along with two other men she'd yet to meet. Margaret claimed an empty chair and sat rigidly.

A moment later, Sophie entered and flashed a smile across the room. "Well, I'm hoping everyone's hungry. I know Bill wanted to say something before we ate…" she said, taking her seat and looking expectantly back to the kitchen.

A long minute passed, filled only by the muffled creaking of the turrets flexing against the ocean breeze far above. Sophie let out a subtle sigh, then cleared her throat loudly. A second later, Margaret heard the clunking of heavy footsteps coming down the service stairwell into the kitchen followed by something crashing to the floor and a yelping swear. It was only after the hum of a spinning lid sank to a dull ring that Bill Emery emerged from the kitchen.

Margaret recognized him from a handful of mocking email chains she and her colleagues had exchanged years before. Aside from the pompous getup of a too-tight evening jacket and decorative silk scarf, Bill was an entirely average looking man. Perhaps a bit on the fluffy side, yes, and with a painfully off-putting goatee that stood out a harsh dyed black against his pale moon face, but he didn't look too bad for only being a few years her junior. Men were lucky that way. *Assholes.*

"Ladies, gentlemen, it is a pleasure to finally meet you all." Bill gave a shallow bow. He had a cheap, theatrical air that reminded Margaret of cheap community theater. "As you have no doubt already deducted, my name is Bill Emery. I want to be the first to welcome all of you to your new home for the next several weeks. I know it's no Four Seasons, but acquiring and outfitting this old monstrosity seemed a better option than spending the better part of the summer sleeping in tents."

As Margaret observed the strange man, she could see the matte discoloration of concealer underneath the sheen of sweat on his temples. Perhaps he hadn't aged *that* well.

"Now," he went on. "I imagine you have a multitude of questions regarding our mission here, but I want to begin by expressing my utmost appreciation for your patience. The project we're about to undertake is not for the weak of heart, and your willingness to sign up for such a, well, *open-ended* operation exhibits — to me, at least — that you all possess that grand spirit of adventure that I admire so much. But, before we begin with our mission, I feel that introductions are in order."

Bill went on to circle the table with his finger, one by one introducing the eclectic mess of people he'd trucked out to this decrepit estate.

"Starting on my right, I would like you all to meet Ms. Margaret Simmons. Margaret is one of the leading archaeological minds in the nation, and you'll all be impressed to know that she spent sixteen years as a professor at Yale."

"It's *Dr.* Simmons," she corrected. "I was only there for twelve years, and it was not an amiable dismissal. Nowadays I waste my life lecturing half-wits at a community college, so don't get your hopes up."

Bill gave a fake sounding laugh, but the subtle squint of his eyes gave away his annoyance. "Very well, nevertheless I'm sure your archaeological expertise will prove an invaluable asset in the upcoming weeks."

Next, he turned to the stubby Italian man who Margaret had shared a ride with earlier that day.

"Here beside her we have Doctor Emilio Bianchi," Bill said. "One of the premier surgeons in Mexico City. Since we have found ourselves exiled so far into the great Canadian wilderness, Dr. Bianchi here has been brought on to serve all of our medical needs."

Dr. Bianchi stood and looked around the table before giving a short bow, careful not to wrinkle his immaculate suit in the process.

"Next is the wunderkind," Bill went on, motioning to a diminutive man with tawny skin and greasy, jet black hair. "Greg Gupta, engineer extraordinaire. With one of the most impressive resumes I've ever come across, he is the recent graduate of a top-tier university. Mr. Gupta will be arming us with an arsenal of abilities and technical knowledge required to pursue such a daunting feat as the one presented to us. I, for one, am excited to see what his brilliant mind produces."

Bill motioned next to Sophie, who gave a smile that didn't quite reach her eyes. "Second to last, but still the head of her class, is Sophie Kensington. Sophie has decided to take a hiatus from the prestigious archaeological graduate program at the University of Wales in order to help us make history."

Bill nodded to the final person at the table. "Lastly, and perhaps most interestingly, our wilderness expert, Mr. Jack Steward, is here to ensure our safety and to help us to navigate the great Canadian forests that surround us," Bill said.

At first glance, Margaret figured the ragged looking man couldn't be more than a decade younger than she was. But upon closer examination she realized he was probably as little as half her age. The wild beard and haphazard mess of chestnut hair aged him in the superficial way that hard labor aged men beyond their years. He might have been handsome with a bit more self-care and a makeover, she mused, but now he looked more like a mountain man than a member of an archaeological team — and the plaid shirt didn't help.

"Aren't you forgetting someone?" A baritone voice came from behind Margaret, startling her. She turned as a tall, tan, thick-muscled man in a tight black shirt and khaki cargo pants entered the room.

Bill clapped his hands. "I'm so sorry, Kevin, I almost forgot to introduce you. Folks, this is my valet and close friend, Lieutenant Kevin Halberd, formerly of SEAL Team Four. He will be taking care of our...

Well, based on my experience with him, Kevin won't have an issue dealing with anything we have trouble dealing with ourselves."

The newcomer took the remaining seat beside Jack and surveyed the table, sizing the others up one at a time. When his eyes finally fell on Greg, his face hardened in a way that told Margaret everything she needed to know about Kevin.

Bill continued with his clearly rehearsed monologue. "As you no doubt know, I am head of the multi-national nonprofit the Emery Foundation for Archaeology and Cryptozoology. And, as of today, I am also your new employer. I know you folks doubtlessly have a great number of questions, but our lovely Ms. Kensington here has gone above and beyond in preparing a welcoming feast for us, so I'm going to try and streamline this evening's agenda in the most effective way possible. So, without further ado, I'd like to open the floor to you all. What are we doing here?"

He let the clearly rhetorical question hang in the air and looked from face to face expectantly. When no one answered, he prompted further. "Come on, folks, any ideas?"

So much for streamlined efficiency, Margaret thought, glaring into the Bill's tiny blue eyes.

"We're here to… find some sort of animal?" Greg asked nervously.

"An animal?" Bill's brow furrowed. Margaret recognized the animated look of confusion for what it was: an act. A poorly done and overly self-aware one too. Like the dramatic way an adult might overemphasize their facial cues when speaking to a young child.

"Yes, an… an animal that should not be here?" Greg stuttered out. "Like bigfoot or a sea serpent — I've read that Nova Scotia is a hub for sea serpent sightings — so I… I'd guess that, due to where we are and the fact that cryptozoology is in the organization's name. Or maybe… Maybe we're looking for a lost pirate treasure?"

"Mr. Gupta…" Bill said with a considerate nod. "Not a bad guess at all. However, I am afraid you are incorrect. Ms. Simmons, perhaps you could share your own suspicions as to why we've all made this grand trek?"

"Once again, it's *Dr.* Simmons. And if I had to guess, I'd say dinner, based on the place settings and decorum," she returned.

Bill laughed, but it was delayed and a little too eager. Margaret felt good knowing that he knew she wasn't making a joke.

"Straight to the point, just like your articles. I have to say, I am a massive fan of your work on the Yazoo people's folklore and traditions. The way you reconstructed an entire region's economy utilizing only their midden piles. *Brilliant.* But no, I have not brought you all out here beyond the rural edges of society just to serve you Ms. Kensington's stupendous cooking. How about you, Mr. Steward, man of the wilderness, what would be your guess?"

"I like Greg's idea," Jack said. "So I'll double down on his guess."

Bill's brow furrowed. "I've already told you it's not an animal, and it's not pirate treasure... so?"

"Yeah, well, it feels like you're fishing an empty pond at this point, so maybe it's time to reel it in and move on," Jack responded with a shrug.

Bill looked enchanted. "You, you are a *find,* aren't you?"

Jack's face held a taut grin just as long as Bill's eyes remained glued to him, then gave a covert eyeroll once their employer had looked away. At least Margaret didn't seem to be the only one not enjoying the millionaire's antics.

"Doctor Bianchi?" Bill went on, eyeing the man who had accompanied Margaret from the airport. "Any ideas?"

The round olive-skinned man chuckled. His thick-rimmed glasses reflected the orange glow of the chandelier, casting dark shadows on his face as he shook his head slowly. "Bill," he said softly, the Italian accent thick in his voice. "Enough teasing, please. Tell us."

"Alright, fine. I'm not one to ignore a doctor's orders." Bill held his hands out placatingly to the group. Margaret could see the excitement bubbling just below his surface. "What I am about to tell you is a secret of the most momentous type. I must insist that you do not, under any circumstances, speak a word of it outside of this team until our expedition is complete. Ladies and gentlemen, I present to you the key to our past, and everyone in this room's future…"

Bill motioned to Sophie. She looked up at him for a second, clearly confused, then seemed to realize what he wanted. Leaning forward, she pulled the cloth cover off of the box in the center of the table. Beneath it was a glass case that contained what appeared to Margaret to be a simple bronze spearhead.

Bill flourished his hands at greened hunk of metal in a way that would commonly be accompanied by a *Ta-da!* The room sank into a dense silence as the newcomers shared unsure glances.

"Bill," Sophie said softly. "Maybe we should start with—"

"Ah, of course," Bill cut her off. "Let me explain. It's widely known that 'in 1492, Columbus sailed the ocean blue.' In the modern era it is also known that — centuries prior to Columbus' exploits — a Viking expedition led by Leif Eriksson made landfall on the eastern coast of Canada, making them the first people to discover the Americas."

"The *first?*" Margaret asked sarcastically.

"You know what I mean; the Vikings were the first *Europeans*," Bill defended quickly. "However, one must accept that in the archaeological record, a *lack* of evidence does not in and of itself stand *as* evidence. Who at this table has heard of an ancient culture known as the Phoenicians?"

"Oh, Jesus Christ." The exasperated exclamation spewed from Margaret's mouth before she could stop it. Suddenly all eyes were glued on her.

"Come now, Margaret, not put off already, are we?" Bill asked with a worried look.

"I…" The mental image of the two-hundred-thousand-dollar check that waited for her at the end of the next six weeks' work floated to the front of her mind, and she silently cursed herself. "Never mind."

"Please, if something is wrong, I insist that you—"

"It's just that… Well, *Bill*, I think I have some inkling of an idea of where this is going," she started slowly, picking her words carefully. This wasn't the time for an academic stand against pseudo-history. "I know your focus is on… let's just say subjects generally of a more *controversial* nature. And sure, it is technically *possible* that a Phoenician ship *might* have been able to make it across the Atlantic Ocean at some point, but there is absolutely no evidence that a living Phoenician sailor ever set foot on North American soil. As intriguing as the concept is, the entire archaeological community has come to the same disappointing conclusion that, outside of a few Vikings, pre-Columbian trans-Atlantic travel did not occur. I really hope that this isn't the focus of—"

"Yet there's also no evidence that contact between Native Americans and bronze age Mediterranean peoples *never* occurred at all," Sophie cut in.

Margaret scoffed. "There's no evidence that dinosaurs *didn't* ride horses or know metallurgy, yet I don't see seasoned paleontologists making assertions that there was a Tyrannosaurus Khan."

"And what if a hundred-million-year-old cave painting showed up of just that?" Sophie came back calmly.

"Then I'd fire the moron who authenticated it," Margaret sneered.

"I'm sorry, but can someone dumb it down a little for those of us at the table without an advanced degree?" Jack cut in.

"The Phoenicians were an ancient Middle Eastern culture," Sophie said. "Master seafarers, they dominated the Mediterranean and even circumnavigated Africa. Theoretically speaking, it's possible that they had traversed the Atlantic and established trade routes with the Americas well before the sixth century B.C."

"And, *factually speaking*, Africa is as far as they got," Margaret sniped.

"History is more an ever-evolving stream of theories than a book of *facts*," Sophie said coolly. "Isn't that what you say in your book?"

Margaret's eyes thinned. She couldn't believe that she was actually arguing this. "Why are we here?"

Sophie nodded to the spearhead. "I personally pulled that artifact out of a cave halfway down the cliff face barely a mile from here. A cave, mind you, absolutely chock-full of ancient carvings and runes."

Margaret scoffed. "Well then it's fake. You see it often enough — a hoax pulled off by someone with too much time and money on their hands." She couldn't help but inadvertently glance at Bill.

"Impossible," Bill said. He held up a hand to Sophie in order to keep her from responding, which in turn solicited a flash of anger in her eyes. "I considered the same thing when Sophie first came to me some months ago with this find. Often times those who come to me seeking funding are, like you say, perpetrators of some scam or another. But Sophie's immaculate credentials spoke for themselves, and she convinced me to invest some interest in the cave system she's speaking of.

"Just like its contents, the cave presents us with a conundrum. It rests halfway down the cliff face, so its location alone begs the question of how and why the ancients found themselves there. In an age with relatively few mechanical marvels, what reason would one have to suspend themselves hundreds of feet over crushing waves and jagged stones just to enter a cave? Or to climb up, for that matter?

"What's even more interesting is the fact that when we used sonar equipment to map the tunnel system branching off of this cave, we found that one of its main routes ends in a rather anomalous barrier. A wooden barrier buried far into the cliffside, hundreds of feet underground, and nearly impossible to reach even for us today. Quite frankly, it would take *far* too much effort, money, machinery, and manpower to create this anomaly in today's day an age without drawing significant attention." His words began to build momentum. "Occam's Razor dictates to us the truth: that what we're looking at is an archaeological mystery on par with the construction of the Great Pyramid of Giza. And you, my intrepid adventurers, are the group of professionals that have been chosen to join us in unearthing it."

By the time Bill finished, he was nearly out of breath. He paused with his arms out wide, as if expecting some sort of applause.

An awkward moment passed in silence.

"Nope," Margaret said flatly. "It's a hoax, or busted sonar equipment, or—"

"If that's the case," Bill interrupted her, finally giving in to his annoyance and sighing. "Then you all get to walk away from this summer much wealthier people. Is that enough for you, *Dr.* Simmons, or should I call back one of the limousines to return you to the airport?"

Margaret glanced at the half dozen other people who sat around the table. Each one of the eclectic mix of faces looked back at her questioningly.

Two hundred grand.

Fuck.

"I came all the way up here. I might as well stay," she said, leaning back in her chair. "But since you're paying me for my opinion, I'm going to give it to you: I've seen situations like this before, and they never pan out the way you hope. Ever."

IV

Sophie

SOPHIE KENSINGTON collapsed into the warm folds of the fleece blanket that covered her bed. The blanket — as well as the silk sheets beneath it — had been the only unnecessary luxuries she'd allowed herself to bring along on the expedition. Now their rich shades of lime, teal, and amber stood out harshly against the shadowy browns and grays of the archaic bedroom. The warmth of the bed set mocked the haunting ambiance of the off-kilter roll-top desk and painfully ornate standing mirror opposite her.

Flipping open her laptop, she waited patiently for her emails to load. A circular icon dominated her screen as the shabby roof-mounted satellite worked to connect.

A drawn-out yawn inspired her to check the time. It was painfully late. The last several hours spent stationed by the fireside like some upbeat concierge had crawled along with the speed and joy of a dying animal. Having to constantly invent new bullshit answers to Margaret's obsessive questions over the discovery of the spearhead had drained Sophie. The web of lies she'd had to weave in order to convince the cantankerous professor that the trans-Atlantic Phoenician hypothesis was even somewhat viable had almost gotten out of hand. By the time she'd finally been able to break away from the rude old woman, it was nearly midnight, and she found herself yearning for nothing more than a solo bottle of merlot in the rare comfort of home that was her cozy fleece blanket. Since she didn't have any wine on hand, the blanket would have to be enough.

Her mind drifted back over the night's events, and she silently cursed herself for imagining that becoming professionally involved with a man like Bill Emery could ever be a good idea. But she hadn't had a choice. What they were really after, the thing that had drawn her to explore those treacherous cliffs six months before with nothing but a climbing harness and a student visa, was the type of thing that had gotten her laughed out of every subsequent grant proposal or research funding meeting. It was too big, too outrageous, too important for the academics to even glance at without a dismissive smirk.

And it didn't have a single thing to do with the ancient Phoenicians.

By the time the computer let out its little ping notification, she had almost dozed off.

> *To: SKensington37@student.uw.uk*
> *From: FWilson@staff.uw.uk*
> *Sophie,*
> *I was very pleased to receive your last email. Despite what you may think, I truly believe that endeavors like the one you have embarked upon are crucial for young archaeologists, even ones as talented as you. It's important to get all of that out of your system. I'm sure that someday you will look back on this experience fondly.*
> *With that being said, I've managed to decipher what I believe to be the general meanings behind the symbols that you sent me, but I'm afraid you're going to be disappointed. The presence of such markings carved into a cave in the Americas most definitely denotes an attempt*

to create a hoax. But, either way, I will sacrifice a bit of my objectivity to help out my most talented student — so long as my name stays far away from anything you might wish to publish later.

It would appear that the carving of the triskele adheres to the rules of traditional Celtic symbolism, and if it is in fact specifically Welsh, as you suspect, then it likely denotes some sort of burial site akin to those seen at Newgrange, and probably represents the typical run of the mill rebirth mythology. I wouldn't worry too much about the face carving; as it sits, I'm nearly convinced it's just another — albeit somewhat bastardized — attempt at a Green Man. As you know, guardian figures such as this are common across the entire European continent, so it is not unimaginable that there would be a Welsh connection. At worst it could be interpreted as a warning. Even so, similar warnings litter a number of mounds along the southern coast of Ireland. They seem to be entirely unrelated to disease, poison, or anything genuinely dangerous, and more of a traditional "get off my lawn" type graffiti meant to ward off grave robbers or vandals.

I have to be honest, if the writing was limited to just those items (and if your benefactor wasn't that pseudo-science extraordinaire Emery), I would be far more eager to take this find seriously and per-haps even consider some sort of legitimate Welsh–Indian connection, however my trepidation lies in the remaining markings. They seem to hail from a variety of anachronistic sources, representing everything from Sumerian deities to a sigil associated with the Macrobians, and all the way onward to what you must have recognized as the Greek Asclepius rod. I don't believe I need to point this out, least of all to you, but the only reasonable and scientific conclusion that I can draw from the combination of these symbols in such a small, remote, and frankly unlikely location is that they were placed there recently, likely as some joke or prank by a well-educated amateur.

"Why, thank you so much for that astounding observation, professor.

I never thought of that. How could I ever function without your supreme wisdom and flawless fucking guidance?" Sophie muttered to herself.

Sophie, please take the next bit with a grain of salt. Though I may be a wrinkled old bag, I too was once a young archaeologist driven by a passion to uncover the great secrets of the past, and I can see myself falling into a situation very similar to the one you have found yourself in. The fact is that Mr. Emery is a hack — you must realize this. His "expeditions," as you call them, are little more than flights of fancy and a halfhearted attempt to live out some adventure fantasy. I'm afraid that despite your current conviction regarding this site, his reputation of buffoonery within the academic community will once again prove true. I urge you to—

"Hey, what are you up to?"

Sophie jolted at the sound of Bill's voice.

"Uh, hey, what's up?" she mumbled, quickly exiting the email and closing her laptop. She hadn't heard him crack the door, and couldn't help but let a scowl escape as he shouldered it the rest of the way open and waltzed in.

"Did you get a response from that professor of yours?"

She knew that Bill almost certainly had Kevin monitoring the satellite's dataflow, and that he'd probably end up with access to the downloaded email anyways. "I have… Let's just say he's not a fan of yours."

"Most professors aren't." Bill smirked. "Call it the curse of a free thinker. What did he say about the symbols?"

"He more or less just confirmed what I already suspected," she said. "Bit of this, little of that. He thinks some of the Celtic bits are meant to be curses, but he also was pretty clear that he believes it's a hoax."

"Curses, really?" Bill snorted. "What kind?"

For a second, she considered adlibbing a long-winded tale about plagues or pitfalls or giant boulders — just because — but she decided it wasn't worth the effort. "Just about all big finds have them here and there. Superstitious nonsense meant to fend off would-be grave robbers and such. I wouldn't give it too much worry."

"Good, good," he muttered, settling in the musty old chair beside the bed.

A combination of the late hour and his soft tone made his proximity unnerving. She tried to ignore the uncomfortable feeling brewing in her stomach.

"That tells me that we're on to something," he said. "It means there's something down there worth protecting."

"Not necessarily," she replied, scooting away from him toward the foot of the bed and sitting upright. "But it is a good sign. If the markings are in fact as old as I believe they are, then they were put there for a reason. I'm guessing whoever—"

"How are you holding up?" he interrupted.

"I'm fine," she said offhand. "But I'm guessing whoever carved those symbols was copying more than a few of them from some other source. Their root cultures span too far across time for us to reasonably assume that there is some cohesive singular system of writing taking place here. If I'm correct about Maedig—" Her words were cut short as he leaned in and placed an unwelcomed hand on her knee.

"Of course you're right," he began softly, his voice carrying a patronizing hint. "Listen, we're here. You seem so stressed and high strung. You can afford to let loose a bit. We'll break ground tomorrow, and it will be no time before we have our answers. In the meantime, it's important to me for you to know that I'm *here* for you. Whatever you need."

He finished the statement with a gentle squeeze that sent a surge of hot fury coursing through her. *Are you fucking kidding me?* She almost said the words out loud, and a huge part of her wished she had, but then where would she be? *Out on your ass,* she reminded herself, *with no equipment, no funding, and no claim to the site.*

"Thanks," she said with a forced smile that must have looked as fake as it felt. She stood and casually began pacing, half-consciously taking a path that placed as much furniture between the two of them as possible.

She shouldn't have been so surprised. After all, she'd been aware of his intentions since she'd first come to him in a last-ditch effort to secure funding to excavate this site barely two months before. If she were being honest with herself, the thought had crossed her mind that those intentions were the real reason that Bill had agreed to sponsor the dig in the first place... but he'd yet to be so brazen as to actually *touch* her. It seemed that that phase of creepy courtship was over, and Bill thought that the vista of a secluded Victorian mansion was to be a romantic one. She gagged inwardly at the notion.

"How do you think things went tonight?" Bill asked, settling deeper into the chair, apparently not put off by the new distance between them.

"Fine, I guess."

"Just fine?" he asked.

There was one major thing that hadn't sat right with her. "I'm worried about the professor, Margaret."

"What about her?" Bill asked, leaning back smugly and unwrapping a piece of gum.

Ew.

"She's smart," Sophie went on, trying to ignore her disgust. "Smart enough to know we're full of shit with the Phoenician angle and the spearhead. Or, at best, she thinks we're dopes. Either way, she wasn't buying what I was selling down there."

"That's fine, as long as she doesn't know why."

"I still don't understand why we have to lie to them at all." Sophie stopped pacing and stared at him. She'd only arrived at the manor a day before the others and had since played along with Bill's odd ruse, but now she needed some answers. "I understand being secretive while recruiting — the last thing we need is someone else rolling up and trying to contest the dig site. But these people, they're here already, and they're going to find out what's actually down there as soon as we do. Why fake the spearhead? What's the point of hiring professionals if we're going to lie to them about the job?"

"Trust me, *this* is not the group I would have recruited if I was looking for professionalism." Bill chuckled. He stood and crossed the room. Before she could naturally resume pacing, his hands were on her shoulders, gently holding her at arm's length. She held back a grimace and fought the urge to knee him in the crotch.

"They're nobodies," he went on with a thin smile. "That's why they're here. Drunks, junkies, outcasts, losers, all disgraced in their own right. The Phoenician lie is perfect because it's big enough to motivate them, but small enough to keep them from getting greedy. If what we think is down there really *is* down there, then security is as paramount a concern as the effort of recovering it. String Margaret along as far as you can. In the end, she's just here to lend credibility to the find. But the others, they don't need to know a damn thing until we've secured the artifact. After all, if we're right, the last thing we want is to have some sticky-fingered nobody trying to steal our find, right?"

She forced an awkward nod and tried to ignore his wafting peppermint-dogshit breath.

"It's not like we're being insidious or anything," he went on, trying and failing to reassure her. "They will serve their purpose and be rewarded handsomely, and then you and I can reap the rewards of our hard work."

My hard work, she wanted to say. *Your investment.*

"And what of Kevin?" she asked.

"Kevin stays in the loop. He can be trusted. He's gotten me out of more than a few pickles in the past, and I'm sure he will again. Now, I've been thinking about *us*…"

The floorboard flexed under his feet as he began to lean forward, and she thanked whatever gods were present that she wasn't backed into a corner. With a quick cough and a spin, she was free and walking toward the door.

"I'm off to have a smoke," she called over her shoulder. "I'll see you in the morning, Bill."

She didn't wait for a response, instead turning down the tight hallway and briskly jaunting down the old staircase. It was late enough that the others were all in bed, so she didn't bother to glance around the ancient foyer before throwing open the front doors and wading out into the cool summer night air.

How the fuck had this become her role?

She snatched a pack of cigarettes out of her pocket and dug into it so hard that a number of them broke.

She was the one who'd catalogued the lore, who'd made the connections, who'd discovered the goddamn cave — all on her own from her dingy student apartment in Cardiff, nonetheless. How the hell was she suddenly the one responsible for cooking meals for a gaggle of degenerates and playing the unwilling damsel in some fat rich prick's fantasy? She was smarter than everyone here; her academic record stood as evidence. And besides, this was her find, *her fucking find!* How the hell was it fair that she needed to enlist the aid of a private sector asshole when so many stupid expeditions were sponsored every day by grants and universities? But oh no, of course she gets the one advisor who refuses to acknowledge her fucking work.

"Fat old shit!" she hissed under her breath, imagining Professor Wilson's face as she lit the menthol cigarette. Bill's face materialized next, with his flicking eyes and pouty face. She jabbed her knee in the air and imagined him crumbling into a blubbering pile at her feet. "Fuckin' asshole. Keep yer goddamn hands to yerself!"

"I'll do my best," a man's voice came from the darkness.

Her whole body flinched. The cigarette flipped from her shaking hands, bouncing off the porch's timeworn timbers in a tiny eruption of glowing embers.

"Sorry," the voice came again from the end of the porch. When she squinted, she could make out Jack's scraggly silhouette.

"You scared the shit out of me," she said, trying to keep her tone cool, but her hand was clamped to her chest to keep her heart from exploding out of it. "Damn near gave me a heart attack."

"How do you think I feel?" he asked with mock sincerity. "You come exploding out here whispering curses and doing ju-jitsu — I thought I was a goner."

"Fair," she smiled. *Back to the game*, she thought. *How's this one going to try and slither his way in…*

But to her surprise, he simply nodded and returned to staring out over the late-night landscape.

A few moments passed. She retrieved her dropped cigarette and tried to focus on her senses. The acrid taste of the smoke, the cacophony of tree frogs that filled the night air, the treetops' faint blueish outline in the distance… but every few seconds her mind would once again find its way back to the problem that she knew she'd soon be forced to confront: Bill.

What the hell did she do to deserve this? Two years… *Two fucking years* she'd worked with Professor Wilson on his projects. Then the moment she has something worth university funding, he decides that she's not worth listening to? Forget her grades; her translative work alone should have proven the value of her judgment and she *wasn't even a bloody symbologist!* How the hell was it that the only way to get something funded in this world was to put her tits on a tray and play the same sickening goddamn role—

"Any chance I could bum one of those?" Jack asked from across the porch.

"Sure," she snapped, then immediately felt bad. This guy hadn't done anything to deserve it, not yet at least. She held out the pack as he walked over. She immediately noticed that there was something off about his gait. As her eyes drifted down to his legs, she realized why.

"I haven't had one of these in ages," he said, plucking one of the thin off-white cigarettes from the pack and taking a lighter from his pocket.

"Oh yeah?" she asked, tearing her eyes away from the thin metal prosthetic and raising an eyebrow. "You just carry a lighter with you for fun?"

"Something like that." Jack chuckled as he lit the cigarette. He drew in deeply and grimaced. "Oof, menthol, huh?"

"Let me guess, cowboy killers for you?" she asked.

"Yeah, but I went through a clove phase in middle school, so there's that." He smiled, then turned and sat down on the porch steps.

She watched him for a moment, waiting for him to beckon her over beside him or spout some sassy remark about how he wouldn't bite. But he just sat there, staring out into the darkness, seeming completely at ease with the silence.

When did I get so jaded? The question evaporated from her mind as a hundred instances of patronizing old pricks flowed in to replace it. Then another face followed: Margaret's. The scowling crone's apnea-ridden snores drifted from one of the upstairs windows. Sophie let herself imagine *that* future… She shivered the thoughts off and decided to take a seat on the other end of the step.

"So you're a hunting guide?" Sophie asked, more as a means to escape her own head than out of a genuine desire for conversation.

"I was, for a long time. Not so much anymore."

"And how does one find themselves in that line of work?"

"I suppose the same way one gets into any line of work."

Sophie snorted. "Okay then, *why* get into that line of work? It's not the most typical nine-to-five these days."

Jack shrugged. "I don't know. I supposed there was one time when I really could have used a guide myself."

"Oh yeah?"

"Yep," he responded flatly.

She waited a moment for him to go on, the slightest bit curious. Only when it was clear that he wasn't going to did she push. "Anything bad come of it?"

"Yeah. I, uh… I ended up losing my best friend."

"Losing?"

"He froze to death."

Sophie felt her face flush, and she was embarrassed at her own prying. "Jesus, I'm so sorry. I didn't mean to—"

He turned to her and gave a sad grin. "I'm not sure how it's your fault."

"I mean… I'm just…" she stuttered.

"I'm kidding. Thanks. I'm sorry too." He pulled a flask from his short's pocket and took a long drink. She found herself surprised at how disarming this stranger's distant demeanor was. When he offered her the flask, she took it.

"I'm surprised you could go back out into the wilderness after something like that," she said, unsure of whether it was a good idea to keep the conversation on this topic.

"I couldn't for a while. Then after I finally did, there was a time where I didn't really want to ever come back out."

"So, what? You became a guide so you wouldn't have to?"

"Maybe." He shrugged again and paused. "I think a part of me thought that I might be able to stop that same thing that happened to us from happening to someone else. Then there's a whole 'nother part of me that thinks I'm just loathsome enough to keep forcing myself back into the wild, closer and closer to that time when it all went wrong. Some masochistic bastard burrowed in my soul, cutting away bits one thin slice at a time."

An indignant owl hooted from somewhere in the abandoned turrets above them. Sophie, lost in Jack's words, flinched at the abrupt noise, drawing a loud creak from the ancient porch. Jack's eyes paused their distant scanning and glanced over at her. They were sad, tired, and not at all sober.

Sophie spoke hesitantly. "Do you mind if I ask you what happened?"

His vision wandered back to the nightscape before them. She could see the internal battle raging in his mind. After a long pause, he finally shook his head. "Not much of a story, really. It was after my last semester at Montana state. My buddy and I went on a hunting trip to celebrate our graduation. It was real fucking cold that weekend, early January and all. The sky was just brewing snowstorms. But we were young and dumb, and I don't think for a second we believed that we could die from something as common as the cold. Fuck, I don't think we believed we could die at all. On the first evening I made a bad shot on an elk. It was maybe three hundred yards out when I fired. Just as that rifle kicked, I saw him start to bolt. Big old bull with more points than I could count. I just remember thinking how proud my old man would be if I brought that rack home.

"Anyway, round hit him in the guts. After a full day and a half tracking that poor thing, Sam started asking if we could go back. Then, when the going got harder, he stopped asking, started pleading. I just kept telling him what my old man had always told me: 'You finish what you start. Only true scum leaves an animal to suffer.' So, what was supposed to be a day and a half trip suddenly turned into two days, then three. It'd already started to snow by the time we finally found the elk's body. We probably would have been fine if it was just the snow, but the wolves were already there picking at the carcass. They tracked us for days. At first, we'd just hear them calling in the distance. Every time a little closer. Then came their scouts. One or two at a time, like phantoms in the night, harassing us, testing our defenses. Toying with us.

"All in all, I was out there thirteen days. Sam died on day seven. I couldn't stop the wolves from getting at his body. The wardens ended up recovering him in the spring, what little was left at least. I don't know exactly when my foot froze, or why Sam had it so much worse. Some snowshoe-ers found me in a heap on the outskirts of a farm. Apparently, I'd walked over eighty miles in those last six days. Even came within spitting distance of a town. Guess I was too fucked up to realize it."

His voice trailed off. She sat staring at him for a long minute, perplexed and entirely unsure of what to say.

Suddenly he looked over and his eyes widened apologetically. "Wow, sorry about that. I don't think I've ever actually told anyone that story. Guess I got carried away."

"No, don't apologize," she insisted.

"How about a change of topic? Maybe something less depressing?" He smiled and plucked another cigarette from the pack between them. "What's the deal with this whole Phoenician thing? Are you guys for real with all that?"

Sophie rolled her eyes dramatically. "Ugh, I could go another twenty years without ever speaking about that goddamn thing again."

"That Margaret really put you through the ringer tonight, didn't she?"

"Mhmm." She took another drink from the flask and stayed silent, reluctant to revisit the night's events. Jack seemed to sense this, and she was relieved when he changed the topic.

"Alright then, I told you my story. What's yours?"

"Nothing nearly so intense," she admitted after wincing away the burn left by the cheap bourbon.

"I'm easily impressed." He held his hands up, gesturing around them. "And it's not like there's much else to do around here."

She gave an uneasy laugh. Her mind raced for some interesting way to explain what she had always considered to be a less than interesting life. "I'm afraid I'm just a typical farmgirl-turned-academic and now I'm here, hoping this whole endeavor will finally get me my doctorate."

Jack stared at her for a second. Then he raised an eyebrow. "Okay. I gotta be honest, I'm not *that* easily impressed…"

She laughed, genuine this time. "What? What do you want from me? I'm still young. I'm allowed to be boring! I went to school, I got good grades, I got accepted into the program I wanted to, and now I'm here. Trust me, I've got no story worth telling."

"Oh, come on. Everyone's got *some* story worth telling," he insisted.

"My life's been spent in the library, Mr. Steward, not out having adventures. The only stories I have worth telling are old myths and legends."

"Well then tell me one of those," he said. "And please, just Jack. Or 'you' or even 'asshole.' Anything besides '*Mr. Steward.*'" He mimicked her accent when he said the name. She gave him an annoyed look.

"Okay, *asshole.*" She did her best American impression. "I don't know, I guess…"

She mulled over the countless mixed and matched stories she'd absorbed and catalogued over the years. There were the common ones, from Arthurian legend to Cúchulainn, and all the fun tidbits of what their pop culture replications had continually gotten wrong. Then there were the more obscure things, like the Tuatha Dé Danann, or the Branches of the *Mabinogi.* As she pondered, her eyes drifted to Jack's mechanical limb, and a particular piece of lore she'd catalogued years before stuck out in her mind.

"Have you ever heard the legend of the accursed huntsman?" she asked.

"Jesus, you go right for the throat."

She made an apologetic face, but he laughed it off and urged her to continue.

She focused her memory on wrangling together a half dozen renditions of the popular Celtic–Germanic tale into one solid narrative. After a moment, she cleared her throat and began:

In a time long forgotten, there was a village on the edge of the Rhine. These were the days long before kings had laid claim to the game of the forests. A time when the beast of the land roamed in abundance and seldom subjected themselves to captivity. It was a time when the hunt wasn't sport — it was a way of life.

In this village, there was a young boy who loved to hunt. Every morning he would leave behind his humble riverside home and traverse the vast fields and forests and bogs in search of prey. Every evening he would return with only his bow and a great sadness, for young boys make poor hunters.

But his young boy was not put off. As he grew, so did his skills, until every evening he would return to his village with a greater kill than the day before. One day, when he had just passed the cusp of manhood, he hid in the stones of an old mountain pass with his bow. The hour grew late and the air cold, but he did not relent. He waited patiently. It was in the last moment of sunlight that out before him trotted the most magnificent stag anyone had ever laid eyes on. This majestic beast strode into his range without so much as a second glance, and he buried a perfectly placed arrow deep into its heart.

It took four men to haul the meat down from the mountain, and the village rejoiced. They drank and made merry, crowning this young man in the countless tines of this stag's antlers to celebrate his great skill. But the young man sat silently through it all, and in the morning, they found him there still. For a week he did not speak, and the villagers worried. Finally, a traveling shaman passed through the village. He spotted the young man and asked what had happened.

"I've killed the greatest—"

Jack doubled over laughing.

"What?" she demanded.

"Nothing!" he insisted, coughing a few times. "Nothing, it's just... I like the dude's voice, that's all."

Truly channeling her grandmother, she'd unintentionally slipped into a deeper voice for the young man without even realizing it. She gave Jack an annoyed glare before going on.

"I've killed the greatest stag in the land," the young man professed to the shaman. "Now what am I to do? Nothing I accomplish from today forward will ever compare."

The shaman heard the pain in the young man's words, and he left to make council with the gods. A day later he returned and told the boy, "The gods have offered you a deal. They have seen your great skill and patience. They will allow you greater beasts than that which you have killed, so long as you heed the law of nature and respect the beasts of the land."

The young man stopped weeping, and the next day he rose with the sun and went in search of a greater stag. That evening he found one and slew it, and once a year for the rest of his life he would find greater and greater prey, until finally he had grown old and decrepit.

It was in the old man's final years that the wandering shaman returned. The old man recognized the shaman and gave great thanks for his role in speaking to the gods. Then the old man made another request that a proposition be made to the gods that he might be allowed to hunt until the end of time. The shaman warned him against it, but the old man insisted, and the shaman passed on the old man's request.

Years passed and the old man grew ever older, but his fingers never lost the strength to draw his bowstring. His wife dies of old age, and his children too grow old and wither away in death. The same comes of his grandchildren and their children, until his line of offspring are no more his than any others. The years strip from him his fat, then his muscle. They leave him little more than a sallow tarp of thin flesh stretched tight against jutting bone.

One cold winter, his village is razed in war. Legends and rumors of curses follow him wherever he goes, and he finds himself driven into the forest to live as an outcast. It's not long before the animals learn his scent above all other smells. They scatter before he can ever come within range, and he begins to starve.

Only one beast dares to come near him: a stag. But not just any stag. He recognizes it as a mirror image of the first great stag he slew all those years ago. It darts in and out of the underbrush just beyond his arrow's range. Every day he hunts it and every night he sleeps, and soon he wishes for a death that will never come.

The world he knows continues to disappear around him — every morning a forest has been logged or a new village erected. He grows ever older, but no longer in the manner that most men do. His joints don't ache and his back doesn't hunch. Instead, his wrinkled face shrivels inward. His features condense with age into a tiny, sunken pit of eyes and mouth in the center of his raisin head. His skin turns to wet paper and his fingers grow long and crooked, hooked forever around that accursed bowstring. The antler crown that he'd once worn so proudly sinks into the mottled flesh of his scalp, the long dead stag's skull fusing with his own.

He loses the will to sleep, instead wandering the night forests, hunting desperately for the damned stag that darts ceaselessly beyond his range. The daylight slowly becomes his enemy. His skin blisters and burns in the sun's radiant embrace, so he hides under leaves among the roots and worms, only rising at night to chase the one stag that endlessly taunts him.

"Even now," Sophie concluded, staring out onto the sprawling lawn before her. "They say you can find him in the forests along the Rhine, and on a windy day you can hear his cries as his leafy blanket is blown away."

For a long moment, silence dominated the porch, interrupted only by the ocean breeze sifting through the overgrown grass.

"That's it?" Jack burst out.

"I thought it was pretty good," she said, a little indignant.

"Well, yeah, I mean, that was great. It's just… I don't know, I figured there would be some kind of redemption, you know?"

"Nah." Sophie shrugged. "These old stories are of a time before forgiveness."

"No shit…" he muttered. "I guess it's a decent lesson in appreciating what you have."

"Maybe." She suddenly realized how efficient the whiskey had been, how warm her skin felt and how loud her heartbeat was in her ears. "Maybe it was more literal than that."

"What do you mean?" Jack asked.

"Would you do it?" Sophie asked quietly, her mind drifting to the dark cliffside cave only a mile away. To what she believed was buried within.

"Do what?"

"Take that deal. Not the whole monster thing. If given the choice, would you accept eternal life?"

Jack laughed. "Hard no. There are times where I think I've had enough of this world already. Forever sounds like hell to me. How about you?"

"I don't know. Maybe," she answered honestly.

"Well, I doubt you'll ever have to make that choice," Jack chided.

Right then, she desperately wanted to share with him the truth of what they were searching for, but despite the inclinations of the moment, Bill's warning about trusting the rest of the team hung in the back of her mind. The stakes were simply too high for her to let her guard down.

"Yeah..." Her unsure voice trailed off into the night.

V

Bill

"A FINE vintage, I must say." Dr. Bianchi relaxed in his seat, rolling a deep crimson port around the edges of the snifter in his hand.

Bill grinned as he crossed the threshold into the third floor drawing room, making sure to pull the door securely shut behind him. The several bottles of wine that decorated the shelf in the corner were hardly a fine vintage. In fact, they were a cheap Bulgarian knockoff of the popular brand their labels had been designed to mimic. But nobody needed to know that. Wine was wine, and if one of his employees revealed themselves to be an undercover sommelier, then Bill could always play it off as some fun anecdote rather than what it really was — him being stingy.

"Indeed it is, my friend," Bill agreed. He glanced around the darkened room, checking again to make sure no undesired ears lurked in the shadowed corners and that the two thin doors to the hallway outside were securely sealed. After crossing to the bar, he poured himself a short glass of 12-year scotch and claimed a mildewy chair across from the doctor. He then beckoned to Kevin, who stood by one of the shuttered windows overlooking the moon-washed sea, lazily blowing plumes of cigar smoke through one of the broken slats. "Come now, Kevin. Sit, relax, take a load off."

Kevin obliged, silently stubbing out his cigar. Bill could tell from the muscle-bound valet's exaggerated movements as he crossed the room that he was already a few bourbons deep.

The three men sat in familiar silence before the hearth as the last handful of desperate flames danced around the edges of a charred log. Its suffocating orange embers gently pulsed against the soot-stained walls of its brick den, as if it were the decrepit manor's very heart weakly grasping to hold onto life.

"This whole operation gives me flashbacks of Angkor." Bianchi grinned at the other two, exposing a brilliant row of perfectly set veneers. "I almost noted it earlier at dinner, but as you asked, I've been sure to keep our last professional rendezvous to myself."

"And for that I thank you," Bill noted, reflexively glancing at the sealed door. It looked thick enough to protect them from prying ears.

"Yeah, well it's good to be out of the jungle this time. And to work with a more… English speaking team." Kevin chuckled. "Though we've got a lot of young ones this time around. It kinda feels like the grown-up table at Thanksgiving in here. If we got that nasty old woman up here, we'd have the full Over 40 club."

"She is a bit off-putting, isn't she?" Bianchi agreed.

"Margaret Simmons is beyond off-putting," Bill snorted. "But she's somehow still relatively well respected among the mainstream circles. Even now, after her dramatic downward spiral, I imagine her validation of this find will carry some weight with her former know-it-all peers and their little journals."

"A very valid thought," the doctor said approvingly, the port bringing out the flushness of his cherub cheeks. "I must say that there is one role that I haven't quite figured out. We have a doctor, an engineer, two archaeologists, and then a… well, a wilderness guide?"

"A hunter," Bill corrected.

The doctor paused. "Yes, but why exactly does that—"

"I'll let you in on a secret, doctor," Bill interrupted. "Mr. Steward's purpose here is quite specific. He's here for his skills, not his knowledge."

"Bill..." Kevin cautioned softly.

Bill waved him off. "Oh, it's alright, Kevin. We've trusted the good doctor before, and Bianchi knows the deal. We might as well fill him in." He narrowed his eyes at the fat, little Italian man and stated matter-of-factly, "The spearhead is a lie."

Bianchi let loose a high-pitched grunt and nodded. "I figured you'd have *something* up your sleeve this time around, but I will admit that that's a big *something*."

"Indeed," Bill replied, feeling a small amount of pride in intriguing the doctor. "I won't bother you with too many details tonight — I doubt *you* would find the truth much more interesting than the lie anyhow. But I will tell you that what we're after, what Ms. Kensington has convinced me is buried in those cliffs, is far more valuable than some lost Phoenician sailor's booty. It's something that will validate a lifetime of searching. Something that, to the right people, could be worth trying to make off with. Mr. Steward is here to ensure that, should some member of this team get sticky fingers, they will not have an easy time escaping with the product of our hard work." He punctuated his words with a friendly smile, but he could tell from Bianchi's exhale that the doctor understood the connotation. Bill felt no need to let the little Italian imagine he was above being hunted down — should he get sticky fingers.

"And he's agreed to this?" Bianchi asked.

"No, but money has a way of making decisions like that easy for men of little means," Bill said.

Kevin grunted. "If that time comes, I still don't think the drunk bastard is gonna go for it. Seems a little too high on his own shit if you ask me."

"He's a destitute, alcoholic hermit that wallows life away in a cabin in the woods. In my experience, men like that will do whatever is asked of them for the right price," Bill assured him.

"But surely Kevin possesses the adequate skillset to track down and apprehend some would-be thief?" Bianchi asked.

"Kevin can also cook, but I wouldn't ask him to make me a dinner," Bill said. "Besides, I don't pay Kevin nearly enough for the value he already brings to these expeditions. No need to expand upon those responsibilities."

"Of course." Bianchi nodded. There was a pause, then his tone shifted almost imperceptibly. "Speaking of payments, I heard a rumor that a number of the workers in Angkor have been quiet vocal about not receiving their—"

"It's a government issue," Bill cut him off, a flash of annoyance cutting through his otherwise pleasant mood. "You know as well as I do how bureaucrats love to screw things up. I'm sure you found your own compensation for that job perfectly satisfactory?"

Bianchi stuttered defensively for a minute. "Well, of course, Bill. I didn't mean it like that. Plus, you know I don't do these jobs just for the money."

A pallid memory of the Angkor expedition three years before flashed through the back of Bill's mind. The doctor's mobile lab, the locals and their accusations, the claims of missing bodies, his dismissive laughter rolling through the tropical air…

Bill immediately dismissed the memories — just as he'd dismissed the accusations in real time. Too often in his experience the locals of some third world dung pit would attempt to extort some measly cash with overblown accusations and threats. Less advanced people always targeted doctors as evil witches. Why would that worthless village outside of Angkor have been any different? Besides, there had been no evidence of wrongdoing on the doctor's part, only empty words blurted in a language Bill barely understood. No, the doctor was a solid hire. A man of extreme discretion well versed in lifesaving medicine and, perhaps most importantly, the type of solitary man nobody would miss in the off chance that things went sideways.

Bianchi cleared his throat. "Whatever brought your interests all the way up here into the Canadian forests must be a great treasure indeed," he said, clearly looking to change the subject.

"Yes," Bill said.

Kevin shot Bill a snarky grin. "Yeah, well, she's not hard on the eyes, that's for sure."

Bill laughed. "Don't be crass, Kevin."

"A woman?" Bianchi's brow raised.

"The redhead." Kevin bounced his eyebrows playfully. "She came to Bill with this whole story about some artifact being up in these cliffs and, brother, I've never seen our man Bill here so eager to sign on."

"Enough," Bill snapped. He could feel his cheeks flush. "We're here because I believe in the integrity of her research. This isn't about romance, or legends, or magic of any sort. For once, it seems we might have stumbled across a legitimate archaeological find."

This wasn't the whole truth, of course. Bill was honest enough with himself to know that he didn't give much of a damn about legitimate archaeology. Of course he was here for those other things — romance and legends and adventure. But even if this cave did end up just being an archaeological find of value, he would still enjoy the validation of rubbing it in the face of his detractors. Especially that loathsome old bag sleeping a floor below.

"Oh, that's all this is about then? You don't believe in legends all of a sudden? How about Indian curses?" Kevin prompted.

Bianchi perked up, and Bill suppressed the urge to hiss at his valet. The hulking SEAL veteran had a habit of getting mouthy after one too many drinks. He'd have to have a word about it in the morning.

"Of course not," Bill said, waving a hand dismissively. "I don't believe in any of that local hocus pocus. I simply believe that whatever's buried in that cave system has value, and if it really is the inspiration of Bran's Cauldr—"

"What curse?" Bianchi blurted out.

"It's nothing," Bill insisted.

"It's not *nothing*," Kevin said, motioning to the house around them. "I mean, *something* killed these sorry fuckers."

"Nobody knows what happened to the Clayborns." Bill glanced at Bianchi with an assured look. "And there's no reason to believe that they were *killed*."

Kevin scoffed. "Except, you know, all the evidence… and police reports…"

"Kevin, perhaps it's time for some water?" Bill offered sternly.

"Forgive me," Bianchi chimed in. "But am I to understand that this house was the site of a crime?"

Kevin made to answer, then seemed to think better of it, instead settling deeper into his chair.

"No, good doctor," Bill said. "The story Kevin is referencing is little more than a spooky tale told at the local pubs about the creepy old manor on the cliffs. The fact of the matter is that for most of the past two centuries, this land belonged to a wealthy Scottish family named the Clayborns. They were a strange, reclusive folk. Fishermen by trade, and traders by necessity. They founded this estate sometime in the nineteenth century. It stayed in their family until about thirty years ago, when the last of their clan finally perished—"

Kevin snorted.

"Okay, fine." Bill rolled his eyes. "The locals seem to believe that they were killed, but technically they disappeared—"

"Except for all their blood…" Kevin cut in again.

Bill sighed, then glared at Kevin, who shrugged. "Yes, except for some supposed traces of blood found about the property. I believe Kevin has subscribed to the theory that they were killed by local wildlife, or *monsters*, if you're privy to the Indian folklore. Many around these parts seem to be. A fun campfire story, but likely little more, I'm afraid. Either way, the land was forfeited to the First Nations as an extension of their reservation after they petitioned the Canadian government, sighting it as religious territory."

"And they sold it to you?" Bianchi asked skeptically.

"Yes," Bill lied.

"Fascinating. Absolutely fascinating. Not to mention incredible luck."

Kevin snorted. He knew just as well as Bill that there was an absolute lack of luck involved in their failed negotiations with the First Nations. *Sober up, you goddamn idiot.*

"Indeed, incredible luck," Bill said. "But, as it is past midnight and the morning is coming quickly, I believe that this is where I must bid you gentlemen adieu."

"Until the morning then." Bianchi drained the remainder of his port. He said his goodbyes and gave a curt bow before shuffling out of the room.

Bill made to leave, but Kevin cleared his throat and motioned him to pause. "Just gimme a second, Bill, if you don't mind."

"Yes?"

"It's just that I checked my account this morning, and the last installment from the Guatemala job still hasn't hit. Is there a problem with Bernard again?"

Bill felt his blood cool and butterflies manifest in his gut. "No, nothing to worry about. You know how he is. Accountants, always wanting to double and triple check. We need to focus on our work here, and the minute we return stateside I'll deal with Bernie and his finicky damn numbers games."

Kevin glanced around the room, taking a moment too long to respond. "Okay."

"Okay," Bill repeated with a curt nod, then turned and swept out of the room. He traversed the long corridor that bisected the third story, pausing only for a second outside of Sophie's bedroom to listen for any sign of life. Deciding that she was likely fast asleep, he made his way down the stairs and to his own room on the second floor.

The bedroom he had claimed as his own was easily the most up-to-date of the musty old rooms. One could tell from the only slightly chipping paint and the (extremely relative) lack of dust that whoever lived here last had no doubt used this as their master bedroom. The maroon walls were still decorated with the dozen or so lopsided portraits that hung at seemingly random intervals along the walls. The Clayborns stared down with disdain — a series of stone-faced wrinkly men passing judgement on him as he prepared for bed.

The portraits weren't the worst of the room's decorations, though. The worst part of the manor's master bedroom hung above the bay windows overlooking the ocean: an exceedingly dreary rendition of a rolling nightscape dominated by a red-eyed wolf. The tempest of blackish blue oil paint with its two tiny, blood red dots never failed in giving Bill the creepiest feeling whenever he let his eyes wander over it. He had considered taking it down when he'd first moved his things in, however some small part of him actually liked the tiny spur of fear the painting induced. It was harmless after all — just a stupid painting.

Bill took his time unraveling his silken scarf and undoing the glinting buttons of his evening jacket. After he had fully undressed, he pulled a moist wipe from the drawer underneath the vanity and swiped away the layer of concealer that filled the cracks and crevices of his aging face. When he was done, he stared at himself in the mirror and forced a smile.

Of all the thousands of ways that this endeavor could go wrong, none had happened yet. The cast was set. The tasks allotted. Now all that was left to do was manage this stable of nobodies. As long as no one found out about the fact that they were illegally occupying and excavating on reservation land, nothing could ruin his perfectly laid plans.

The small satellite phone still buried in the pocket of his evening jacket buzzed.

Shit.

There *was* one other thing that could ruin it all.

Bill tapped the twenty-digit password into the satellite phone's small screen. He scrolled through the five newest text messages, all sent from the same source: his accountant, Bernard.

Bill, pick up.

Answer the phone goddammit.

What the fuck is this charge to a limo service in Nova Scotia? I told you not to use that card.

Answer your phone.

What do you not understand about the word BROKE?!?

"Arrogant, bean-counting prick," Bill muttered.

He deleted the messages, then re-locked the phone and placed it on the vanity. Once again, he looked at himself, this time noting the slight tremble in his left eyelid. He focused on stilling it. Bill Emery didn't shake, no matter the risk.

At least that's what he told himself.

And there was no question that this, perhaps his last adventure, was one hell of a risk… because no one in this manor was getting paid unless there truly was a treasure buried in that cliff.

Or, he mused, maybe even something better.

Either way, Sophie had better be right.

VI

Jack

"I CAN'T feel my fucking hands, man," Sam whimpered.

Jack could barely see his best friend's face in the dim orange glow of the fire, but he could hear the pained tremble in his voice.

"It'll be okay, Sam. Your sister knew where we were going. They must have sent out a search party by now. We'll be okay." The words sounded hollow, even to him.

Sam didn't respond, but Jack could hear the steady staccato of frail gasps escape the dark figure curled in the snow beyond the fire. Jack winced as he tossed the last scrap of map into the dying flames. They licked at the thick paper for a moment before catching on the edges. In the resulting plume of light, he could make out Sam's features.

Sam wasn't crying, as Jack had thought. Instead, his face was pulled taut. Flexed in a look that might — in a different time — have denoted concentration. Only the young man's distant, bloodshot eyes gave away the truth. It was a look of pure terror. Seeing it made Jack want to vomit.

He'd never seen Sam afraid.

"Jack, what do you think happens when we go?" His words came out slowly and broken by violent shivers.

"We keep going south," Jack said for what must have been the hundredth time. "Like we've been saying, bud. South is the ranger station. South is warm. We'll be okay."

"No," Sam said. "When we *go*."

"We'll start again soon. We're going to burn the fire as long as we can, warm our bones, then I'm going to make a sled with some branches and—"

"What if it's nothing?" Sam croaked.

"I'm going make a sled for you. We can't keep stopping like this."

"I'm scared of that the most, you know. If it's just... There's no hell or heaven, no rebirth, just... everything is gone and... your soul just sort of evaporates..."

"Sam, stop!" Jack felt the anger creep into his voice. "We're going south, and we're leaving soon. You need to be ready. You hear me?"

"Nothingness is worse than hell, Jack. I think it's worse than anything. Just nothingness, black, empty nothingness..."

Jack struggled to his feet. He couldn't stand to listen anymore. There was shit to be done. "I'm getting those branches, Sam. Stay close to the fire and try to stoke it if it gets low. I'll be back soon."

"I can feel it coming, Jack," Sam continued, finally starting to sob openly.

Jack trudged away, trying to tune out the sobs against the howl of the midnight wind and his own crunching footsteps.

The forest was a cold blue outside of the firelight, and as Sam's whimpering grew more and more distant, Jack felt his own eyes begin to well up. He cursed as he wrenched at the few pine saplings that stuck up from the knee-deep snow. There wasn't enough for what he needed, and the few he did find were brittle and looked like they would snap rather than bear a man's weight. Finally, he came across a dead bow that jutted out from a tree trunk. He yanked at it but stumbled back when the rotted wood crumbled under pressure.

"Just one fucking thing—*Just one fucking thing go right!*" he screamed into the night, hopeless fury building in his chest. Hurling the mess of weak sticks down, he collapsed into the freezing embrace of the snow. He lay there for a long moment, curled in a ball like Sam; weeping, frozen, broken, waiting to die.

He almost accepted it then.

Death.

Wretched, numb, hollow death.

It felt inescapable, lost out there in that icy hellscape, and if the wind hadn't died down at just the right moment, he likely would have just welcomed it with open arms. But the wind did die, and in the first instance of stillness he had felt in days, Jack heard the distant echo of Sam's screams.

He bolted. There was no hesitation. No pain or thought, just pure adrenaline. His legs ached as he charged back through his own snowy tracks toward the bloodcurdling noise. Bursting through the wall of snow-laden pine branches, he caught sight of a sleek black streak as it darted away from Sam's thrashing form and disappeared into the underbrush.

"Help! Jack!" Sam screamed. He hurled handfuls of crumbling orange embers into the trees where the shape had disappeared.

Jack dove down beside him, ripping Sam's smoldering polyester glove off to reveal spots of melted plastic clinging to the blueish black mess of Sam's frozen digits.

Jack fell back, stunned by the severity of frostbitten appendage in his grasp, but then some primal part of his brain cut through the blathering screams of his companion and caught the rolling growl coming from the surrounding darkness.

"Sam! Shut the fuck up!" Jack grabbed the rifle from his pack, but the fire was gone, and it was too dark to see any targets.

"Fucking wolf, Jack!" Sam was shouting. "It was here, man! It was fucking—"

"Sam! Enough!" Jack roared, then he caught movement in his peripheral. He spun and fired blindly. The deafening gunshot echoed through the valley, and the howl of the wind was replaced with the high-pitched song of his inner ear cells dying.

Everything went still for a long minute.

"Kill it, Jack." Sam's voice was weak, disoriented, and drawling. "You killed it, right?"

"Shhh!" Jack hissed, listening intently for a yelp or a whimper, but there was nothing.

"Jack… kill it…"

"We have to move, make for open ground. There's too much cover here for 'em. I need you to walk, bud, until we can find enough shit for me to make a sled," Jack said. He turned back to Sam and froze.

The wolf had managed to yank one of Sam's boots off in their struggle. His sock had gone with it, and the foot that now sat exposed in the moonlit snow was black and dead.

"I just want to sleep a little bit, dad," Sam muttered.

"What? It's me, man." Jack leaned in close. Sam's eyes wandered vacantly over his features.

"I just… I need sleep. Where's mom?"

Jack felt his lip begin to tremble. "She's not here, bud. It's Jack. Your family's close though. We're gonna go find them."

"Jack!" Sam said weakly, but there was a spark of excitement in his eyes, like two friends meeting for the first time in years. "Man, where are we?"

"We're almost home, Sam. But I need to carry you, okay?" Jack's voice cracked, and he crouched and hoisted his best friend over his shoulders.

"I don't like this, Jack," Sam wheezed pathetically as they began their slow shamble toward the ridgeline ahead. "Why'd you do this to me?"

Why'd you do this to me?

Why'd you do this to me?

The words echoed all around Jack, stabbing violently through the strained muscles of his chest and piercing his soul as blackness enveloped him.

Why'd you do this to me?

Why'd you do this to me?

WHY'D YOU DO THIS TO ME!

THE DARKNESS broke and he was on his back, soft blue moonlight illuminating the wood grain of the ceiling. In the distance, a wolf's howl echoed through the open window.

The howl lingered in his ears for a moment too long — like some half-forgotten puzzle piece thrown into the wrong box, blurring the terrifying memories with reality. But the howl wasn't real — he knew that for certain. It was part of the dream. There were no wolves here, not in Nova Scotia.

Jack fought against the cramping muscles in his forearms to release the damp sheets from his grip and sat up, swinging his legs over to sit on the edge of the bed. His breath came hard, and he slapped himself to clear the haunting call from his mind. His other senses were working though; he could feel the uneven floorboards under his foot, smell the sweetness of the summer air, taste the smoky residue of the cigarettes on his breath. Other than his lying ears, it seemed he'd gotten away clean, woken up lucid and oriented instead of terrified and lost.

Yet somehow it was just as bad.

He worked to slow his breath as he attached his prosthetic, then crossed the room and threw open his duffel bag. He fished around in the various side compartments until he found a large Mason jar marked *Apil Pi*. It had been a gift from a good ol' boy he'd tracked a wounded moose for a year before. As of yet, he'd been hesitant to sample the absurdly strong concoction due to the old man's casual warning of blindness.

Eyesight was overrated anyways. Right now, he needed something strong and efficient.

A bit of the moonshine spilled onto his shaking hands as he unscrewed the lid, but otherwise the thin liquid went down too easily. Its warm apple overtones seduced him into taking an extra-long swig, then another, and after raising the jar to his lips a third time, he had to force himself to stop. He needed to be able to function in the morning. Somewhat, at least.

He placed the jar back in the suitcase and opened the rifle case beside it. Skipping over the long deer rifle and his father's stubby old lever gun, his hands found their way to the single action revolver that lay nestled between them and an accompanying box of .357 magnum.

Sitting back down on the edge of the bed, Jack turned the cool metal of the pistol over in his hand and slid open the loading gate, then filled the chambers. By the time he had finished the familiar procedure, his hands had stopped shaking. He pulled the hammer back the rest of the way and stared at the gun for a long, long time.

It could all be over.

It'd be easy.

It'd be… a relief.

"Not yet," he whispered to himself, bringing the hammer down carefully and placing the pistol on the bedside table. He crossed the room to the open window, letting the cool breeze wash over his bare chest. The moon hung low in the sky, casting the overgrown lawn and forest in a silvery hue.

"Not yet," he whispered again, this time more confident.

He had debts to pay. Wrongs to right. Two hundred grand could never bring back a lost son or brother. But it might be able to save a daughter.

Still, he thought, looking back at the pistol, it was comforting to have the option.

He caught movement in his peripherals, and his eyes snapped to the moon-washed tree line.

There was something there.

A shadow, massive and pure black, skulked low and long against the edge of the forest. It hung in his vision for less than a second before it evaporated into the trees.

"It's just a shadow," he hissed to himself. Just some cruel trick of the moonlight, a hateful mirage from the abyss of his own tortured mind. There were no wolves here.

There couldn't be.

There were no wolves in Nova Scotia.

DAY 2

*"Sometimes legends make reality, and become
more useful than the facts."*
— *Salman Rushdie*

VII

Greg

Take me out to the ball game,
Take me out to the crowd.
Buy me some peanuts and Cracker Jack,
I don't care if I never get back…

GREG WOKE with a start. The song was distant and tinny, but it still managed to summon the sickening image of blood-matted hair and spasming death throes. The boiling memory of the moment's emotions — rage, fear, hatred, and the sickening aftertaste of guilt — all brought a shiver of horrible awareness with them. While he hated reliving the experience, the horribly familiar song that had been playing over the car's radio that chilly morning all those months ago always ripped him back to reality. That's why it made such a damn good alarm.

But he'd set the alarm for six, and the sun was already cutting strong yellow bars through the drawn curtains. Struggling out of the mess of covers, he realized his mistake. His phone lay near the foot of the bed, almost completely dead and playing the tainted tune on repeat through his knotted headphones.

"Shit!" He snatched the phone and checked the time. 8:52. Bill had told them they were to depart for the dig site at nine sharp.

Greg scrambled out of bed, almost falling several times as he yanked a random assortment of clothes from his bag and pulled them on. How had he forgotten to unplug the headphones? *The alarm doesn't work if the headphones aren't in your ears, idiot!* What the hell had he been thinking?

Wait, what time *had* he gone to sleep?

He paused in the middle of struggling to identify which sock went on which foot and thought back to the night before. He'd been playing that stupid block game on his phone at around four in the morning, and he'd had his headphones in, listening to the new-age techno-punk band he'd discovered on the train, then he must have drifted off... But he wouldn't have done that since he'd only gotten caught up in the game while taking a break from figuring out how to install a coded VPN server on his laptop...

He glanced over at the computer that still sat open on the floor and wondered if the program he'd modified had worked. Bill and his apparently outrageously overqualified valet Kevin had added a very obvious and quiet simple monitoring program to the satellite internet modem, but despite it being pretty industry standard for creepy internet monitoring software, Greg had found himself experiencing undue difficulty circumnavigating the code. He'd written a go-around, but who knows if it worked. Right now, he didn't have time to check it to see if his hard work had gained him free and unrecorded access to the web. Hell, even if he did have time, he wouldn't risk entering his *real* name into the search engine, as had become his morning ritual since his panicked flight from the drowsy little campus in upstate New York two months prior.

He figured out the socks, smoothed his hair, and popped three pills rather than his regular two. Today called for focus.

The savory scent of breakfast foods welcomed him as he descended to the main floor of the manor. The other adventurers (a moniker Bill had insisted on using the night before) stood or sat in various locations around the kitchen and dining room. Margaret dominated her entire section of the heavy oak table with nothing but a black coffee, her bleary-eyed scowl scaring off any potential neighbors. Jack and Sophie sat beside each other nearby, and Bill hunched over the ancient kitchen range, cheerily humming some upbeat song while burning eggs. Dr. Bianchi and Kevin hovered over the serving platters and picked at the sparse remains.

By the time Greg had retrieved a plate, the only thing that was left over was a pile of Bill's burnt eggs and a single slice of bacon. *At least there was that*, he thought.

As Greg reached for the strip of bacon, Kevin's hand snapped out and snatched it from the tray.

"You snooze, you lose, pal," the much larger man said. His wide, flat face seemed to rest in a mean grin, and he gave Greg a condescending wink as he shoved the bacon in his mouth.

Greg felt a bubble of rage deep in his chest. He always seemed to stumble into people like this. Big, arrogant, meathead bullies. They'd ruined his life so many times, systematically disassembled him from the ground up and stomped on the bits. No matter where he went, it seemed he could never escape the torment of muscly jerks with massive egos.

Fuck you, idiot. He wanted to growl menacingly. Instead he glared at his feet, took a small serving of burnt eggs, and went to sit beside Jack.

"Ah, our last intrepid adventurer has joined us!" Bill leaned through the door to the kitchen as Greg tried to stomach the scorched yellow chunks on his plate. "How are the eggs, Mr. Gupta?"

"They're very bad," Greg responded before realizing this wasn't a moment that called for honesty.

"Oh… uh… My apologies." Bill gave him a queer look before disappearing back into the kitchen.

"Can we get a move on already?" Margaret called after him, roughly massaging the dark bags under her eyes.

Bill gave a muffled response, but Greg's focus had shifted to Jack, who took the pieces of untouched bacon from his own plate — as well as a sausage and a slice of orange — and silently transferred them over to Greg's. This was a far better gift than the whiskey.

"Well?" Margaret demanded.

Bill's head slid back into view. "I said that we can depart once Mr. Gupta is ready, Dr. Simmons. Let's let our young companion here finish fueling that genius engineer brain of his. We're going to need it today, after all."

"No, I'm good!" Greg proclaimed, furiously shoving the bacon, sausage, and a bit of eggs in his mouth and pushing the plate away. "I'm ready when you are, Ms. Simm — sorry, I mean *Dr.* Simmons."

She gave him a dispassionate glance.

"Very well." Bill disappeared again amid the sound of clanging pots and clattering dishes, then strode confidently into the room. "Sophie, Greg, Dr. Simmons — we'll go ahead and call the four of us the excavation team — when you're ready, please grab whatever you think you may need for the day and meet me at the UTVs out by the carriage house."

They all gave various forms of agreement and stood, except for Greg, who turned to Jack.

"You're not going with us?" Greg asked.

"A good question," Jack muttered, then motioned to their employer. "Bill, a quick word?"

Bill strode over as the others funneled out of the room, leaving just him, Greg, and Jack standing in a close circle.

"Greg just bought up a good point. What exactly is my day-to-day role here? I mean, what am I supposed to be doing while you all are off doing your thing?" Jack asked Bill.

"Well, Jack, I'm glad you asked," Bill said, patting Jack on the back. "In truth, I see you as a bit of insurance. I wanted a man of your abilities present in case the rurality of our location became an issue. However, I must admit that I chose you namely due to your more recent occupation.

Our food stores here are plentiful, but the local government has been kind enough to grant us several out-of-season hunting permits. Perhaps some fresh local venison might hit the spot tonight, eh?"

"You're paying me a small fortune to hunt deer?" Jack asked skeptically.

Bill chuckled, then motioned to Greg. "Consider Mr. Gupta's role. He's being paid the same amount as you, only his job is to use his skills as an engineer in order to help myself and our companions overcome whatever obstacles may arise. You've been employed for the same purpose: to use your skills to help me overcome obstacles. As it sits, no obstacles have arisen, so perhaps a good deer hunt might be just the thing to kick things off. I'd say Kevin would join you, but he's got a full plate shoring up last minute logistics today. Perhaps the doctor might care to accompany you?"

"If you say so," Jack responded flatly.

Greg couldn't help but notice the skeptical look on Jack's face as Bill nodded and strode out of the room.

"What did he mean by 'obstacles'?" Greg asked once they were alone.

"I don't know," Jack muttered. "Whatever he meant, I get the feeling I'm not gonna like it."

GREG CLUNG for dear life to the roof strap of the bouncing four-seater UTV. Beside him, Sophie must have noticed because she eased off the gas a bit. He tried to flash her a thankful smile but quickly found that looking up from the small open-air vehicle's dashboard for even a second made his stomach turn. Instead he mustered a small "Thanks."

"We're almost there. Don't worry!" she called over the engine's roar.

He gave a fleeting thumbs up, but then the UTV hit another bump, and he was once again clinging to the roof strap with both hands.

"Is he gonna make it?" Bill shouted from the other UTV driving beside them.

Sophie called something back that Greg didn't make out. Rather than try and respond, he closed his eyes and focused on not vomiting up the breakfast meats that boiled in his stomach.

Several excruciatingly long minutes later, the vehicles came to a halt at a vibrant green cliffside field overlooking the ocean. A long, steel storage container, like the type one might find stacked neatly on the deck of a cargo ship, sat near the cliff's edge. Greg barely had time to appreciate the picturesque scene before him before he felt overcome by the dizzying sensation of nausea. He leaned on the UTV's side, urging the others to go on so that he might take a moment to ease his roiling stomach. The others dismounted and made their way over to the storage container.

"Take your time, Greg!" Bill called out as he helped Sophie unlock the creaking latch.

Greg waved, then waited for the storage container's massive doors to swing open and shield him from view before vomiting. He took another several minutes to recover, then joined them around a small card table that had been set up outside the container's opening, still wiping the burning stomach fluids from the corner of his mouth.

"That's not really an option," Sophie was saying to Margaret in a tone that seemed overly polite.

"Why not?" Margaret asked. "They do this all the time in central Europe. You know how many otherwise inaccessible underground caves have been excavated by drilling? What you're suggesting is one little fuckup away from suicide."

Sophie gave her a placating look. "Dr. Simmons, I promise you we have given this the utmost consideration—"

"With all due respect, I'd like to give it my own considerations," Margaret snapped.

"Mr. Gupta," Bill interjected before Sophie could respond. "Perhaps we could get an engineer's perspective. Sophie, if you wouldn't mind explaining the situation once again now that our more mechanically inclined friend has joined us."

"Sure." Sophie shot an annoyed look at the back of Bill's head. "What we're working with here is a beehive issue. Basically, this entire cliffside is littered with caves and caverns like you'd see in a honeycomb. Our entry point, where I discovered the spearhead and carvings, is a small opening about halfway down the cliffside — maybe seventy-five yards from the top. After the opening is a decent sized antechamber which leads downward into a maze of tunnels." She unfurled a laminated map that glinted in the morning sun. "This is a sonar map we took of the caves. As you can see, the system is massive. Too massive, even, for a full sonar reading." At this, she pointed to the edges of the map where the lines denoting the tunnels faded away. "Furthermore, this is only one level of this single tunnel system, and based on the geology here, we're guessing there are far more systems down there than just this one."

"Get to the good part," Margaret said with an eye roll.

Sophie pointed to a fuzzy gray line on the opposite side of the map from the cave entrance. "This is our target. The sonar system we used can generally detect the density of the materials it picks up on." She outlined the hard, black lines of the tunnels with her finger. "All of this is stone. But this gray part at the end, we believe this is wood. Now, Greg, there can't be this much wood down there naturally, not in this shape and volume. It's simply not possible. We believe that whatever this is must be *man-made,* and—"

"No, I meant the part where we die horribly," Margaret interrupted again.

Greg could tell from the growing vein in Sophie's temple that her blood pressure was rising with every interruption or rude quip, but her tone remained cordial. "The issue Dr. Simmons is referring to is the tidal flush. After the first cavern, there is a steep drop off from the main chamber that falls below the high tide mark. As you probably know, Nova Scotia is subject to some of the highest tides on the planet, so… as far as we can tell, many of these tunnels are susceptible to flooding for the four hours preceding and following high tide."

Greg felt a claustrophobic knot in his gut tighten as he looked over the spiderweb of tunnels presented on the map. "So… We, uh, we have two separate four-hour windows a day to get… how far is it?"

"About a quarter mile as the bird flies, but the route is much longer when you take into account all the ascending and descending," Sophie confirmed.

Greg wanted to throw up again.

"And back," Bill added.

"Or we tunnel down," Margaret offered. "Measure out exactly where that hunk of wood is and dig a nice clean hole straight to it. That way we maybe don't get trapped in rapidly filling tunnels of subterranean hell. Just a thought."

"That's a bad idea," Greg said, then almost flinched as Margaret's glare snapped to him. "If… if the cliffside is as porous as this is showing, then, you know… we, uh… we don't really want to go hacking away at it. Beyond the threat of creating a new fault line, we need to worry about the actual ground stability. Digging a hole that far down would probably be just as dangerous as spelunking in it, and definitely more expensive."

Margaret's face soured even more. "So we're just going to try and hoof it there and back and beat the tide?"

Sophie shook her head. "No. We've done the math, and the time limit is too restrictive to even think about taking this head-on." She pointed to inside the storage container where an organized pile of steel pulleys sat atop several large pieces of machinery. "That is exactly why we brought on an engineer."

All eyes turned to Greg, and his stomach tumbled once again.

VIII

Jack

"CAN IT not smell us?" Dr. Bianchi whispered.

Jack shushed the doctor without taking his eye away from the scope. The crosshairs continued to bob slightly despite the steadying brace of the rifle's sling wrapped tightly around his arm. Still, he felt confident enough to begin squeezing his finger. His lungs emptied as the pressure on the trigger increased, and the crosshairs came to a slow halt.

The shot was deafening, and in a wooded clearing eighty yards away, the massive buck staggered, then dropped. Jack worked the bolt quickly to chamber another round but otherwise remained still.

"Jeez Louise, that was much louder than I exp—"

Jack jutted out an insistent finger, once again silencing the little round man kneeling next to him. He kept his eyes on the mass of white and tan fur that lay barely visible between two distant birches. Short, violent waves rippled across its skin as the animal's muscles spasmed, but after a few seconds it went still.

Concealed by a large rhododendron, Jack and Bianchi stayed frozen and silent in their position for several long minutes. Jack could feel

Bianchi's mounting confusion next to him, and every time he felt as though the man was about to speak out, he would raise his finger again to silence him. Finally, once Jack was satisfied that the animal had passed, he slowly rose.

"You ever been caught off guard by a loud noise, doc?" Jack asked softly, slinging the rifle over his shoulder and starting toward the body. "The sound echoes off everything around. In this case the trees, rocks, hills… Unless you're expecting it, there's damn near no way to tell where a noise came from out here. Now, let's say you wing a deer with a bad shot. He's stunned, in pain, his fight or flight drive is kicking into sixth gear by the time he gets back up, but the noise is gone, and he has no idea where to go."

"So, we're just playing the odds that he comes running in our direction?" the doctor asked, a little disappointed.

"No. The opposite. We don't want him to run at all. If there's no pursuit, most of the time he'll pause and try to orientate, and we get another shot. Even if he takes off, we have to wait, so that the deer doesn't sense pursuit. If he senses a predator giving chase, then the adrenaline kicks in with full force, tainting the meat and driving him a whole lot farther and harder. This way when he does die, it's much closer and easier to track."

As they entered the clearing, the doctor gave a long, impressed whistle. But it transformed into a grunt as Jack's hand slapped against his chest.

"Stop." Jack eyed the freakishly large animal before them. It lay in a twisted heap, legs curled and crossed and head jutting so far back that the massive rack of antlers threatened to stab into its own spine. A myriad of thick scars carved paths through the blanket of rust-colored fur, crisscrossing and intersecting like a map of chaotic, source-less rivers. This wasn't normal, not for a whitetail. Jack's well-versed understanding was that wild animals seldom survived major injuries, almost always succumbing to blood loss or infection.

No, Jack thought. Despite its healthy, almost youthful appearance, this deer was both far larger and more weathered than any of the hundreds — maybe even thousands — he'd encountered before.

His eyes drifted to the bullet hole. It had been a clean shot, the 30-06 round leaving a circular, red entry wound just behind where the deer's foreleg met the torso. A thick pool of blood had already begun to seep out from underneath the body and soak into the spongey bed of moss. There was no discernable movement or signs of life, but that meant nothing. Jack's focus shifted to the deer's bulbous eyes: they were clamped shut. He shoved the rifle into the surprised doctor's arms, stepped forward, and drew his father's long, antler-handled Bowie knife from its sheath.

"What are you—" the doctor began.

"He's not dead."

"How—"

"The eyes," Jack hissed as he padded a wide circle to approach the deer from behind.

"So just shoot it again?"

In the old days, Jack would have done just that. Any sane hunter knew the dangers of entering within the striking distance of a mortally wounded animal — especially one with at least two dozen spear-like tines attached to its skull — but Jack had taken that second shot enough times before to know that a hair of miscalculation would result in a painful and violent death for the animal. Despite the fact that he'd rather endure a gored kidney than watch that happen again, he'd have been lying to himself if he didn't also acknowledge that a part of him considered that maybe the deer would be doing him a favor, should it manage to take him with it.

The doctor stood by anxiously as Jack knelt behind the buck and readied the knife. When he was sure of his target, he swiftly reached out and grasped the base of an antler. The deer's eyes snapped open and it gave one short-lived attempt to throw its head. But Jack's knife was too quick, and before the antler had a chance to wrench out his control, the blade slid between the vertebrae at the base of the animal's skull and twisted. The result was a sickening pop, then the panic disappeared from the suddenly lifeless eyes, replaced by an eerie, mechanical twitch.

Nearby, the doctor let out a quiet, deeply unsettling moan.

Jack decided to ignore the noise. In his experience as a guide, he knew that people often displayed a tendency to react in strange ways when dealing with death. But when the groan came a second time, just as Jack began the long cut along the deer's sternum, he was forced to look back. The diminutive man's normally warm features had taken on a new look, cold and hungry as he glared unblinking at the carnage in what Jack figured was morbid fascination.

"You alright, doc?"

The doctor didn't respond, and Jack noticed his fingers slowly rubbing together. Then, after a few seconds, the trance broke, and he glanced up to meet Jack's eyes. "Oh, erm— Yes. My apologies, it's just… fascinating."

The way the final word dribbled out of his mouth sent a creeping shiver down Jack's spine. *No more hunting trips with the doctor*, he noted silently, turning back and beginning the painstaking process of field dressing.

"RIGHT OUT here, Kevin. You *must* see the size of this thing!" Bianchi had disappeared into the manor's front door, but his enthusiastic shouting was still clear.

Jack stood under one of the few trees that grew immediately beside the house. He tried to embrace the burning fatigue in his arms as he yanked at an old rope looped over one of its branches. After a strained effort, he managed to hoist the deer carcass to a hang and secured the slack. He collapsed back against the tree's trunk, staring up at the gutted carcass swaying above him. The deer was even heavier than he'd initially thought; the long trek towing it back had put that into perspective. A part of him wondered if this buck might be some sort of record — probably not for the continent, but maybe for Nova Scotia. He shut his eyes and banished the thoughts from his mind. Records were for pricks.

"Not bad," came Kevin's voice alongside the thump of his heavy footsteps. Jack didn't bother to open his eyes.

"It was quite the shot!" the doctor proclaimed, and Jack could make out the lighter, quicker thumps as his short legs worked to keep up with his much taller companion. "We must have been a hundred and fifty, maybe even two hundred yards away, through thick brush, and—"

"Eighty yards," Jack cut in, finally regarding them as they surveyed the draining carcass. "And I had a clear target."

"Still," Bianchi insisted with continued enthusiasm. "It was extremely well placed."

"I've seen worse," Kevin said with a smirk. "Decent, for eighty yards. You've been hunting a long time, huh? What was your longest kill shot?"

Jack shrugged, then clumsily rose to his feet and began skinning the deer.

"Oh, come on, if you had to take a guess," Kevin insisted.

"Seven, maybe eight hundred on the open plains. Wouldn't risk it again, though. No need." The freshly honed knife cut easily through the fascia and exposed the still warm muscle beneath. "Doc, would you be a pal and go grab some freezer bags? I think I saw some in the pantry earlier."

The doctor gave a giddy nod and scurried off. His stubby figure looked almost comical as it bounded away, especially contrasted against Kevin's bulk.

Kevin shrugged nonchalantly and made a show of staring off over the nearby oceanside cliffs. "Makes sense. No need to reach out too far if there's no real danger. There's just a different mentality when the target can shoot back, you know? Longest for me? Let's see… Shit, I once took out a haji at damn near a half mile with a .50 cal."

"Neat," Jack said flatly.

"Yeah, well, you might feel more comfortable at a distance if you upgraded your kit a little bit," Kevin went on, nodding to the old wood-stocked deer rifle leaning against the tree. "That Elmer Fudd stuff will only get you so far. I've got a handful of toys upstairs I could introduce you to, maybe teach you a thing or two. Ever shot a .338 Lapua?"

"Nope."

"Okay, how about an AR-10?"

"Yeah. Not for me."

"Oh man." Kevin sucked his lip and cracked his neck dramatically. "Fuckin' love that shit. No better weapon to take on the most dangerous game, if you know what I'm sayin'."

"I'm not sure I do," Jack said.

The sarcasm seemed to evade Kevin, and he gave Jack a condescending look. "I mean, you know, the *most dangerous game?* Humans, bro."

Jack gave an empty "ahhh" without looking away from his work.

Bianchi came trotting back, bags in hand, and there was a prolonged silence. Jack figured some of his blatant disinterest must have started seeping through Kevin's thick skull because when the man spoke again, his voice was more aggressive and seemed to be for the benefit of the more easily impressed doctor.

"Been a while since I've been hunting," Kevin began, circling around and lightly slapping the side of the hanging carcass. "Used to be a pro at cutting these things up. Deer got boring though. Last time I went was with a few of my spec ops pals out in Wyoming. The Rockies — roughest land in the country. Out there hunting *grizzly*. You ever hunted grizzly, Jack?"

"Nope."

"Yeah, tagged one, clean shot: *pew!*" Kevin mimed a rifle shot. "Dropped like a sack of potatoes. Real rush, man."

"Cool."

"Yeah, it was." Kevin scowled. His next words came as a challenge. "So, Jack, what's the most dangerous game you've hunted?"

"I don't know."

"If you had to guess…"

"If I had to guess… Deer."

"*What?*" Kevin laughed. "You're kidding. Your whole job is hunting, and you've never killed so much as a bear?"

"I've killed bear."

"Wait, you've killed—" Kevin's eyes narrowed. He clearly suspected he was being taken for a ride. "So you're trying to tell me that you think a *deer* is more dangerous than a *bear*? Yeah, okay."

"In my experience, they have been."

"Bullshit. A bear has claws, fangs. Shit, they're apex fuckin' predators," Kevin spat.

"You said 'most dangerous,' not 'best equipped.'"

"What?"

Jack sighed and turned to face him. "How far away were you when you shot that bear?"

"Uh…" Kevin stuttered. "Maybe, like, three hundred yards?"

"So it didn't charge."

"Nah, dropped clean." Kevin gave a proud smirk.

Jack pointed his bloodied knife at the half-skinned deer beside him. "I finished this one with a knife. One little fuck up, and I'd have a belly full of holes from those antlers. You understand? It's all about context."

Kevin's eyes narrowed. "What the hell does that have to do with—"

"This isn't combat. You didn't *fight* that bear. It probably didn't even know you existed when you killed it, and even if it did, there was very little, if *anything*, it could have done about it. You either harvested it for a purpose, or you murdered it for ego. Either way, it was a one-sided fight and that animal didn't stand a chance. A twelve-year-old girl can shoot a bear. It doesn't take much. The only danger we face from these animals is the danger we bring on ourselves through stupidity or lack of preparedness. I'll take a grizzly at three hundred yards with a rifle over a wounded, cornered buck up close and personal with a broken bowstring any day."

The half confused look on Kevin's face shifted slightly toward anger. "I don't—"

"Look, man," Jack cut him off again and pointed to the deer. "I'm pretty beat from hauling this thing back. You're a pro at this, right?"

"Of course," Kevin insisted, puffing out his chest.

Jack fought the increasing urge to throw a punch and instead motioned to the knife on Kevin's belt. "You mind finishing up here? I figure we can have the backstraps fresh tonight and freeze the rest. And make sure you don't waste any. Bill said we have a limited permit for sustenance hunting while we're out here."

Kevin fumbled for a response, but before he could pick any in particular, Jack strode up, clapped him on the back with a bloody hand, and gave him a wide, disingenuous grin. "Thanks, pal. I'm gonna head in and wash up. Doc, what do you say we figure out how to work that coffee maker?"

The doctor joined him and together they walked up the porch and to the front door, leaving Kevin standing there, motionlessly surveying the hanging carcass.

"Not a fan of that one, eh?" the doctor asked with a smile as they entered the house.

"He's got too much to prove," Jack said. "In my experience, it's guys like that who ruin the game for everyone."

The doctor let out a chuckle. "Surprising. I thought the two hunters here would get along."

"That guy's no hunter," Jack said, glancing back out the window at the man frozen in front of the swaying deer. "Look at him; he has no idea what to do with that thing."

"Well, if he's hunted bear—"

"That whole story was bullshit."

"How do you know?"

"It's illegal to hunt grizzlies in that part of the Rockies."

The doctor laughed. "Next thing you'll tell me is that he wasn't even a Navy SEAL."

Jack crossed into the kitchen and flipped on the coffee maker. "I don't know, doc. But if that prick was really a SEAL commander, then I'm Mickey fuckin' Mouse."

IX

Margaret

A SALTY breeze cascaded over the oceanside cliffs a mile north of Clayborn Manor. Legs dangling off the cliff's edge, Margaret sat apart from the other three members of the excavation team. The thunderous crashing of waves far below drowned out all the surrounding noises of the morning. The only sound that conquered the raw roar of the ocean below was the rhythmic whisper of her own breath. For the first time that day, she felt the comforting embrace of solitude.

She glowered at the cloudy afternoon sky while rolling half a pill between her fingers. It hadn't taken her long that morning to realize that she had extraordinarily little interest in the mechanical bickering between Greg and Bill. When she'd finally abandoned the conversation an hour before, Greg had been stumbling through some stutter-ridden tangent about actuators and pulleys and creating a system of cable elevators or some other nonsense.

"Do you want to see it?"

Just as in the bathroom the evening before, Sophie's voice startled her, even more so this time due to Margaret's precarious perch. She turned to regard the young woman who had silently manifested behind her. "Don't you know not to sneak up on— Ugh, never mind. See what?"

"The cave. I'm sure you noticed the rigging is already set up." Sophie motioned to two frighteningly bare steel cords that dangled over the rocky ledge nearby. "Have you ever rappelled?"

"It's been a while…" *More like twenty years.*

"Well, it's up to you, Dr. Simmons. We can't get too deep into the tunnels yet, but I'd be happy to show you what we've got so far."

Margaret paused, feeling the hard edges of the pill concealed in her hand. She'd been hoping to pop it soon and enjoy an afternoon free of cravings, maybe even have a few glasses of wine later… but spelunking called for coordination.

"Fine. Let's see the damn thing," she muttered, discreetly tucking the half pill into her breast pocket as she climbed to her feet.

THE HARNESS dug painfully into Margaret's hips as she and Sophie descended the rocky cliff face side-by-side. Every so often, her foot would slip off some loose earth or slick stone, sending her heart spasming up into her throat. It wasn't until the two women reached the cave's mouth and had their feet back on solid earth that she finally looked down — and immediately wished she hadn't. Nearly 200 feet below them at a sheer drop, furious, white-capped waves thundered and smashed against the broken stones that littered the immediate shore. From the clifftop above, the frenzied battle between land and sea had felt distant and romantic, but now, after dangling so precariously above it, it was simply terrifying.

"It's best not to look down," Sophie called over the din. Her voice echoed eerily back at them from the muted darkness of the cave beyond.

"Too late for that shit," Margaret muttered, fumbling with the zipper of her pocket with trembling hands. As soon Sophie turned away, she popped the half dose of oxy and swallowed hard.

"The entry chamber is just through here!" Sophie called over her shoulder as she walked deeper into the dark maw of the cave.

Margaret gave the crashing waves one final, horrified glance then turned, clicked on her headlamp, and followed Sophie.

The cave's entrance was little more than a pockmark on the massive cliff face, only six yards across and half that high. However, after a few swift strides across the smooth floor, Margaret found that the cave opened dramatically.

The antechamber Sophie led her into was damp and filled with the echoing whistle of the wind against the cave entrance. Easily the size of a small lecture hall, it dwarfed Clayborn Manor's cavernous foyer — though it gave her a similarly eerie feeling in the way the darkness hungrily consumed the few rays of daylight that managed to penetrate this far in. The cave walls were rough and cracked, and a number of young stalactites hung above the uneven floor. As she followed Sophie deeper into the cliff's face, Margaret could make out small pockets of inscriptions dispersed along the walls.

"Over here." Sophie shielded her eyes from the bright beam of Margaret's headlamp as its light snapped to her, then pointed to a shadow on the wall. "This is where I found the spearhead. Note the symbols here."

Margaret crossed over to her, the headlamp's beam cutting through the darkness like a scalpel. The strange array of markings etched into the solid stone wall were each barely larger than a closed fist, and similar to the ancient Phoenician letters she'd studied in graduate school. However, they varied just enough from the traditional forms that she couldn't decipher their meanings. After taking in the images, she leaned in close and observed the more mechanical aspects of the carvings themselves. The lines were clean and precise, cutting straight into the stone at a ninety-degree angle. This was granite, which meant etchings like these would require either an absolutely absurd amount of time with ancient methods, or, in most cases, the use of hardened steel tools. Steel tools that the Phoenicians wouldn't have had. As she angled the light into the corners of the letters, she noted the distinct residue of dull red ocher, an ancient coloring agent, still wedged in the lettering's deepest recesses.

"What's it say?" Margaret asked.

"I was hoping you could tell me," Sophie muttered. "There's more."

Margaret stepped back, letting the beam of her headlamp cast a wide, arcing light over the cave walls. Dozens of similar carvings littered them, each etched with the same precision and care as the last.

"Jesus… What's the connection?" Margaret asked, feigning ignorance of the glaringly obvious answer.

"I don't know. I imagine they're just symbols these Phoenician explorers picked up along the way," Sophie offered.

Bullshit. Margaret almost spit the word out loud. This little brat was supposed to be a brilliant young archaeologist? She knew exactly what the connection was. Hell, even that buffoon Bill could have seen it. Sophie was clearly playing dumb.

But why?

"I think you're right," Margaret lied, pointing to a triangle, circle, and square all encased in larger circle. "That looks like one of the seals of Tyre. It would've been sacked in the same era that the spearhead came from. You don't think… Perhaps the people who left the spearhead here were Phoenician survivors fleeing Alexander the Great?" She made sure to give the question a false air of hope.

"Dr. Simmons, I think you might be on to something…" Sophie said, and while the inflection of her voice seemed genuine, Margaret caught the smallest movement in the peripheral light of her headlamp: a disappointed head shake.

Sure I am, you little shit.

"Perhaps we should continue. We can get another thirty meters or so before the first steep drop-off," Sophie offered, motioning to a small opening in the back of the cave.

Margaret strode up to opening. The light of her headlamp dissolved into the darkness of the long, winding corridor. Even from here she could make out the distant gurgle of rising seawater filling the tunnels deep below. "Eh, why bother?"

Sophie paused. "I thought you might want to see—"

"With any of it, I mean," Margaret muttered, eyeing the inky void beyond the flashlight's beam one last time before turning back.

"I'm sorry?"

"You should be. For wasting my time." Margaret pointed to the symbol she'd purposely misidentified. "An alchemy symbol? Really? And the philosopher's stone at that. Little bit of a fucking anachronism for Phoenicians, hm?"

Sophie's words jumbled out nervously. "Well, I mean, nobody has an actual date on when the alchemical symbol was first—"

"Are you even an archaeologist? Or just a full time grifter?" Margaret asked. Sophie tried to protest but Margaret waved her off and continued. "I mean, fuck Bill. He's a creep anyways. If you can take his money, go for it. I won't rat you out. But I also won't drown in some subterranean shithole on your fabricated goose chase. Good luck running your scam. I'm leaving."

"Wait!" Sophie called as Margaret made to cross back to the cave opening. Margaret ignored her until she heard the slapping of running feet and felt a firm hand on her shoulder.

"Please," Sophie insisted. "Just let me—"

Margaret spun and knocked her hand away. "You touch me near that edge out there and you'll see how mean an old bitch I really am, girl."

"I didn't mean..." Sophie began, but when Margaret raised a threatening finger, Sophie's voice dropped off. The desperate look on her face melted away, replaced by a tired exasperation. "Fine," she groaned. "I'm tired of this bullshit anyways."

Sophie plopped down a stony outcropping and pulled out a pack of cigarettes. After lighting one, she eyed Margaret. "You think I'd have involved that chauvinistic prick if I had a choice?"

Margaret snorted, shaking off her surprise over Sophie's sudden shift in character and looking at the girl with a hint of newfound respect. "Well, at least you own up to it. The carvings aren't half bad, I have to admit, and the ocher was a good touch—"

"I didn't carve a damn thing." Sophie took a deep, frustrated breath. "Look, lady, Bill wanted to run with some flimsy story to keep you all in the dark about what actually brought us down here, but the man has about three brain cells and two of 'em are devoted solely to being a pervert. I figured, nay, *hoped* you'd see through that Phoenician nonsense. Why do you think I brought you down here on day one? So you could see this for yourself, maybe even understand the *actual* importance of what this place is."

Margaret stood silently, trying to gauge Sophie's new angle of approach, what she was trying to do, and —more importantly — why?

"Imagine, just for a second, that this isn't a hoax. You understand what all this would mean, don't you?" Sophie asked.

"You want a theme?" Margaret asked, figuring she might as well indulge the young con artist. "They all relate to medicine and restoration. The alchemical symbol for the philosopher's stone, the Celtic cauldron, the Grail… symbols of elixir myths, stories of endless youth and health, of raising the dead… half of which weren't even around when the Phoenicians—"

"Forget Phoenicians," Sophie interrupted. "The spearhead was bullshit; some old Greek hunk of bronze Bill managed to get his greasy sausage fingers on. Why do you think we wouldn't let you take it out of the glass case? I mean, *come on…*"

"Look, kid." Margaret pushed a hint of venom into her tone. "I'll admit that I'm liking this brash side of you a bit more than the bubbly dish maid, but maybe reel in the attitude a bit."

Sophie snorted and threw her hands up defeatedly. "*So* sorry. I guess I'm just a bit pissy about the prospect of being stuck as the lone woman here with that rich turd Bill and his gaggle of halfcocked cronies."

Margaret scoffed. "Appealing to my sense of sisterhood? That's a low blow. But it only works if you can't walk away either. Run your little scam, but don't try manipulating me into running it with you."

Sophie took a long drag from her cigarette. "Look, I've put myself in your shoes, and I understand that there likely isn't a damn thing I could say right now that would convince you I'm being honest. I'll tell you anyways: Everything you see in this cave, it's *real*. All of it. And I didn't stumble across this place — this was four years of obsessive research, dissecting myths, and wading through more bullshit academia than any sane person should be subjected to. I backtracked a hundred interconnecting legends from the Welsh and Irish all the way through the Mi'kmaq, and it brought me here. *I* found this place — *all on my own* — and couldn't get so much as a dollar to excavate it from a single one of your beloved institutions. You can be like your peers and blow it off — but just know abandoning this site will be your greatest professional regret."

"It's a nice story…" Margaret started, then she considered the younger woman's face. She wasn't pleading or hopeful — she was genuinely annoyed. Sophie's attitude reminded Margaret just enough of her own youthful struggles to be taken seriously in the world of academia that she decided to humor her. "There's really an anomaly down in those caves?"

"Yes."

"What's behind it?"

"I don't know."

"Okay, what do you *think* is behind it?"

Sophie took a deep breath, seeming to prepare herself for the impending rejection. "Bran's Cauldron."

Margaret didn't stifle her laugh. "*What?*"

"You sound like my advisor."

"Maybe there's a reason Bill Emery is the only one who would listen to you." Margaret shook her head. "What in the ever living fuck has led you to believe that an old British zombie pot is buried here — in Canada?"

"If you really want to know then you'll stop sniggering." Sophie's voice carried a hint of disdain.

Margaret steeled her face and raised an eyebrow. "Well?"

"First off, it's a Welsh legend, not British."

"Potayto, potahto," Margaret muttered.

"No, that'd be the Irish," Sophie deadpanned.

Margaret couldn't help but grin. A tiny bit of the tension that filled the yawning cave dissipated.

"Secondly," Sophie went on. "I— well, there's no short way of going about this. Have you ever heard of the twelfth century Welsh prince named Madoc?"

"*Oh God…* The one from the Welsh–Indian legend?" Margaret scoffed. "I hope you've got more than that."

"What I've got are three published papers on related subjects, and I'm either one successful dig or an unenthusiastic blowjob away from a PhD, so please, just indulge me for two minutes," Sophie snapped back.

"Fine." Margaret was surprised at how much she suddenly liked this girl.

"Growing up," Sophie began. "I heard the same age-old Welsh–Indian legend as everyone else: in the twelfth century, a Welsh prince named Madoc fled his homeland after the death of his father and sailed west, where he discovered new lands and, in some renditions, the fountain of youth. Every historian with an ounce of professional respect has come to the same conclusion — that it all boils down to little more than nonsense Revolution-era Anglo-centric propaganda claiming that the Americas were originally discovered by a Welshman. But Thomas Jefferson didn't consider it propaganda. In fact, he charged Lewis and Clarke to seek out the remnants of the lost Welsh–Indian tribe during their famous journey west across America.

"During my undergraduate, I got stuck working on a project research-ing and cataloguing Lewis and Clark's scattered efforts to prove what even they considered a largely crackpot theory. In order to prove my hypothesis — that the story was nothing but nationalistic nonsense — I pored through hundreds of texts detailing both ancient Welsh and Native American myths and legends looking for similarities and potential connections, all the while fully believing that I was wasting my fucking time. So, you can imagine my surprise upon discovering that there *were* connections. Only a few weak links at first, entirely built on a timeline that made absolutely no sense — they hinted at some connection having been forged between the two ancient peoples long, *long* before the twelfth century." Sophie paused to give Margaret a poignant glare.

"So I started to backtrack these connections through the Welsh written records," she recounted. "The further back I got, the weirder shit became. I discovered that the twelfth century prince Madoc wasn't the first 'Madoc' who supposedly sailed west in search of the fountain of youth. Half a millennia before, in the seventh century, came the legend of Maedoc of Ferns. This Maedoc — different spelling of course, but the same etymological name — ended up as a Christian saint. But before *that*, he was a figure shrouded in mystery who was said to have ridden a serpent west from Wales and across the ocean, again in search of the fountain of youth. It felt like coincidence at first, but then when I pushed even *further* back, into the earliest written records of the island, I found something else. Something that made it all come together."

Sophie paused again, but this time, an almost wry smile spread across her face. "In the oldest renditions of the *Mabinogion*, the most ancient of all Welsh stories, the last of King Bran's inner circle fled west over the sea following his death, bringing with them the cursed cauldron of rebirth. Those men were led by none other than a druid priest named Maedig..." At this, she look up at Margaret. "Madoc, Maedoc, Maedig, all fleeing west, all related to a great life-giving magic. Twice is a coincidence, thrice is a pattern."

"There have probably been ten thousand 'Madoc's in history," Margaret said. She was intrigued, but if this girl's theory was really built on the similarity of three names spaced a millennia apart, then she'd misjudged Sophie's intelligence.

"Aye, but what we're talking about is not a repetition of events, it's the natural evolution a character takes in an oral tradition. There weren't three Madocs; there was one, and his story was retold constantly and always in new ways in order to keep the legend alive with changing times. My research led me to believe that if there *was* a historical figure, he most likely existed in the first century. Right around the time that the Romans invaded the British Isles. Whoever he really was, he took something of great value — likely a talisman or even some sort of pre-Medieval technology — and sailed to new lands in the west two thousand years ago.

"I scoured the records of coastal tribes up and down the east coast for any legends of someone or something coming from the ocean and assimilating into their society. There were none. But there was one *very specific* legend that the Mi'kmaq had allowed a young colonial librarian to record. It told of pale spirits that emerged from the waters maybe a mile from where we stand now. They rejected the friendship of the locals, instead burrowing into the earth like bugs, souring the land."

"You did all of this this from a library halfway around the world?" Margaret asked. She was half impressed, half skeptical as hell. "Then what? You just happened to find this exact cave on Google maps?"

Sophie snorted. "You're closer than you think. I took a break from school, flew across the ocean, and blew most of my savings spelunking every cave I could find in this cliffside for a month. I was about to give up when I found this one."

"Ballsy," Margaret admitted.

"But finding the cave was only the first step. What's here, that's the real mind fuck," Sophie went on, the tempo of her voice quickening. "You can trace a singular line through history, from Utnapishtim to Herodotus and the Macrobians to the Ark of the Covenant, all the way through the *Alexander Romance*, the Holy Grail, and finally to the second branch of the *Mabinogi*. They're all connected — sequential even. From the beginning of recorded history all the way until the first century. Then chain just ends. At that point, literature and history don't place anyone actually possessing this life-extending thing anymore, only that people and cultures were searching for it, recounting legends about some great treasure lost to time. What I've found in my research has led me to believe that it was then, the first century AD, that this druidic priest Maedig fled Wales and made landfall along these very cliffs. I think he brought something with him, something that, through the chaos of history, had wound up in the possession of the Welsh. Something that we know as Bran's Cauldron, though I doubt it's as simple as an iron pot. Whatever it was, Maedig hid it here almost two thousand years ago. Those carvings aren't forgeries, Dr. Simmons — they're warnings. Warnings he and his men etched into these walls in order to protect whatever it was they sealed down here."

"Wait, you're telling me that think you've found the fountain of youth?" Margaret scoffed.

"I don't think there's actual magic here," Sophie added quickly. "I'm not *that* much of a lost cause. But I do believe there's something here that those ancient people attributed great value to. I think a group of desperate men in ancient times found this place and gave up their lives to hide something. Something that, no matter how mundane or genuinely inert it may be in reality, may have inspired some of the great myths and legends of our ancestors."

Margaret sighed. As much as she had begun enjoying the little sprite's antics, they weren't enough to buy her time. "It's a good pitch, but I'm afraid I'm not sold, Sophie. Maybe if I was your age, I'd—"

"Fine," Sophie cut in quickly. "Fine. I'll tell you what. I can't convince you, but maybe I can buy you. No offense, but you're an addict, yeah?"

Margaret paused. "What the fuck did you just say to me?"

"You're a pill head, an opiate addict, right?" Sophie must have noticed the growing red of Margaret's face as rage flushed to the surface. "Oh, come on, you think I didn't see you pop that pill not ten minutes ago? I mean, it's dark as hell down here and your pupils are fuckin' pinpoints. I just… All I'm saying is that we're all adults here. Adults who stand to make a lot of money. More money means you can skip out on that garbage community college gig you're barely surviving on and do whatever the fuck you want. *Ingest* whatever the fuck you want. How much did Bill promise you? Two hundred thousand?"

Margaret was once again silent. She battled the desire to reward an arcing slap to the suddenly too-confident, young Irish woman seated on the stone before her. Sophie met her furious gaze without blinking.

"Even beyond splitting the find, he's contracted me for twice that," Sophie said. "Four hundred thousand American dollars. I'll sign my paycheck over to you before we even begin. *That's* how confident I am in this dig. If there's nothing here, I'll walk away with fuck all but a handful of 'I told ya so's from everyone I went to for funding before I stooped to Bill. Imagine what you could do with an extra four hundred grand. It's yours, but only *if* you stick around and help me do this."

"Do what, exactly?" The words barely managed to slip through Margaret's clenched jaw, but the idea of the mounting sum lubricated their path.

"Get through this damn cave, for a start."

Margaret shook her head. "If you really believe all this nonsense, then why do you need me?"

Sophie smiled, and Margaret could tell the younger woman knew the money had hooked her. "They say you're one of the foremost minds in the study of ancient Native American culture. We're standing on ancient native soil. If there's one person in this whole gaggle who Bill brought on that I'd like to stick around, it's the woman with the education and experience to actually be an asset."

There was a long silence as Margaret pondered her options. Her next words came out slow and stern. "You'll sign a contract *today*, entitling me to your sum. Also, you won't say a goddamn word to anyone about the pills."

"Deal!" Sophie hopped up, a satisfied grin on her face. "But I should warn you, I think Bill already knows. I'm pretty sure he has dirt on the whole crew — but you didn't hear it from me."

"Fuck Bill." Margaret held out her hand, and Sophie took it in a firm grip and shook.

"Fuck Bill," Sophie repeated, her grin spreading. "…But not literally. Also, I get to call you Margaret from now on. You're not my goddamn professor."

Despite everything, Margaret couldn't help but give a small grin of her own.

Sophie

"ALRIGHT, LAY 'em out and show me what you've got," Jack said, tossing his own cards down to reveal a pair of threes.

Sophie watched Greg's face sink as he gently slid his own cards onto the table in front of him. A two and a seven. Nothing.

"That's alright, bud. You'll get it next time," Jack prodded reassuringly, motioning to Sophie. "Let's see 'em, cowgirl."

She stifled a grin as she flipped over her cards, instead shooting Jack a teasing *boo hoo* face. He rolled his eyes and shoved the pile of chips that centered the table toward her.

The three of them sat in plush, wingback chairs around a small coffee table in the center of the bottom floor's cavernous foyer. The mildewy scent of the timeworn furniture intertwined with the rich bouquet of antique wood, the savory scent of the crackling hearth, and the wafting ozone that drifted in through the occasionally billowing curtains. Together the smells blended to create a surprisingly comforting aura that reminded Sophie of donning an old, comfortable shoe.

Nearby, Margaret sat beside the fireplace, scrolling obsessively through something on her tablet. Sophie figured it most likely had something to do with case law regarding pre-payment contracts, as just few hours before she'd signed a document Margaret had drafted entitling the older woman to her upcoming paycheck.

"So, you and Margaret have to get to a wall buried half a mile deep in some maze of tunnels, huh?" Jack asked nonchalantly as he shuffled the cards and doled out another hand.

"More or less," Sophie said curtly. The whole team had already had a long conversation on the subject over dinner a couple hours earlier, so she figured this line of questioning was just some sneaky attempt for Jack to throw her off her poker game.

He smirked, tossing a handful of chips to the center of the stained old table. "How's that gonna work?"

"We'll see," she said, raising him.

Greg let out an almost imperceptible groan and folded. Jack clearly noticed the defeated nature of the noise because he folded as well and shifted his shoulders ever so slightly toward the younger man.

"What do you think, Greg? First impressions of poker?" he asked sincerely.

"It's fine, I guess," Greg muttered.

"The trick is confidence, my friend. Let me show you." Jack stood and made for the dining room, giving Greg a light slap on the back as he passed. "But first, tell me again how you're going to pull this whole thing off. I didn't quite catch it all earlier."

Jack had listened intently at dinner and doubtlessly understood every word that had been spoken. Sophie knew this because she'd noticed him sketching the cliffs schematics in a small notebook as she'd explained the pulley system. She now saw his question for what it was — an attempt to ease Greg just a tiny bit more out of his shell.

"Well… the, uh, the whole goal is safety," Greg started. "We need to get them in and out of there during a very short window. The generator we install up top will power a series of winches, which will in turn raise and lower the cargo from the mouth of the cave itself. That part, is, well, you know, the easy part. Once they're in, the plan is to install a bunch of pulley-bound cables at the numerous points in the cave system that offer a more vertical challenge. That will allow the ladies— sorry, the *archaeologists*—"

Sophie gave an appreciative smile. Greg seemed like a sweet kid. Maybe a little touched, but sweet nonetheless.

"—to use basic, battery-powered ascenders to more effectively traverse the lower tunnels. Using the sonar map, I think the installation of a sufficient pulley system should only take five, maybe six low tide excursions before they're able to reach the end of the tunnel. So, you know, given hard work and a lack of complications, we may be able to get to the wooden anomaly within the week."

"Awesome." Jack returned with a stack of glasses and a sloshing brown liquor bottle. "We're lucky you're here with us, bud. I personally don't know many folks who could pull something like that off."

Jack eased back into his seat with a grace that still surprised Sophie — especially given his disability — and doled out three aggressively poured shots. "Take this. It's the secret to a good poker face." He held one out to Greg with a slight nod.

"Aye, getting too drunk to see your cards means you can't give them away," Sophie said with a wink at Greg, who hesitated only a second before joining the other two and upending his glass.

The rum was sickeningly sweet. It clung to her tongue like molasses and she had to shake her head to keep from heaving. Greg coughed loudly, and Jack made a disgusted face.

"The hell are you trying to poison us with?" Sophie demanded.

Jack cleared his throat several times as he tried to hold himself together and stared at the bottle with a look of betrayal. "It's Bill's rum. I figured he wouldn't miss a few shots' worth. But my God, is it cut with straight antifreeze?"

Greg had shut his eyes and was rocking back and forth slightly. Sophie knew that look: he was trying to keep from vomiting.

"Forget that syrupy garbage. Watch my cards, *Greg*, I'll be right back." As she stood to leave the table, she shot Jack a dramatically suspicious look which he returned with a toothy grin. Seconds later, as she quietly jaunted up the stairs toward her room, she realized that that look — along with most of their interactions since the night before — was probably seen as pretty transparent flirting to the others.

A massive part of her didn't care. So what if she wanted to flirt with a man on an archaeological expedition? It's not like the majority of academics hadn't indulged in some fling while out in the field for a prolonged period. Who was to say she couldn't hit on who she wanted to? Or fuck who she wanted to? Or reject who she wanted to?

But that was the crux of the issue, wasn't it? The fact that Bill's prior advances had gone unreciprocated hadn't seemed to get through to him. Not until earlier that evening after dinner, when Sophie was hurriedly clearing the dining table and fantasizing about never scraping another plate again, when Bill had surprised her in the kitchen with gentle hand laid on her lower back as she bent over to pick up an onion skin that had fallen on the floor.

Six words had escaped. Jagged and furious, they'd erupted from deep in her belly and entered the world loud enough for the rest of the team, all scattered among the other rooms, to catch clear as day.

"Keep yer fuckin' hands to yerself!"

At a bar in Dublin, she'd once watched one of her friends knee a handsy bouncer in the crotch so hard that even she had flinched. The pathetic horror on Bill's face as those words slammed into him might have dwarfed the pain that bouncer had felt. Shortly after a stuttering, disingenuous apology, he had disappeared upstairs to lick his wounds.

Rejecting Bill was an absolute. She would never sell out her dignity regardless of the price. A part of her had felt victorious in asserting that fact. However, openly flirting with Jack did make her wonder if it was really a wise choice to be rubbing it in. As she reached her room and dug an old bottle of her hometown's famed whiskey from deep in the closet, she made the decision to ease up on her banter with Jack. She'd gone ages without bothering to indulge that part of herself, so it shouldn't be that hard to keep up.

GREG'S SQUEAKING belly laugh filled the room. He plucked his third serving of Sophie's whiskey from the table and drained the glass, then hiccupped and laughed harder.

Jack and Sophie were laughing too. Greg had just successfully won his fourth hand in a row. Of course, he hadn't *actually* won, but after realizing just how excited he got after winning the first one, the others had begun ignoring the cards and just giving him the pot.

Across the room, Margaret sucked her teeth as Jack poured Greg another splash.

"What?" Jack laughed, turning her way. "Not a fan of the devil's nectar?"

"You're going to kill the damn kid," Margaret muttered.

"Come now, Dr. Simmons, how can you still be that cold when you're that close to a fire?" Jack came back. "Join us. Maybe you could teach him a thing or two about handling his liquor."

Margaret shook her head without looking away from her tablet.

Greg took a steadying breath and turned in her direction. "I don't like drinking, but this stuff is really—*urp*—really good. You should come have some."

She ignored him, and Sophie indulged the urge to pipe in. "Can I ask what's got you so enthralled over there, Margaret?"

"It's Miss *Doctor* Margaret," Greg slurred, but Sophie waved him off.

Margaret sighed. "Do I really have to go upstairs to be left alone?"

"Yeah, probably. Or you could join us." Jack brandished the bottle at her. "I don't think we can consider each other housemates until we've had at least *one* real drink together."

Sophie watched as Margaret pinched her eyes shut and threw her head back. After a moment, the older woman rose with a grumble and crossed to the table. Jack pulled up a seat for her and poured an extra-large serving of whiskey. She shot it without so much as a flinch.

Greg immediately leaned in to stare at her tablet. "What's a *mag-bolognian?*"

"Mabinogion," Margaret corrected absently, then glanced up at Sophie. "The Second Branch of the *Mabinogi*, to be more specific."

The warmth of the alcohol in Sophie's blood dissipated. She felt her upper lip twitch.

Margaret must have noticed the tick because her own mouth lifted into a sly crescent. Her annoyance at being bothered was clearly feeding her spite. "You've heard of it, of course."

"Of course," Sophie said, silently swearing to herself.

"I haven't," Jack said, turning in his chair. "What is it?"

Sophie glared into the shrewd professor's eyes from across the table. "Just another old story," she said.

"Really? Hell yeah! Let's hear it then." Jack reclined in his seat and grinned.

"No, it's not that interesti—"

"I'd love to hear your version," Margaret said coolly without breaking eye contact with her.

Seriously?

Sophie let out a resigned sighed. She didn't like the idea of Margaret exercising some sort of manipulative power over her, but in her current state, she also couldn't think of a good reason not to share the age-old tale.

"Sure." She cleared her throat and shut her eyes, preparing the tale she knew by heart. "Fuck it. Why not..."

Long ago before the mutterings of Christ, kings and gods bartered and battled, and mortality and magic were equally vague in their existences. These were the days of King Bran the Blessed, a warrior giant in both reputation and magnitude. He towered over his people, shading them from the jagged arrows of the world with his wisdom and grace.

One cold winter morning, Bran sat along the cliffs of Wales, watching the ocean's barrage against the stones of his kingdom. On the horizon, a fleet of Irish ships approached. Not knowing whether they came as friend or foe, Bran met them on the shore, alone and bearing a great sword on his shoulder. The strangers debarked their ships, and it was revealed that Matholwch, the young Irish king, was among them.

Matholwch was a decent man by reputation, and it was only by reputation that Bran knew the Irish king, so he led the visiting sailors back to his hall and poured them mead and served them meat, and they all made merry. As Bran warmed to the young king Matholwch's nature, he offered a proposition: Matholwch would marry Branwen, Bran's beautiful sister, and thus their two kingdoms would be united. Matholwch eagerly agreed, and the plan was set.

But Bran was not Branwen's only brother. While they were both sired of the great spirit Llyr, their mother also bore two mortal men. One of those men was Efnysian. Efnysian was human, yes, but he was no normal child. He was wild and conniving, wicked for the love of bloodshed. When he discovered that the king had bartered off his half-sister, he grew furious. In an act of rage, he slunk through the Irish camp with a hooked knife and mutilated their most prized steeds.

Upon waking to the carnage, Matholwch made to abandon the deal he had struck with Bran and sought to prepare for war. Bran was shocked to learn of his half-brother's actions and swore to replace the ruined horses as well as award gifts of gold and silver in order to mend this fresh wound. But Matholwch was not sated by the new gifts nor the promise of Branwen's hand, and for the first time, Bran grew wary of his new ally.

But King Bran was ever the cautious man, and he had a plan. He had in his possession something ancient and holy, something that had been gifted to him for safekeeping many years before by refugees seeking solace from the lands across the southern sea. These refugees had given Bran a great golden cauldron that was believed to hold the very soul of a god in its ancient belly. Any man who drank from its waters would not only be healed of wounds and sickness, but he would also be returned his youthful vigor.

Bran had hidden this treasure away the moment it had been gifted to him, for it had come with a warning that nothing but blood and greed had ever come from its use. Thus, Bran had treated the cauldron as a burden that he wished not to bear. In turn, he become the protector to this ancient and horrible device of the gods from those that might abuse it.

On that night, as Matholwch decried the act of violence against his stables, Bran saw in the Irish king a young man who'd fought no battles nor suffered any famines, and he knew that — should he give his sister's hand over to this man — a lesson in strength needed to be learned.

So Bran passed that ancient burden to the Irish king, hoping that the trials and tribulations that would no doubt arise from its possession might strengthen the young ruler. And Matholwch, in his greed for power, accepted it gratefully, forgiving Efnysian's slight and returning to Ireland alongside his new bride.

Seasons passed with little more noise than the faint hiss of the growing crops, and Branwen enjoyed her new life alongside Matholwch. It was not long before they had a son named Gwern, and they were happy.

But not all in Ireland were as happy. A lifetime of peace led the people to forget the horrors of war. Old feuds that should have been long extinguished were reignited, and rumors of rebellion circulated the small island nation. Stories of Matholwch's forgiveness of the Britons' slight were whispered by firelight and with an air of disdain.

Quickly, the young Irish king's reputation dwindled to that of a weak ruler unfit for the crown.

Out of fear of the rising tempest among his own people, Matholwch did what cowards so often do: he placed the burden of fault upon his wife. He blamed her for the actions of her half-brother Efnysian and for the resulting insurrection. Unable to bring himself to kill her, he confined her to the scullery as a slave and ordered her to receive daily beatings from the cook.

Branwen suffered this tortured existence for some years until she came upon an injured starling that had become trapped in the kitchen's thatch. She nursed the small bird and trained it to seek out her brother across the sea, then released it with a message securely nestled under its wing.

The great king Bran was furious at the news of his beloved sister's imprisonment. He raised the greatest host the island had ever seen and crossed the sea to destroy Matholwch and free Branwen, leaving only seven lords behind to protect their homeland. But when their ships made landfall, they found no Irish enemy waiting for them on the shores. Instead, they were greeted by abandoned villages and scorched fields. Once more, Matholwch had proven himself a coward; the Irish hid beyond the river and sued King Bran for peace.

A runner came to Bran bearing Matholwch's offer. In exchange for peace, the Irish king swore he would relinquish his rule as king of Ireland, ceding his power to his infant son Gwern, Bran's nephew, and Branwen would be freed from her captivity. Furthermore, the Irish would construct for Bran the greatest hall ever built, so long and tall that it could fit all of his glorious power.

Bran considered the offer. Eager to avoid the bloodshed that would result from a true battle, he sent the runner back with his answer, and a peace was made. Within a fortnight, the Irish had completed the grand mead hall they had promised.

But the Irish king's intentions were not as pure as he'd let on. In secret, he ordered one hundred armed Irish warriors to conceal themselves in sacks of flour hung from the rafters. Upon the muttering of a secret word, they would burst forth and ambush the drunken Britons during their victory celebration. The plan was clever, and it may have worked if not for the suspicious Efnysian. Never one to trust the word of another man, Efnysian snuck into the hall under cover of darkness. He saw the hanging bags for what they were, and one by one silently drove his spear through their hearts.

The next day, Bran and his host entered the hall and feasted and made merry. It was only by the actions of the wicked Efnysian that Bran was spared when the secret word was muttered, and not one Irish warrior fell from the sky.

However, ever the prideful monster, Efnysian does not leave this story a hero. He grew drunk and irate, and took great insult when his nephew Gwen, only a toddler then, would not look kindly upon him. In a fit of unbridled rage, he hurled the boy into the crackling hearth at the center of the great hall.

The great hall exploded into violence. The ring of swords and whacks of axes filled the air and crimson blood flowed thick over the freshly hewn beams. Being greater both in size and ability, Bran's forces quickly seized the upper hand.

Matholwch saw this and knew his nation would be destroyed that day. Desperate and scared, he recalled the magic cauldron he'd been so eager to accept all those years before. He ordered his men to drag the mighty golden pot to their front lines, and one by one they began tossing the wounded Irish warriors into its roiling depths. Wounded men became whole again and rushed to rejoin their brethren. But in the blood-soaked mayhem of war, the Irish couldn't always distinguish between the wounded and the dead. Soon the cauldron was full of those whose souls had already departed, but by then the tides of battle had already begun to turn, and the Irish pushed forward, no longer in need of the cauldron's magic.

It was then that the bodies of the dead began to rise.

Screeching monstrosities emerged from the blood-blackened waters of the ancient cauldron. Many little more than limbless, blinded, torn bodies, they bore the punishment of the wounds that had taken their lives and sought retribution on those who had torn them away from the next world. Their haunting cries filled the hall as they crawled and shambled into the rear of the Irish ranks — tearing and biting and clawing, indifferent to the screams of their former kin. The Britons fought forward, sandwiching the Irish and cutting them down all the way to the last man. But soon the Britons' swords began to fall on the moaning corpses of those who had been dragged back into life, and the battle was renewed.

By the time the battle finished and the last of the abominations was slain, the only souls left standing in the hall were Branwen, two Britonian warriors, and Bran's most trusted advisor, the druid Maedig. Even Bran lay among the dying. With his final breath, the last true king of the Britons ordered the survivors to gather the ancient cauldron and to bring it and Bran's own head back to London to be buried in secret.

That evening, as the trio of men hauled the cauldron aboard their ship, Branwen collapsed in the sands on the beach. There she died of a broken heart, the final casualty in the first of many battles that would soon consume the island.

Sophie let her voice trail off with the conclusion of the story.

"What happened to them?" Jack asked after a moment. "The last three, I mean."

Sophie shrugged. "Most versions of the legends have them returning to England to find their homeland conquered by a foreign host in their absence. Some of these renditions claim that they were successful in following the dead king's orders, while others say they fled west across the sea."

"Well, I've never heard the latter." Margaret's tone bordered on accusation.

"I imagine there are at least a couple things you've never heard of, *Margaret*," Sophie came back snidely. After telling the long story, she was far too tired and tipsy to deal with the older woman's attitude. The two women glared at each other for a long moment.

Greg broke the tense silence with a belch. "I don't feel good," he announced, wobbling in his seat.

"*Oh shit*. Okay, bud, let's get you to the head," Jack said, grabbing the inebriated Greg and quickly escorting him away from the table.

Once they had disappeared up the stairs, Sophie turned on Margaret.

"That good enough for you, *professor*?" she asked.

Margaret looked Sophie up and down, then gave a little smirk. "Not bad. A little flowery for my taste… but to each their own." She stood and tucked the tablet under her arm. Before departing for her room, she paused and placed a hand on Sophie's arm — a surprisingly affectionate gesture. "You really believe there's something related to that cauldron down there, don't you?"

"Is that so stupid?" Sophie asked.

"Maybe it is," Margaret admitted. "I don't know. Maybe I'm just jealous."

Sophie took a long slug straight from the bottle of whiskey as she watched Margaret leave.

Not even a full minute later, Jack came tromping back downstairs, his gracefulness apparently overtaken by the glowing embrace of alcohol.

"I'm having a smoke. You want one?" Sophie called to him before he even reached the bottom stair. She didn't wait for a response, almost stumbling as she stood and making her way out into the pea soup fog that filled the night air.

"You really are trying to give me cancer, huh?" Jack asked once he'd joined her on the porch.

"Yeah, well it's a good thing we have a doctor here."

"Eh…" Jack made a squeamish face. "I'm not so sure I'd want ol' Emilio Bianchi as my primary care."

"And why's that?"

"I don't know, just a gut feeling." Jack took one of the cigarettes she held out. "You're trying to get me hooked again."

"Yeah, then I can start sellin' 'em to you for a fiver a pop. Pretty sure I'm the only one out here with a stash after all."

Jack snorted and handed her the nearly empty bottle she'd left on the coffee table. "Let's say I did want to run to the store for some cowboy killers. How far do you think that might be?"

"A store? Hell, closest decent-sized town is a couple hours through some rough roads, but I suspect you'd be able to find a gas station before that," she said.

"And what vehicle would I be able to take? The single cab truck with no keys, or maybe one of the UTVs? You know, the ones with the built-in GPS kill switch?" Jack's voice dropped ever so slightly, and he stared her straight in the eyes.

Sophie squirmed under his gaze. "I think there's an old timey bicycle buried somewhere in the back of the carriage house too," she offered with a placating smile.

Jack didn't return the smile. Sophie wasn't sure if Bill was just a complete idiot when it came to ruses, or if the group he'd chosen was just exceptionally cautious. Either way, she didn't like this pattern of being forced to answer for the tubby magnate's tricks.

"It's all that obvious, huh?" she asked.

"It's hard not to notice when you're in a cage. The GPS modem for the UTVs, is it in the house?" he asked.

"I imagine so."

"And how far from that modem will those UTVs get before they shut down?"

"I'd say don't push out past three miles unless you want to walk back."

Jack paused. If he was angry or annoyed about the situation, he didn't show it. "I get it. I mean, it'd be pretty easy for one of us to grab some priceless artifact and run off. I don't know what they normally do in situations like this, but I imagine it involves less of a focus on entrapping the worker bees and puts a bit more of an emphasis on security and accountability. The way this whole thing is set up… it's got me wondering exactly how legal this endeavor is. We gonna get in trouble for what we're doing?"

Sophie sighed. "Look. It's not like there's anything super wonky going on, it's just…" Her words drifted off. What was she going to say?

"Will it affect the pay?" Jack asked after a few seconds.

"What?"

"Whatever laws Bill's skirting, will this whole thing come to a head with the Canuck government taking the money he'll owe us?"

"God no, nothing like that," she insisted. "I don't know much of his business' inner workings, but I do know that he bought this land from the reservation. Beyond that… shit, his reputation for paying on time is probably the only thing that keeps his whole foundation thing rolling. You don't need to worry about the money."

"Alright." Jack sat down in one of the porch's old rocking chairs, popped off his prosthetic, and began massaging his stump through the tight nylon sleeve.

"Are you going to bring it up to the others?" she asked. The thought of Margaret's reaction when she realized that they were essentially trapped wasn't a pleasant one.

"Depends," Jack said, leaning back and taking a swig from the bottle. *Here we fucking go.* "On what?"

"How good your next story is."

She snorted, and something inside her relaxed. "Really? You think you can extort another tale from me?"

"Well, the last two were so good, and you said you have a lot, so I figure it's a cheap price."

"Oh, so now my services are cheap?" She feigned offense as she sat in the next chair over.

He opened his mouth to say something, then clearly thought better of it and smiled to himself instead.

"What?" she demanded. He simply shook his head. "What!"

"Nothing! Just… I want to hear a story, that's all."

"You were gonna make a dirty joke, weren't you?" She reached over and slapped his arm hard, and he held back a laugh. "Let's hear it then!"

"I promise, I wasn't going to say anything, I— *ow!* I just want to hear a story!"

She snatched the bottle away from him and tried to give a mean glare, but from the look on his face, she could tell hers was transparent. "No. No more stories."

They shared a comfortable silence, passing the bottle back and forth as the oceanside fog rolled over the creaky old porch.

"I'm not gonna lie. The past few days, I keep asking myself 'what the fuck am I doing out here?'" Jack admitted. He replaced his prosthetic and stood, then crossed the porch to lean on the railing once again. "This whole thing — it doesn't really make any sense to me. I get you being here, and Margaret, and even Greg, but why a hunter? So far, Bill's just got me wandering around, doing my own thing. I keep waiting for the other shoe to drop."

Sophie watched his silhouette against the moonlit clouds of mist and fought the urge to join him. She'd made her decision already. It wasn't going to happen.

But the whiskey had other plans.

She stood and followed the magnetic pulse that placed her at the railing beside Jack. It had been a long day. She was tired. She was sore. The inside of her chest felt warm, and her head felt like it was filled with the same haze as the balmy night air.

The simple fact was that she was lonely. Over the past two years, it had been so easy to ignore the growing emptiness in her chest, to ignore the yearning for genuine human connection beyond the occasional fling or seldom (and often fruitless) date. Surviving in a constant state of forward momentum had given her little other chance to find someone — not to mention being constantly surrounded by creeps like Bill — and it had dulled her appetite in general. But here, now, she felt something emanating from this strange man beside her. Maybe it was real, maybe it was just a pent-up result of neglecting that part of herself for so long. She didn't know. What she did know was that it wasn't something she was used to — actually *believing* someone. And that was what she'd begun to feel with Jack.

Trust.

They stood together, side-by-side and almost touching, staring out over the lawn and distant forest. The stars above seemed just the tiniest bit brighter, even despite the fog, and she found her hand gliding over the rough wood of the railing until it lay gently on his. He turned, and she leaned forward, closing her eyes as their bodies pressed together. Just as their lips came flush together, a distant howl cut through the otherwise silent bubble that encompassed them.

Jack's breath stopped dead.

When she opened her eyes, his face was ghost white and jaw clenched tight.

"What is it?" she asked softy.

"Did you hear that?" he pulled back and surveyed the horizon.

"I did. What was it? A coyote?"

Jack stayed silent, glaring into the darkness. She glanced down and saw that his hands were shaking.

"Jack, are you—"

The howl came again, emanating loud and crystal clear from the forest.

"Is that—"

"Yeah." Jack breathed the word. He almost stumbled as he turned on his heel and strode quickly inside. She watched him in shock.

"What the fuck…" she muttered after a long, dumbfounded moment. She made to glance back at the direction of the call, but her eyes caught on a pale blob in one of the nearby windows. Bill's face was thick with childish jealousy. His beady eyes burned into her for only a microsecond before he disappeared behind a flourish of curtains. This time the phrase was more of a hiss than a mutter. *"Oh, what the fuck!"*

DAY 7

*"We are always paid for our suspicion by finding
what we suspect."*
– Henry David Thoreau

XI

Greg

THE FIRST week in Nova Scotia had passed quickly as the new residents of Clayborn Manor settled into their daily routines. Every morning Greg, Sophie, Margaret, Bill and Kevin would ride the UTVs the mile out along the cliffs to the dig site. As soon as the tide dropped below a certain point, the two women would descend into the caves and set about the demanding process installing the complex cable and pulley system that Greg had designed.

Greg didn't particularly like the manner in which the group had become divided. Sophie was pleasant to be around, and Margaret, though grating at times, had her moments. However, between Bill's bloated arrogance and Kevin's increasingly open disdain of him, Greg couldn't imagine two people he'd less like to spend twelve hours at a time with. And the doctor, well, the doctor had become little more than a shadow in the back of Greg's mind. He'd sometimes see him at a meal or wandering the manor's shadowy halls, but for the most part, the Italian kept to himself.

Perhaps worst of all was Jack. He was a person Greg had come to think of as something akin to a friend in those first few days, but now he had become almost entirely absent from the group's activities — withdrawing from the group as a whole, skipping meals, and only appearing on the rare occasion when Bill hailed him over the radio.

But Greg had more to worry about than his absent friend and the suspicious doctor. By the time midweek rolled around, the two spelunking archaeologists had managed to master the system of drilling and tapping, just as Greg had come to master directing them by way of radio through the labyrinth of caves below his feet. By the seventh day of the expedition, Greg found himself stationed in the hot sun above the clifftop as the two archaeologists reached the anomalous barrier.

"It's wood alright," a breathless Sophie crackled over the radio. "Ten feet wide, maybe eight feet tall. Construction looks like it's just stacked logs. They're soaked through, half pulp on the surface but—" She grunted and cut off, and Greg could hear that she was stabbing at the wet wood with a knife. "Yep, still solid after a couple inches. I'm guessing it's pretty thick from the width of these logs."

"Good thing we have chainsaws." Kevin chuckled from where he was seated atop a stack of gear crates overlooking the ocean. Bill gave a bemused grunt from his own seat in a folding chair staged in the shade of the storage container.

Greg ignored them and keyed the radio. "What about the edges? Are there any gaps where we can get some leverage?"

"Uhhh…" Sophie's voice came in and out of static. "No, the logs disappear flush behind the edges of the tunnel. The way they're set — like they were pushed tight against the walls from the inside — makes them look like whoever put them here either entombed themselves or found another way out."

This was precisely what Greg had been worried about: a sheer wall. "Is there anything else?"

"No, not really—"

Margaret cut Sophie off. "Yeah, there are some symbols carved here in the wall, which means that someone spent a decent bit of time down here chiseling. They're heavily eroded though… Are we below the high tide line here?"

Greg checked the schematic. "It's hard to tell. It looks like you're just at it, maybe a few feet below but that depends on the exact sea level and strength of the swells."

"Greg, how are we going to get through this barrier?" Sophie asked.

"I need to know how thick it is. Do you have that long drill bit I gave you?" Greg asked. Unless one of them had taken a fall and snapped it, there was no reason why the duo shouldn't have brought along the three-and-a-half-foot tool he'd given them that morning.

"Yeah," Sophie came back after a second.

"See if you can get through to the other side. Make sure you're careful to take note of exactly how deep the bit is when it breaks through."

"Okay," Sophie affirmed. "Give me a second."

The radio went silent. Greg spent the next several minutes nervously looking over his notes and trying to avoid being pulled into Bill and Kevin's petty banter. Kevin was once again voicing his objections to Jack's newfound habit of carrying a revolver on his side, which was met with little more than a series of exasperated sighs from Bill. It was true that beyond just becoming increasingly absent, Jack had become a bit testy after the first couple days of the expedition. Greg had considered that maybe the missed meals and growing bags under Jack's eyes had been the result of him running low on booze. Greg had seen similar effects on his grandfather when he'd been forced to "dry out" (as his mother had called it). But the one thing Greg's theory didn't account for was all the time that Jack now spent in the forest. Most mornings, Jack would already be gone before the others rose, and at night he would return well after dark, filthy and clearly exhausted. Kevin had taken to often and loudly asserting that Jack might be losing his mind.

"Greg," Sophie's voice finally came back. "You there?"

"Yes," Greg answered. "Did you get through?"

"Greg?" Sophie's voice came through the radio once again.

Greg cursed the old Motorola. He wished he could kick the relay antenna they had set up near the mouth of the cave but settled for a violent shake of the handset. "Sophie, did the drill make it through?"

"No, it didn't break through. Based on what it kicked back, the wood gets dry maybe a foot in, but it's definitely more than three-and-a-half feet."

Shit.

"How much does the thickness of that barrier matter for what you have in mind?" Bill asked, startling Greg. He hadn't noticed that Bill had crept up on him and was now standing over his shoulder.

"A lot," Greg insisted, maybe a bit too shortly based on Bill's ensuing frown. The truth was that he didn't really have anything in mind. Each time he approached the problem from a new angle, he found himself running into the same roadblocks. "I need to know how thick it is," Greg said into the radio. "Can you, you know, try cutting away at the wet stuff to get the drill farther in?"

"Miles ahead of you," Margaret's panting voice came over the radio amid wet *thunk*s of a climbing axe against soaked wood.

Greg once again put the radio down and turned to his notes, carefully pretending to be absorbed in contemplation in order to deter the other two men from initiating conversation. It wasn't so much Bill he disliked communicating with as it was Kevin. Over the previous week, the hulking troglodyte had continually reinforced Greg's opinion that he was little more than a run-of-the-mill bully.

"So, what's the plan, Greg?" Bill asked after a far too brief moment of silence.

Greg wiped a bead of sweat from his upper lip and steadied his breath. "Uh, well… it really depends on that wall. If it's over four feet thick, then I'm not sure we're going to be able to make it through anytime soon. We also have to consider that at that width, it may be load-bearing, and that just destroying it outright would cause some sort of cave-in. I have the feeling this is going to require some very specific tools in order to be accomp—"

"Slow down, son!" Bill laughed out, holding out his hands. Greg realized he'd been spitting out the words so quickly that they'd been little more than a jumble.

"Sorry, it's just… I mean, it's— err… We need to handle this quickly or else—"

"There's no rush," Bill insisted. "Whatever we need to get through there, I'm sure you can figure it out."

"Well, Bi— Mr. Emery, I mean, there *is* kind of a rush," Greg corrected. "I've been keeping close tabs on the weather and tides and… I'm sure you know that hurricane Mallory changed course again last night, and now it's headed northeast along the coast. The current projections put it *here* by Tuesday. It… it might downgrade to a tropical storm by then, but even so…" Greg watched the mental math play out on Bill's face. "That means we have four days — eight low tide periods — to get through that wall."

"Why not just wait until after the storm?" Kevin chimed in.

"Yeah, I guess we can," Greg said. His words came rapid again, and his hands started to tremble. "But we run the risk of the storm surge weakening or even dislodging the pulleys we've already set up. Furthermore, if we start the process of breaking through that wall now, the storm surge could come right through those tunnels and break it. If that happens, then whatever's inside will, more likely than not, be washed away or destroyed. No one really predicted the storm would shift this way. I mean, had I known, I would have suggested we postpone setting those cables until afterwards, but… well… we just didn't know."

Bill gave Kevin a scathing glare that made Greg assume it had been Kevin's job to monitor the weather.

"We're through!" Sophie's voice crackled. "Not as bad as we thought. Looks like… a smidge over four feet thick. We're going to take some pictures and head back. We're already in the red zone on time down here. Greg, is there anything else you need?"

"Yeah…" Greg darted into the storage container and shuffled through the mess of papers and tools on the long foldout table until he found the sheet of graph paper. "I need some quick measurements of the exposed wood."

Sophie quickly went through and relayed the numbers to Greg, who was only half paying attention to jotting them down. Outside the storage container, Bill was quietly chastising Kevin. Just as Sophie finished and the two archaeologists began their journey back, Greg heard one of the two UTVs rumble to life. A moment later, Kevin was tearing away across the grassy clifftop lawns toward the manor.

"He's off to double check on that hurricane and make some calls," Bill said politely, giving the departing vehicle one last annoyed look.

Greg turned his attention back to the sonar map. Over the next forty-five minutes, he and Bill sat in silence as they followed Sophie's radio check-ins until the archaeologists closed in on their final ascent.

"How far back in workdays would it set us to wait until after the storm?" Bill asked hesitantly after the last radio check. Greg could tell he'd been working the question over in his mind, brooding on it and trying to digest it himself before deciding to pose it.

Greg considered the question. "Between waiting for the storm to subside, then re-securing or replacing the pulleys… a week and a half? Two weeks? Maybe more… and… and that just puts us back where we are now. Still, I really do think that it's probably the best plan."

Bill stared out over the ocean. "No. We need to push through now. How fast can you get us through that barrier?"

"It, you know, it depends on which route we take—"

"The fastest route."

"Well…" Greg's voice cracked a bit. "If we can get our hands on the right gear, maybe two low tide periods? It depends how much we want to budget for a larger drill—"

"You'll use what you have here," Bill said offhand, motioning to jumbled mechanical contents of the storage container. "This should be plenty to get done what we need."

Greg almost laughed at the absurdity of the statement. "What?"

"We don't need to order anything new. There's enough equipment here to get us through the safe at Fort Knox. Figure it out."

Greg felt a lump in his throat and looked back at the random mess of gear piled in the back of the storage container. There were old air conditioners stacked on top of sun-bleached generators, a crumpled mass of diving gear, half a dozen pieces of heavy-duty mining equipment, and a mismatched heap of odds and ends. The sudden realization of what this massive steel box actually contained smacked Greg in the face: they were leftovers from Bill's previous adventures.

"Mr. Emery, it's just, you know, a— a fact. I can't make something that can, like— for safety's sake alone—"

Bill was, like most people, larger than Greg, so when he stepped close and placed his hands on Greg's shoulders, it didn't feel like a calming gesture. "I believe in you, Greg. Just build me something that will work."

Greg wasn't sure if it was the tone of his voice or perhaps the light breeze that flowed over the picturesque clifftops where they stood alone together, but a shiver ran down his spine. "I— I can't, Mr. Emery. It's not— It wouldn't be safe—"

"Oh, I think you can." Bill chuckled and pulled back, retreating to the stack of crates that had been Kevin's perch and taking a seat.

Greg let out a long breath, but it did little to calm his nerves. "Mr. Emery, I think… I… I have to ask, why are we using this leftover equipment? If we could just order some—"

"Waste not, want not, young man," Bill said with a hint of annoyance. "You don't amass wealth like mine without saving where you can."

Well that's not at all true, Greg thought. He knew from his research into Bill's exploits that the man had a habit of overspending, to the point where he'd been subtly investigated by several governments as a potential money laundering operation or drug trade facilitator based on the absurd amount of money he would dump into their local economies for seemingly superfluous purchases.

Greg also knew that over the last handful of years, the Emery Foundation had, for the first time, begun lobbying for grant funds. Normally this might signify a faltering business, however even the rumor writers on the internet considered it laughable that Bill Emery could squander an estate as *massive* as the one he'd inherited.

But those random internet personas didn't *know* Bill Emery.

Suddenly the small things that had been chewing at Greg began to line up: the dilapidated state of the manor, the shim sham team of nobodies, the secondhand gear…

Was it possible…?

"Mr. Emery, it's really, *really* important that we have the right equipment for this. I can only do so much with what we have. Maybe I could take a look at the financial side of this expedition and move some numbers around, see if we can't get some more liquidity—"

"Enough." Bill sounded annoyed. "Stay in your lane, Greg."

"Mr. Emery, are you… are you broke?" The question slipped out before he could stop it.

Bill burst out in a deep belly laugh so suddenly that Greg flinched. It wasn't a sincere laugh. It was a manufactured guffaw that made Greg feel queasy. He cast a wary glance at the distant manor on the horizon.

The militantly silent drivers…

The secrecy of their destination…

"Are we… are we squatting?"

Bill's fake laugh grew for a moment, then it cut off cold when Sophie's voice cracked through the radio. "We're almost at the mouth of the cave. Go ahead and get the generator running to pull us up."

Before Greg could respond, Bill had darted from his seat with surprising speed and snatched the radio away from him.

"Sounds good, Sophie, but there's a little issue with the generator. Kevin let the oil get too low. Just give us a moment to get it going again." Bill waited for Sophie to give a resigned reply, then placed the radio on the seat behind him and stared hard at Greg.

"Does anyone here know?" Greg asked. The spike of fear he had felt moments before was suddenly mixing with the faintest hint of anger, just enough to maybe — for once — stand up for himself.

"Know what?" Bill asked.

"Mr. Emery, don't—"

"Ugh, you're a smart kid. What do you think?" Bill cut him off with a dismissive hand wave.

No. Of course they don't know. Why would they? Maybe Kevin, yeah, but if so, he probably had his own guarantees from whatever remaining little chunk of money Bill might have stashed away.

But Jack?

No.

Sophie?

No.

Margaret?

Definitely not.

Not even the doctor would have agreed to sign on if it weren't for the exorbitant price Bill had offered—

"Have you ever visited Ithaca, New York, Greg?" Bill asked casually.

Greg's stomach plummeted.

"There's a little school there — maybe you've heard of it — Cornell?"

No.

"I only ask because there was a very interesting news story that came out of that little college town a few months back," he went on.

The shiver turned to a tremor, and a hot, heavy feeling rushed to Greg's head. The world was unsteady, and he felt his mind begin to spin out from under him. His legs started to give, but suddenly a plump hand was clenching the front of his shirt, holding him up.

"You really think I don't know all about you, Greg Gupta? Or should I say *Arjun Bandi*?" The disdain with which Bill hissed Greg's real name brought a bubble of sickness into Greg's throat. "Why the hell do you think I hired you? A monkey could have seen through those fake credentials you applied with. How *stupid* do you think I am?"

Greg heaved, and Bill tossed him to the ground just in time to avoid the torrent of hot bile. Before Greg even had the chance to finish coughing up the last of his vomit, the hard tip of Bill's right dress shoe caught him full in the ribs, sending him tumbling. He cried out in pain and tried to crawl away, but Bill was immediately there, towering above him with a foot planted firmly on his sternum.

"Stop moving," Bill commanded, and Greg immediately surrendered. As he stared up at the hateful look in Bill's eyes, he couldn't stop the hot tears from welling in his own.

"Please…" Greg begged, but Bill's heel dug down harder.

"Shut up," Bill snarled, and Greg could feel the tiny specks of spittle raining down on him. "You're a killer— *Look at me!* You're a killer, yet you're laying here crying like a baby. Man up. *Now!*"

Bill removed his foot and bent over, seizing Greg's limp arm and violently yanking him to his feet. "You listen closely now, *Arjun*. We both know you never graduated, and we both know *why*. But the things I've read about you say you were some kind of genius before you snapped. So now you're going to be my little pet and use that innate talent to get me what I want."

Greg whimpered, then nodded. His tear-blurred eyes fixed on the grass at his feet. "You were never going to pay any of us, were you?"

"Money, money, money," Bill spat. "That's all anyone cares about. Well, I *believe* that there's something down there, exactly the type of thing I've spent my life searching for. If we find it, then taking part in this endeavor will have been payment enough. Do you understand?"

Greg nodded.

"Good." Bill took a step back and smoothed his shirt before continuing in a calmer tone. "Now, there's no reason we can't still have a symbiotic relationship, *Greg*. The way I see it, we both have things we'd rather be kept secret, and I think that in keeping each other's secrets, we can both walk away from this relatively happy. You, a man free to continue his life on the lamb, and me with prize in hand. Does that sound like a good plan to you, Greg?"

Again, Greg nodded.

"*Speak!*" Bill barked.

"Yes," Greg breathed.

"Fantastic!" Bill proclaimed with a grin. "I'm so glad to hear that, Greg. I would hate to have to call those decent folks at the FBI. I hear their deals aren't nearly as good as mine. Now, get those two broads up here and figure out a way to get us through that wall before the storm hits, or I'll have Kevin throw you off that fucking cliff."

XII

Jack

SIGHT, SCENT, silence.

The mantra had been beaten into Jack's head at such an early age that he couldn't remember a time when his mind had operated without it. Looking down at his mud-splotched jeans and red plaid shirt, he knew he'd already broken the first tenant of the hunter's holy trifecta. The not so occasional whiffs of the previous evening's whiskey seeping from his sweat glands let him know he'd also doubtlessly broken the second. However, even with the often clumsy and forever unfeeling metal appendage suction locked to the stump beneath his left knee, he knew he could still abide by the last law. And the last law was all that really mattered: silence.

He picked his steps meticulously. The forgiving floor of pine needles that dominated the immediate forest surrounding the manor had eventually given way to dense underbrush littered with rotted leaves. Offering little more sound than the hushed, steady rhythm of his own breath, Jack stalked ever deeper through the crowded trees of the Nova Scotian forest.

It had been almost a week since he'd heard the wolf's call. Still, every day he'd wake before the sun and head deep into the forest, searching for some sign, some spore of the creature that haunted his nightmares with its bloodcurdling howl. Throughout the days, Bill's obnoxious voice would often come crackling over the radio, disrupting Jack's search with some nonsense task or another. But not this morning. The radio at his side was switched off. The dig team was scheduled to reach the barrier at end of the tunnel, and Jack was confident they'd have too much on their hands to worry about an unanswered call to their resident hunter.

Today was his day to find the answer to the question that had been eating away at him since that terrifying night a week before.

He stalked low and silent through a patch of young fir trees, eventually crossing the narrow stream that had previously marked the boundary of his excursions. He mounted the crest of a low hill and came out overlooking a small bog.

Only a handful of dead pines scattered the mossy sea of stagnant muck. It hadn't rained all week, so the softened earth still bore the marks of all the animals that had passed over it in that time. Tracks of every type littered the mud, from chipmunk to deer, and even a long line of wide, deep pits that revealed the presence of moose. As Jack's eyes darted from track to track in the mud before him, the sickening feeling in his stomach grew.

Was it possible he'd just made it up?

No. Sophie had heard it too.

Heard what?

The wo—

It could have been anything.

His mind focused on those words. He'd been so sure that night. The howl had sounded so painfully clear it had made him sick with a deep dread. The type of harrowingly malignant dread that he hadn't felt since he woke up in the hospital in Montana, leg amputated and Sam's weeping mother beside his bed.

But there were no wolves in Nova Scotia. Not anymore at least. If there were, he wouldn't have taken the job.

Could it have been something else? Some owl's hoot that had hit his ear wrong? Some stray dog howling for its master?

That night, after he'd wrangled in his mind, he considered the possibility that the call had come from a coyote. But Jack knew a wolf's howl like he knew his own name. That was no coyote howl. Besides, in all of his tracking over the past week, he'd yet to see any sign of the less than discreet little beasts.

Another possibility had been knocking incessantly on the back of his mind. As much as he'd tried to stop it from entering, it had broken through the door: *could the whole thing have been his imagination?*

The idea of his nightmares blending into his waking hours had him considering the pistol at his side. If his grip on reality had finally started to slip so much that he was hallucinating, then his participation in this expedition — and the world of the living, for that matter — might have to be cut short.

No.

Sophie had heard it too.

There was something here.

He wasn't losing it.

...Maybe.

He pushed the thoughts away. He had a purpose, clear and singular, and as long as he could keep his shit together until that was achieved, everything would work out.

His eyes paused on a particular set of tracks a few yards away. The gait was short for what he was looking for, but as he approached the divots, his heart began to pound faster. They were deep and had the distinct four toed shape of a canid. Entirely unconsciously, he slid the short 45-70 rifle from his shoulder and racked the lever. After checking to make sure the massive buffalo round had seated itself in the chamber, he cast a wary look around the rich greens and browns of the bog before crouching to examine the fine details of the tracks.

The toes were close to the center pad, and the spread was altogether significantly longer than it was wide. It was a large coyote. Not a coydog, not a coywolf. Simply a coyote.

Still, he didn't move until he'd double- and triple-checked. Only once he felt confident in his assessment did some small tension in his chest let go, and he couldn't help but smile inwardly. As he stood, he followed the path of the tracks with his eyes and let the relief he felt wash over him as he began to laugh.

No shit, dumbass.

He hadn't hallucinated it after all, simply misheard some lonely coyote's howl. That had to be it. He wasn't losing his mind; he just made a bad call. He'd let his fear take control of the situation and mislead him. It was nothing more than a loud, lonely little critter.

After all, there are no wolves in Nova Scotia.

But the relief was fake, and he didn't believe it for a second. But it still felt good.

Fifty yards away up an east-facing hill, Jack's eyes caught on the base of a fat sugar maple. The unquestionable red of blood stood out harshly against the rich earthy tones of the undergrowth.

Ever so slowly, he followed the coyote's trail through the sucking mud toward the massive veins of blood-stained roots. He tried to imagine what small game this coyote could have taken down to make such a violent mess. He was still several yards from the tree when he finally managed to see the broken mass of gray fur half hidden behind a wall of ferns.

The coyote's corpse lay in a torn heap, the deep crimson blood that stained its fur still wet.

The warm summer air went cold, and the strong taste of copper filled Jack's mouth. Suddenly the silence of the forest around him rang so loudly in his ears that the oak leaves rustling in the cool breeze above threatened to deafen him.

In a staggered row beside the corpse were the massive, indisputable tracks of a very, *very* large wolf.

Sam's face, shredded to little more than a meat-flecked skull, flashed into his mind. The wardens hadn't recovered Sam's body until the beginning of the thaw, not long after Jack had woken up. The coroner had asked Jack to identify Sam's remains in order to save the grieving family from having to see the mutilated thing their son and brother had been reduced to. Sam's face had been almost unrecognizable to the point where it could have been just another gore-striped skull from a movie — had the wolves not left his eyes.

No one could explain it to Jack, not the coroners or the game wardens. Animals ate the soft tissue first *every time*. Yet for some reason, those hellish beasts had left Sam's sky-blue eyes, offset and lolling, as if to issue some cruel taunt.

Now, standing over the freshly killed carcass of what had to be the largest coyote he'd ever seen, Jack found himself fixated on its eyes. They were open, terrified, and all too familiar.

The creature that did this wasn't a just an animal.

Animals didn't do this.

This was a monster.

The same type of monster that took Sam.

The type of monster that could take him, or Sophie, or Greg, or any of the others.

A wave of hatred coursed over Jack's body like a scalding shower, washing away the crippling fear he'd felt for so long. Without a second thought, he clicked the rifle's safety off, checked the revolver at his side and the antler-handled Bowie next to it, and began tracking the wolf inland.

XIII

Margaret

"SO, WHAT'S the plan?" Margaret asked from the cracked door of Greg's room. She chuckled inwardly at the way he jumped in surprise before turning to look at her. Then, seeing the boy's face, her mirth melted to pity. "You alright, kid?" she asked, crossing into the room and looking over his shoulder at the chaotic mess of half drawn schematics that littered the desk.

"Yes, yes, Dr. Sim— err, Margaret." His voice was hollow, more scared than normal, and Margaret wondered if the deep bags under his eyes were from the early mornings or just pure manifestations of stress.

"I just wanted to check in, see how you were planning to get us through that wall." She circled the desk and sat opposite him. Even in his entirely disheveled state, Margaret noticed Greg's fleeting glance, and she had to withhold a smile.

Still fuckin' got it.

Normally she would have assumed there was some toilet paper hanging out of her shorts, but not this evening. This evening, she had popped a whole pill, and the world was her oyster.

"I…" Greg swallowed hard and cast a paranoid glance at the door behind her. "I don't know if I can really get through that wall, at least not with what we have."

"Well, then we'll make Bill double down on whatever it is you *do* need."

"No!" Greg's eyes went wide with desperation for just a second, then shot down to the paper in front of him. "I— I just meant that I, you know, I can't… I need to take some parts from some other things. I saw an old hydraulic pressure washer in that storage container somewhere, and there's a chance I can pull the components to get a makeshift hydraulic intensifier pump going if I pull apart one of the UTVs… maybe. I think I can make this thing work."

"And what exactly is 'this thing'?" Margaret gingerly reached out and plucked the scribbled-on graph paper from his grasp. On it appeared to be a 3D schematic for a something similar to a circular railroad track.

"A uh, a water jet cutter," Greg said sheepishly. "Like a super powered pressure washer mounted on a track, that way it can cut a precise path through a thicker obstruction. If I can get it to a high enough PSI, then it should be able to cut through the wood at the full four-foot distance required. I don't know if I can get it to be the right pressure though, so it might be a bad idea."

"You can build this?" she asked, raising an eyebrow. "With just the junk around here?"

"I hope so…" he muttered, then more confidently, "Yeah, yeah, no, I can."

"And this big circle here…"

"That's the, uh, a rail system. Basically, you guys— girls— err, women, um…"

"…Archaeologists," she provided.

"Yes, I'm sorry, I— You archaeologists, you and Sophie, you'll have to strip the waterlogged, rotted stuff from the face of the barrier then assemble and secure the rail system against the wood with screws. Then the water jet cutter will get clamped on the rails, and a motor will pull it along the track and, you know, cut the outline of a passage."

Margaret didn't try to hide the fact that she was impressed. "I have to admit, that's pretty goddamn clever, Greg. One thing though: how do we get the thousand-pound cork out of the bottle once the cutting's done?"

"That's actually what I was just working on now." Greg's voice grew a little stronger with her praise, and Margaret wondered just how much the negativity of the environment in general affected his anxiety. Maybe someday he'd learn not to give a fuck about the opinions of others, or maybe he could miss that lesson like she had and just take a fuckin' oxy.

Enough, she chastised herself. This evening she was going to be happy, goddamnit.

"Here." Greg shoved a paper over to her. Even for an archaeologist, the markings on it were nearly indecipherable. "Basically we're going to run a, uh, a steel cable through all of the pulleys you've already set up down there, and then hook it up to the winch that we normally use to haul you gu— archaeologists up and down. We have an inch-wide drill bit that should make it through the center of the cut out area — the cork, as you said. So I'm going to make you a retractable claw type thing." He made a fist with one hand and wrapped his other hand around it. "You'll drill a hole in the cork's center then feed the retracted claw through—" He jutted his fist forward so that his other hand was clenched around his wrist. "—and when it's on the other side, it will open up and catch." His fist sprung open. "And then we use the winch and motor up top to pull the cork out."

She eyed the schematic for a long time, until finally the markings began to make sense. "This is actually kind of brilliant."

"Thank you."

The unexpected confidence in Greg's voice caught her off guard. When she glanced up at him, she could tell she'd made the kid's month. Some evil part of her clawed at the sea of opiate-induced happiness, writhing and fighting to surface long enough to bring the little brat back down to earth. But instead, she just smiled and decided to let that gurgling bitch drown. At least until tomorrow.

"You're sure this will work?" she asked, returning the paper and sitting back in her chair.

"You know… yeah, yeah I am. It'll work."

She had to admit: confident Greg wasn't entirely unattractive.

"Where did you go to school, Greg?"

As fast as it had come on, the confident look on his face melted, and his shoulders deflated. "Oh, uh, Co— err, Colorado State," he sputtered.

And just like that, the attraction was gone.

"That's not a bad program. My ex-husband taught at Boulder before we met. Would never shut up about the Rockies. You much of a hiker?"

"No, no. I… uh… I'm not an *outside* kind of guy, really."

"You don't say." Margaret paused and searched the muffling opiate fog of her mind for the name of an old acquaintance. "Daniel… Daniel Hargrave? Harkest? Har-something. That name ring a bell?"

"No. Sh— should it?" Greg looked nervously at her.

"You know, what's-his-name. The head of the engineering department at your alma mater. He was buddies with my ex. Nice guy, real handsome."

"Oh, uh, yeah, yeah Daniel— Professor, uh, I forget his name too," Greg stuttered, then groped at the table, searching for a paper. "Look, I— I really should get back to… this stuff and…"

An urgent awareness penetrated the pea soup oxy-fog. Some primal, tribal warning of insincerity sent alarm bells ringing in Margaret's mind. "Daniel Harkstaff," she lied. "That was it."

"Oh, yeah, definitely. Professor Harkstaff," Greg repeated quietly, eyes glued, unmoving, to the paper in his hands.

"Did he ever get that wild mane of his cut?" Margaret asked dreamily, then gave a shy laugh. "We used to tease him and call him Fabio. Not just because of the hair, if you catch my drift. I mean *that build*…"

"Uh… No, no it's still— He's still real, yeah, you know. Like Fabio."

Margaret's memory held the image of Daniel as a bald, slight man who might have been the furthest possible thing from Fabio ever conceived.

"Yep. Good guy," Margaret went on. "Did you get a chance to work with him?"

"Oh, uh, no. Not really, I was just an undergrad—"

"I mean besides Introduction to Materials Engineering. Isn't that a mandatory course? I remember he always insisted on teaching that one himself."

"Oh, yeah, no. I took that one with him but, you know, I— I doubt he'd remember me." A thin sheen of sweat had started to glisten on Greg's forehead, and a pained look had overtaken his face — almost as if he were holding back tears. His darting eyes made Margaret wary. It was time for her to make an exit.

"Have a good one, Greg. If you talk to Professor Harkin any time soon, tell him I say hi," she said as she stood, changing the name for one final test.

"I will," Greg said, his voice finally beginning to crack.

Margaret crossed out of the room and shut the door, then stood silently for a moment and listened to the muffled sobs within.

XIV

Jack

IT WAS dusk by the time Jack first caught sight of the ravine. It wound like a great snake through the forest floor. From his position atop a nearby mound, Jack thought that its weather-hewn stone walls looked more like blasted highway-side cliffs than a natural geological occurrence.

Over the last several hours of tracking, his anger had largely burnt away, leaving the ashy remains of fear and anxiety paramount in his chest. Ignoring the growing tightness in his lungs, Jack pushed forward. Silently, he followed the lone wolf's tracks down a gradual incline and into the yawning mouth of the crevasse. Soon he found himself surrounded by the ravine's jagged stone walls. The thin passageway, lit only by the fading remains of daylight twenty feet above, closed inward to a point where Jack figured he could have touched one side with an outstretched hand and the other with the tip of rifle's barrel. But he didn't test this. Instead, the rifle stayed glued to his shoulder, its barrel darting over every shape and shadow as he glided forward between the boulders that littered his path.

The wolf's prints nearly disappeared as mud gave way to slippery moss-coated stones, but Jack knew there was only one direction the animal could have been headed: deeper into the growing dark. The orange glow of the deciduous canopy above limited his vision to only a few yards, but he continued, staying low to the ground.

The gentle gurgle of a stream echoed from ahead. A few strides later and he was stepping through ankle-deep rushing water. When he took a bounding step over a rock at the stream's edge, the boot on his prosthetic slipped on the wet stones and sent him careening into the craggy wall with a painful thump. He froze, listening for any sign of movement.

There was only the trickle of the stream.

He took a deep breath and recovered. Then, as the steady throb of his heart slowed, he heard it.

It was like the crackling groan a rotten tree trunk lets out as it finally collapses. Only this was not a falling tree. It came in short bursts — furious bouts of tearing and ripping that Jack couldn't come close to placing. There was another sound woven in with the tearing, though. A sound that Jack knew all too well.

A growl.

Jack glanced down to check the rifle and realized for the first time just how dark it had grown down in the belly of the ravine. Even in the shadows, though, he could see the tremble of his hands.

Are you really going to do this?

He took a deep breath and let it leak out slowly. He focused on the weight of the rifle.

You are the predator.

Don't hate what can't feel hate.

It's only an animal.

Leave.

Let it go…

…

Deep down, he knew only one living thing was going to walk out of there.

Fuck.

With as much stealth as he could muster, he advanced down the rocky path. Each step felt like a bound into hell. Every fiber of his instincts begged him to turn back. He ignored them. In only a few strides, he was approaching an opening.

The ravine ended in what Jack could only describe as a cellar hole. Spending most of his life in rural New England, he'd seen plenty of them before. Deep, stone-lined pits dispersed in the wilderness, seemingly at random like centuries-old scars pockmarking earth, all that was left of people long dead and forgotten.

But Jack had never seen a cellar hole quite like this. This pit was circular, a good thirty feet wide and nearly as deep. A portion of the pit's side had collapsed into itself, leaving a rocky slope on one side. The rest of the walls, as well as the floor, were lined with moss-coated shale and granite and clumps of bright yellow wildflowers that Jack couldn't place. At the pit's center stood a single, massive oak, wider than the fattest sugar maple he had ever seen.

A flash of movement caught his eye, and he snapped the rifle up. He watched through the peep sight as a torrent of dirt shot out from behind the bulbous trunk, then another.

The growling was loud now, filling the pit alongside the horrible ripping and tearing. Dusk's glow had almost entirely faded, and Jack knew this was it. He steeled himself.

Now or never.

"Hey, bud," Jack called quietly.

The air froze over with silence. Then, ever so slowly, a shaggy mass slunk into view.

It was monstrously large. Larger than any wolf Jack had ever imagined in his worst nightmares. Its snout was scarred badly, with flashes of pale skin shining through the dark gray fur. Lips pulled back menacingly to reveal bright pink gums and long, spittle-dripping fangs.

Jack focused past the rifle's front sight post and on the two blood moon orbs that stared back at him.

The eyes… they weren't supposed to be that color.

Nothing was supposed to be that color.

Jack wasn't sure who was more surprised by the gunshot, himself or the wolf. The beast recoiled and let out a furious grunt as the massive hollow point bullet impacted. Jack slammed the lever forward and back and fired again. This time a chunk of moss exploded up from the earth at the wolf's feet. It spun and bounded away up the collapsed section of stones. The distinct echoing clack of bullet on stone filled the void left by the deafening booms. Once again, Jack recycled the action and fired. Then again, and again, taking blind shots into the undergrowth above, where the wolf had disappeared into. Finally, the rifle clicked empty. With as much speed as he could muster without being clumsy, Jack plucked his remaining bullets one by one from their leather holder on the rifle's stock and reloaded the tube.

For the first time since killing the deer a week before, absolute silence reigned over the forest above him. Keeping the rifle up, Jack inched forward. His eyes darted from the rim of the pit above him down to the splatter of blood that soaked the stones where the wolf had been struck. There was no movement in the brush. No distant whimpering or whining. Just dead silence.

Jack examined the crimson liquid's consistency. He'd hit a lung; he could tell from the bubbling froth that floated on the blood's surface. With a 45-70 hollow point straight to the boiler room, the wolf likely made it less than fifty yards before dropping dead.

A large part of him felt vindicated. Perhaps even victorious.

Another part of him felt ashamed.

"It was just an animal," he muttered. "And you had to kill it because you're just a fuckin' pus—"

The words caught in his throat as his eyes drifted to the root-bound earth beyond the overgrown oak and he realized what the tearing noise had been.

Massive chunks of wood were ripped away from the earth, forming a pit of torn wood and upturned black soil. Veiny roots the thickness of Jack's thigh were gnawed clean through. At the pit's bottom, the mesh of intertwining roots was marred with blood, clearly from the wolf's broken claws.

"Holy shit," he muttered to himself. Jack had seen enough erratic animal behavior in his time as a guide to fill a book, but nothing like this. He surveyed the quickly darkening pit, searching for anything to give him a clue as to what the hell had prompted this animal to commit itself so wholly to such an entirely unnatural task.

And then he saw them.

Barely visible through the wear of time, a rough carving of three twisted figures stood out on the pit's shale façade. The figures were hunched together, antlers extending from their skulls and intertwining. The chiseled holes of their eyes still had an ancient red hue. As Jack stared at the primeval markings, a horrifying realization set in: he should not have come here.

A dazing impact sent him sprawling. Suddenly he was pinned on his back as the rifle skittered away across the stones. Deep-set molars crushed down on his forearm, and he cried out. But his muffled screams were trapped between the furry, thrashing mass atop him and the hard, root-bound earth below. Jack's hand slapped at his waist, blindly searching for his pistol, but all he found was an empty holster. Sheer adrenaline dumped into his veins and he struck out blindly. His fists thumped fruitlessly against the beast's side. Hot, fetid breath rolled over his skin and filled his nose as drops of his own blood rained down on him.

Through the violence and chaos, his eyes still managed to latch onto the blood moon eyes that stared back at him with animalistic hatred.

Then the edges of his vision began to blur.

He groped desperately for something, *anything* to fight back with. His grasping hand found only dirt and flimsy torn roots, but soon fell on the smooth bumps of an antler handle.

XV

Greg

GREG CRUMPLED forward over the pile of schematics and let the turmoil in his chest boil to the surface. He clamped a clammy hand over his mouth to suppress the gasping sobs that raked his body.

Margaret *must* have known he was full of shit. She hadn't even really tried to hide her suspicion. He had seen it on her face, heard it in her voice, and now she was going to start digging. How hard would it be for her to discover his real identity?

It'd been over an hour since she left his room. In that time, he'd all but abandoned his work on the water jet cutter. Not because he had the time to put off the ungodly amount of math and engineering left to be done, but simply because his hands had been shaking too much to write, his brain too electric to think.

Driven by the horrible lead sinker of apprehension in his stomach, Greg pulled his laptop in front of him and powered it on. He entered the half dozen passwords to bring him to the desktop, then, his fingers still trembling, opened the command prompt and typed a series of commands. A second later, he had bypassed Bill's cheap network monitoring software and was connected to the internet via a migrating VPN that would allow him to maneuver the web without having to worry about his ISP being traced back to the satellite mounted atop the manor.

"Arjun Bandi." He breathed the words as he typed them into the search bar. He hadn't dared to Google his real name since he'd crossed into Canada, and now, as his finger hovered over the enter key like the lever of a hangman's drop-door, he wished he didn't have to.

But he needed to know what Margaret could find if she decided to start sniffing around.

He pressed enter. The slow satellite connection took its time loading, then a handful of news stories popped up. He clicked the latest one.

Reward Increases for Information on Cornell Killer

Tuesday, state police reported that they are officially raising the reward for information leading to the arrest of Cornell student Arjun Bandi from ten thousand dollars to twenty thousand dollars. This news comes almost three months after the nineteen-year-old engineering student, set to graduate this year, was caught on video driving a midsized sedan into a group of four students, leaving one dead and another in critical condition.

Sources say that Bandi's behavior was likely the result of the combination of bullying and a history of mental health issues. The accused's mother, Lajita Bandi, confirmed last Wednesday that despite being highly sought after by several ivy league programs and being considered a "genius" by many of his professors, Bandi had several severe social issues that she believes stemmed from his advanced placement in school.

"He graduated high school at fifteen," Lajita Bandi says. "We understood he had troubles then, but not like this. I think college was worse because he was still a child and the others were adults. He suffered from it, but that is no excuse for his sins."

Bandi had a history of behavioral issues in school, including lashing out against peers, but never as severely as what took place on May 15, only a week before graduation. According to those who were closest to him, Bandi's attack on the Cornell campus seemed to be unexpected. "He had so many problems," his mother recalls, "but I still cannot believe he would do a thing like this. I didn't believe it."

Bandi's parents are cooperating with the police and asking that anyone who has information about him to come forward. "He is no son of mine," Lajita Bandi says. "The son I know is not evil. He did not know evil. The person who killed that young man, he is evil."

Inserted under the article were two side-by-side photos. On the left was a photo of Greg's high school graduation. Flanked by a beaming mother and dispassionate father, he looked like a child graduating elementary school. Only the size and maturity of his fellow students meandering in the background gave away the truth. The photo beside it was of his parents standing before a row of microphones as they offered a public apology for their son's crime. It was taken recently, and it contrasted harshly with the image of a happy family. His father's expression hadn't changed much, but his mother's face struck a dark chord in Greg's soul. She was stone-faced and cold. Her eyes were dry, and her lips pulled in a tight line. There was nothing there, Greg realized as he stared at the photo, there was no love or warmth left in that face. Not for him at least.

The broken sobs that had been hiding just beneath the surface of his own face returned, and it was a full minute before he managed a long, quavering breath. He hadn't seen his mother since weeks before the event, so he'd never been able to explain himself or ask forgiveness or even say goodbye. For the past few months, he'd been wandering, faking his way into odd jobs — more often than not the less-than-legitimate type — only to flee at the first sign of trouble. All he'd wanted this whole time was an opportunity to go back, to be with his family, for his mother to hold him and tell him everything would be okay. He'd figured maybe if he made enough money, they would come with him to somewhere he'd never be found, maybe they could start over, go back to the way things were before…

But the look in his mother's eyes extinguished this dream. He was dead to her.

For the first time in his existence, he was truly alone in the world.

Totally alone.

And in danger.

His heartrate doubled. The anxiety Margaret had induced earlier that night came flooding back to overtake his sadness. His hands felt numb and he could taste the bile teasing at the back of his throat. He fought to keep from vomiting.

Normally it wouldn't be such a big deal. Normally a mistake like the one he'd made with Margaret would simply mean it was time for him to run before he was found out. But he couldn't run from here. There was nowhere to go. And Bill… Bill had Greg under his heel. One slight misstep, and Bill could crush him like a bug.

Greg swallowed hard and shut his eyes. When he was a child, before the pills, his mother had taught him how pattern breathing and meditating could reduce anxiety. Now, with his heart nearly bursting, he focused on his breathing.

In, then out.

In, then out.

Slowly his heart rate dropped, and by the time the anxiety had returned to its regular levels, the reasonable aspect of Greg's mind knew what had to happen.

No matter what, there would be no fairytale ending for Greg. He needed one thing: Time. Time to figure out what to do next. Time to figure out where to go. Time to figure out what he could possibly make of his life now that he had nothing to go back to.

As long as Bill's polished boot heel was hanging over his head, he would have no time.

Greg was going to have to do *it* again.

Only this time, it would have to look like an accident.

The computer pinged, denoting that one of the computers connected to the network had come online. Greg opened his eyes and saw the small rectangle in the bottom corner of his screen come to life. As part of his hacking, he'd built a backdoor into Bill's own monitoring software that allowed him live access to the other computers on the network. He expanded the small rectangle to full screen. It was Margaret's laptop. She pulled up Google, then slowly began typing.

"Don't do it," Greg pleaded, tears welling in his eyes as he watched in agonizing dismay. The words began to appear in the search bar.

He figured he could stand to hurt Bill. Bill was bad. Bill was a monster. But Margaret… he couldn't do something like that to her—

No.

The image of his mother's stone-faced glare flashed in his mind.

He was really, truly alone now, and the only person who could protect him was himself.

He watched as Margaret finished typing "Greg Gupta Colorado State" into the search bar and clicked "search." Thankfully, only various fruitless results popped up, but he steeled his mind nonetheless. How hard would it be for someone who reconstructed entire civilizations from a few scattered rocks and bones to discover his grand secret?

There was only one way out of this mess.

Margaret was going to have to join Bill in his accident.

The tears came again, but this time his face was stone, like his mother's. He turned to the schematics that littered the table. He knew what he had to do.

XVI

Margaret

IT WAS late by the time Margaret managed to find Daniel Hindberg's Colorado State profile. The full moon hung lazily over the cliffs outside, its silvery glow leaking in through her bedroom windows and blending near perfectly with the cobalt background of the college's staff website. Daniel still looked much the same as she'd remembered him from twenty years before — maybe a bit more distinguished in a Ben Kingsley type of way — but still thin and mostly bald. Needless to say, he was not at all Fabio-esque as Margaret had claimed. It didn't require the brunt of her deductive reasoning to know that Greg was full of shit about his education.

But why?

Probably the same reason she was here, she mused. Quick cash. Maybe he was just another clever engineer with a degree from some shittier school who knew he'd be overlooked if he didn't beef up his resumé. It probably wouldn't've been hard to fake credentials enough to slip them past that idiot Bill, after all. She tried to imagine a more ominous reasoning behind the young man's fake identity and actually laughed out loud. That boy was couldn't hurt a fly.

Her back ached from sitting at the edge of her bed, and her fingers felt cold and brittle from ticking away on the keyboard. She checked the clock. It was well past midnight. The excavation team had to be ready for the next incursion into the caves by a quarter after five, and she knew she'd have to be well rested. Especially since the next morning's endeavor likely involved beginning the process of hacking away at the wet, half rotted remains of the subterranean wall's surface in order to reach a solid enough base for Greg's water jet system to bolt onto.

She laid back and closed her eyes. Maybe an hour before, she'd taken an extra half pill, and now the wonderful chemicals swirled through her bloodstream, delivering contentment and the most pleasant tingle to every bit of her body. Despite this, after ten relaxing minutes, she found that she couldn't sleep.

This happened sometimes when she was high. Sleep would evade her for a night or two, and while sometimes it would hinder her teaching schedule or grading time, she mostly thought it as a little treat. A time when she'd get the pleasure of experiencing hours of euphoric calm alone and undisturbed in the darkness. Now wasn't the time for that, though. There was no question that she would need every ounce of her strength in the coming days. She knew she needed to find a way to break the cycle of insomnia before it even began. Reading sometimes helped — on the page, not on a screen. The only problem was that she hadn't packed anything boring enough to sedate her pleasantly humming mind.

She pulled on a pair of shorts and a raggedy T-shirt. The nighttime house was the perfect level of warm as she padded down the stairs in her slippers and into the foyer. She looked over the barren bookshelves in the drawing room and in the various drawers and crannies, searching for something old and boring to read.

But there was nothing. Either some vandals had come through at some point in the house's three decades of abandonment and snatched up every scrap of history that wasn't too heavy to carry, or Bill had had the place cleaned out before their arrival. For some reason, Margaret suspected the latter.

After giving up on her fruitless search of the drawing room, she walked down the first floor's central hallway. All of the occupied bedrooms were on the second and third floors, so she didn't bother knocking as she tried one door after another. Most of them were unlocked and revealed little more than barren cobwebbed and dust-coated floors. Finally, she reached the last door. The patinaed brass doorknob held fast in her hand as she tried to turn it.

Interesting. This was the first locked door she'd encountered in the dingey old manor.

She crossed the house to the kitchen, returning with a tiny crumpet fork, a flathead screwdriver, and an inward grin. It only took her a few moments to pick the old lock. It was a skill she'd picked up from an exceedingly handsome historian she'd shared a hotel room with in Cairo decades before. She still felt the same little rush of pleasure as the final pin slid into place that she had when he'd first taught her.

The door let out an eerie creak as she eased it open. The room beyond, the only room that Bill had bothered to lock in the whole house (at least as far as she knew), looked to be a long-abandoned study. The blue hue cast from the moon illuminated the tall bookcases packed full of dusty tomes, and a beautiful hardwood ship desk centered the dusty floor. Piled atop the desk was a mountain of books, bound scrolls, and loose bundles of century old paper.

So, this is where Bill stashed all the goodies.

"Jackpot," she muttered as she pulled the little clamshell phone from her pocket and powered it on. It pinged as it tried and failed to pull a signal, but she only needed it for the light of its luminescent screen.

Most of the first layer of the papers she sifted through were water stained to the point of being illegible. Even those few that still maintained their jagged scrawling were in such heavy-handed cursive that she knew it would take hours to decipher a single page. It didn't matter. Most of them seemed to be letters and shipping documents, some bore the seal of banks and others of merchants, all their various dates ranging from the turn of the nineteenth century onward.

She quickly lost interest in the randomly assorted legal documents and manifests and moved on to the warped shelves of the bookcases that armored the walls. Many of the books had already passed the point of recovery, but there were still a few whose spines held strong enough to be able to pull them free. Margaret's fingers wandered gingerly over one such book. Its golden letters glinted in the electric light of her phone screen: *De Danorum. Beowulf.*

She gently pulled it free and examined the inlayed patterns that decorated the dark leather cover. Its scent wafted into her nose as she cracked the pages apart, smelling of mildew and freshly tilled earth. The text was fully in Latin, and the first page placed the date of publishing at 1815. Based on a combination of instincts and her own little bit of knowledge in the world of rare books, she knew this was a once in a lifetime find.

Amazing.

No wonder Bill had lock all of this up — this book was an artifact in and of itself. It belonged in a museum.

The museum of Margaret Simmons' fucking house, she thought with a smile.

She tucked the priceless first edition of the epic Anglo-Saxon poem under her arm and let her eyes wander over the countless eroding books before her. She wondered how many lost treasures lay hidden among those shelves.

"You'll find out tomorrow," she whispered to herself, vowing to return and pick the shelves dry. "But you need some fucking sleep, you old bag."

She turned to leave, then paused when she spotted a drawer peeking out from beyond the back of wooden chair tucked into the desk. She pulled away the chair and found that the drawer bore an antique brass keyhole. The drawer held fast when she tugged at the petite knob and wondered if Bill had bothered checking it — or any of this stuff for that matter. No, it was likely that this tiny portion of the manor had remained sealed since the lives of the Clayborns. Her interest piqued, Margaret once again dug the crumpet fork and screwdriver from her pocket.

Inside of the drawer were a number of commonplace personal valuables and knickknacks. An elegant scrimshaw pipe and matching pen, a gold-plated pocket watch, a rusty pocketknife, and the decaying remnants of a lock-clasp journal. Margaret pulled the journal out of the drawer and into the phone's light. Though the lock itself was still engaged, the leather flap that had bound it crumbled and broke in her fingers. She opened the journal.

The name Clara was scrolled in bold cursive along the top of the first page beside the date: January 3, 1807.

In Clara's first entry, she revealed that the diary was a gift from her brother, Lord Thomas Clayborn the Third, given to her on her sixteenth birthday. The writing itself wasn't so much in the form of a diary entry as it was a letter meant for the girl's mother, who had clearly already passed on at the time of its writing. She pleaded and prayed for all manner of things a young Catholic woman of the time might: good health, fair fortunes to her brother, to escape the dreary country life, but mostly, she wished for a handsome husband to rescue her from her horribly boring life.

"*Blech.*" Margaret made a dramatic gagging sound. She flipped to the next page, only to find it stained and mostly illegible. The third page was worse, and by the fourth, it was clear that some past reader, perhaps Clara herself, had spilled a significant amount of coffee or tea on the journal while perusing the whining prattle of a pre-Victorian teenage girl. As Margaret reached the latter half of the entries, the few bits of writing that remained visible through the blotched ink began to take on a shakier script as if written by a weaker hand. Only the last few pages had escaped the damage largely unscathed. Most of them contained a repeated checklist of the manor's doors and windows, each column marked systematically with dozens of checks and dates. Wrong dates, Margaret noted, since the year written was 1973. In her old age, Clara must have been a bit senile. Assuming that she'd mistakenly written 1973 rather than 1873, that would put her at... eighty-two during these last entries. Only a few decades older than herself, Margaret thought with self-loathing disgust.

The last page of the journal had one final entry. It was a poem, written in the smoother hand of a youthful Clara — clearly a piece of work she'd copied into the rear of the journal as a means of easy reference.

Ere she went, to the forest heart
Where grew the king of the great oaken beam,
Thick in the belly, lost in dream.

Down went Mary, rollin' her cart,
And that where it found her, tore her apart,
O'er the wind came her bloody scream.

Dare we not go, down past the stream,
For that is the bounds of wickedness start,
Down is the grail in Eden's heart.

Where devils sleep, wicked things dream,
In the lowland with black mountain hawkweed,
Drawn are those who follow the dark.

Where God almighty lays his tests
Reveals the heathen heart 'neath Mary's breast.

—Clara

"Are you kidding me?" Margaret muttered. She re-read the poem again and again, each time stopping on one particular line: "Down is the grail in Eden's heart."

"Are you *fucking* kidding me?" she released a frustrated groan.

Of course.

How could she have not seen the glaringly obvious truth?

Of course Bill hadn't bothered to do his due diligence.

Of course the answer to the whole goddamn expedition was right there in that pile of shit manor.

Of course it was all *bullshit*.

This wasn't Sophie's hoax, or even Bill's hoax.

It was some goddamn Victorian era nutjob's hoax.

Down is the grail in Eden's heart.

It made so much sense. This was all just some rich, nineteenth century ass-wipe cult of Scottish hillbillies scrawling nonsense into cave walls about the Holy Grail or the fountain of youth or whatever nonsense they considered it.

It's not like this would be the first time this happened. People in the nineteenth century were *assholes*, every archaeologist knew that. She couldn't even begin to count all the stories she'd heard of supposedly ancient excavations revealing that an entire dig was based on nothing more than the casual flight of fancy of some bored Victorian era asshole.

Of-fucking-course.

Margaret fumed, her anger piquing to a point where it drowned out the calming waves of pleasure that stemmed from the opiates' embrace. She wanted to scream, to run up to Bill's room and force feed him the goddamn journal that he was too stupid to find in the first place. Her gut filled with a roiling anger, not just at the doughy little turd, but also with herself — because some tiny part of her had actually started to *believe* this bullshit wild goose chase.

She shook the journal in frustration, imagining it was Bill's throat, then tossed it onto the desk and collapsed into the wooden chair.

"Fuckin' fuckity fuck fuck!" she hissed over and over.

It took a few minutes, but finally her blood began to cool, and the opiates once more did their job. It was as she sat there, staring blankly through the mountain of old documents and ledgers and imagining the various ways in which she'd like to kill Bill, that she noticed the words scrawled in panicked bold across the journal's back cover.

Thomas should not have gone into the garden. That devil which slinks and slithers now knows his scent. I'm sorry, mother, I cannot let him in.

"Oh, so spooky. Demented old bitch," Margaret hissed. "Little fucking prankster weren't yo—"

A lonesome creak echoed outside the room.

Margaret froze.

From down the hallway and through the foyer she heard the faint groan of the manor's front door easing open, then shut. Something was out there. Someone.

One of the floorboards — in the foyer from the sound of it — creaked underfoot. Then there was silence.

Margaret held her breath.

It wasn't that she cared if she was caught down here in the study. Bill had technically never mentioned the room nor told them *not* to pick locked doors. Also, and more importantly, Bill could go fuck himself. The reason Margaret felt the icy needles of fear pricking the nape of her neck at that moment was that she had been *sure* that she was the only one awake when she'd come down from the second story. Now something had entered the house from the outside. Something that, from the sound of it, was moving with purposeful stealth.

Her hands were shaking as she plucked the small, rusted pocketknife from the drawer and unfolded it. It felt like little more than a butter scraper as she held it out in front of her, but it would have to do. She sat completely still, the crashing beat of her own heart deafening her to the silence that filled the room. The shadows beyond the cracked door of the study were still as she glared into them. An hour passed, or maybe a minute, she had no idea, before she finally worked up the courage to slowly stand. As softly as she could manage, she padded across the dust-coated room and poked her head out of the door.

The hallway was still and silent, as well as the sliver of the foyer she could see into. She let another chilling minute creep by before she eased herself through the cracked door and walked slowly forward down the hallway and into the sprawling foyer. The moonlight that leaked in from the unshuttered windows revealed that the front door was closed. It also revealed a trail leading from the entry toward the kitchen. She immediately recognized the dark, splattered droplets for what they were. Blood.

Her whole body spasmed in panic as a loud squeal came from the kitchen. She darted behind one of the twin wingback chairs and made herself as small as humanly possible, then listened as the gurgling splash of water revealed the truth.

It was just the rusty old kitchen sink.

Whoever was in the kitchen was splashing water, and she could hear them muttering something. Using the noise to cover her movement, she darted across the foyer and into the dining room, which gave her a clean vantage into the kitchen. The dull orange glow of the kitchen's dying bulb barely illuminated a darkened figure hunched over the sink, but Margaret recognized the outline of a wild mane and unkempt beard.

"Jack?"

He spun, his hand darting to the pistol that hung on his side. Their eyes met and he froze. Even in the darkness, she could see that they were wild and terrified.

"*Fuck!* It's me Margaret!" she hissed, stepping out into the light with her hands raised in front of her.

His posture deflated, and he shook his head. "Goddammit, I could have shot you," he said.

"What are you doing sneaking around down here like a—" She paused as her eyes were drawn to the crimson stains that covered his left arm and smeared his clothes. "What the hell happened?" she demanded.

Jack let out a dismissive grunt. "It's nothing." He turned back to the sink and began scrubbing at his bleeding forearm.

"Like hell." She crossed the room for a closer look. "You need medical attention."

"I'm fine. It's superficial."

"It's not," she snapped. "Let me see it."

He hesitated, then held out his arm. The flesh was red, swollen, and spotted with dark blue and black bruises. Several rows of jagged punctures ran along his arm just below the elbow. Margaret instructed him to flex his hand, then one by one checked his fingers' range of motion. As far as she could tell, the tendons and muscles of the forearm were undamaged despite the ugly flesh wounds.

"You still need a doctor," she insisted.

"You won't catch me near that creep Bianchi." He went back to scrubbing at the wound with a dishrag. "Anyways, I thought *you* were a doctor."

She rolled her eyes. "Funny. How the hell did you manage to get bitten by a dog all the way out here?"

"Wolf," Jack corrected.

"*What?*"

"It was a wolf."

"I heard you. I just… I seem to remember you specifically stating — *quite adamantly* — that there are no wolves in Nova Scotia."

"Well, there weren't supposed to be," Jack muttered. He looked up and met her eyes. "Something weird is going on here, and I don't like it. We're being lied to. *I'm* being lied to, and I've had damn near enough of it. I need you to be honest with me: this isn't just some spot where Phoenician sailors washed up a couple thousand years ago, is it?"

Margaret sat at the kitchen table and considered her answer. "No," she finally admitted. What was the point in carrying on Bill's pointless lies?

"You gonna fill me in, or are you just gonna sit there and—"

"Bill's got some sort of paranoid scheme he's running here," she said, interrupting him. "Sophie convinced him that there's something big down in those caves. Something similar in nature to the fountain of youth. The best I can figure it, he's lying about the Phoenician angle because he's scared someone will try and poach his find."

"What is it Sophie thinks is down there?" Jack asked. "Let me guess, the cauldron from that story?"

"Yeah, maybe." Margaret failed to hide an approving glance.

"I figured there was a reason you two were staring daggers at each other that night," Jack said, then winced in pain as he scrubbed a little too hard. "You believe them?"

"Hell no." Margaret shook her head. "I said it in the beginning, and I'll say it again. It's a hoax."

"You think Bill's trying to fake a find?"

"No. At this point I'm guessing it was the Clayborns that cooked something up."

Jack scoffed. "Why?"

Margaret poked her chin toward the south end of the house. "Bill locked up all the old documents that came with the house without going through them. There was a journal, some girl that lived here around the time this place was built. She says some stuff about the grail and what not, seems to be the God-fearing Catholic type given the context and time period. If I had to guess, the Clayborns put those symbols in that cave and built that wooden wall is on the other end of those tunnels. Rich people used to love to do shit like this when they were bored, which was almost always. Add in a bit of religious extremism and *voila*, a waste of my fucking time is born."

"And you told the others about this?" Jack asked, turning off the water and pulling one of the first aid kits from beneath the sink.

"No, I just found it. Bring those bandages over here."

"Are you going to?" Jack asked, sitting at the table opposite her and laying a roll of bandages out between them.

Margaret helped him roll the bandage tightly around his arm. "Why wouldn't I?"

"I don't know." Jack winced as she pulled the last bit of gauze tight and secured it with tape. "I feel like there's a real fucked up rift in communication around here."

"You can thank Bill for that," Margaret muttered.

"Is it possible that there's really something down there?"

"What, some genuine find of historical significance? I guess anything's possible."

"No, I mean something… something with *real* power."

Margaret eyed him for a long second, trying to figure out if he was serious. "I didn't peg you for an idiot, Jack. Maybe I was wrong."

Jack pulled a flask from his pocket. He took a long drink and offered it to her, but she declined.

"I never claimed I wasn't an idiot, but I will tell you what I've seen in these forests. The things here — the animals, the trees, even the underbrush — it's all just so oversized and healthy. It's like it's, I don't know…" His voice trailed off. He gave her a forlorn look.

Margaret sighed. She *hated* lecturing outside of a class, but there was a time and a place for it. "Which came first, the chicken or the egg?"

"Huh?"

"The egg came first," she stated. "Because there were dinosaurs popping out eggs millions of years before the first thought of a chicken. It's a *really* simple answer to a question only debated by morons who don't understand evolution. The same lesson can be applied to ninety-nine percent of the hocus pocus that surrounds archaeological finds. Let's say that the things here really *are* bigger and healthier than elsewhere in this area. Well, a number of scientific theories could account for how that started. Food source abundance, a perfectly balanced ecosystem, some later stage extinction of a major subspecies that occurred in the surrounding area, or even just a mineral rich spring. If we imagine that however many lifetimes ago, the first Native Americans to establish themselves here noticed that this one area was even a bit more abundant in whatever way, it's likely they would attribute that to some sort of mythological or folkloric meaning which, in turn, would likely lead to the preservation of this area. Now, fast forward to some loony Scottish traders who catch wind of this dramatic Native folklore of an unnaturally bountiful land. These nineteenth century nutbags obviously draw some correlation between their own mythology — AKA the Bible — and the Native American one. Now you add in a couple generations' worth of devolving belief, a little education, and a bunch of very bored people spending cold winters and dull summers out here in the middle of nowhere, and you end up with the spiteful masterpiece of bullshit you'll find in those caves."

Jack leaned back in his chair and crossed his arms, drawing a wince as he brushed the bandage.

"You see, Jack," she went on. "It's easy to look at the result of a perfectly sensible series of events and imagine some supernatural cause. But in reality, the only reason anyone ever thought there was any sort of magic here is because the forests and animals have been left the fuck alone long enough to create a healthy ecosystem. Take it from me: no matter how enticing the idea of it can be, there's no such thing as magic."

Jack cocked his head. "You teach that lesson at Yale?"

"Eh, more or less. Aspiring archaeologists tend not to take it too well. Too many of them are there for some romantic Hollywood nonsense anyways."

He didn't say anything for a moment, instead examining on his new bandages. After a while, though, he spoke up. "Are you going to leave?"

"I'm considering it," she muttered. "But there's a lot of money involved."

"Same." Jack took another drink.

"One thing is for sure: I don't trust Bill," she said, casting a loathing glare upwards in the direction of his bedroom.

"Neither do I." Jack nodded and followed her gaze. "Or Kevin, for that matter. That prick wouldn't shut up about how many guns he's got stashed away in his room up there. I'll tell you from experience that getting firearms through Canadian customs is no easy task. Even if he could get a permit for something, the shit he says he's got is not even remotely legal in these parts."

"You think they're dangerous?" She'd never actually imagined that those two could be capable of committing actual violence.

"I think they're stupid, which generally means the same thing."

"I tend to agree."

"Well then we should watch each other's backs," Jack said flatly.

"What do you mean?"

"You ever handled a deer rifle?"

"I've never even shot a gun," Margaret said with a hint of pride that suddenly felt painfully off, given their situation.

"Well, I'll show you the basics. That way if anything gets, you know… at least you'll have something to fall back on."

"I don't need a gun—" she started.

"No one needs a gun until they *need* a gun," he said matter-of-factly. And if I were you, I wouldn't trust Kevin as the only person to *have* a gun. We'll put it in your room, that way if shit hits the fan, you can do something about it."

Margaret wanted to laugh at the idea. To tell this bloodstained bumpkin to go fuck himself and that he was being absurd. She might've, had she not been wishing for a rifle a mere ten minutes before.

Beyond that, it didn't seem *that* crazy. Who knew what kind of terrible tricks Bill would end up revealing down the road?

DAY 9

XVII

Greg

IT TOOK Greg two full anxiety-ridden days to fashion the water jet cutter from the miscellaneous equipment at his disposal, then another full day to perfect the rail system it would be mounted on. In the meantime, Sophie and Margaret had managed to strip the waterlogged mush of wood and algae from the barrier's surface and measure out the appropriate drill points for the rail. The team planned out a number of scenarios based on the various possibilities of what they would reveal beyond the wall. Greg had watched Margaret nearly throw a fit at the idea of not waiting out the storm, but in the end, Bill's insistence on keeping to the schedule had won out.

It was just after dawn on a damp, foggy morning when everything came together, and the entire team — besides the doctor — found themselves perched atop the cliff with dreaded Hurricane Mallory hanging menacingly just off the coast.

"This morning, we make history!" Bill had excitedly announced after a brief overview of the plan at breakfast, then again as they made the trek out to the dig site, and a third time once they'd all settled into their rolls. The closer they got to the tide drop, the more he'd begun to sweat.

Now he tugged nervously on the steel cable that would suspend him over the sheer drop. "Are we sure it will hold?" he asked, his voice trembling a bit despite his attempts at bravado.

Greg nodded, keeping his gaze lowered until Bill had turned his focus back to the too tight harness cutting canyons in his paunch. The man looked like the chubby caricature of a nineteenth century tiger hunter, all done up in a khaki adventurer's suit with freshly shined boots and more pockets than could ever be filled. *He even has the subjugated local Indian boy to complete the look*, Greg thought with a grimace. All Bill was missing was a monocle and an elephant steed.

"You sure you don't want me to come with?" Kevin asked for the dozenth time.

Bill shook his head. "No, no, Kevin, I think there will barely be enough room for the ladies and I, and I'm not missing out on whatever's on the other side of that barrier. You stay up top and make sure everything runs smoothly."

Margaret and Sophie exchanged a look at the way he said "ladies."

Archaeologists, Greg thought, *not ladies. They don't like that.*

Bill should be smarter, especially since he was headed down into those deep, dark tunnels where anything could happen. Where the only thing standing between Bill and a horrible fate were those archaeologists — and Greg's equipment of course.

"Let's go! We're wasting time we don't have!" Margaret snapped at the group.

Bill muttered something to himself, then attached the carabiner to his harness and approached the edge.

"We're ready!" Sophie shouted as the three cave divers, each loaded with various pieces of gear, lined up on the cliff's edge and leaned back against the support of the cables that held them. Greg, sitting over the winch controls thirty feet away, could barely hear her over the thunder of the storm-driven waves far below.

"No funny business, kid," Kevin muttered into Greg's ear.

"N— no funny business," Greg repeated obediently, then gave the spelunkers a thumbs up and pressed the button to begin slowly unwinding the mechanical winch, lowering them down the cliff face.

No funny business.

Not yet.

It took an extra ten minutes longer than usual to lower the trio to the cave mouth, as Bill's trembling command to "slow down" rattled through the radio at least half a dozen times during the 200-foot journey. The whole time, Greg imagined Margaret's frustration and considered the far-out fantasy that maybe she and Bill might just kill each other down there, entombing Greg's secrets on their own accord.

Once the trio was safely unhooked, Greg released the pressure on one of the winches. The steel cable unwound freely as the team in the cave below slowly towed it, alongside a water hose and power cord, deeper into the abyss.

Greg kept his eyes glued to the lights and switches on the control board before him. He'd rewired the panel — which was originally meant to control a small, unmanned submarine — to control the multi-cabled winch system, the water pump that led from the clifftop reservoir, and, when the time came, the waterjet itself. It wouldn't be unimaginable that something could malfunction, not with this jerry-rigged setup.

"That a .357?" Kevin said suddenly.

Greg looked up to see that Kevin was looking past Greg.

"Yeah," Jack said.

Greg turned his head to where Jack paced the cliff's edge a dozen yards away, eyes slowly scanning the area as if preparing for some imminent threat.

"Cool gun. Those single actions though... kind of an antique if you ask me." Kevin stood and slapped the large pistol at his own side. Greg recognized the hulking semi-automatic from one of his video games. "I prefer something with a little more *oomph*. Ever fucked with a Desert Eagle?"

Jack barely bothered to shake his head and continued pacing.

"Well, we could trade for the day. It might be fun to pretend I'm a cowboy." Kevin chuckled, but when Jack once again didn't respond, his face morphed into a scowl. "You have some kind of problem, Jack? I'm over here just trying to be friendly—"

"You should give up," Jack cut him off.

Greg's position between the two men suddenly felt unsafe, and as he glanced between them, a scene from a lion documentary he'd watched years before flashed through his mind. Kevin flexed like the proud, young challenger — despite the at least ten years of actual seniority he held over Jack. He stood tall with his chest puffed out and thick, muscular arms crossed and flexed. Meanwhile, Jack mirrored a weathered pride leader. Thinner and scarred, but cool, confident, and terrifyingly comfortable with the situation. Greg didn't need to overthink it to pick which one he'd bet on. Kevin was intimidating, yeah, but Jack was downright scary.

He hoped Jack wouldn't blame him for the accident that was about to happen.

The silent standoff ended quickly when Bill's voice crackled through the radio regarding some frivolous concern. Kevin resumed his seat atop the crates and Jack resumed his pacing, and Greg tried to ignore them both and mentally prepare for the events to come.

It was nearly an hour and a half before the underground trio reached their destination. Based on Margaret's exasperated attitude over the radio, Greg guessed that Bill's inability to keep up was the root of the issue. In another thirty minutes, they had the water cutter mounted to its circular rail system, which was in turn bolted to the barrier.

"It's going to— It'll travel along the rail under its own power, okay?" Greg reminded them.

After they had all responded — Sophie politely, Margaret sarcastically, and Bill anxiously — Greg hit the switch to initiate the water pump, then tracked the pressure as the long hose the team had towed with them filled with water.

"We've got water," Sophie called over the radio after a few minutes. On command, Greg flipped the switch atop the generator to push power to the water cutter below. Sophie came back over the radio.

"Yeah, it's powering on…" A thunderous noise sounded through the speaker that made Greg flinch, and the radio went silent.

It took Kevin a millisecond to react. He eyed the radio, then Greg, then the radio again and made a stupid face. "What the… What the fuck happened?" He grabbed the radio, and an edge of panic rang in his voice as he spoke into it. "Hey, what's going on? You okay?"

Silence.

"Hey!" Kevin called louder into the receiver, but when he still received no response, he turned furiously toward Greg. "What did you do, you little fuckin' haj—"

"Hey!" Sophie's voice cut him off, barely audible over a loud background hissing. "This thing is loud as shit, Greg. What the hell?"

Greg slowly reached out and keyed his radio, afraid a sudden move might set off Kevin. "I— I'm sorry. I should have considered how loud it would be in… in an enclosed space."

Kevin sat down, and from the dirty look he shot over Greg's shoulder, Greg was suddenly aware of just how close Jack was standing behind him. He wondered if it had been a move made to protect him, or perhaps it was made with the same intentions as Kevin.

"Don't worry about it!" Sophie was shouting so loud that Greg had to turn his radio down. "It's working! Goddamn, this thing can cut!"

Yeah, it worked. It was precise, too, Greg thought with an inward flinch. Exactly five degrees off at an outward angle. Just enough so that what *should* have been a perfectly cylindrical cork would have a diameter about nine inches wider on the far side than the near side.

Greg felt a growing tingle in his gut, but it wasn't the familiar run-of-the-mill anxiety. It was something else, something hot and rotting. Something he'd only felt once before, months ago, when the airbag had deflated, and he'd watched in horror as Edward Nichol's pinned torso twitched atop the hood of his car. Greg's mind had gone blank on that chilly May morning when he'd spotted his relentless oppressor jaunting down the sidewalk. He'd been pointing to Greg's rundown sedan, spouting some snarky comment and laughing with the others. Something in Greg had broken in that moment, and he had turned that mocking laugh into a scream.

After the fact, Greg had repeatedly told himself that the car had somehow accelerated itself. But it hadn't. He'd pressed down on that pedal. He'd turned that car off the road. He'd embraced the pure rage and finally struck back against the bully who had ceaselessly tormented him for years.

Afterward, there was no feeling of vengeful catharsis like he'd expected. Only sickness, horror, and guilt.

He'd never meant to do it.

It'd just… happened.

Now that same rot that he'd felt on all those months ago once again grew in his belly as he considered what he was about to do. He knew Sophie didn't deserve to die. She'd been nothing but kind to Greg. The truth was, none of them really *deserved* to die, but Greg didn't have a choice. They'd trapped him there — *Bill* had trapped him here — and Margaret just had to ask so many damn questions. What else could he do?

Greg tried to suppress the growing ache and checked the time against his charts. The cutter would have made it somewhere between eight inches to a foot deep by now. He tried to turn his focus to preparing the winch, but one thought hung heavily in his mind. He pushed it away, attempting to repress it as he had the last few days. But it couldn't be contained, clawing its way back to the forefront of his skull: in less than an hour, he would truly become a murderer.

Greg couldn't bear to imagine himself a murderer. What happened before… it wasn't planned or orchestrated or premeditated or whatever the courts called it. It had been a moment of weakness and rage, a second of terrible judgment and pent-up hatred that he knew would haunt him until the day he died. *That* was a mistake, but this was different. Killing the trio in the caves… this was premeditated. This was self-preservation. This was murder.

The image of Margaret's face bloodied and porcupined with wooden slivers forced its way into his mind's eye. He almost gagged. Then Sophie joined Margaret's face, bloated and drowned, fish-nibbled eyes still bugged out in abject terror.

Despite the cool, damp morning breeze, Greg began to sweat.

It was too late anyway, he thought. He'd already pulled the trigger. The cutter would finish within the hour, then the women would feed the grappling hook through the cork's center, and then he'd engage the winch that would wind back the steel cord attached to said grappling hook — but the uneven cork wouldn't budge. Greg would push the pressure up higher and higher, feigning panic at the failure of his contraption, and when the time came, he would remove the power inhibitor from the circuit beneath the panel, immediately tripling the tow force of the winch. Then cork would pop — *really* pop — and if Greg's math held up, the immediate wall surrounding the cork should explode into a thousand broken dagger-like splinters of half petrified wood. Even in the slight chance that the spelunkers could avoid the massive wooden projectile and accompanying shrapnel, the cork only needed to travel a mere fifteen feet before it would wedge itself in the increasingly thinner tunnel, trapping them there to drown in the rapidly approaching tide.

"Something wrong with you?" Kevin demanded. Greg realized that between the trembling hands and sheen of sweat, he must have looked absurd. Guilty even.

"Yeah, I— I just, I, well, nerve— nervous. I just want it to w— work, you know?" Greg felt like he might cry. He glanced back at Jack, hoping maybe for some comforting nod or word of encouragement, but was met instead with an untrusting glare that made his already upset stomach tighten. A terrifying thought crossed his mind: what if Margaret had talked to Jack, revealed her suspicions? What had they figured out? How would Jack react when—

"Get your shit together," Kevin commanded.

"I— yeah, no I don't— I think the uh, the…" Greg's heart was going to explode, he was sure of it. His hands were hot and trembling as they floated over the controls. Suddenly, the tunnel-like focus he'd had while protecting his identity opened up to encompass the complexities of the overarching situation, and with it, a horrifying realization rolled front and center: he had made a horrible mistake. He couldn't do this. He couldn't murder.

But for all his planning and machinations, Greg suddenly realized he'd never built himself a way out.

There had to be a way to call it off without revealing himself. A way to shut it down and get them out of there before the cutter got any farther through. Something that would allow him to get down there and fix it. A way they couldn't argue with or fight against, but also something passable enough that he wouldn't be figured out…

What could go wrong? What could go wrong… the generator, the winch, the reservoir, the cutter, the water pump— the water pump! Of course! There was no water cutter without water. He'd need to cut the supply off just before the jet cutter itself. If the jet cutter were to remain on without the water source, it would seize, and he might be able to weasel his way down there to fix it with the afternoon's low tide period and recalibrate the jet's angle… But then there'd be the issue of him getting down there — Greg didn't do well with tight spaces, or heights, or climbing, or hiking, or—

"Greg, my God! Kid, you're going to get a promotion!" Bill's excited voice came over the radio. "This thing must be cutting two feet deep already!"

Greg eyed Kevin, who was looking away over the cliffs, lost in some bored daydream.

This was it.

He had to do it now.

As subtly as he could, Greg reached under the control panel and felt for the circuit under the pump switch. It took him a minute to find, but thanks to his own meticulous organization when soldering the panel's connections together, he felt somewhat confident when he came across the thin double wires. He gave the left one a short tug, but it stayed in place. Grimacing and trying to hide the motion, he yanked harder, and the rhythmic hum of the reservoir's water pump cut off.

"What the hell?" Kevin muttered, trying to place the change in noise. "Greg! Something just shut off."

"W— what was it?" Greg jolted back into place and flashed a curious look.

"I don't know! What was making that, you know, like..." Kevin imitated the pump noise.

Greg waited several long seconds, still feigning confusion. Only once he was sure the water had had time to clear the long, thin underground line did he fake the spark of realization. "Oh no! You mean the pump—"

"What the fuck happened?" Bill shouted through the radio. "Turn it off, turn it off!"

Greg slapped at the controls in fake panic until all the board's lights had cut off. "I don't know what—"

"The fucking water cut off!" Margaret's enraged voice took over the radio. "Jesus Christ, it sounded like this piece of shit was going to explode! What the hell is wrong with this rinky dink—"

Greg quickly rolled the volume down on his radio and rushed over to the pump, pretending to search for an issue. Kevin fumed nearby, arguing back and forth over the radio with Margaret, insisting that it was just a temporary hang up and that he'd make sure it was back up and running in a moment... but Greg knew better. He'd take his time to figure out the severed connection, and by then he'd have come up with some half-truth about needing to fix the locked cutter himself.

Greg glanced over to Jack, who now stood beside the control panel. In his panicked state, Greg had forgotten about the silent hunter pacing along the cliffs behind him. Slowly, Jack knelt and looked under the control panel. After a long second, Jack gave a stone-faced glare that evaporated every feeling of comfort he'd ever instilled in Greg. Without a word, Jack turned and resumed his pacing.

It didn't matter. Greg was going to fix it, and no one was going to die. Not today.

XVIII

Bill

"I NEED you to cut me a goddamn break!" Bill clenched the satellite phone in a white-knuckled grip as he paced furiously along the cliffs directly behind Clayborn Manor.

Bernard Guthrie let out a sigh on the other end of the line. His voice was thick with a New York accent and ripe with an exhausted tone of defeat. *"Bill, bud, there are no more goddamn breaks. You exhausted every single line of credit I could scrape up on your last trip."*

"It wasn't a trip, Bernie. It was a non-profit scientific expedition — and the legal team cleared at least half of those debts."

"No, your legal team sent out cease and desists to all those local contractors you never paid," the seventy-seven-year-old accountant came back. *"They didn't clear a thing. Just because they're not American doesn't mean those debts aren't still owed. And on top of that, you now owe fifty grand to the lawyers for that whole debacle anyways."*

Bill made to hurl the phone over the cliff, only barely stopping himself in time. He glanced nervously back in the direction of the manor to make sure no one was watching. "Fine. Fine. Pay the bloodsucking lawyer. Pay the foreigners. Write everyone a goddamn check. By the time this expedition is done, we'll have the capital to pay them all back and then some. I just need a cash infusion to keep me going — that's all. Come on, Bernie, something's come up — a fucking hurricane of all things. An act of God! I need time to reset and regear. It'll be worth it, just liquidate some more of the old man's assets or—"

"*Bill, what don't you understand?*" The gravelly voice shifted from exhausted to exasperated. "*There are no more assets — it's all gone. For the past fifteen years, you've been bleeding the stocks, dumping properties, and burning through cash like a fat kid in a fuckin' candy store. You're done, you're out, kaput, no more. I don't know how else to fuckin' tell ya, kid. It's over. You might be the first person in the history of capitalism who's managed to completely burn through an inheritance that massive in such a short time. It really is incredible.*"

Bill battled to keep the tremble of anger out of his voice, but it still managed to spill out with his words. "Do not speak to me like that."

"*Look, Bill,*" Guthrie said. "*I promise I'm not trying to be an asshole. Really. You know your father and I went way back, and I really do get a kick out of all the weird stuff you do. But my god, man, I don't know how else to get through to you. I've been on your case about this since the old man passed, and now the piper's come to get his payment. I'm sorry, my friend. There's no more money.*"

"Fine. Fine, just get us a loan then—"

"*Are you deaf? Nobodies. Gonna. Lend. You. Shit. You're not just broke — you're in the hole for a fat sum already. It's over!*"

Bill bit his tongue. "That's temporary, goddammit. What I've uncovered here is—"

"*It could be the fuckin' Holy Grail, and still no one would give you a penny until you could prove it. How is this not clear?*"

The volcano of frustration that burned in Bill's belly bubbled up to his face and he had to blink away furious tears. He took a deep, calming breath, then spoke as evenly as he could. "Bernie, a quarter million would give us the time and equipment we need—"

"Bill, no bank in the world would—"

"I'm asking *YOU*, Bernie. You."

There was pregnant pause.

"Bill…"

"Please!"

"No."

"Bernie—"

"You made the choice to sink what little you had left in your rainy-day fund into transporting all that gear and all those people up there to God knows fuckin' where. And I mean that literally, 'cause even I don't know where exactly the fuck you are. That was your decision, Bill, and I advised you against it. I can't in good faith lend you money."

"You can't, or you *won't?*" Bill spat, his patience breaking. "Are you forgetting that *my* family made you a wealthy man? Where do you think you would be without us looking out for you? And when I simply ask for a *little* gratitude—"

Bernard's patronizing cackle drowned him out. *"There it is. That's what I've been waiting for. All these years I've been working with you were a favor to the old man. I can't do this anymore. Goodbye, Bill."*

"Bernard, don't you *dare* hang up on me! I will—"

"Listen to yourself. I'll tell you something, kid, and it's been a long time coming: You're a loser, Bill. You lost your father's respect a long time ago, then you lost his business, then you lost his fortune, and now you've lost the last hint of good reputation he brought to your family name. I don't owe you shit besides maybe a few million 'I told ya so's."

"How dare you—"

"Take it from me, kid: you're fucked. By the time the dust settles, you'll probably end up a good eight figures in the negative. You know what happens then? You get tossed into a place that rhymes with snail and take it up the keister 'til you rot to death. You better have some fun playin' fantasy in the woods while you can, cause I'm through with you. I'll send you your bill along with the invoices regarding your debts to the Chicago condo, but remember that you've only got it paid through the end of the year."

"Now you listen here—" Bill snarled, but the line clicked, and a blank dial tone replaced the patronizing accountant's voice. Bill wrung the phone between his hands and let loose a furious groan.

Bernard was right, of course, and deep down in the unexplored depths of Bill's psyche, he knew it.

But the only part of Bill's mind that engaged at that moment, as he stared out over the ocean and eyed the distant thunderheads, was the furious rejection of reality in favor of the much more palatable idea that the geriatric ingrate was simply incompetent. That, despite the lack of immediately accessible liquid assets, Bill *must* have some untapped account to pull from, some forgotten about vacation home or a misplaced portfolio.

But after several minutes of failed brainstorming, the roiling anger in his gut began to evaporate into a dense fog of anxiety.

There must be *something*.

Anything.

There fucking *had* to be.

Oh, God, *please* let there be something else.

"Everything alright?" Kevin's voice broke his trance.

"Uh—yeah, no, everything is fine," Bill stuttered, collecting himself and shaking off the aura of fear that surrounded him.

Kevin strode up beside him, the sound of his movements shrouded by the distant thunder of waves far below. "You good?"

"You just startled me," Bill assured him.

"What was that all about? You looked pissed."

"Why were you watching me?" Bill demanded.

"It's my job," Kevin said.

"Yeah, I guess you're right." Bill tried to box off the sickening apprehension inside of him and step past it. "The call was nothing — well, no, it was important. There's an issue with customs regarding the possibility of bringing in more gear to get past this hurricane issue."

Kevin chuckled. "We snuck all this stuff up here, I'm sure we can do it again."

"It's not that easy." Bill paused, his mind racing for a better excuse. "The fisherman we hired before won't do it again. He says it's too risky. I'm afraid I don't have any more transport contacts I can trust to be discreet."

"It's too bad the Indians wouldn't just sell you this shithole," Kevin muttered, looking back at the decrepit manor.

"Just be happy that they don't even come around this area. If they found us here, we'd be royally screwed."

"They really are that scared of this place, aren't they?" Kevin asked.

"Just the same goofy local superstitions as always, my friend," Bill said reassuringly. Having no desire to bullshit with his valet, he turned and began back toward the manor.

"My grandfather was like that," Kevin said, causing Bill to stop and turn back. The hulking man now had his back to Bill, instead facing the ocean. "Superstitious, I mean. You know, a lot of the stuff out here reminds me of him."

"The grandfather that raised you?" Bill asked. He didn't actually care, but he'd always been the type to observe courtesy.

"The same. He was a fisherman on Cape Cod. Real old school guy. He would've fucking loved this place." Kevin paused, seeming to gather his thoughts. "He was a real good man. I mean that, like, seriously good. The dude was the definition of stand up. He always made sure I was taken care of and had everything I needed. He taught me what he felt I needed to know, and he always treated me with respect."

"He sounds like a wonderful person." Bill tried to sound sincere. He had no idea what Kevin was on about, and with the series of cascading failures regarding the dig and his financial issues hanging over his head, he didn't really care.

"Yeah. He was. But deep down, I could always tell that he fucking hated me." Kevin shook his head. "I don't know, man. There was just something about me he really didn't like. He never said it. Ever. He never even hinted at it as far as I remember. He just saw something in me that filled him with some bad feeling. In the end, I have to give him credit. He fought that bad feeling every damn day. It's taken me a long time, but now I think I know why: in that old man's mind, he owed me a debt for his part in bringing me into this world. He despised me, but I was his responsibility, and I carried his name, so he squashed that hate as far down as he could and treated me well. Then one day all that hate and resentment finally took on its own life in the form of cancer and killed him."

"Uh, I don't think that's how cancer works—" Bill started.

Kevin finally turned back Bill. His face was cold and expressionless. "In the end, I took two lessons from my grandpa. First, you always pay the debts you take on. Second, if you feel hate, let it out — better it hurts someone else rather than you."

Bill felt the fine prickle of chill run down his neck.

"I didn't know that, about your grandfather." Bill worked to keep his voice even. "That's tragic. Whatever his issues with you were, I'm sure they were entirely misplaced. Perhaps—"

"I *still* haven't been paid for Guatemala, Bill," Kevin said calmly. "Or my down payment for this job. You need to tell me what the problem is. I know it might not seem like much for you, but that money is everything to me. I have a kid and a bitch ex-wife waiting on her alimony. You have to call Bernard and get it sorted out. This week, if not today."

"Of course." Bill nodded vigorously. "I… My sincerest apologies, old friend. It's not like him to make mistakes. I think maybe his age is getting to him. I'll have to find a new accountant. I'll tell you what, would a five percent bonus help mend this rift?"

Kevin considered, then slowly nodded.

"Excellent. Again, I'm very sorry about this. Now, if you don't mind, I have to go make sure the others are ready for this afternoon."

Bill could feel Kevin's eyes boring into the back of his head as he walked away, and one absolute truth became suddenly and terrifyingly clear in his mind: either they made it through that wall in the next several hours and recovered something precious enough to validate his lies, or he was infinitely, unequivocally fucked.

XIX

Sophie

SOPHIE LEANED against the side of the manor's detached carriage house, soaking in the fleeting rays of noon sun and furiously puffing her third cigarette in a row. It'd only been an hour since she'd returned to the surface, but she'd already gone through nearly half a pack.

How the hell had this whole expedition devolved into this? A water cutter pieced together from spare parts, storm dependent timelines, towing Bill's chubby childlike ass through the caves… A large part of her wished she'd agreed with Margaret in the beginning and that they'd dug straight down — yet somehow she knew that Bill would've found a way to mess that up too.

It should've been so goddamn *easy*. Get a capable crew, throw some money into tools, work on a decent timeline in the right season, and *bam* it comes together. But no. Not with Bill. The moronic man-child needed his dramatic secrets and absurd workarounds, not to mention that, despite his reputation, he was somehow the cheapest rich man Sophie had ever met. Now here they were, stuck between a rock and a fucking hurricane. And the idea of spending an extra two weeks shacked up with this misfit crew felt about as enticing as a cow's visit to a meatpacking plant.

"Fucking Bill," she muttered. "Piece of shit…"

As if called upon by the ghost of annoyance's future, Bill's voice drifted from somewhere inside the decrepit manor, calling her name. It came again, and again, and finally he emerged onto the porch, calling once more and looking around before catching sight of her. "Sophie, a word please?"

She neither moved nor tried to hide the furious grimace on her face. After a pause, Bill seemed to think better of taking a proverbial stand and instead shuffled down the porch steps and over to where she stood. She watched his approach closely, noting with every trudging step how much she hated him. He was no longer in his great white adventurer getup, instead having switched over to a button-up and evening jacket combo that seemed more appropriate to this century.

Good. That meant he didn't plan to accompany them back down into the caves that evening. Maybe they could actually make decent time and excavate something before the storm surge washed the whole goddamn cavern clean.

"Sophie, I've spoken to Greg and he seems to think that it was a pump malfunction that caused the water cutter to seize. He's insisted that he must be present to manually fix the machine itself, so he will be accompanying you and Margaret this afternoon instead of me. As much as I would love to be there, there's only room for three on that trip. I'm going to need you to be my eyes and ears down there, okay?" Bill's voice was soft in a way that verged on apologetic.

"Fine."

Bill paused, then stuttered over some half words before finally saying, "Sophie, I hope you know that even if we have to pull back and wait for the storm to pass, we'll make it through, you and I, and retrieve what's on the other side. I promise that, and a promise from me is one you can count on. We're in this together."

"Fine."

Bill's face gave away a hint of annoyance, but he covered it quickly. "I'm just saying, it will all work out. Sometimes these things just happen—"

"This didn't just *fuckin' happen*, Bill." Sophie felt the blood rush to her face. Furious words tumbled out before she could stop them. "Look at that!" She pointed an accusatory finger at the half disassembled UTV several feet away in front of the carriage house. "Why the fuck is our engineer making our most important tool out of goddamn scraps?"

"Sophie…" Bill's brow furrowed, and her name came out of his mouth slowly, as if in warning, but all she wanted to do was shove it back in with her fist.

"Don't you fuckin' '*Sophie*' me! What even is all this? Half of this crack team you've assembled seems to actually be on crack, and the other half is either so goddamn detached or underfunded that we're on the verge of completely screwing up what should have been one of the easiest goddamn digs of the century!"

"Sophie!" Bill barked, but she wasn't done.

"*Bill! Bill!*" she snapped back. "Why the hell are we using spare parts, *Bill*? I'm sick and goddamn tired of this roundabout bullshit and half thought-out trickery! Margaret knows what we're looking for. I had to tell her the minute we got into that damn cave. Put Greg down there and he'll find out the minute we break through that wall. Hell, I wouldn't be surprised if Jack's figured it out by now because it's pretty fuckin' obvious we've been full of shit this whole time! I'm done lying, and I'm done pretending to be okay with this goddamn circus you're running here! We're on the verge of discovering something huge, something that could rock our entire understanding of human history, and instead of focusing on the issue at hand, I'm stuck babysitting some horny old bastard — who's also somehow in charge!"

She sucked in a harsh breath and glared at him, waiting for some rebuttal. He silently glared back. They stood like that for a long moment, and for the first time Sophie found herself with a hint of respect for Bill — even if it was entirely based on the unkempt malice that he was barely hiding. At least something about him wasn't full of shit.

"Why, you little…" Bill started through gritted teeth.

"Everything okay?" Jack's voice came around the edge of the open carriage house door, startling them both.

"Fine," Sophie responded as he emerged from around the corner and surveyed the situation.

With a nondescript grunt, Bill glared at each of them in turn then turned and stormed back to into the manor.

"That sounded fun," Jack muttered.

"Oh, fuck off." Sophie collapsed back against the exterior carriage house wall in exasperation, closing her eyes and taking a long drag of her almost burnt out cigarette. When she opened them, she realized Jack was gone. "Goddamnit, I didn't mean…" She groaned and considered the manor, then gave a resigned sigh and followed Jack into the carriage house.

He didn't look up as she entered, instead focusing wholly on filling a gas can from the massive 500-gallon reservoir in the corner.

"How much of that did you hear?" Sophie asked over the glugging petrol.

"Does it matter?" Jack asked.

"I don't know, does it?"

"Am I still getting paid?"

"I imagine so, yes."

"Then I guess it doesn't matter."

The deadpan delivery of his responses struck a disheartening chord in Sophie's mind.

"Then what's wrong?" she asked.

"With me? Nothing."

Jesus Christ. "Look, there's something I need to tell you. This whole dig, the Phoenician thing, it's—"

"Margaret told me."

Of course she did. "Jack, I figured you wouldn't even care after our last conversation—"

"I don't." Jack capped the gas can and loaded it into the back of the remaining UTV, then climbed aboard.

"Oh, come on now, don't be like—" She winced as the roar of UTV's engine in the mostly enclosed bay cut her off. Jack checked the dashboard and shifted it into drive.

Seriously? Sophie chastised herself, then stepped up, grabbed the roof strap of the slowly rolling UTV, and swung herself into the passenger seat. If Jack was surprised by his sudden companion, he showed no sign of it.

"Where are we going?" Sophie shouted over the engine as they emerged onto the lawn and picked up speed.

"The woods," Jack said.

She gave him an annoyed look. *I get it,* she wanted to say. *I get that you're pissed, but we have bigger fish to fry, so get over it.* Instead she sat silently, staring out over the approaching forest and wondering if it was even possible to undo the damage already done.

It took just under five minutes for them to reach the tree line. Jack was forced to drop the vehicle to a slow saunter as he picked a course through the thin pine forest. After twenty minutes of zigzagging through rough, pathless terrain, the duo arrived at a singular, massive tree in the center of a small clearing.

"Jesus," Sophie muttered as Jack cut the power and they both disembarked from the UTV. "It looks like a goddamn redwood."

The statement was an exaggeration, of course, but as she approached the huge pine's base, she couldn't help but wonder if some ancient strain of DNA was shared between this tree and those on the west coast.

"Yeah, she's a big one alright," Jack said offhand.

Sophie let her eyes glide upward in wonder from what she figured must have been a six-foot diameter base all the way to the distant green frilled top above. "Why do you think it got to be this big?"

Jack didn't answer. When she finally glanced back over, she caught his figure disappearing into the brush, heading off in the direction of the cliffs. She groaned, gave one last look at the magnificent tree, and broke into a trot to catch up with him.

"Look, Jack, I know you're upset with me for lying, but I promise I didn't do it because I wanted to. Bill insisted we get everyone to believe the dig was for some Phoenician nonsense so that no one would draw attention to what we were really looking for. He's afraid of someone hijacking his glory if this all works out. All I care about is that we find what's down there. I'm sorry I upset you, but we need to talk—"

"That's fine. I'm not upset," Jack said over his shoulder without slowing.

"Oh, come on!" She was getting frustrated. Despite Jack's disability, she was having a hard time keeping up with him in the thick underbrush. "What happened to the guy I met last week? If you're butt-hurt, then at least get mad."

Jack gave a dry snort and continued, pausing to hold back a particularly thick and springy barb-covered stalk for her to pass. "I wouldn't say I'm butt-hurt."

She passed him, then once he'd released the thorny branch, she turned and put a hand on his chest to keep him from moving forward. "Will you just listen to me?" she insisted.

"I have been." He gave her outstretched arm a dismissive look and went to gently brush past.

She felt like pushing him down, slapping some sense into the stubborn woodsman, but a secondary instinct took over, one born from a combination of stress, frustration, and desire.

He was caught off guard and almost stumbled when she grabbed him and yanked him toward her. She pulled him close and kissed him hard on the lips. He froze, hands jutting out to the sides awkwardly as she embraced him, then, after a second, she released and stepped back.

"There. Can we fuckin' talk now?" she asked sternly, feeling a rush of achievement based on the surprise still painted across his face.

"I... uh..."

"Look." Her voice softened, and she stared him straight in the face. "I lied to you. I lied to everyone because it was my job and it was getting me where I needed to be. On top of that, I didn't know you, or anyone else here really, and I didn't care to. But things have changed." She brushed away pieces of dirt and sticks that had caught themselves on her t-shirt. "Jack, I'm going back down in that hole in a few hours to retrieve something that I believe is incredibly important, something that I believe many people have killed and died for over the centuries. Bill's been… I just don't trust him — not that I ever did — but there's something extra shady about him now that we're close to the end of this thing. He's more nervous, like he's got more to lose. I need to know who I can trust once we get that thing topside."

"Trust is a two-way street, Sophie." The shock of the kiss had already faded from Jack's face. "I came here for a cash price. The way it sounds, you're asking me to put some loyalty to you above that price. Give me one good reason why the hell I should trust you."

Sophie didn't have a real answer. Rather than bullshitting one, she figured now was the time, if ever, to be honest. "I don't know. I don't have anything I can say to make you trust me, just like I don't have any real reason to trust you. But the one thing I'm trusting is my gut, and my gut tells me you're the one person here who isn't a piece of shit. What does your gut tell you?"

"What does my gut tell me?" He scoffed, then paused and his face tensed. He stared into her eyes so hard that she felt like she might be able to see beyond their darkened depths and into the very soul that hid behind them. A pleasant shiver ran down her spine.

But there wasn't time for this. At least that's what a part of her mind was screaming at her. The other part didn't know what it wanted. It was too full of worry and doubts. About the storm. About the team. About the climbing and the equipment and the faulty goddamn water jet. Mostly, it was filled with the fear that whatever it was — if anything at all — that was buried in that cave might be as worthless as every one of those professors and universities had claimed.

Jack reached out toward her face, and she instinctively batted his hand away.

Now is *not* the time.

Goddammit.

She pounced on him. Her momentum sent him stumbling backwards. Together they tumbled, hitting the forest floor hard, but neither of them noticed the impact. Every bit of their attention was focused on tearing away the thin layers of fabric that separated their bare skin. She felt the warmth of his chest pressed against hers and felt her own raging pulse in his grip as he grasped the back of her neck and pulled her in close. Their bodies tangled together into a roiling storm of trembling limbs and gasping lips, and the forest around them disappeared.

THEY LAY still, staring beyond the canopy above at the masses of slowly moving gray clouds that dulled the harsh afternoon sun. Somewhere in the distance, a bird sang. Even farther off, they could hear the gentle roar of the waves crashing against the cliffs.

"I hope you don't think that was just meant to earn your trust," Sophie said, lighting a cigarette and relaxing atop the bed of clothes and pine needles.

"I'll be honest, I'm having a hard time thinking at all right now," Jack said with a laugh.

She grinned, savoring the warm touch of the few rays of sun that penetrated the leaves above. "Well, I just need you to know that things might get weird here soon, especially once we get this artifact up. I wanted to make sure that we both agree that all *this* that just happened… this is unrelated."

"Yeah, I'd say we're in agreement there."

"Good." She smiled and gave his arm a gentle squeeze, relishing the feeling of closeness that she'd been missing for so long. But there wasn't time for romance — there wasn't even time for what they had just done — not with the afternoon's excavation looming over them. She reluctantly rose and started to dress. "We've got some things we need to figure out, especially with Bill. I get the creeping feeling that he's going to try to nab whatever we bring up and bail on us."

"Makes sense why he'd hire such a crew of misfits. He can leave us high and dry with some cash and walk away with all the glory," Jack muttered.

"Maybe. Either way, I know for a fact that he's up to something, or at least hiding something."

"Agreed," Jack said, taking a moment before moving to dress. "I have to ask: what exactly do you think it is that's down there? Margaret gave me the broad picture, but she kept saying you're the expert."

"I'm not entirely sure. The fountain of youth?" She was only half joking. She pulled on her shirt as she considered a real answer. "Honestly, it's probably just some old artifact. Maybe a statue or a carving, or even a mummy. Really all I expect is some*thing* that was created thousands of years ago and preserved throughout time by various cultures. The *what* isn't as important to me as the *why*. Why would one physical object captivate such a varying audience and be so sought after in the ancient world? If I'm right about this artifact's roots, then how did it inspire so much awe and bloodshed, and in the end drive whoever brought it here to give up their lives in order to hide it away?"

"Margaret thinks it was the Clayborns playing a prank," Jack said.

Sophie nodded. "Yeah, she told me, but I think she's just looking to confirm her own bias. What about you? What do you think is down there?"

"I'm starting to suspect that it's not a hoax, but that it'll still be a disappointment."

Sophie stared at him skeptically.

"The trees," Jack said, nodding back in the direction they had come from. "The big ones, like the one we just found. I found dozens of them in a winding path that goes miles back. They get smaller as they go on. It's almost like they're connected. You see things like that sometimes in nature, where a row of vegetation inexplicably cuts a perfect path through a desert. Normally it denotes an underground river or stream. Here, I'm thinking it might be the same idea. These massive trees, maybe they're following some subterranean spring, absorbing something from it. Not to mention the wolf—"

"The wolf?" Sophie cut in, her eyebrows rising in surprise.

"Yeah. The wolf. The same one we heard that first night. A couple of days ago I tracked it inland to an old cellar hole that sits right on this line of massive trees. It was digging at the base of one of those trees. Burrowing for something."

"Jesus, Jack, you could have told the rest of us," Sophie hissed.

"Well, that's the pot calling the kettle black if I've ever seen it," he came back.

"Touché" She touched his bandaged arm. "Is that how this happened?"

"Yeah," he said. "But that doesn't matter. I did some research after Margaret told me what we were really looking for. Of all of the elixir myths, the fountain association is the most common. A handful of sources even pointed to mineral rich springs that sported some restorative properties as the root of these legends. That's why I was coming out here. Right around here is where the line of overgrown trees stems from. And right here, where we are right now, is smack dab above that cave you're trying to break into. I'm starting to think that's what the wolf was after, some water source that's running below that tree and stems from here."

Sophie wasn't surprised that she hadn't recognized their location. She'd only been out there once with Bill the day before the others had arrived, and to her it looked like any other patch of forest. But what Jack had brought up was intriguing. Maybe even possible. Most myths, no matter how convoluted, were rooted in some kind of truth, after all. She would be lying to herself if she hadn't fantasized about it, even been half convinced of the reality of the whole thing before the expedition began. But now, on the threshold of breaking through the final barrier, the cynical likelihood of reality had eaten away most of those hopes and left her far more worried about protecting the artifact than imagining what, if any, power it might have. If this really was just some mineral rich spring, she was fucked.

"I guess we'll know by this evening," she said with a wink before helping a half-dressed Jack to his feet. "Please, keep an eye on Bill. I don't think either one of us can trust him."

"Yeah, I will." Jack looked at her. "I'm pretty confident that Margaret's alright, but you keep an eye on Greg. He sabotaged the jet cutter this morning — pulled a plug under the control board."

"What?" The accusation caught Sophie off guard.

"Saw him do it, but I can't put together why. Margaret seems to believe he's not who he says he is, and she's no fool. I'd say keep him close down there in those tunnels. Maybe don't let him behind you near any steep drop offs…" Jack let the implication hang in the air.

"Jesus Christ, this shitshow just gets worse by the minute, huh?" Sophie checked her watch. "We need to get back. It'll be time to gear up soon."

Sophie turned to head back toward the UTV, but Jack caught her arm and pulled her back.

"Whatever ends up happening, we'll come back to… you know… *this* later, right?" he asked, then kissed her hard.

She smiled after he drew away. "Yeah."

XX

Greg

"QUIT LOOKING down and give me your damn hand!" Margaret snapped.

Greg tried to comply, but his gaze was locked downward on the terrifying expanse of nothingness that stretched out beyond the weak beam of his headlamp. The stench of saltwater and stale air mixed with the sound of distant gurgling as the porous cliffside ceaselessly drained, and the overwhelming awareness of the inescapable stone walls all combined to create a knot of sickening unease in Greg's gut. Even if he wanted to do as Margaret commanded and let go of the electronic climbing tool that had zipped him up the last of many steep inclines, he doubted he could. His hands might as well have been bound in iron to the mechanical ascender.

"Come on!" Margaret slapped the wet floor of the tunnel above him and hissed. "You're as goddamned bad as Bill!"

Her words were well placed. They managed to strike a tiny spark of indignation. Greg forced his eyes shut and banished the horrifying blackness from his mind, then, one finger at a time, he released a hand from the ascender and accepted Margaret's waiting grasp. With a rough tug, Greg was mostly over the ledge. He wriggled forward on his belly, fighting to get the last bit of his legs onto solid ground before even attempting to clamber to his feet.

"At least you're lighter than that fat shit," Margaret muttered.

Sophie glanced at her watch then gave Greg a cold, calculated look. "Let's get a move on. It's almost six, and most of the estimates have that storm hitting us in a few hours… I don't particularly want to know what a storm surge looks like down here, do you?"

Greg eyed the slick walls of the narrow tunnel around them and imagined the flood of foamy seawater crashing through it. The thought made him shudder.

The trio continued through the last stretch of the journey. Finally, after almost a full hour of hiking and climbing through tunnels often so low that even Greg had to crouch, they arrived at their destination.

Greg found himself surprised at how small the cavern that housed the wooden barrier actually was. In his mind's eye, and even on paper, the dimensions had felt so much bigger. Now, standing before his mounted contraption and facing the impatient glares of two very annoyed archaeologists, he felt as though the tide-hewn walls of the ten-square-meter room were slowly closing in.

"You going to stand there and gawk, or are you going to get us through?" Margaret grumbled, pointing at the water cutter.

After a short hesitation, Greg crossed over to the device and began the process of unlocking the jammed piston inside. Then, in a way that he hoped looked accidental, he bumped it off its current heading. He made a show of swearing before remeasuring the cutting angle. He had figured neither of the other two would be paying too much attention, but when he finished and turned back, he found them both staring at him, arms crossed, and brows furrowed.

"Is it going to work?" Sophie asked.

"Y— yes, it sh— sh— should." Greg gave a fake shiver in an attempt to cover his nervous stutter.

Margaret grunted. "Are we good then?"

"Yeah, yes. We're good." Greg glanced back at the circular track and imagined the wood it was mounted on exploding into vicious shrapnel. Had he really planned that to happen?

Sophie keyed her radio. "We're good, Jack. Turn it on."

Jack came back, distant and tinny through the speaker, "Roger that. Here she goes…"

Greg jumped as the water hose snapped taut, then he saw — a second too late — that Margaret and Sophie had already covered their ears. The noise of the water cutter was sudden and deafening, somewhere between a close passing train and the wet whistle of a whale's spout amplified through a subwoofer. Panic overtook Greg, and he collapsed into a fetal position before even realizing what had happened. He curled inward, clutching his ears and squeezing his eyes shut so hard that they ached. In that moment of sheer fright, he couldn't help but imagine the terror that Sophie, Margaret, and Bill would have felt that morning if he hadn't abandoned his original plan. Even beyond the damage of the shrapnel, the cork of petrified, compacted wood would have been utterly impassable and easily trapped them there until the tide had seeped through its cracks and filled the small chamber. As he lay on the wet stone floor, his mind conjured the panic, the *horror* of clawing desperately at the sealed tunnel, gasping for air as the chamber pulsated with the rhythm of the filling waves. It was a long moment before he was able to shake the horrible image away and pry his eyes open.

The dinky, makeshift water cutter clicked along its four-foot-wide circular path in the pale electronic light of their headlamps, a laser-like jet of water cutting a thin incision deeper and deeper into the stacked log wall as it went. It was a slow process, made even slower by the tightening feeling in his gut as the walls began to feel like they were closing in. He shifted to sit against the wall and rocked back and forth slowly, forcing himself to consider every horrible detail of how this all could have played out. If at some point he had really been willing to let that horrible thing happen… maybe he did deserve to be thrown from that cliff.

"Greg, this chart you left says it should be close!" Jack's voice was barely audible over the water cutter, even with the radio volume maxed out.

Greg uncovered an ear just long enough to check his watch. Jack was right, and if his math was also right, then any minute now the water cutter should begin to break through to whatever was on the other side of that wood.

The sound in the chamber changed, first alternating between loud and muffled as certain areas of the wood gave way before others, and after a few more passes, the sound of the water jet dulled almost entirely, leaving behind only the deafening rhythmic hum of the compressor itself. Two hundred feet above, Jack turned the machine off, and the three in the tunnel worked quickly to dismount the water cutter and feed the reinforced grappling hook and its attached steel cable through a small hole in the barrier. Once the mechanical arms had unfurled on the opposite side of the cork, Sophie radioed Jack and the cable began to wind back. All three of the spelunkers backed away from the marred wooden wall, and after a moment, the steel cable sprung tight.

Nothing happened.

There was an eerie groan from the ancient wood as Jack increased the pressure. Sophie kept on the radio, goading Jack to increase the pressure further and further, to a point where Greg started to wonder if he'd made an actual mistake with the cutter's angle. The horrifying idea that he'd stumbled right into his own trap filled his mind.

Just as he was about to speak up, the four-foot-wide wooden cylinder budged, then, with a loud creak, began to dislodge. Greg watched in the dim light of his headlamp as the cork slid away, revealing dozens of thick wooden timbers petrified together in one solid piece. Minutes later, the end of the cork crashed to the ground. Sophie called on Jack to loosen the winch, and together, she and Margaret rolled the massive wooden cylinder to the side of the cave, exposing the almost perfectly cut wooden tunnel and the black expanse beyond it.

"Last bets on what's in there?" Margaret proposed in what Greg took as a somber attempt at humor.

Sophie ignored her, her eyes wide and focused entirely on the blackness beyond. She reached into the pockets of her climbing vest and retrieved a pale glow stick, cracked it to a bright, glowing green, and tossed it through the hole. It hit the ground with a wet clack, illuminating an expansive, perfectly flat stone floor beyond.

"Here we go," Sophie whispered, then ducked and crawled through the circular portal.

Margaret went to follow close behind, then paused and glanced back at Greg with a distrustful look. "You first, kid."

"W— wha—" Greg tried to find the words to protest, but Margaret cut him off with a stony glare. Bowing his head, he shuffled forward and climbed through the opening, Margaret hot on his heels.

"Holy Mother of God…" Sophie's voice trailed off as he came out on the other side, then she exclaimed in amazement, "Hoax my ass! Margaret! Are you seeing this?"

The cavern Greg found himself in wasn't so much a cave as it was a finely hewn dome. At least a dozen times the size of the previous chamber, this one had an almost perfectly flat stone floor that gave way on all sides to an evenly sloping walls and ceiling that were entirely covered with a myriad of markings and symbols. He flashed his headlamp along the floor's edge and knew immediately from the crisp angle where it met the wall that this was no natural occurrence.

"What is this?" he asked, dumbfounded. "Where the hell are we?"

Sophie laughed, and when Greg looked over at her, he saw a look of genuine, glorious happiness splayed across her face. Next to her, Margaret seemed more stunned than anything.

"Wha… What the fuck…" Margaret finally got the breathy words out, every bit of her cocksureness dissolved.

"I told you!" Sophie yelled, her gleeful voice echoing around the chamber as she seized Margaret's shoulders and gave her an excited shake. "This, this is *something*, something *big*!"

Margaret's lost expression hung on for a second, then melted away into a toothy grin that matched Sophie's. "Holy shit. Holy shit, holy shit, holy shit!" Margaret exclaimed. "We need to document *everything*. Hold on!"

Margaret fished a digital camera from her pack and immediately set about photographing the thousands of symbols scattered along the walls in a series of blinding flashes. Meanwhile, Sophie laughed like a schoolgirl as she danced across the room, cracking half a dozen more glowsticks and scattering them across the floor. The chemical light dissolved the darkness into an alien green glow.

Awestruck himself but still more confused than excited, Greg tried to make sense of the room they were standing in. Whoever had built it must have closed off the tunnel early on in its construction to avoid the tidal flush, Greg figured, so there must be another way in and out. As the archaeologists darted around amid the strobing camera flash, Greg meandered along the wall until he found his target. A small, stone-packed hole in the wall that stood about three feet above the ground. Greg figured it was just big enough that, when clear, a man might have been able to slip through it.

"Guys, I found the exit," he called to the others, but they seemed too wrapped up in their excitement to bother responding.

What was this place? Why would someone go to all this effort to build this subterranean dome? Were they hiding something? Who were they? Greg didn't know much about whatever Native American tribes had inhabited this area, and even less about Phoenicians, but he couldn't fathom why either would waste their time on something as superfluous as this.

"Margaret, do you see anything?" Sophie asked. "Outside of the wall carvings, I mean."

There wasn't so much as a pause in the camera flashes as Margaret gave an absent grunt.

"Greg, what about you? Anything that looks like, like an object or something? Some… I don't know… *anything*?" Sophie asked, her voice growing slightly desperate.

"No," Greg answered. She seemed intent on looking for something specific, but what?

As his hearing finally recovered from the deafening blast of the water cutter, Greg caught the sound of trickling water. He followed it to the opposite side of the room until his headlamp caught the telltale glimmer of running water.

"Here," he called to Sophie. "There's some sort of spring."

Sophie trotted over and together they approached the thin, quickly-moving stream. It fell from a narrow crack in the wall and disappeared into a carved, funnel-like hole in the stone floor. Sophie bent and examined the funnel closely. "My God, Jack was right. Whatever it is, it must be below us."

"W— what are you talking about?" Greg didn't like not understanding what was happening. It made him feel open. Exposed. Much like how he'd felt when he was suspended above the furious ocean by nothing more than a thin steel wire.

"You'll see, trust me," Sophie responded offhand, turning both her focus and flashlight to the floor. "Look for anything on the floor, a symbol, or even a seam maybe."

It was only minutes before Greg found exactly that — a perfectly straight crack in the floor near the center of the room. As he brushed away years of chalky dust, he realized another seam ran parallel to it, then two more connected them in a two-foot by two-foot square. He called Sophie over.

"Hell yes! Do you have a pry bar, something to wedge in there?" she asked excitedly.

"No, I— I wasn't told that I would need one—"

"Never mind," Sophie said quickly and brushed by him and back out the wooden portal. He heard the whir of an electric screwdriver, and a second later she reappeared with a foot-long piece of the water cutter's rail system. She crossed the room and grabbed one of the few loose stones that littered the floor. Placing the curved end of the metal bar on the ground, she brought the stone down hard to flatten its edge.

The camera's pulsating flash paused, and Margaret's worried voice sounded nearby. "What the fuck are you doing over there?"

"Making a prybar. Margaret, what's our time look like?"

Greg could see the bright blue light of Margaret's watch flicker on the other side of the room. "Shit, we're already cutting it close. Quit fucking around and help me document this stuff."

"I will in a second. I just need to make sure this isn't something important," Sophie called back, bashing the metal rod one last time before giving its now flat edge a satisfied look. She then jabbed it violently into one of the thin crevices. "Greg, hold this while I drive it in."

Greg did as he was told, and Sophie once again began striking the metal rod with the rock, this time hammering the flattened portion down into one of the cracks. Once she was satisfied with its depth, she seized the bar from Greg and wretched it back. There was a loud scrape as the thick stone slab lifted and Sophie wrestled it to the side.

"He was fuckin' right!" Sophie almost giggled as she hunched over the square hole and shined her flashlight down into it. From where he knelt, Greg couldn't see into the hole itself, but heard the distinct gurgle of flowing water from its shallow depths.

"Who was right about what?" he asked insistently, trying to be more aggressive in the hopes of actually eliciting some response.

"Maybe it's something, I don't know, scientific in nature that…" Sophie started, then the mask of utter joy on her face crumbled, replaced with a look of dread.

"Greg," she whispered, her face growing pale as she slowly looked over at him. "Get the Geiger counter."

"What?" Greg asked. It took him a second to understand the implication of her request, but his suspicions were confirmed when his headlamp caught on the matte surface of what could only be lead on the inside of the stone lid she'd pushed aside. He wrestled his pack off and jabbed his hand inside, searching among the assortment of tools until he found the smooth plastic device. Silently he tossed it to Sophie, doing everything he could not to imagine the increasingly real possibility that they had just inadvertently and inescapably doomed themselves.

Sophie slowly raised the Geiger counter in front of her and clicked it on. Despite the continuous flashing from an oblivious Margaret in the background, a horrible stillness settled in the air as the handheld machine blipped and the meter went through its warmup. Finally, the device emitted a long tone, indicating it was ready. Sophie slowly extended it to just a few inches above the water.

"Oh, thank fucking God…" she groaned after a second and collapsed back onto the ground. "Holy shit, that scared me."

Greg's hands relaxed, and he realized he'd been clenching his pack in a white knuckled grip. "Why would they put a lead lining on something like this?" He paused. "And what the hell *is* this?"

"There's something glistening in the water." Sophie said after letting out an exasperated sigh of relief, then sat up and winked at him. "Only one way to find out what." She began rolling up her sleeve.

"No," Greg squeaked. "It— it could still be dangerous, even if it's not radioactive. Whatever it is, they buried it down here for a reason."

"We only have a few minutes before we have to start back, Greg, and this whole place—"Sophie motioned around them"—is going to get washed out by that storm surge, so unless *you* want to reach in there—"

"I will," Greg said to his own surprise. Some manifestation of guilt over nearly killing the two archaeologists must have bubbled to the surface because a moment later, his sleeve was pulled up and he found himself crawling over to the hole.

"Greg, come on. You don't have to do this…" Sophie gave him a funny look, completely taken aback by the situation.

"I do," Greg insisted — almost firmly.

Why though? he asked himself, and the same words played across Sophie's furrowed brow.

Because you're a piece of shit, and if anyone triggers some booby trap and dies down here, it should be you, a furious voice answered inside his head.

He glanced down into the hole. A gently flowing stream of water rushed by nearly a foot below. The light of his headlamp reflected against the smooth, gliding surface of water but did little to penetrate it. Somewhere deep down in the hole, a small round object glinted.

Fighting every instinct that told him not to, Greg shut his eyes and plunged his hand beneath the quickly moving surface.

There was a feeling Greg remembered from childhood. He had never quite been able to place it in any specific event or memory, and even though he couldn't recall or describe exactly how it affected him, he'd always looked back on it with longing. He didn't remember it with a hunger or desire like he might remember a hot mushroom and onion pizza after skipping a meal. No, it had left its mark more in the way of some phantom emptiness of what *was* but could never again be. Greg had always imagined this feeling was what people meant when they talked about happiness. Real, true, unadulterated happiness. Like the kind he'd read about in books or saw in movies. Like the kind Sophie had felt moments before. It was a feeling he'd always missed as an adult, and as of recently he'd been sure he would never feel it again.

But as his hand dropped below the flow of water and into the recess beneath, along the smooth lead floor, then finally closed on a flat, egg-sized object at its center, he was filled with *that* feeling in the most pure, indescribable way he could ever imagine. It rushed over him in the same way the water rushed past his arm, washing away all of his anxiety and terror. It filled his chest with euphoric glory and his mouth with the sweet taste of strawberries. It was magnificent, orgasmic in a way that surpassed sex, and he didn't attempt to stop a weak moan from escaping his lips.

"What is it?" Sophie asked. She sounded worried. She sounded a thousand miles away. He would've answered if he could, but there weren't words. No, not for this. How do you describe something… something so… incredible?

Cradling the egg-shaped stone delicately, he drew it up from beneath the water and held it out for her to see. It was smooth and shimmery like polished opal, but dark as the cave walls around them, almost black in the dim light of Sophie's headlamp. Between bleary eyed sobs of happiness, he watched the confusion play out over her features.

"It's wonderful," he whispered as she reached out.

But then Sophie recoiled, her eyes suddenly wide with terror. Then she was screaming. The panicked, animalistic noise flooded over Greg's body, washing away the euphoric feeling and leaving a cold, naked, shivering sheen of nothingness. His palm began to ache. Then it burned. Then a searing pain like nothing he'd ever felt before cut through the burning. He looked down, expecting to see flames, but instead watched in horror as his hand darkened, shrank, contorted, and shriveled into a sinewy, jerky-like husk. The pain clawed its way up his arm, dark veins of dead tissue growing like snakes under his suddenly pale skin. He flailed to release the stone, but the room was a dark blur, spinning and lopsided. Gravity evaporated and his head hit something hard. He saw stars, and all he could hear was screaming, and then there was nothing.

Jack

"SOMETHING'S WRONG," Bill shouted over the howl of the ever-increasing wind.

Jack didn't argue, shielding his face from the harsh gust and calling again into the radio. "Sophie, Margaret, do you guys copy?"

The storm had come on far quicker than expected. They'd watched it skim over the thrashing waves from miles out. Now, twenty minutes after they'd lost contact with the cave diving team, its gale force winds had begun to sweep over the cliffside.

Bill had to pin his Scally cap to his head with his hand as he shuffled over to Jack. "Why did we lose contact?" he asked for the umpteenth time.

Jack fidgeted with the dial that controlled the radio relay attached to the cave mouth below. The light on the panel indicated that it was working, but, since the events of that morning, Jack had lost faith in Greg's custom-made equipment. "I'm guessing the relay went down. The wind's hitting the cliff face almost head on; it could've knocked the antenna off."

Bill swore, then looked out over the ocean at the rapidly approaching tempest. "Do you think there's a chance…" he started, then seemed to realize who he was talking to. Without another word he leaned into the wind and stumbled over to Kevin, who stood just inside the storage container.

Jack watched them speak, but he didn't need to be a lip reader to know what Bill had been about to ask. *Do you think they could've found another way out?* In other words, was it possible the trio of could have managed to steal whatever it was they had recovered?

Kevin shook his head repeatedly and the two argued. After a minute, Kevin grimaced, and with a final, resigned sigh, he dug out a climbing harness from one of the nearby boxes and began strapping in.

"No!" Jack called out, leaving the control panel and crossing over to the other men. "I'll go."

"What?" Bill was taken aback, but Kevin gladly handed over the harness.

"Do you know how to work the winch?" Jack asked.

"I can figure it out," Kevin said. "How are you going to climb with… you know?" He eyed Jack's prosthetic.

"I just need to get to the relay at the mouth of the cave," Jack said, pulling the harness straps tight. "Even if it's damaged, I should be able to communicate with them from there and relay back to you two myself. Just standby at the controls."

Kevin nodded, and Jack attached himself to the smaller secondary winch and unlocked its mechanism. Pulling the slack behind him, Jack approached the cliff's edge and looked tentatively over. Far below, massive waves smashed against the jagged stones at the base of the cliff. Jack swallowed hard, then turned back and signaled Bill to lock the winch once more. He gave the cable a firm tug to make sure it would hold before leaning back over the ledge.

"Kevin, are you ready?" Jack shouted over the wind and waves.

Kevin shook his head and motioned that he couldn't hear him, so instead Jack gave him a thumbs up. Kevin nodded, and the winch began to slowly unravel. In a second, Jack was horizontal, feet planted on the cliffside and cable digging into its edge. He forced his legs to relax, and he was dangling over a terrifying expanse of salty, swirling air.

As if on cue, the rain started. It came in wind-driven sheets. Thick, stinging droplets barraged Jack's exposed neck and arms as he glided downward. Within seconds he was soaked and half blinded, and then a gust of wind lifted him away from the wall. He felt himself spinning on the cable, and he reached out blindly, searching for the rocky face of the cliff. His hands found only air and he felt the momentum of his swing shift before the stone wall crashed into his back, leaving him half dazed and scrambling to grab onto something. But the stones were too slick, and a second strong gust tossed him into another wild swing. He forced his eyes open against the onslaught of wind and rain just in time to cover his face before he smashed back into the cliff again. His arm absorbed the blow, sending a jolt of pain all the way to his shoulder. Before he could recover, he was once again airborne.

"Drop me!" His hand scrambled to key the radio attached to his shoulder as he braced for another impact, but this time he only glanced off the cliff, swinging like a pendulum in the opposite direction. "Drop me to the cave now!"

Kevin's response was garbled and drowned out by the crashing, howling elements.

"Drop me or I'll fucking die!" Jack roared back. Once again, he hit the stone face, this time shoulder first. His head whipped to the side, cracking against the unforgiving rock. Stars filled his vision, and suddenly his stomach hit his throat. He was freefalling, no longer drifting left or right, but plummeting straight down as the shroud of unconsciousness threatened to take him.

"Jack!" Kevin's panicked voice was distant and muffled. "Jack! Jack, are you there?"

The soaked stone wall of the cliff rematerialized in Jack's vision. He was hanging limply by the harness, once again caught in the wind, but no longer swinging wildly. He grabbed the cable and heaved himself upright. Both above and below him, the sheer cliff seemed to go on forever, except for a small cavity maybe a dozen feet below where he was currently hanging.

"Lower me more!" he shouted into the radio. There wasn't a response, but within seconds he was descending, and a minute after that he managed to swing himself inside the cave entrance and collapse on its beautifully solid floor.

"I'm in!" he shouted into the radio, then held it close to his ear to hear over the whistling of the wind on the cave's entrance.

"...find... ...che... ...relay..." Kevin's broken voice came back.

Jack slapped the radio, then searched around the cave mouth for the relay transmitter. There was nothing there, and the horrible thought that perhaps this was the wrong cave entered Jack's mind. But then he spotted the power cord and water line riveted above. "Kevin, I don't know if you can hear me, but the transmitter's gone. The wind must have taken it."

"...oger... ...bring you up?"

"No, I'm gonna wait for the others. The surge is pretty bad down below. If there's a chance the tunnels flooded early, they might need a hand."

Kevin gave a short, garbled response and Jack started into the antechamber. The howling wind glanced off the cave's mouth, and as he moved deeper into the cliff face, the tempest's fury died to little more than a background hum. Amid the loose equipment that lay in disordered piles around the antechamber, Jack found an emergency kit, including a headlamp and a spare ascender. He marveled at the small device, then stared into the abyss-like blackness of the tunnels with a newfound respect for the archaeologists. He wasn't claustrophobic, but it would take a hell of a lot more than two hundred grand to get him to go crawling through that mess.

"...ucking help!" A voice suddenly crackled through the speaker.

Jack froze. "Margaret?"

"...own here now!" It was Margaret, and she sounded frantic.

"Margaret, are you okay? Is someone hurt?"

"Greg's... ...ucked up... ...get the doct..." she shouted, and in the background of the transmission, Jack heard the gushing sound of water.

Fuck.

"Kevin!" Jack called into the radio, unhooking his harness from the outside cable and continuing forward. "I'm headed in. Get the doctor on standby. Repeat, get the doc on standby!"

There wasn't any response, and Jack prayed Kevin had heard him. He mounted a headlamp on his brow and attached the ascender to his harness.

"Margaret, are you there?" he called as he entered the darkness of the first tunnel.

"...ere... ...can't carry... ...ater..." her inaudible voice crackled through the speaker and echoed through the narrow tunnel.

Jack moved forward as quickly as he could. The terrain sloped heavily and at times haphazardly, and the fused metal of his left ankle tripped him up more than once. Just as he reached the first sheer drop off, Margaret's voice came through clearer.

"He's going into shock!"

"Can you hear me?" Jack radioed back as he secured the ascender onto the cable that hung from the ceiling. From the darkness below, a loud gurgling came as his only response. The ascender locked into place and he hesitantly hung his weight from it. He pressed the down button and slowly began sliding down the cable, trying not to think of his perilous descent of the cliff face minutes before. "Guys, can you hear me?"

"Jack? Is that you?" Sophie's voice sounded pained.

"Yeah! How far are you from the cave mouth?"

"I don't know — close! Greg's hurt. We need help getting him back!"

"I'm on my way." Jack tried to sound reassuring but wasn't so sure if he was successful. He zipped down the line and suddenly recoiled as his already soaked foot plunged into a pool of surging seawater. He cast the headlamp down to see that the storm surge had already begun to fill the tunnel below. After a readying breath, he lowered himself the rest of the way into the turbulent, waist-deep water, unattached himself from the cable, and waded forward, praying that the unfeeling hunk of metal and plastic that made up his lower leg wouldn't get trapped in some submerged crevasse or under an immovable rock and anchor him in the rising waters.

Fifty yards later he found himself up to his chest in the rapidly filling tunnel and facing a wall of smooth stone. Another cable led straight up the stone face, and, as he wrestled to lock the ascender onto it, he heard a shout from above.

"Jack! Is that you?" Margaret's shout echoed down. He cast his beam upward and spotted the beam of her own lamp far overhead.

"Yeah," he spoke into the radio. "Listen, this tunnel's filling quick. If these ascender things have a fast setting on them, you better use it."

"We have a problem," Margaret came back. "Greg's in shock. He can't operate on his own."

"You're gonna have to double up then. We've got like five, maybe ten minutes before we're stuck swimming back."

"We've *been* doubling up, but the goddamn ascender keeps failing under the weight. Sophie already sprained her ankle on a fall. This drop is sixty feet, it would kill us." For the first time since he'd met her, Margaret sounded like she might lose control.

"Listen, Margaret," he said calmly, despite the situation. "You need to risk it. If the ascender gives, the water might cushion the impact, but if you don't get down here and back through this tunnel right now, you're going to be trapped, and you're going to die."

There was silence, but then Jack heard a click and a whirring above.

"She's coming down with Greg," Sophie's voice — strained with pain — came through the speaker.

"Are you okay?" Jack asked into the radio, watching the headlamp above grow as Margaret and Greg descended.

"Yeah I am. I… I think my ankle might be broken," Sophie muttered, then laughed. "But hey, you were right about the underground stream."

It took Jack a second to remember what she was talking about. "No shit. You can tell me about it later. Right now, I need you to attach to the cable and get down here. The water's already almost at my neck."

"I need to wait until they're clear of it. The cable might not hold the weight of all three of us," Sophie insisted.

Jack swore silently and fought the urge to yell at Margaret to hurry. She was getting close, maybe twenty feet above, when Jack made out her form, Greg curled around her like a large child.

"You're good! Get the fuck down here!" Jack called to Sophie once Margaret reached the water. He helped Margaret unhook and told her to keep moving. She had to fight to keep above the turbulent water, but still managed to give him an appreciative glance before disappearing with a ghostly, shivering Greg in tow. Minutes later, Sophie had slipped down into the water beside him. She looked shaken and in pain. Her skin seemed extra pale in the reflection of the foamy ocean water, and her bun was half undone, leaving her normally bouncing red curls splayed ragged and wet against her face and shoulders.

"Jack, before we get up there—"

"We need to go now, Sophie!" He pulled her forward. The top edge of the fifty-yard tunnel had almost disappeared beneath surging waterline, and Jack had to help Sophie keep her head above water as they clawed their way through. He didn't know how far they'd made it before the air pockets disappeared, but by the time they erupted from the turning mess of salty brine and latched onto the cable, they were both gasping for air. Sophie clung to him as he attached the ascender, and together they lifted up and away from the roiling cave and into the cool, airy tunnels above.

Margaret was waiting for them by in the back of the antechamber, furiously batting at her radio and screaming obscenities in response to Kevin's broken words. She glanced up momentarily as they emerged, but quickly did a double take.

"Sophie, your ankle?" One of her eyebrows raised suspiciously.

Jack looked over and realized that the limp Sophie had been sporting minutes before in the tunnels had entirely disappeared.

She looked at Margaret and Jack in turn. "I swear to God, it felt like it was broken—"

"It doesn't matter, let's just get the hell out of here." Margaret grabbed Greg, who was slumped in a huddle mass beside her, and yanked him to his feet.

"Hold on," Jack started, and when Margaret ignored him, his voice rose to a bark. "Margaret, stop!"

She glared back at him, and he returned the look. Pointing to the mouth of the cave, he shouted, "It's a fuckin' hurricane out there. You go up now, and those winds will scatter your brains across that cliff, you understand?"

Margaret glanced over her shoulder at the opening. Wind howled over its edge and sheets of rain splashed inside. She looked back, defeated. "Then what the hell are we supposed to do?"

"We wait. There's enough stuff down here to keep warm and dry, and when the storm slows down—" Jack started, but Sophie cut him off.

"We can't. Greg's hurt. Bad. We need to figure out a way up."

Jack wanted to argue, but instead crossed to where Margaret still supported a half limp Greg. "What happened?"

"His arm," Margaret said, gently coaxing a silent, violently shaking Greg to reveal the withered end of the appendage. "He's in shock. He needs the doctor."

The sight of the shriveled, blackened hand struck a horrifyingly familiar chord of memory that drained the blood from Jack's face.

"What is it?" Margaret demanded.

Jack shook away the sickening image of Sam's frostbitten hand. "Nothing. I… I have an idea. Can shithead hear us?"

Margaret smirked at Jack's use of the moniker she'd assigned to Kevin. "Barely, but I think he can hear us better than we can hear him."

"Okay." Jack moved forward from the antechamber to the mouth of the cave. The wind mixed with the crashing waves in a violent crescendo which drowned out any hope of effectively communicating, but he saw what he needed. Moving quickly and cautiously, he grabbed the loose winch cable he had used to descend the cliff face and clipped it to the nearest of the rivets that held the water and power lines in place. Rain slapped him as he gave the cable a hard tug, and when he was confident the rivet would hold, he retreated to the antechamber and keyed the radio. "Kevin, can you hear me?"

A garbled, but positive response came back.

"Listen, I need you to pull the secondary winch tight, but not too tight. Get it good and taut. We're going to use it as an anchor line."

There was a pause, then Jack looked out to the cave mouth as the loose cable began to retreat upward until it pulled hard against the rivet.

"Good!" he said into the radio. "Now listen closely. We're going to send Margaret and Greg up together. Greg needs a doctor, okay? You can send the cable back down for me and Sophie after he's taken care of. Did you get all that?"

"…oger, g… …it…" Kevin was shouting over the wind.

"Alright." Jack turned to the others. "We're going to hook Margaret and Greg to the winch. Margaret, I need you to reattach your ascender, set it to free fall, and hook it onto the anchor cable. The wind out there will whip you all to hell, but hopefully that will hold you tight to that anchor line and the cliff face as Kevin hauls you up. In theory, it should keep you from being bashed against the rocks. Sound good?"

"Sounds like a bunch of bullshit," Margaret came back, but after a second, she scoffed and laughed. "Yeah. Yeah, fuck it, why not?" She eyed Sophie. "You want to hold onto it, or send it up with me?"

Sophie considered her question, then pulled a wet bundle of cloth from her pocket. "Take it, but be careful. And don't let Bill know."

Margaret pocketed the bundle. "Help me strap in, then find some way to stay warm down here until we get Greg settled. Some form of friction might help." She gave the pair a knowing smirk.

Jack and Sophie both exchanged a quick accusatory glance. Margaret let out a chipper laugh. "Fucking kids… Alright, Jack. Let's try this stupid plan of yours."

They moved to the mouth of the cave. The wind whipped and whistled against the steel cables above as Jack wrestled to secure one of them to Margaret and Greg's harnesses. Meanwhile, Sophie attached the ascender to the anchor cable. A minute later, they were set, and Jack dropped back beyond the deafening noise to radio Kevin to engage the winch.

"Just do it slow," Jack said. "She's going to be loosely attached to that anchor line. The last thing you want is to go too fast; you'll run the risk of breaking her harness if that ascender catches."

"…eah, I go… …on't worry…" Kevin came back.

Jack looked back to Sophie and flashed a thumbs up. Sophie responded in kind before finally finishing the web of cables and harnesses by attaching Margaret's climbing harness to the ascender. When they were strapped in, Sophie held up her fingers in a countdown from five, and Margaret nodded along with her. Greg hung silently at Margaret's front, hunched and cradling his arm as his body was racked with violent shivers. As Sophie's last finger came down, Margaret pushed off from the edge, sending herself and Greg swinging out over the open air.

Greg's head snapped up as his feet left the ground. His eyes flung open, wide and bloodshot, and his mouth gaped in panic as he drifted away from the cave and into the air. Jack watched as Greg's hand, his good hand, shot out in a desperate, grasping attempt to stop his momentum. The clawing fingers found purchase on Sophie's outstretched hand, and before Jack could even understand what was happening, Sophie had disappeared, tumbling over the cave's edge.

XXII

Margaret

"SHE FUCKING fell!" Margaret shouted as Kevin helped to haul her over the edge.

"What?" He gave her a queer look and tried to shield his face from the onslaught of nearly horizontal rain.

"Sophie!" Margaret pointed back over the cliff. "She fell!"

It took Kevin a moment to digest her meaning, then his eyes snapped wide with shock.

Bill was yelling something indistinguishable from the mouth of the storage container, but Margaret ignored him, instead turning her attention to unclipping Greg's limp form from her harness. The wind was cold and the rain blinding, and it took her longer than it should have to unscrew the carabiner's safety and release the crumpled young man into Kevin's grasp.

"What's wrong with him?" Kevin demanded.

"His hand!" Margaret shouted, then immediately took a cautious step away from the ledge as Kevin went to examine the withered appendage. "Just get him to the storage container. We need to bring Jack up!"

Kevin nodded, then swung Greg up in his arms like a child and carried him back to the shelter of the steel box.

Margaret stayed back, dropping to her belly in the soaked moss and crawling to the cliff's edge. The thick sheets of rain dashing off the cliffside made it almost impossible to see down, but after a long minute, she was sure that Jack had not followed her up.

The crackle of her radio was nearly drowned out by the howling winds. She glanced back at the storage container and saw Bill still waving his arms. With a final glance down into the mashing blur of distant waves, she edged back from the ledge and stood.

"What happened to Sophie?" Bill demanded as she entered the storage container.

"She was helping me strap in and she fell," Margaret responded over the clatter of the elements against the steel roof, giving Greg a sidelong glare.

Bill's features condensed into a look of shock. "Is she, I mean..."

"She's dead," Margaret said flatly. A part of her was shocked at the coldness in her voice, but she knew this wasn't the time to mourn. If her own personal meltdown could wait, then so could Bill's. Right now, lives were still at stake.

"Where's Jack?" Kevin asked. He had moved the control panel into the shelter of the storage container and was now plucking away at it with a painstakingly confused look on his face.

"He hasn't called in?" Margaret asked.

"He told us to let the line go full slack right after we started hauling you in." Kevin darted to the mouth of the steel box and eyed the winches outside. "Looks like it quit unraveling though."

"Jesus Christ," Margaret whispered. "He wouldn't..."

"What?" Bill shuffled in front of her.

"Just… Just engage the winch. Pull that cable up now!" she commanded. Kevin did as he was told, and the cable outside began to rewind.

"You don't really think he—" Kevin started.

"Yeah," Margaret cut him off and shook her head. *Fucking madman.*

"Margaret." Bill stepped directly in front of her. "Margaret, what did you find?"

"What?"

"In the cave, what did you find?"

"It was a dome, lots of writing, all sorts of…" she sputtered out, her mind racing to recall the specifics through the adrenaline-induced fog. "Lots of shit, Bill. We'll deal with it later. We need to get them—"

"Was there an artifact?" he asked hungrily, his beady eyes glowing.

She tore her eyes away from the cliff, lowering them to glower at his excited face. The small, cloth-wrapped stone hidden in her breast pocket began to feel as if it was radiating heat. She silently swore to herself that she'd rather join Sophie than hand it over to Bill. "Are you kidding me? Sophie's dead, and Jack too probably, and you're asking about what we *found*?"

Bill's eyes narrowed for half a second, then he stepped back and held up his hands. "I'm sorry, I'm sorry. I don't deal with these types of situations well. We don't know that, you know, that she's dead…"

"What, you think those rocks down there are made out of fucking pillows?" Margaret came back.

"I'm sorry!" Bill insisted again. "Kevin, we need to get Greg to the doctor. Go get the UTV."

"Negative, not yet," Kevin said, cranking the power of the winch up a notch. "We're pulling something up."

Margaret looked back at the cable that trailed over the cliff's ledge. It was taut, like a fishing line with a catch, and slowly slid back and forth along the ledge as whatever — *whoever* — was attached to it swung below.

"Reel it in faster!" Margaret shouted, knowing painfully well just how horrible the free-floating swing was on the other end. She sprinted back out to the ledge, dropped to her knees, and stared over it. Swinging like a pendulum far below, Jack cradled Sophie's limp form in his arms.

"SLOW DOWN!" Margaret shouted from where she crouched awkwardly in the UTV's rear bed.

Kevin glanced back at her, but didn't ease off the gas.

"Slow the fuck down, you moron!" Jack roared from his position beside her. He leaned over where Sophie's supine form lay draped across the back seat and jabbed Kevin's shoulder. "You hit a bump and you'll fucking kill her!"

Ever so slightly, Kevin eased off the gas. Clinging to the bars of the UTV, Jack looked like he might go for the pistol on his belt. Kevin must have seen his face in the rear-view mirror because a moment later, the vehicle slowed to a more reasonable pace. Margaret leaned over Greg, who was huddled in the back seat with Sophie's legs draped over his lap, and surveyed the young woman.

One of her arms was horribly broken. It looked like there was an extra joint midway down her forearm, and the skin around it was twisted and growing increasingly dark. Her clothes were torn and soaked with a briny mix of seawater and blood. The jagged gaps in the fabric exposed a multitude of rough gashes and lumpy disfigurements. Margaret had the sickening suspicion these were the markers of more broken bones jutting out against their fleshy encasing. Sophie's neck was limp, and a long, thick bruise encircled it like a strangling python. Yet, through it all and against all odds, Sophie was still pulling in shallow, hoarse breaths.

"How did you find her?" Margaret leaned over and shouted to Jack above the engine.

"She got caught on a ledge, maybe a hundred feet down from the cave. If she'd missed it and hit the water, I never would have," he answered, staring at Sophie.

"Well, let's hope the luck keeps up," Margaret said.

"She was still barely conscious when I found her," Jack said quietly enough so that only Margaret could hear. "She just kept insisting you not to give *it* to Bill."

Margaret's hands tightened inadvertently on the UTV's cage. "I won't," she promised.

Minutes later, they arrived at the manor. Dr. Bianchi exploded out of the front door, a fold-out stretcher precariously balanced over his shoulder as his stubby legs worked overtime to bring him to the UTV. Margaret and Jack loaded Sophie's broken form onto the stretcher and carried her inside. Bianchi led them up the stairs and through the dreary manor's dark halls to the clean second story room that had been designated for artifacts. Now, a handful of medical instruments stood waiting beside a table. Ever so gently, they eased Sophie onto the table and stepped just outside the room while the doctor began his assessment. After a brief once-over, he turned to the group and gave them an annoyed look.

"Some privacy, please! She is not an exhibit!" he snipped, slamming the door.

They stood crowded around the door, waiting pensively for some report or command, but it was eerily silent all around them. The only noise came from the steady *pat-pat* of rainwater that dripped from their soaked clothes and the howling wind that was beating against the old manor. Seconds stretched into minutes. Margaret felt hopeless, unable to shake the horrible image of Sophie's mangled body from her mind. Beside her, the frustration slowly bubbled over Jack's calm façade. He finally knocked on the door and tried the locked handle. Somewhat calmly, he called to the doctor, "Doc, either let me in or I'll let myself in, bud. You understand?"

A second later, the door cracked open, and the normally soft Italian face glared out. "This woman is in critical condition. Do not—"

Jack shouldered the door open and strode past him. Sophie was lying on her back, a pale sheet covering up to her shoulders, clinging to her as it absorbed more and more seeping blood.

"You can't expect me to believe you can save her by yourself, not here," Jack said harshly, eyeing the doctor with a look that drained the little man's furious attitude.

"Well, s— save her, no," the doctor stuttered out, his accent growing a hint thicker under duress. "We need to stabilize her for transport. She needs a real hospital, and even then, it's a long shot."

"Fine. Bill, help me load her in the truck—" Jack started.

Bill cut him off. "In an open bed? In the middle of a hurricane? Bouncing over rough dirt roads?"

Jack glared at him. "We call in a helicopter then—"

"Pft! Again, in a hurricane?" Bill shook his head. "I doubt even think an ambulance could make it out here."

"Well, we'll find the fuck out, won't we? Get me the phone."

Kevin spoke up from down the hall. In all the commotion, Margaret hadn't even noticed him leave the group. "I just checked it — the line's down. The winds must have taken out the dish on the roof."

Jack's face began to glow red. He turned to the doctor. "Do everything you can," he said through gritted teeth.

"I will, I promise." The doctor gave a nervous head bow as Jack stalked out of the room.

"Where's the phone?" Jack demanded.

Kevin gave Bill a sideways glance before he answered. "The dining room."

Margaret followed Jack, Bill, and Kevin down the stairs, through the foyer, and into the dining room. Jack immediately grabbed the phone from the table and left the room, searching for a signal. Margaret's focus shifted to Greg, who was curled up in a corner, silently rocking back and forth. She took one of the dusty old blankets from a pile in the next room and draped it over his shoulders. He recoiled at her touch, then slowly looked up at her. His eyes were spiderwebbed with thick red veins, and his normally dark skin had taken on a ghastly pale sheen.

"How you holding up, kid?" Margaret asked in her softest voice.

His lip quivered and he let out a weak whimper.

"I need you to let me see it, okay?" She crouched down and gently grasped his elbow, manipulating the makeshift bandage she'd fashion in the cave to expose the withered claw of human jerky that his hand had become.

"What the hell is that thing? Is that his hand?" Bill asked over her shoulder. Greg let out another whimper and withdrew back into himself.

"Goddamnit, Bill," Margaret hissed, standing and turning. "You're a little fucking thick, aren't you?"

Bill paused and stared at Greg for a long second before Margaret's words seemed to penetrate his awe. He turned his beady eyes to her, and his face took on a grimace. "Excuse me?"

"The boy's in shock, you moron. Don't g—"

"Since when does an employee get off speaking to their superior with that tone?" Bill exploded. "You've forgotten your place here, you old—"

Margaret slapped him, and in a second, Kevin was between them.

"How fucking stupid are you, Bill?" Margaret snapped. "Don't you ever speak down to me. Your incompetence just got that girl killed!" The heat in her face melted the wall of ice into tears, and alongside the salty droplets came a torrent of realization. In all the movement and panicked rushing, Margaret had not had time to process or even realize what had really happened. Now, in the lukewarm air of the manor with no noise outside of the heavy patter of rain and occasional crack of distant thunder, her mind finally wrapped itself around the fact that the young girl in the other room was dying.

Bill gave a confused look, clearly taken aback by her tears. He took a moment to compose himself before sitting at the table and bowing his head. "I'm sorry, Margaret," he began softly. "Truly, I... I don't know how to say this. I've never been in a situation like this, and I'm fighting to understand it and come to terms with it myself. Please, I was wrong to speak that way just now, and I know I'm coming off as a callous ass. I just... I'm not sure how else to maintain control, and I'm afraid that if we lose control, we won't be doing anybody any good. You understand, don't you?"

For once, Margaret thought she saw a grain of honesty in the pudgy man. She wiped her eyes clean with a dirty sleeve and cleared her throat, then sat across from him. "What's done is done. The only thing that matters now is that we do everything we can to get her out of here. You know the logistics and area, so you tell me: what can we do?"

Bill considered the question, then looked at Kevin, who shrugged.

"I think we need to stabilize her, if possible, then wait for the storm to subside," Bill said.

"That could take days," Margaret protested.

"I don't see another option. I'm open to ideas, but..." Bill's voice trailed off.

They sat there for several long minutes, Kevin leaning against the wall and Greg huddled in his corner. Jack's cursing echoed from all around as he relentlessly darted room to room, floor to floor, searching for a signal on the satellite phone. Eventually Bill cleared his throat.

"Margaret... I... I need to know exactly what you found down there. You mentioned writing..."

Margaret glanced up at him. He was nervous, but the tiniest bit of excitement bled through onto his pale, moon-like face.

Disgusting.

"Only symbols," she offered. "It was a manmade dome hewn into the stone, completely littered with pictographs and writings."

"But nothing else? Such as, perhaps, an artifact?" Bill prodded.

"No," Margaret lied. She had to stop herself from unconsciously brushing a hand against the pocket that held the wadded stone.

"Margaret, by now you know what we were really looking for, don't you?" Bill's voice was slowly sinking back into its pandering tone.

"Yeah." She narrowed her eyes. "And just like I told Sophie, it's an absurd myth. A wild goose chase. Things like this always have been, and they always will."

Bill glanced down at her hands. He clearly wanted to say something, to push some line of questioning, but she could see his hesitancy.

"What?" she demanded.

He looked at her a bit cockeyed, then let out a deep breath. "People like you have always considered me a fool for believing in ventures like this. The way I see it, throughout most of human existence, people lived in a different reality. A reality not governed by elitist cynics touting the word *factual* as if their half-proven theories governed it. People *believed* in things. They had different truths than we do now. I've always tried to respect those truths of our ancestors, which is why I considered that maybe it wouldn't be so outrageous that they were really onto something here." He paused for a moment, and Margaret watched as several emotions — anger, desperation, confusion — crossed his face.

"Cynics, I always figured, have a much easier life than those of us with hope. Sophie wasn't a cynic. I think that when we started, she really believed *it* was down there. You know, *it*, whatever you want to call it— the singular *it* that's been searched for since the dawn of our species. The key to longevity and power and health. The one thing in the world that could save us from death. After listening to her pitch, she convinced me of the same thing. Despite what she might have thought in the end, *I* still believe. I believe it was there. I believe you found it. I believe you brought it up. And I believe you're hiding it from me now." Bill's eyes darkened.

Fuck.

"Well, you're wrong," Margaret said matter-of-factly.

"Then why aren't your hands shaking?" Bill asked, his eyes narrowing to match hers.

"What?" she glanced down. He was right — her hands were perfectly still.

"My mother was like you in her old age. An addict, I mean. She started taking the pills by the handful after a bad surgery, and even after she healed, she just couldn't stop."

Margaret made to stand up, but Bill slammed his fist down on the table, freezing her in place.

He glared at her, continuing with a voice the was calm but razor-edged with anger. "There's a difference between older junkies and the younger ones, you know. The kids, they learn to hide it well, since they're always under the scrutiny of so many: parents, teachers, police... But older folks, they never really learn to hide it. They just come to *think* that their half-assed efforts are working since the truth is that nobody really cares enough to intercede. They're all too old for anyone to really give a shit about, too set in their ways. Margaret, your tells are transparent. When you're high, your pupils are saucers and your voice flutters like a happy little butterfly, and when you're low, you're nasty and mean and your hands twitch like a dirty old vibrator. Yet ever since you've come back up from that cave, I've seen nothing but a well-rounded, poised, almost healthy older woman. Why is that?"

Margaret felt the tiniest flush of adrenaline creeping through her veins. She glanced up at Kevin, who towered over her only a few feet away with his hands casually positioned on his hips, mere inches from the pistol on his side. Tiny waves of warmth radiated from her breast pocket, and her mind focused on the weight of the stone.

"I know you have it. It's not too late to tell the truth," Bill whispered. "You're not a thief, Margaret. Not yet. Give it to me."

Margaret looked from Bill to Kevin, then shut her eyes and growled. *Fuck this.*

A china teapot was a few inches from her hands, and it felt smooth and cool in her grasp when she propelled it toward Kevin's face. But he caught her arm mid swing, and she was launched backwards by overwhelmingly powerful hands. She crashed violently into the hutch behind her, barely managing to recover in time to see Kevin baring down on her. His face was distorted in a grimace and his hands were clenched in cannonball fists. He pulled back to strike as a surprised shout erupted behind him, then something brilliant exploded over his head. Light reflected against heavy chunks of glass as they rained down on Margaret, and Kevin collapsed in a heap. Jack stood over him, the remaining neck of a wine bottle in his hand. Without a moment's hesitation, Jack spun and slammed Bill's face to the table. The short, thick muzzle of his revolver pressed so hard into Bill's temple that a white ring grew in flesh around it.

"Please, stop!" Bill begged, spreading his hands across the glass-littered table in submission. "I promise I can help her! I can help Sophie!"

"How?" Jack demanded, jabbing the barrel in harder.

Kevin stirred from his daze, his confused, droopy gaze lolling around the room before landing on Jack. He struggled onto his back and made to reach for his own pistol but froze as Jack's gun aligned with his head. The three distinct clicks of the revolver's hammer echoed off the walls around them.

"Test me. Go ahead," Jack growled. Kevin slowly withdrew his hand. "Your gun. Take it out with two fingers and slide it to Margaret. Keep in mind: if I get nervous, you die."

Kevin complied, slowly drawing the pistol with his thumb and pointer finger and sliding it across the floor into Margaret's waiting hands.

"Good," Jack said, hauling Bill to his feet. "Margaret, do you know how to use that?"

She eyed the gun. It felt massive in her hands, but still comforting. "Just like the rifle you showed me?"

"Yeah, same thing. Make sure the safety shows red. If he moves, don't hesitate — just empty it into his guts," Jack said, then dragged Bill into the foyer.

A moment later, Jack returned for Kevin, and Margaret helped him bind the two men in wingback chairs with a healthy amount of rope. Bill pleaded several times, but Kevin seemed too concussed to contribute more than the occasional groan. Once they were confident that the two men could not shimmy out of their bindings, Jack and Margaret returned to the dining room.

"So, what really happened down there?" Jack asked, quiet enough that Kevin and Bill couldn't hear.

"I don't know," she answered honestly. "I was focused on the walls, the writing… They found something, some hole in the ground down there. This was inside." She plucked the bundle of cloth from her pocket and unraveled it on the table between them.

The egg-sized stone was smooth and gray, with tiny, glinting speckles of crimson spattered across its surface. Jack instinctively reached out to examine it, but Margaret grabbed him. "No." She met his eyes and shook her head, then nodded over to where Greg was huddled in the corner.

"Jesus Christ, this is what did that?" Jack asked, looking down at the stone with newfound respect. "How?"

"I don't know," Margaret said. "It was encased in lead, but Sophie told me they tested it and it wasn't radioactive. Hell, even if she were wrong, I don't think a stick of pure plutonium would do *that*." She motioned to Greg. "At least not that quickly."

"What did the writing on the walls say?" Jack asked. "I mean, this thing clearly does something. Maybe it's possible that—"

"Jack, it's not magic," Margaret interrupted, fishing in her pack for her camera. "Whatever this is, you can't let yourself get swept up in some fantasy."

"We need to find out what it is," Jack said. "Especially if it's capable of doing that to Greg. We could all be in danger just being around it. Translate what you can. I'm going to find out what that blowhard knows."

Margaret found the camera and pulled it out. She began scrolling through the photos, searching for something she could translate. Meanwhile, Jack disappeared into the foyer, and between Greg's whimpering gasps, she heard him begin to interrogate Bill.

XXIII

Jack

"YOU SAID you could help her." Jack sat on an ottoman, eyeing Bill with disdain.

"I did— I can. Just… just untie me and—"

"Stop. This isn't a bargain." Jack kept his voice even.

Bill nervously wrestled against the ropes, his expression caught somewhere between fear and rage. "Untie me, Jack. Goddamnit! What is wrong with you? *I don't like this!*"

"I don't like being lied to. Margaret doesn't like being assaulted. Sophie doesn't like dying. And as much of a thug as he is, I don't think Kevin likes being a patsy. We're all doing things we don't like today, Bill, so how about you try not being an asshole and tell me how you can help her. I don't want to have to hurt you."

Bill's face tensed, but he stopped fidgeting. "Are you threatening to… to *torture* me?"

Jack let out a long breath and considered the question. Was he? He knew it was wrong, but the image of Sophie's broken body flashed in his mind, and with it, nothing else really seemed to matter. He looked

Bill square in the eyes. "No, I'm telling you — flat out — that if she dies, I'm going to shoot you in the stomach and let you bleed to death."

The words had been intended for intimidation, sure, but deep down, Jack knew some part of him meant it. Apparently so did Bill, because his shoulders slumped against the ropes and whatever fight was left in him seemed to drain away. Kevin, still too dazed to contribute, groaned loudly beside them.

"I don't know if I can help her," Bill admitted. "I… I believe there's something that can… that can… I don't know. Whatever they found down there, whatever did that to Greg, it's got power."

Jack eyed him suspiciously. "It's a rock. A river stone. How the hell is a rock going to help Sophie?"

Bill's eyes lit up. "They did find it! My God, let me see it—"

"What do you know about it?" Jack demanded.

"It's *it*. The thing we — the collective *we* — have been searching for for over a thousand years. The Ark, the Grail, the Fountain of Youth, Bran's Cauldron… as far back as you want to go. Please, just let me—"

"It's a fucking rock," Jack said. "Tell me something that's real, like how the hell we're going to get her to a hospital. A guy like you must have had some sort of evacuation plan in place, even if it was just for yourself."

"No, Jack, I'm all in on this one," Bill insisted. "The Indians believed in it, the Clayborns too. That's why they built this house here. Why else do you think there's a Victorian mansion out here in the middle of nowhere?"

Jack leaned closer. "Believed in what?"

"*It*, Jack, *it!*" Bill insisted, nodding to the other room.

Jack leaned in threateningly. "Speak plainly. What did they know about it?"

Bill squirmed. "I'm not one hundred percent sure. The Mi'kmaq claimed it was cursed and refused to let anyone on it, but then came the Clayborns. The Clayborns didn't think it was cursed, they though it was a gift from God. They believe the Indian myths — legends of massive animals that live forever, streams that washed away age, monsters and curses and all that type of hocus pocus. They spent generations obsessing over it but never got anywhere — at least not as far as I could find. It was all just folklore hooey and it mostly disappeared when the Clayborns did. Then the Mi'kmaq petitioned the Canadian government to expand this into reservation territory and take it back. That's how Sophie found this place; she followed the legends of the Welsh prince across the ocean, hunted through thousands of old myths, made the connections between the *Mabinogi* and the First Nations' legends."

A puzzle piece fell into place in Jack's mind. "The tribe didn't sell you this land, did they?"

"No. But they'll never even know we were here!" Bill insisted. "They never come near this land; they're terrified of it. They still claim it's cursed. I tried to have my broker approach them, but they wouldn't even entertain the notion of it."

"That's why you trapped us here…"

"You signed up for this, Jack! Don't paint me as a villain. You're a goddamn adult — all of you are — and you all took on a clear-cut job in coming here."

A sudden burst of rage coursed through Jack's veins, and he fought to hold back from striking the bound man before him. "We signed up for an excavation, not a goddamn horror story. You tricked us, you little shit, and now you sit here and act like it's all part of a fair deal while a woman bleeds out in the other room."

"Use the stone!" Bill said excitedly. "Use the stone, Jack! It's real. The natives, the Clayborns, even Sophie knew it!"

Jack stood, knocking the ottoman back and drawing his revolver. He leveled it with Bill's stomach.

"No, no! Wait! Just try it! Please, for the love of God!" Bill squealed as he recoiled farther into the chair.

Kevin stirred, lolling his head over to see what was happening. "What's… what's going on…"

Jack lowered the pistol and regarded Kevin. "You're going to explain to your intrepid employer here what happens when someone takes a bullet to the stomach. In detail. You understand?"

Kevin gave him a confused look. "Okay?"

A nearby thunderclap shook the room as Jack swept out of the foyer and back into the dining room. Rain pelted the bay windows behind Margaret, who was still sitting in the same spot at the table, intently scrawling notes onto a yellow pad as she clicked through the photos on her camera.

"He believes it's real," Jack said in a low tone. "Apparently we're also trespassing on a Native American reservation."

"Splendid…" Margaret muttered, squinting to make out the image on the camera's tiny screen then jotting something down.

Jack hesitated, eyeing the stone. "Is it possible?"

"Is what possible?"

"That it's, you know… real? If it could do that to Greg's hand, then, I don't know…" His voice trailed off.

Margaret grunted. "You know, at this point anything's possible. This writing, it's just…" She shook her head, brows furrowed in concentration.

"What?" Jack asked.

Margaret looked up at him and made a face like she was lost for words. "I… I don't know. It's hard to translate, mostly broken Latin mixed with a lot of pictographs I've never seen. It doesn't make any sense at all. Except… Sophie claimed the people who did this were led by a druid priest, a man misrepresented later in history as the Welsh prince Madoc.

"The druids were eradicated in the second century and left behind no written records. But almost every historian will agree that while the various druidic orders had no written language of their own, it's more likely than not that they *were* literate in other languages and simply refused to record their own information in order to horde and protect their secrets."

"Margaret, we're running low on time here," Jack prompted.

"Yeah, yeah, I know. But it's just… this writing, it reads like someone only partially familiar with traditional literacy — almost like the pictographs are filling in holes and gaps in the language. If a person were to write *this* way, with *this* efficiency *that* far back in history, it would make sense that it was a druid… But that's not all, that's not really even the start. There are thousands of these symbols, all perfectly etched in the stone in a way that would have taken even a decent sized group of artisans longer than a single lifetime to achieve. On top of that, the work it would have taken to hew the dome itself… we're talking a major architectural occurrence, Jack. Something that a required a massive undertaking. Something that I cannot explain."

"So, what are you saying?" Jack asked.

"I'm saying I have questions," Margaret said slowly. "I'm saying…" She glanced over at where Greg wallowed in the corner, then over to the stone that sat between them. "You asked me if I believed it was possible that, you know, *it* holds some sort of power. Two hours ago, I would have laughed in your face. Shit, I *did* basically laugh in your face a few minutes ago. Now, I'm telling you that I don't know. I just— I have questions…"

Jack considered her words. If Margaret, the Ivy League archaeologist and devout realist, would admit her faith had been challenged, they who was he to question it? "What have you translated so far?"

"Not much." Margaret scanned over her notes. "A lot of warnings, curse-type jargon. Here's one symbol that keeps showing up every so often in various contexts— Here, this one."

She pointed to the small screen. On it was a carved symbol resembling a cooking pot.

"And that's repeated?" Jack asked.

"Just about every few rows, and so far, it's the only line I've seen more than once," Margaret said.

"Well? What the hell does it mean?" Jack asked.

Margaret shrugged. "It looks like a cauldron, which would make sense given the story that brought us here."

"So you think there's another artifact down there? An actual cauldron?"

"Trust me, there was nothing else in that cave."

"There has to be," Jack insisted. "Think of that story, the one about the Irish and the British. If this could do that to Greg's hand, then maybe there's something that does the opposite, something that actually heals, *just like that cauldron.*"

"I mean, we could have missed something, but you can't get back down there anytime soon, that entire cave system is flooded," Margaret said, but then paused. "Although…"

"What?"

"There was a spot on the wall that Greg found. It looked like someone might have burrowed out. It would make sense that there would be a second entrance into that place, after all, but God knows where it would come out."

The trees.

The underground spring.

The stone-walled pit.

"I know where it is." Jack stood.

"Where?" Margaret asked.

"That whole row of giant trees was leading straight away from the dig site. There must be some sort of underground spring. Maybe it's manmade, maybe the result of a passage or tunnel of some sort that ends where I killed the wolf. If there's another entrance, that's gotta be it."

"There *is* mention of a wolf in the carvings." Margaret scrolled through the camera for a second, then squinted at the screen. "It's a shit photo; the flash reflected back. I see *lupus* — that's Latin for wolf — but the rest is pretty fuzzy. I'd have to try to manipulate the image on my computer."

"Take a guess, what does it say?" Jack snapped.

"It's mostly blurred. Something about guard or guardian, then… no, I can't make it out."

"Good enough for me." Jack pointed to Kevin's pistol, which still sat on the table in front of Margaret. "If they try and get loose, use it. Remember, they won't hesitate to fuck you up."

"Be careful," Margaret said.

"I'll do what I can," he responded, eyeing the raging storm through the window. The wind had picked up, and from all around the house came the chaotic clatter of loose shutters bashing against old walls and the incessant staccato of heavy rain. One of the turrets flexed, releasing a squeaking groan. It almost felt like the old house was warning him. But the weather wouldn't stop him. Nothing would. He knew what had to be done.

"Hold down the fort and try to figure out what that says. I'll be on the radio."

XXIV

Margaret

MARGARET WATCHED Jack leave. Not a minute after the front door slammed shut, Bill's whining voice called from the foyer.

"Margaret, please, just untie me and we can talk."

"Shut up, Bill!" she called back. She looked down at her hands. He'd been right — her shake was gone and amazingly so was her craving. At first, she'd figured it was just adrenaline, that she was distracted by everything that had happened over the past few hours. But now, with every reason for her body chemistry to have returned to normal, she realized that the call of the bitter, chalky opiates no longer drew her in.

"Please, Margaret, I can't feel my feet. At least loosen the knots, please!" Bill went on.

She ignored him and tried to focus on her work. But the whiny stream of meaningless words persisted, blending together into little more than a string of reminders of how stupid and malleable he apparently thought she was.

"Margaret, my left arm, it's numbing… there's a pain in my chest…"

Really, Bill? Did he really think she'd fall for cheap pity tricks like some B-rate actress in a noir thriller?

"Margaret, please, my circulation. I'm… I'm feeling light-headed… Please…"

Finally, she couldn't stop herself. She stomped into the foyer and slapped Bill hard across the face. "I said shut your fucking mouth, you pathetic worm!" she hissed. "How little respect do you have for us? I already let your stupid antics almost kill me six different ways today, and if you imagine for a second that I'll toss some pity down on you over a punishment you've earned, then you've got another thing coming, you understand me?"

Bill scowled, his victim façade evaporating in an instant. "You goddamn people. All so self-righteous in your contempt of me. I *saved* you. I bought you and brought you into the fold on this, and you repay me with treachery and dec—"

Another hard smack silenced him, then another brought a howl of pain, and the third was with a closed fist and left a crimson streak under his nose.

"Enough! Stop!" Kevin shouted.

Margaret turned to him. "Who are you? Huh? What do you owe this piece of subhuman garbage?"

"I don't owe him jack-shit," Kevin said, eyeing her with contempt. "He's my employer, and when I take a job, I have the professional integrity to actually see it through. Apparently, I'm the only one here who understands that you don't get to turn on the boss just because a job might get dirty."

"You're a lap dog," Margaret snapped. "Don't get your delicate ego twisted into seeing yourself as a good guy here."

Kevin took a breath like he might say something, but instead just glared.

"Fuck you both," she muttered.

"I see things have devolved a bit," Dr. Bianchi's soft voice drifted from the staircase.

Margaret spun and looked at the round figure. His smock was dabbed with bloodstains and his gloved hands were held up in front of him to avoid contamination.

"I—" Margaret started, but she didn't have the words to finish the sentence.

"I won't judge," the doctor said, surveying the two bound men. "My only priority right now is Ms. Kensington. I come to ask for some water; I need to finish bathing the exposed wounds."

"Sure," Margaret said slowly.

"Dr. Bianchi, please, for the love of—" Bill began to say, but Margaret silenced him with a raised backhand.

"Given the circumstance, I must fall upon the Hippocratic Oath," Bianchi announced, his eyes drifting to the massive pistol tucked in Margaret's belt. "But Ms. Simmons, please, I would appreciate it if you did not create more patients for me. I have my hands quite full already."

Margaret looked him over. He was entirely too calm considering what he'd walked in on. But then again, who was Margaret to judge? "You got it, doctor. Just water?"

"Yes, a large bowl please," he said, then turned and disappeared upstairs.

"You've got to be fucking kidding me," Bill whimpered under his breath.

"You reap what you sow, Bill." Margaret glowered and made for the kitchen.

"What did I do to all of you?" Bill desperately called after her as she placed a large soup pot in the faucet and turned on the tap. "You act like I killed your damn puppy! Sophie pushed this excavation forward harder than I did, yet here I am as the sole villain. We all came here because we were desperate, we were all willing to sacrifice something to regain what we've lost, and here we are, with the greatest find of the last two thousand years, and you've all turned on me!"

Margaret dropped her head in her hands and sighed. "No, Bill, we found a poisoned stone that almost killed Greg, and some cryptic message about a second artifact, which will doubtlessly lead to a clue of a third. It's all just another old sham, you understand that? Not worth a young woman's life, if you ask me or any other sane person."

"A second artifact? What do you mean?" Bill's voice dropped.

Margaret sighed. Of course he'd perk up at that. Never mind the woman dying upstairs or the traumatized kid in the corner with the withered hand...

The water dribbled out of the tap, and the pot filled slowly. If only this shitty steel pot was the cauldron, she thought defeatedly.

The simplicity of it struck her off guard. Her mind stumbled over itself, then retraced its way back to the beginning. She turned and left the room. Hunching over the dining room table, she stared at the stone. Sophie's words played in the back of her mind, something she'd said in their retreat through the tunnels about Jack having been right about a stream. She shut her eyes and thought back to the dome-like cave, to the moment after Greg had passed out, before she and Sophie had hauled him back through the tunnels. There had been the hole, something glinting at the bottom, the trickle of water...

No shit.

The Holy Grail. Bran's Cauldron. The Fountain of Youth.

Different receptacles, but same contents.

Trusting her gut, she stalked into the kitchen and tore through the drawers until she found a pair of barbeque tongs. Using them, she plucked the stone from the table, crossed back to the sink, and dropped it into the nearly full pot of water. It let out a sharp clink as it hit the bottom of the metal pot, then sat still, glinting under the water's disturbed surface.

"Fuck it," she whispered, closing her eyes and imagining Sophie's broken body. She plunged her hand into the water and gripped the smooth stone.

At first there was nothing, then in a fraction of a second, the most pure, utter, incredible joy wove its way from Margaret's fingertips to her chest. Her heart fluttered, and she felt as if years of built-up grime and debris had suddenly flushed away from her soul. Her mouth filled with the taste of fresh strawberries and her ears rang with the most beautiful silence. It was euphoric, better than a thousand tiny white pills in a way that was entirely unmeasurable. Her skin tingled and she felt it pulling taut all around her, like some invisible blanket squeezing snug, warm, and fresh against her bones. The feeling was incredible, but somewhere in the back of her mind, the image of Greg's disgustingly disfigured hand flashed as a horrible warning. With a hesitant burst of control, she released the stone and stumbled back.

Reality crashed back down onto her. The patter of rain filled her ears, and the musty scent of old wood and fresh ozone filled her nostrils. The air was thick with storm in a way she'd been too numb to feel for decades. She stared at the bowl and the stone inside and realized her vision was so much clearer than it had been a moment before. The tightness of her skin remained, and when she looked down, she didn't find her hands and body a shriveled mess of dried, blackened leather — no, they were perfect. The wrinkled old hands had transformed, reverted to the beautiful, youthful hands she barely remembered. Slowly she looked up at her reflection in the window above the sink and gasped. The woman who stared back at her was twenty years younger.

"Water, please!" Bianchi's shout echoed from above.

Bullshit. It wasn't real. It couldn't be real. Margaret slapped herself in an attempt to reconnect with the harsh reality of her situation, but instead found herself marveling at the feel of her own soft, smooth cheek. It wasn't possible. Nothing could do this. It was absurd to imagine that something like this could actually exist. Yet here it was, and here *she* was, looking and feeling barely more than half the age she'd been a moment before.

Holy mother of shit.

It's real.

"Margaret!" the doctor shouted again, his voice growing hoarse.

Sophie. Sophie was dying. Shit. If this was real, then maybe it could… yes. It was real. It was *real.*

Margaret's brain felt like it was short circuiting. She stumbled forward and pulled the bowl from the sink, then carried it out into the foyer and up the stairs. Both Bill and Kevin gave shocked responses to her transformation in the background, but the only thing that filled Margaret's ears was her own whispering voice. "*It's real. It's real. It's real.*"

Sophie was still spread across the table when Margaret entered and brushed by the doctor. He tried to protest, but she silenced him with a hand. Slowly, she scooped handfuls of water from the bowl, feeling the tingling power in each one, and bathed Sophie's wounds.

"What in the hell happened to you?" the doctor gasped, staring at Margaret's youthful face as she worked. "Margaret? You're… Margaret, that is you, right?"

Margaret dripped a small amount of water into the corner of Sophie's mouth, then turned and smiled. "Yeah, doc." She had to stop herself from crying. "Same old me."

"Hardly…" the doctor said, bewildered.

Once the water began to run low and she was confident in her work, Margaret took the bowl and retreated to the door. "Just keep her heart beating. Do whatever you have to, but keep her alive, okay?"

The doctor nodded, still in shock over her appearance. She dropped back into the hall with the bowl in her arms and pulled the radio from her belt.

"Jack, are you there?"

A long fizzle sounded on the other end before his voice broke through. "Yeah, di… …igure out what it said?"

"No, but I found the missing piece. It's water. I think it's going to be okay." She laughed and realized her cheeks were wet with tears of joy.

"Water?" Jack's voice was barely audible. "What?"

"It's okay! You can come back now!" She laughed harder, making her way down the hall to the bathroom. "We figured it out, Jack. It's amazing."

"Sophie okay?"

"I don't know," Margaret admitted. "I… we can only wait and find out."

"…an't understa… …ere's something out here. The wolf was digging for someth… …st figure out what it says."

"Okay, okay." She took a deep breath and steadied herself, then looked full in the mirror. There she was. The beautiful girl she remembered. It was stunning. *She* was stunning. Puffy red eyes from crying. Rosy, tear-streaked cheeks. Full, quivering lips. It was the most wonderful thing she'd ever seen.

"…igure it out, Margaret!" Jack's voice was barely more than static now.

"Yeah, I… I will," she promised, then shook her head to clear it. "I'll do it in a second, hold on."

She hurried down the hall, through servants' stairwell, through the kitchen, and to where Greg huddled in his corner. The steps came easy and painless, her newfound springiness propelling her in a way she'd forgotten years before.

"Here, drink from this," she insisted, but when she tilted the bowl toward him and he saw the stone sitting in its bottom, he recoiled with a terrified whimper. After a few more attempts to coax him, she gave up, refilled the pot, and hurried back upstairs. She placed the lifesaving liquid outside the doctor's door and used a piece of cloth to pluck the stone from the water. Tucking it back in her chest pocket, she darted into her room to grab her laptop, then headed back to the dining room. Once she reached the table and settled into a seat, she opened her laptop and connected it to the camera. A second later, she was viewing the images in high definition. She clicked through until she found the right one, then increased the brightness and contrast until the blurred symbols began to take shape.

"Are you there, Jack?" she called through the radio. There was no response. "If you can hear me, it says… it says the wolf is the guardian awakened. No, no wait… the wolf… *awakens* the guardians. The wolf will awaken the guardians. Yeah, that's it. Did you catch that?"

The radio remained silent.

"Jack?"

XXV

Jack

THE LAST gloomy hint of dusk had fully disappeared, absorbed by the roiling black clouds of the storm. Despite the thick forest canopy above and the wiper blades that blurred across the UTV's windshield, Jack could barely see through the mess of darkness and heavy rain. Pine saplings and dead logs crashed and crumbled under the small four-wheel-drive vehicle as he sped through the forest, jerking the wheel back and forth in a white knuckled grip to avoid the thick tree trunks as they emerged into the short reach of the headlights.

He broke through an opening in the forest and pressed harder on the pedal, accelerating up a muddy incline. Reaching the top of the wooded hill, he pulled to a halt and checked the coordinates on the built-in GPS system. The numbers took a long minute to load, and when they finally blipped up bright and blinding blue against the darkness around him, he knew he was close.

"Margaret, can you hear me?" He had to use his jacket to shield the radio from the clacking of the rain on the UTV's roof. There was no response. He cursed to himself, then squinted through the headlight's beams, trying to make out a clear path forward. The hill he'd just climbed gave way to a muddy downward slope, and just ahead, maybe a hundred or so yards away, he spotted the massive pillar that marked his destination. The sight of the overgrown oak's trunk emerging the end of the ravine brought with it a curdling ache in his gut, and his hand unconsciously brushed his still painfully swollen and scabbed forearm where the wolf had latched on.

He eased onto the gas, angling the UTV toward the closest thing to a path available: a patch of thin saplings. The engine hummed and all four wheels engaged, pulling it forward a few feet — then the engine cut off. Jack's stomach dropped as the headlights evaporated, and suddenly he was rolling down the hill in complete blackness, rapidly picking up momentum. He slammed on the brakes, but it did little more than tear at the soft, muddy earth. He made the split-second decision to bail, but before his body could comply with his mind, a violent impact launched him forward. He hit the windshield shoulder first with a loud crunch.

For in indeterminable period he lay draped over the wheel, head pounding, and eyes filled with unfocused darkness. Eventually, the world seeped back in. Flashing lightning cut through the black night, cold rain dribbled down through the cracked roof, and the stink of motor oil filled his nose.

"What the… what the fuck?" he finally managed to cough out, carefully testing his bruised shoulder and eyeing the spiderwebbed glass. He groaned as he slowly sat up. His whole body already felt pulverized from the cliff face, and now this. He was surprised he was still alive.

He tried the ignition. Nothing happened. A red light on the dashboard lit up. He rustled through the glovebox until he found a headlamp and shined it on the tiny, blinking red writing beneath:

GPS LIMITER ENGAGED

You're fucking kidding me.

"Margaret?" Jack keyed the radio repeatedly. "Margaret, if you can hear me, I need you to turn off the GPS limiter on the UTVs. You need to find the modem. Make Bill tell you how… Smack him or some shit. Please, tell me you can hear me."

Nothing.

"Marg—" he started again, then swore and tossed the radio down. It was no use. She had more important priorities right now anyways. What was he really expecting to find out here? Some magical nonsense that could make thousands of years of medical development obsolete? Why had he even—

Because there was nothing else, he told himself. He had no other path, no other options. There was nothing else he could do to help Sophie, but this was better than standing by and waiting for her to die. He'd done that before, back in Montana all those years ago, and he wasn't about to let it happen again. At least out here, he could lie to himself. He could try to contribute, to *do* something. If the stone could do that to Greg's arm, then maybe… maybe there was a chance that it *was* what Sophie thought it was, and that whatever this second piece of the puzzle was… maybe it could help her.

He leaned into the backseat and grabbed the wood axe he'd dug out of the carriage house. It was old, dull, and rusted, but it wasn't like he had many options at this point. Climbing out of the vehicle and into the torrential rain, he shouldered the axe and carefully made his way down the rest of the muddy hill and toward the ravine.

The energy of the forest was different than it had been the last time he was in this area. Now, despite the rolling thunder and endless drumbeat of heavy raindrops on leaves, the world around him was cold and dead, silent. The animals had all retreated to their shelters in the face of mother nature's fury, and some voice inside of Jack told him to follow suit. But he trudged on, pushing into the mouth of the ravine, then forward through the tiny, cascading waterfalls that fell from the ledges above. Each step brought with it a stinging, sulfurous cloud of terror-soaked *déjà vu*.

"It's dead, you idiot. You already killed it," Jack breathed to himself so quietly that it was drowned out by the storm. "Dead and gone. It was just the one, an outlier, just the one."

His hands wrung tight on the axe handle as he crossed the flooding stream and closed on the final bend. The axe felt weak and toy-like compared to his rifle, and as he reached the place from which he'd fired on the wolf before, he found himself unconsciously brushing his fingers against the revolver at his side. But other than the branches tossing in the wind and the blur of rain, there was no movement. There was nothing there but the tree. His chest relaxed and he released a breath he didn't even realize he'd been holding.

He crossed to the edge of the pit where the wolf had torn into roots and dirt. The hole was only a couple feet deep, and maybe twice as wide. If there was a second piece to this puzzle, it was here. It *needed* to be here.

Jack brought the axe down on the ragged mess of springy wood, but the roots simply bowed against the blunt steel edge. He swung again, this time finding purchase in a thicker root and chipping off a sizable chunk. His third swing ate through a handful of thinner, spidering roots, and by the twentieth, he had made some minor progress. His breath started to come ragged after a few more swings, and rather than take a moment to catch it, he imagined Sophie's broken body and swung harder. The thick root broke and bent away, exposing another one twice its size. Jack didn't stop; he swung harder and harder as the muscles in his back and arms began to burn.

Why'd you do this to me?

Sam's whispered words drifted into Jack's mind like a poisoned fog. He hacked harder at the ground as they intermingled with the image of Sophie, of the dubious sideways glance she'd given him when he'd first seen her, of her glinting smile as she laughed in the cool blue light of the moon, of her unnaturally canted head, strangled by the dark necklace of bruised flesh. He shut his eyes and swung harder, and harder, and harder until his hands rang with numbness and his bruised shoulder gave out.

He collapsed to his knees and pounded the torn roots and soft earth with his fists. His breath came hard between gasping sobs, and finally he fell back against the muddy pit wall and screamed in futile rage.

He lay still for some time, choking through sobs as his eyes raced to produce hot tears faster than the rain could wash them away.

What did it all matter? Why was he even here, chopping at some fucking tree, digging a hole in solid earth and searching for some goddamn buried treasure? The horrible feeling in his stomach told him the truth. His effort was stupid. He was there for himself.

Jack sat up and let the defeat wash over him. He spitefully refused to look at the hole as he stood. A part of him was ashamed for the whole endeavor, but as he turned to leave, a flash of lightning revealed a wet edge glinting between the roots. Slowly he turned back and bent to examine it.

It was a piece of hewn stone, laid flat on the earth under the criss-crossed roots. He brushed a clump of mud away and revealed a worn symbol carved into its surface.

"No fucking way," he muttered, then laughed and shouted, "No fucking way!"

Despite his sore muscles, the sight of the symbol renewed his strength, and he hacked at the closest roots, exposing a worn edge. He followed it, chopping the roots that bound the stone to the forest floor. Once he'd finished, he used the axe's dull blade to trace the stone's outline. It was some sort of lid, like a capped portal. He jammed the blade in and torqued it, raising the thick stone enough to get a hand under. Then, with all his strength, he heaved and lifted the slab away from the hole. His muscles strained, and he fought to flip the massive cap away from the opening.

Lightning flashed through the broken foliage above, casting the whole pit in sharp relief. In the flash, he could see the figures carved into the shale façade glaring down at him, long limbed and threatening. In an instant, the blanket of darkness once again fell over the forest. But the figures stayed, burned into his mind's eye, and some primal voice furiously commanded him to run.

The wolf's dead, he thought, muffling the feeling and heaving harder, lifting the stone edge as high as his waist.

He saw it before he felt it. A pallid blur flashed in the corner of his vision, emerging from the darkness of the cavity below. Long and muddy, it grasped his lower leg in a painfully tight grip. His heart leapt into his throat and he jerked away, but the sallow hand locked around his calf only gripped harder. The stone slipped from his hold and came down hard, pinning the veiny, pale arm that extended out of the black hole. From deep in the recesses below came a heinous, animalistic shriek, and the hand flexed, talon-like fingertips digging into his flesh before releasing. The sickly appendage yanked back against the pressure of the offset stone, writhing in the mud for a moment before disappearing into the blackness. Jack stumbled and fell backwards as the stone slid back into place. He lay at the edge of the pit, frozen in shock, entirely too stunned to react. Everything in the pit felt distant, slow, alien. It was as if some projectile launched from the far-off universe of absurdity had crashed through his mind, shattering his lens of reality.

Then the stone began to shift.

XXVI

Sophie

Blue.
Rich, deep, pure blue-green.
Velvety smooth.
Bubbling.
Foaming.
Rushing.
Fine sand gently rubbing between toes.
Warmth.
Caressing, cascading, soul-mending sun heat.
Warmth soaking from smooth stone into the soles of her feet.
Radiant heat gently seeping from the inside out.
Breeze.
Cool.
Disarming.
Alive.
Bones, shifting.
A mother's voice, goading her, laughing, playing, dancing.

A beach.
Her beach.
Happiness.
Pure.
Unimaginably pure.

"SOPHIE? CAN you hear me?" The gentle, Italian-edged voice echoed in the distance for a moment, then it came again, louder, closer. "Sophie, if you're awake, I need to know. Can you hear me?"

The beach began to fade away. She fought to grasp onto it, but the harder she clutched at it, the further it dissolved in her groping fingers.

"If you are awake, please, try to open your eyes."

The beach was gone, misted into spotty, red blackness. But the warmth remained.

"Well, maybe it's better that you stay unconscious, for the beginning at least."

A quick, sharp pain on her chest. The sting was fleeting though, dissipating back into the warmth.

"Marvelous. Simply marvelous. I wonder…"

She knew the soft voice. It was the doctor. He was happy. She was happy. It was wonderf—

A burning pain ignited her hand. She tried to thrash and scream, but nothing moved. Her body refused to respond to her call. The pain came again, and she made to rip her hand away, to clutch it to her chest, but again the call went unanswered.

Slowly, painstakingly, and with every bit of focus and strength she could muster, she willed her eyes to open. At first, they didn't respond just like everything else, but after a moment, her eyelids drifted lazily upward, exposing the dazzlingly bright white of the ceiling above.

"So true, regeneration is still beyond our grasp. Even so…" the doctor muttered to himself nearby.

She tried to lift her head, but just shifting her eyes down took every ounce of energy she had. She could make out the top of his bald head, giddily bouncing around as he sat beside her, loudly shuffling through his various medical instruments. The pain throughout her hand ebbed, slowly becoming more concentrated until she knew it had resonated from her pinky finger. She tried to move it but couldn't.

"If it can't regenerate, then perhaps it isn't linked to DNA. You can't rebuild the house if you can't read the blueprints," he mused, then his sweat-glinted forehead turned toward her. "Oh my! Sophie, you've woken up. Incredible!"

He rolled toward her on his stool and propped her head up. She could see her own body now, naked and half covered in a thin, white sheet. Despite the warmth that still ebbed inside of her, the sight of the gashes and dark oceans of damaged flesh made her feel ill.

"Yes, you took a hell of a fall, young lady," the doctor said, surveying her with a warm smile. "But whatever that thing Margaret has… it's… well, it's working a miracle."

She forced her eyes to move to one of the torn, red abrasions on her shoulder and watched in amazement as the wound shifted. The darkened, exposed red flesh clumped and hardened into a spattering of scabs with a speed that couldn't be natural.

"I thought she was coo-coo at first," the doctor admitted with a shake of his head. "But then… well, your bones were the first thing to start moving. Thought I was going crazy, or maybe you were having a minor seizure or something when they began shifting around all slow like that…" He reached out and wiped at her shoulder with a damp cloth. The scabs came off clean, leaving not so much as a trace of scarring behind.

She focused on her lips, working to control her mouth and trying her best to harness the air in her lungs. "…What…" was all she managed to get out.

"Oh my, it's so fast!" The doctor tensed and gave her a funny look. "Speaking already — Sophie, tell me, can you move anything below your neck yet? It was, well, perhaps *is,* quite broken."

She couldn't build the energy to respond. She just wanted to shut her eyes again. To drift away back to that warm, wonderful beach. But as she stared at him, she could also see something else in the background.

She let her vision fall to the shining metal tray table and her left hand which lay propped on it. The end of her pinky looked funny. It was wrong, unduly short as if bent away. But it wasn't bent away. A healed nub had replaced everything beyond the second knuckle, and on the tray lay the bloody half digit next to a pair of medical sheers.

She managed a sharp breath, and the doctor followed her eyes.

"Oh, that," he said, then gave her an apologetic look. "Just an experiment. A little one to help us understand the nature of whatever wonderful miracle thing you ladies have uncovered. I'm afraid... I do have a few more questions that I need answered."

"...No..." she got out, and he giggled. It was a sick, twisted giggle that transformed his soft, harmless demeanor into anything but.

"Oh, yes. Yes indeed, young Sophie. What we're dealing with here... We can't just, you know... Let it out into the world without *understanding* it first. Even then, it needs to be *controlled*. You *understand*, don't you?" He grinned at her, then stood and crossed the room to lock the door.

When he returned, he plucked a scalpel from the table and lightly brushed it across her arm. She saw the thin red line before she felt it. It only stung for a few seconds, but then the warmth enveloped it, and she watched it fade away from her skin without a trace.

"Amazing!" the doctor proclaimed. "So amazing."

"...No..." she said again. She meant to scream it, but it only came as a breathy exhale.

Bianchi turned to face her, a twisted pleasure sparkling in his eyes. "Yes, Sophie. *Yes*. You can't tell me no. Remember what I said: life is about *understanding* and *control*. Now you must *understand* that *I* am in *control*. Accept this."

"...No..."

Bianchi rolled his eyes and laughed. "Such a goof. If that's the attitude you want to take, then I'm afraid you won't be recovering from your wounds."

She felt her heartbeat rise the tiniest bit, and next to her, the rhythmic tone of a beeping monitor that she hadn't even noticed before increased.

"Oh, geez." Bianchi raised an eyebrow. "So fast! Maybe… I wonder if motivation plays a part. Perhaps fear?"

He stood and hunched forward, placing his face mere inches from hers. She could smell the sweet, pungent scent of lozenges on his breath.

"Let's see if I can speed it up a bit. What do you fear, Sophie? Are you afraid that I'm going to kill everyone here?" he whispered in an even voice, his eyes bulging behind the thick-rimmed glasses. "That I'm going to inject Margaret with a high dose of Pavulon? That she's going to seize to death right in front of you? Well, I do have both the means and motive… as a matter of fact, the needles already prepped over there on the table for the next time she insists on barging in here. Are you afraid that after that I'll call your little boyfriend Jack for help and do the same thing? Then the others, well… they're already tied up, so to speak. Anyways, slice, slice, and they're gone. And Greg… Maybe I'd just shoot him for fun. Then it would just be you and me. Does that idea frighten you, Sophie?"

A horrible pain almost muted the warmth as he sliced an even deeper line in her arm. Her heart jumped and the machine next to her beeped faster. This time, though, the warmth overtook the pain even more quickly, despite the severity of the wound, and after a few grueling seconds, there was no evidence left of it.

"Amazing!" Bianchi almost shouted, then nervously eyed the door. "Oh, I shouldn't be so loud. I have much more work to do before the big finale."

"…Why…" she managed to gasp out.

He gave her a curious look. "Why? Why? *Seriously?* Young lady, think about what you've discovered. You think I, or anyone here, is just going to let something that is a *literal* miracle just drift off in that moron Bill's hands as some prize for a wasted lifetime of buffoonery? Or yours, or Jack's, or Greg's? So it can be plucked away and sit in a lab and be dissected and disseminated to the inbred gargoyles that make up today's elite? It de-aged that old hag Margaret — *de-aged*, goddamnit! It's… well, I'm tempted to call it magic. You think I'd give *that* up? Ha! No, dear girl, no. It's mine. I will take it."

They stared at each other, and Sophie saw in his big brown eyes that the sick creature was telling the truth.

"Now, onward!" he proclaimed. With a gleeful twitch, he resumed shuffling through the bag of instruments before him, humming some forgotten showtune and erupting in fits of mad giggles every so often.

Sophie felt sick watching him. Not physically — the warmth still resonated strong and ripe inside of her — but the image of the little goblin hunched over his satchel twisted in her thoughts like a rotten piece of meat ready to be purged. Soon she couldn't take it anymore. She let her eyes drift away, then forced them shut and found the red-black blanket of spackled darkness welcoming. She tried to move her arm once again, but it lay still, numb, and seemingly dead at her side. It was an unfamiliar feeling, but something about it rang a distant bell of memory. She fell inward, working to discover the source of the familiarity, and found herself recalling a terrifying moment from her childhood.

When she was little, she'd suffered from sleep paralysis. It had only happened a few times, but at only six-years old, she was so terrified that she would stay up until the late hours of the night, fighting off sleep in fear of the ominous, unmoving shadow that haunted her episodes. She remembered her grandmother calming her, telling her the secret that allowed her to finally sleep peacefully.

"Wiggle your big toe, Soph. Give it a good, hard wiggle, and it'll snap ya right out of it, ya hear?" the old woman would tell her. "Even if the damn thing don't work, keep goin'. Only way to keep the night witch away is with that little waggle."

Sophie felt a jarring pain in her side. The warmth fought against it. She suppressed both senses, focusing every bit of herself on moving the big toe of her right foot.

At first there was nothing, but eventually she heard a tiny thump. The doctor's stool squeaked as he gave a startled jump.

"What in God's name... You rascal! What a strong girl you are!" Bianchi proclaimed with a laugh. "A little toe tapping to keep the rhythm going? I like it!"

She opened her eyes the smallest bit, guiding them to look at her feet. Her right foot was resting up against the wall. Her big toe was twitching ever so slightly at her command, tapping gently against the ancient wallpaper. She shut her eyes and tried to ignore the pain as Bianchi sliced again, instead focusing everything she had on that toe. The tap grew the tiniest bit louder with each passing minute, and after a short time, Bianchi began humming along.

XXVII

Jack

THE STONE rocked back and forth at first, then began to slowly rise as it was lifted from beneath. The image of the unnaturally long, sallow, squirming forearm and its horrible, mud-drenched hand hung in Jack's mind — not to mention the pain in his leg —, and, in a movement driven purely by adrenaline and instinct, he yanked the revolver from his side and leveled it at the shifting slab. The stone rose higher, exposing a sliver of the dark cavity beneath, and he fired directly into it. Once. Twice. Three times. The third round resulted in a heavy clack as it ricocheted off the stone cap, which quickly fell back into place. Over the storm and through the thick stone, Jack heard another tortured scream.

He leapt to his feet and tried to focus. The fog of panic was dense, but he immediately knew what he had to do. He crossed to the ravine's opening and grasped a flat stone slab several feet wide at its base. He wrestled against its weight. The mud sucked hard against the rock's bottom as he strained to lift, and, with a long, grueling shove, Jack managed to upend it. He let it fall forward, reset, and he hauled it up again, rolling it one flip at a time until it came to a crashing rest atop the stone slab. Without pausing to catch his breath, he turned and found another large rock and did the same, flipping it end over end until it came to rest beside the first. Then another, and another. Finally, when he'd run out of stones, he stumbled back and collapsed against the massive oak.

Thunder rumbled overhead, and above his own panting, he heard a grinding sound from the earth deep below his feet. Some faint, shifting rumble.

"Fuck this." He gave the immovable pile of stones a final glance, then blindly stumbled through the muddy ravine. Minutes later, he'd found his way to the UTV. The hope that perhaps Margaret had heard his message and managed to disable the GPS limiter was quickly quashed when he pressed the ignition. The little red icon flashed and beeped. He swore and looked up the hill behind him and tried to pinpoint exactly where he'd been when he last broke through on the radio.

It took him too long to climb the muddy incline. When he finally reached the hilltop, he keyed the filth-covered radio and found himself breathlessly shouting into it, "Margaret, for the love of Christ, please, answer!"

There was a long pause before she responded. "…ack? What's wro…"

"There's something out here, something… something I can't explain! You need to disable the GPS right fucking now!"

"…at are yo… …me?

"GPS! Margaret, disable the UTV's GPS limiter *now*!"

"…iter, I don't know ho… …ven works… …old on."

"Hurry, goddamnit!"

The radio went silent, and Jack stared back over to the ravine below. Another flash of lightning lit the forest around him, and the thousands of leafy shadows suddenly took on a terrifyingly nostalgic feel. For the first time in seven long years, Jack felt entirely defenseless. He was prey once more.

"…ink I got it. The limiter is go… …reset, it'll take a…"

"It'll take what?"

"...few minutes to reset, just standb..."

Jack eyed the UTV. In the light of the headlamp, he could make out that it was resting against the trunk of the thick tree he'd impacted. Twin smeared tire slides wound out behind it in the mud, and he doubted he'd be able to reverse it from its current position. He needed to get it away from the tree to ride it out, and to do that, he had the feeling he'd need a lever. His eyes darted around the hillside for a sturdy branch or a freshly fallen sapling, but he found nothing.

The axe. He needed the axe. It lay discarded back by the pit.

Cursing himself, he flipped off his headlamp and half slid, half stumbled down the hill in the dark. This time he made directly for the opening of the cellar hole, walking along the top edge of the ravine's winding walls. He was more willing to take the long way than place himself in the clutches of the thin, inescapable corridor. When he reached the pit, he cautiously leaned over the ledge, scanning for the axe. He let out a sigh of relief as his eyes glided over the undisturbed pile of stones, but it caught in his throat when he spotted the wide opening torn in the earth a dozen feet away.

A flash of light behind him made Jack jump. He yanked the pistol from his side and spun, only to realize that the not-too-distant UTV's headlights had flicked on. Of course. He'd left the key turned on and Margaret must have managed to reset the modem. The yellow glow of the one headlight not pressed against the maple's trunk illuminated a patch of forest before it, its yellow rays catching and reflecting around Jack.

A dark shadow crossed through the pouring rain between him and the UTV.

Jack instinctually dropped to his stomach, pressing himself against the cold, wet stone of the ledge to avoid the swath of light. Another shadow passed between him and the light, and this time he made out its shape. It was tall, thick, and bipedal. Though it almost had the build of a man, it didn't move like one. Its motions were liquid, smooth, yet quick like an insect. It glided between Jack and the UTV, stalking low and predator-like toward the vehicle. The image of the pale, grimy hand that had emerged from the hole burned in Jack's mind, accompanied by the abject terror born from the distinct and irrefutable understanding of his position.

But he didn't have time for terror. Animals that gave in to terror died first. Jack knew this. He mustered every bit of control he could grasp and stilled himself completely. He watched the shadow as it dissolved into the trees, flanking the UTV, and he turned his mind to focus on the noises around him.

The patter of rain masked almost everything besides the rolling thunder and the smashing of his heart against his ribs, but after a few seconds he was able to make out another noise. Something was moving nearby. At first it was just the snap of a twig, then the slightest sound of suction as a foot lifted from the mud, then a muffled crumple as wet leaves compacted under weight. Whatever it was, it was stalking Jack, and it was close.

He knew he had no choice. They — whatever *they* were and however many of them there were — not only stood between him and the stuck UTV, but between him and the forest at large. He'd effectively cornered himself against the ravine's twenty-foot drop, and he only had three rounds left in his pistol. In a misplaced thought — one rimmed with a mixture of mirth and regret — he decided even he wouldn't place much of a bet on himself given the situation.

Another wet footfall, this time even closer, and Jack knew he had to act. He still held the element of surprise, maybe he could—

No. Not on his belly. Not pinned against a drop off and against unknown numbers. He needed to escape. It was his only option.

As slowly and silently as he effectively could, Jack holstered his pistol and slid backwards along the ground. The gurgling streams of water that washed over the smooth edge of the ravine covered his noise well, and soon his foot was hanging over the ledge, then his knees and his waist. Then his chest was flush with the edge, arms extended and grasping on to cracks in the stone. He froze as another branch snapped in the dark woods far closer than before. His heart pounded in his ears and he tried to stay calm as his one good foot gently scraped the ravine's high wall for a foothold. Finally, he found a jutting stone that would bear his weight, and he slowly released his grasp. In another few seconds, he was pinned to the stone wall halfway down the ravine's drop, one hand latched onto an old root and the other lodged in a cold crevice.

A thin line of water poured like a miniature waterfall from a divot in the ledge above. It cascaded down and beat against his shoulder. The drumming, gushing sound effectively muted the noise from above. It wasn't until he finally eased himself out of the tiny waterfall's path that he heard the distinct huff of something sniffing at the air overhead. He pressed himself as flush as possible to the stone, then a long shadow darkened the headlight's yellow glow directly above him.

Every muscle in Jack's body tensed. A sharp ache seized in his back as his muscles cramped. He ignored it, letting the muscle spasm and explode with pain as he fought to maintain his grip on the stone wall. The shadow above remained there for a long, agonizing minute, then slowly shifted away. Jack listened to the soft footfalls retreat, but still refused to move.

"…id it work?"

Margaret's voice shattered the world around him like a bomb. Then a second noise, a horrible, animalistic shriek, erupted from just over the ledge. Jack grabbed for the radio at his waist, but in his rush to do so, he lost his foothold. For a second, he was hanging from the old root. Then it broke. He hit the unforgiving ground of the ravine hard. The impact stunned him only for a second, then he was on his feet and sprinting toward the ravine's opening as fast as his prosthetic-marred gait could carry him.

"…ey Jack, you the…"

Without thinking, he tore the radio from his belt and threw it as hard as he could over the ravine's far ledge. As he stumbled in front of the oversized oak, he heard the telltale crash of something large charging toward him through the underbrush above. He made to turn, but another savage call rang out on the ravine's far end. He was cut off. With no other choice, Jack bounded forward and dropped blindly into the gaping hole in the earth from which his adversaries had emerged from.

The drop was only a ten feet or so, but still managed to bring a shooting pain to his knee as he splashed down on the wet stone floor. He rolled to his feet and stumbled away from the opening, pulling out his pistol and backing up until he felt a cold rock wall at his back. His heart hammered in his ears. He waited, not even daring to breathe. The room around him was filled with rolling blackness, and ankle-deep water passed over his feet in the lightest current. Jack tried to ignore the creeping knowledge that he was blind in here, turning his focus instead to the small opening above him. He leveled his barrel, waiting for some horrible thing to come clawing its way down. Minutes passed, only rainwater dribbled in through the opening. A flash of lightning spilled through the gap, illuminating the cave just enough for Jack to make out the four perfectly hewn stone walls surrounding him.

It wasn't a cave.

It was a tomb.

XXVIII

Margaret

"JACK, CAN you hear me?" Margaret asked for what must have been the tenth time. "The modem's been reset — the UTV should work… Talk to me if you can hear me."

Once more, there was no response.

Margaret looked over the dark attic around her. Dusty old furniture and antique knickknacks littered the damp space. Sitting anachronistically in the center of the hodgepodge of old junk was the complex box of buttons, wires, and blinking lights that made up the processor for the satellite mounted on the roof. Attached to it by a number of these cables was the GPS modem for the UTVs. It hummed rhythmically, and the little red light blinked above the word "disengaged."

"Jack," she said into the radio again, hoping that the signal went through. "I can't tell if it worked. If you can hear me, try to get somewhere high you can transmit from. I need to know if Bill's instructions for this hunk of junk were bullshit or not."

Still no response.

She swore under her breath, then rose and headed for the ladder that would take her down to the third floor. As she descended, her mind continued to circle back to Jack's last broken transmission. He'd said there was something out there with him, something he couldn't explain. Her mind raced to imagine what the seasoned outdoorsman might have come across that would lead to the amount of fear that she'd heard in his voice. She considered the wolf as she crossed to the stairwell. Could there have been more of them? Jack didn't take a rifle with him. Could he be cornered? Or maybe it wasn't an animal; perhaps he'd gotten lost or stumbled into some pit or over some ledge. The idea of him trapped out in the increasingly violent storm made her squirm.

As she reached the second floor, Margaret noticed the empty bowl still sitting outside of the room the doctor had claimed as a makeshift OR. She padded down the hall to grab it, thinking maybe another dose of the healing water might be in order, when she noticed the faintest rhythmic thump emanating from the wall. She stood still for a moment outside of the door, listening, then tried the handle. It was locked, so she rapped her knuckles softly on the old wood.

"Doctor Bianchi, it's Margaret. Open the door," she called gently.

There was a moment of shuffling, then the lock clicked, and the door slowly swung open. Bianchi sat on his rolling stool, grinning ear to ear and flourishing his hands toward Sophie.

"Oh, dear Margaret, look at you! You're almost as beautiful as the things I've witnessed in this room! Come, come!" He ushered her inside, shutting the door behind her.

Sophie lay on her back with her eyes clamped shut, a pillow propping her head up at an awkward angle. The light ring of bruising around her neck was still there, but the heinous lumps and gashes that had littered her body less than an hour prior had all disappeared. Margaret looked her up and down and spotted the source of the thumping. It was Sophie's foot, rolling lazily back and forth, rhythmically dropping its weight against the water-stained wallpaper.

"Why is she doing that?" Margaret asked.

The doctor chuckled. "Ask her yourself. She continues to drift in and out of consciousness."

Margaret glanced at him. He smiled and motioned her toward Sophie. Something about the situation felt wrong. She couldn't explain it, so she decided to bury it and ignore the creeping unease as she stepped forward.

"Sophie, can you hear me?" she asked, leaning over the supine young woman.

Sophie's clenched eyelids twitched, and her foot stopped. Margaret glanced down at the now still appendage, and when she looked back up, Sophie's eyes had drifted open. Her pupils lolled lazily over Margaret's features for a second before her mouth opened.

"…Margaret…" The word came out breathy and strained.

"I'm here, Sophie, it's okay." Margaret smiled as comfortingly as she could and reached out to clasp Sophie's hand. The limp digits were warm in her grip at first, but then Margaret felt a strange lump. She glanced down and saw that instead of a pinky finger, the hand bore a short, healed stump.

"…behind you…"

Sophie's warning came too late. A sharp pain nipped the skin between Margaret's shoulder blades, followed immediately by a hard pressure in her chest. She spun and lashed out, but the doctor had already backed away. A wide smile splayed across his face, and a long, thin syringe glinted in his hand.

"It will work quick," the doctor began, but Margaret lost the rest of his words as the muscles in her core began to seize and convulse. She tried to scream, but her lungs pulled taut, and she collapsed to her hand and knees. Violent seizures racked her body and she vomited watery bile onto the floor. Somewhere far away, the doctor laughed. Rage coursed through her blood and she made to rise, but the movement brought a horrible series of cascading spasms that sent her tumbling to the floor and twitching like an upturned beetle.

"There, there," the blurred blob that loomed over her muttered. "You should relax, Ms. Simmons. It will be more pleasant. Well, I mean, less *un*pleasant"

Margaret writhed against the encroaching darkness, spitting the froth from her lips and hissing hatefully at the rapidly disappearing blur of evil before her. The light faded further and further away as her body left her control. Then her vision let go, and all that she could sense was her own weakening heartbeat.

That's when she felt it.

The warmth.

It started small in her abdomen, gently easing outward from her center and soothing the spasming pain. It inched out along her limbs, ever so slowly easing the tortured muscles back into submission. She focused on the warmth, embracing it with everything she had, and after a moment, her vision started to return. The dirty pinewood floor stretched out from under her face. Thick, shallow divots ran along the soft boards where the doctor had rolled his stool, and she focused on them, forcing her vision to work itself out until she could make out the stool itself and the pudgy little man atop it. The warmth continued to spread, and soon she had weak control over her body. She strained to rise against the burning protest of her nerve endings.

The doctor let out a surprised squeak as she clambered to her hands and knees. She felt his foot on her side and he gave her a gentle shove that sent her sprawling painfully onto her back.

"Margaret, my God! That dose should have killed a horse!" the doctor said quietly, beside himself with awe. She glared at him as he seemed to reel his shock in and crossed to the table and began to prepare another needle. "No matter. I guess you'll just need a little extra, hm?"

The warmth was stronger now, and her muscles continued to battle the spasms with their newfound strength. Margaret fought to rise once more, clawing at the wall for support until she was on her feet. Bianchi eyed her with annoyance.

"Really?" he asked, pulling the full syringe away from the bottle and squirting a thin line of the clear liquid in her direction. "I'm not a fighter, Margaret, so if you'll please—"

She spit a wad of the foamy gunk that had accumulated in her mouth at him. He gave a cross look. She lashed out, sending a rolling table crashing to the floor at his feet.

His face shifted, taking on a look of determination. "Fine. Have it your way."

Bianchi brandished the syringe and advanced like a slow-moving bull. With only a few steps, he was upon her. A series of heavy left hooks pummeled her ribs, but she managed to secure a two-handed grip on the pudgy fist that held the needle. She absorbed the blows and braced against the wall, struggling to break the meaty little hand's control over the poison-filled needle. His punches stopped, and instead his free hand formed into a clamp that shot up between her arms, fixed around her neck, and squeezed. She coughed against the crushing pressure on her throat. Out of the corner of her eye, she saw something shift behind Bianchi. There was a loud thump as Sophie dropped off the side of the bed. She let out a pained yelp that sounded like the word "push."

Margaret did just that. Flexing hard to keep the syringe at arm's length, she shoved off the wall with all her strength to drive Bianchi back. He gave a surprised gasp as his feet caught against Sophie, and both he and Margaret were tumbling head over heels. Margaret hit the ground hard, and before she could recover, he was straddling her, pinning one of her arms, syringe raised over his head and a furious rage in his eyes. He snarled and brought the syringe arcing down like a dagger. It was all Margaret could do to throw up her one free hand in defense. The thick-gauged needle drove clean through her palm and erupted out the back of her hand. Cold poison sprayed in a thin stream across her chest as he pressed down on the plunger.

She wrenched her arm and managed to free her pinned hand, then immediately grabbed at his groin. He yelped as her grip tightened and twisted the small bulge in his pants, and he released the syringe as both his hands shot down to protect his crotch. Margaret screamed, closed her fist around the plastic tube that protruded from the center of her palm, twisted her wrist, and backhanded his chest as hard as she could. The needle that protruded from the back of her hand drove through the flesh between his ribs, and before he knew what had happened, Margaret sat up hard and headbutted the plunger.

The plunger compressed, emptying its clear contents into the doctor's chest cavity. Bianchi's eyes momentarily widened, then rolled back in his head as he collapsed off of her, his body rigid and twitching.

Margaret gasped in pain, kicking his body away from her before ripping the needle free from her hand. She scrambled across the floor to Sophie. The younger woman's eyes were open and vacant, but the tiniest bit of breath still seeped from between her lips. Margaret looked around desperately, finally spotting a sealed bag of intravenous saline solution that had been kicked under the table in the squabble. She grabbed it and used one of the half dozen scalpels that littered the floor to slice a line across the top, then pulled the cloth-bound stone from her pocket and dropped it into the bag. Liquid spilled over the top as it was displaced, and Margaret prayed that the salty concoction would work with the stone the same way that freshwater had.

She opened the valve at the bag's base and eyed the drip before putting it to her lips. After taking a cautionary drag of the lukewarm saline, the warmth inside her seemed to replenish. Confidently now, she propped Sophie's head up and slowly poured the liquid into her mouth. For a second, the half dead woman wheezed, then she let out a weak cough. Margaret coaxed her to drink more, and she did until the bag was nearly empty and the dark ring around her neck had dissipated.

"Holy fuck," Sophie finally rasped out once Margaret pulled the plastic baggie away. Margaret helped her to her feet, and after a moment of wobbliness, Sophie seemed to regain her balance. She immediately turned and kicked the still twitching doctor hard in the ribs. "You sick fucking shit," she snarled and launched another kick, then another as her strength came flooding back. Then she grabbed a pair of scissors from the table and raised them over her head.

Margaret caught her arm, and Sophie struggled against her, trying desperately to break free and finish Bianchi off, but she quickly gave in and collapsed into Margaret's embrace. Her shoulders convulsed as she sobbed openly into Margaret's chest. Margaret held her tight, staring over the poor young girl's head at the squishy ball of evil spasming on the floor.

"It's okay, it's okay… but we can't just execute him," Margaret whispered as she held a trembling Sophie close. "That's the difference between us and him. We don't do that. We can't do that." She squeezed Sophie and took in her surroundings. The white sheet on the table was blotted with red, and surgical utensils lay scattered across the floor, a number of them glistening with blood. She shivered as she tried to push away the thoughts of the horrors that the younger woman must have endured.

The stone caught her eye where it sat inside the saline bag on the floor. Maybe three ounces of liquid remained in the small plastic bag. Margaret grimaced.

"But we don't have to save him either."

XXIX

"I'M GONNA fucking kill him," Kevin hissed, wrestling against the ropes that bound him to the wingback chair.

Bill glanced over to where his valet was bound beside him. Kevin's muscles bulged out under his too-tight shirt, and thick, pulsating veins erupted along his temples as he struggled against his bonds. Bill hadn't even tried to yank against his own. Instead he focused his energy on his own strong suit: *thinking* his way out of the current situation.

That was the difference between him and Kevin, Bill thought with a sense of satisfaction. The former SEAL might have the skills and aptitude to become a furiously destructive beast. But Bill had something better — the shrewd intelligence necessary to guide the weapon that was Kevin.

"Calm down," he said as he eyed the stairwell Margaret had disappeared up twenty minutes before. "I have an idea."

Kevin stopped squirming and glanced over.

"Gre–eg!" Bill called out gently, his voice lilting the name into two syllables. He wrenched his neck as far as it would go, allowing him just the scantest view of the dining room. "Greg, are you there?"

Silence.

"Greg!" Bill called again, then sighed dramatically. *"Arjun!"*

A weak whimper.

"That's it." Bill gave Kevin a smug wink. "Arjun… Arjun? I know you're there."

Another whimper.

"Arjun, my young friend," Bill went on. "Have you ever heard of a dead man's switch? It's an old tactic that politicians and spies often employ to guarantee against assassination, but in this case, I believe it works just as well against mutiny. Did you really think I didn't prepare for a situation like this? I make a phone call every night at…" He paused his lie to glance at the tall grandfather clock. It read 9:47. "Ten PM," he lied. "And if I miss that call by more than five minutes, a close associate of mine back in the states places a call to a *very* inquisitive organization you might know as the FBI. Ever heard of them? I understand that they're well connected with the Mounties up here. With your status as a wanted fugitive, it would be a real shame if they were to learn your exact location."

There was another muffled whimper, then Greg shambled into sight. His eyes were red and brimming with tears. He glared at Bill like a wounded dog begging to be put out of its misery.

"Get a knife from the kitchen and cut us loose. Then I'll make the call and you'll buy yourself at least another day," Bill prompted.

Kevin grunted. "But the phone doesn't—"

"*Shut up!*" Bill hissed, giving him a glare before turning back to Greg. "Look, I don't think you can make it very far in this storm on foot, especially not with that arm. Are you really ready to face the consequences of your—"

"Get away from him, Greg," a woman's voice came from the top of the stairs.

Impossible.

Bill felt his jaw go slack as Sophie strode down the steps and into sight. "No, not possible," he breathed.

"Very possible, shitbreath," Margaret called as she descended behind Sophie.

"God*damn*" Kevin muttered as the two women came fully into view.

As obnoxiously blatant as it was, Bill couldn't help but agree with his valet's sentiment. Despite Sophie's matted, ragged hair and the splotches of dried blood that dappled her freckled cheeks, she was absolutely stunning. The jeans and button up shirt she wore were clean, but the mud and filth from the cave still clung to her skin. Even so, her pale flesh seemed to glow with a subtle radiance that amplified the leaf green of her glaring eyes. Behind her, Margaret stood tall and magnificently poised. Her short hair remained a spackled salt and pepper, and it juxtaposed perfectly against the beautiful, youthful face beneath it. Bill couldn't help but marvel at the pair of them, and he let his eyes drop down and back up, absorbing every curve as they went.

"Really?" Sophie looked at him in disgust.

"I, erm… Sophie, I thought you were beyond saving! How did— What? How?" was the best he could force out.

"Don't worry about that." Sophie waved him off and turned to Greg. He stared at her in silent horror, but he didn't flinch when she placed a gentle hand on his shoulder. "It's alright, Greg. Really. I understand that it was an accident. The stone we found, it hurt you, but it saved me. Now I get that it's frightening, but you need to try and let it heal you too."

His eyes fell to the floor and he muttered something close to affirmation.

Kevin spoke up. "Sophie, you need to untie us. That lunatic Jack—"

"You shut up, lackey," Margaret commanded. "Greg, what was Bill just saying about with the Mounties?"

Greg tensed.

Bill's mind raced, and when no brilliant idea burst forth, he blurted out the last card he held. "He's a fugitive from justice and wanted in the States! This lunatic ran down one of his classmates in a car—"

"No!" Greg shouted. His voice broke, and he coughed violently on the tail end of the word. A thin spattering of frothy blood landed on Bill's lap, and he recoiled with a squeal.

"Yes!" Bill shouted after he'd recovered from his disgust. "Yes, he did! He's a sick, savage little bastard!"

Greg tried to respond but was overcome by hacking coughs that sent him stumbling. Margaret caught him by the arm and ushered him away toward the kitchen.

"We have to see if this stone can heal the damage it caused," she insisted softly as they went.

Bill craned his neck to watch them enter the dining room. As Greg's coughing subsided, he stopped and called weakly back, "He's broke. None of us were ever going to get paid."

"Liar!" Bill screamed. A sudden hateful brine boiled up inside of him. How dare the uppity little piece of shit— "I should have had you thrown from that fucking cliff, you murderous little… Ass!"

Sophie slid a chair to face him and glared into his eyes. "Is it true? Are you broke?"

"Of course not!" he proclaimed.

"Bill…"

"How could you ask me that? These people are criminals! Imprisoning me on my own property, stealing the product of our hard work— Sophie, don't fall for such an obvious goddamned ruse!"

Sophie seemed unimpressed by his theatrics. "It makes sense… Actually, it makes a whole lot of sense. The shit gear, the desperate team, your little secrets… How much do you even have left? Less than a million? A hundred thousand? *Less*?"

Bill scoffed dramatically. The truth was actually far worse; he had maybe a few thousand in liquid assets, not counting at *least* a million in debt.

Sophie scoffed. "I imagine that'd be a real blow to a fella whose entire life revolves around having your little prick sucked on by money grubbers like Kevin here."

Bill glared at her and waited for Kevin's rebuttal, but there was none. He glanced over at his valet. Kevin was staring daggers back at him.

"Is this true?" Kevin asked.

"Of course not, Kevin. When have I ever lied to you—"

"Is this why I haven't been paid?"

"Kevin, no—"

"You fat old piece of shit! Is this true?" The veins began to bulge again in Kevin's temples and his voice grew louder with each syllable.

"You do *not* speak to me that way!" Bill snapped. "I am your goddamn employer—"

"You owe me over eight hundred grand, you fuck!" Kevin shouted. His chair flinched, and the wood flexed as he lurched at Bill.

"Don't let them turn you against me!" Bill insisted. Somewhere deep down he knew it was too late — the damage was done.

"How much is left, Bill?" Sophie asked flatly.

"Millions," he lied. "Tens of millions. Hundreds of fucking millions, and I'll spend every goddamn penny to destroy every conceivable facet of your life if you don't untie me right this goddamn second!"

Sophie massaged her temples, then leaned back and called to the kitchen, "Hey, Margaret. It looks like you're not getting that check after all."

Bill scowled and strained once more to look behind him. Margaret was gently goading Greg to rest his good hand in a large bowl spilling over with water. He resisted for a second before complying. Only once his hand was submerged did she leave him and rejoin the group in the foyer.

"Fine," she said as she entered the room and plopped down in a chair beside Sophie. "We'll take the artifact as payment."

"Like hell!" Bill growled and writhed against the ropes. They dug into his skin painfully and he immediately gave up. "You're nothing but a band of criminals. Low lives. Junky scum. Sophie, are you really going to lump yourself in with the likes of them?"

"*We're* criminal?" Margaret scoffed. "Says the man who defrauded a half dozen people into trespassing on First Nations land—"

"*What?*" Sophie cut in. Her brow furrowed as she spun to Bill. "You lied about the land agreement? You fucking *lied* about the goddamn land agreement? *Are you kidding me?* You arrogant, stupid old prick!"

"Sophie I…" he started, but his voice fizzled out.

"'*Sophie I*' what?" she demanded.

Bill racked his brain, but it had begun to ache from all the stress and screaming, and at this point he felt nearly ready to resign rather than go on. "Sophie, the truth is… they wouldn't sell it to me."

"So, we're just *here*? Illegally?"

"Yes. But they'll never find out—"

"Anything we find is their cultural property, you moron! We're not archaeologists here, we're graverobbers!"

"We can just say we found it somewhere else—"

"That's not how this works, you thick fuck!" Sophie leapt to her feet, her chair clattering to the ground. She paced across the room, clawing her fingers through her matted hair. "All of this, everything we've found is worthless!"

"Look at Margaret, Sophie!" Bill shouted. He couldn't believe how stubborn she was being. "Look at Margaret and then look in a fucking mirror! You were doomed! Fuck archaeology, fuck the journals and academia. Do you understand what we've found?"

Sophie glared at him. "I do. Better than you. That sick Italian fuck you hired showed me *exactly* what it's capable of. *And* what it's capable of turning people into."

Bill needed an excuse, a lie to buy him time to come up with something better. An idea began to develop in the back of his mind. He spit it out as quickly as it came to him. "Sophie, just stop and listen! Please, I'm not broke," he lied. "The Indians just wouldn't sell it to me." He turned to Kevin, who was still glowering at him. "Really, I swear. This whole project isn't underfunded due to lack of resources. I've earned the reputation of a man who pays his dues, and I stand by it! Things unraveled the way they did because I didn't want to draw attention to where we were. The Indians, they were unreasonable. They kept on about the curse, claiming it was their sacred land and they'd never sell it. I knew what we needed to do, and I knew a bigger team and more resources would lead to them discovering that we were—"

"What exactly was the curse?" Margaret cut in.

"— on their land," Bill continued, ignoring Margaret. "Then we would have been forced to abandon the dig, and we never would have found the stone. Please, Sophie, I…" His voice drifted off as Margaret rose and put her face an inch from his, narrowing her eyes.

"Ignore me again and it will hurt," she promised, and he believed her. "What. Curse."

"Ask Sophie," Bill muttered. "She's the expert."

"The lore I have on the area comes from two hundred years ago, Bill," Sophie said. "You were the one who spoke to the tribal elders. You didn't tell me there was an active oral tradition."

"What does it matter?" Bill sputtered. "It's all just Native nonsense. What *does* matter is that they wouldn't sell me the land. It was because of their hoaky traditions, not because I didn't have the cash!"

Margaret snorted. "I've started to open my mind up to stranger and stranger possibilities. So, Bill, if you don't mind, I'd like you to regale us with this *very specific folklore* regarding the exact area where we recovered a *bona fide* magic motherfucking rock we just pulled out of an impossible, manmade cave."

Bill wanted nothing more than to punch her. "Fine, fine. They claim this land is — what the hell did they call it? — *ripe*, I think. That it's like an Eden, filled will life and abundance, but that it's all a trap. That there's some sort of spirit here that takes the people dumb enough to be drawn in by the, well, *ripeness*."

"What kind of spirit?" Margaret hissed.

Bill sighed. "They said it was like… like the wendigo."

Sophie laughed, and Kevin gave a puzzled look, but Margaret's face went dark.

"The wendigo? What, like in a bad TV show?" Sophie chuckled. "You're literally grasping at straws, Bill. Is that the only Native American monster you know?"

"I swear, it's what they told me—" Bill started.

"I believe him," Margaret interrupted. She gave Sophie a look that melted the smile from the younger woman's face. "Yeah, sure it's become pop-culture by now, but the original legends of the wendigo came from Nova Scotia. Sophie, you told me that in your research you found that this place was supposedly cursed. Did the written record say anything about creatures like this?"

"It said a lot of things, and yeah, there were stories of monsters, just like with every curse… but Margaret…" Sophie raised an eyebrow.

"What the hell are you people going on about?" Kevin demanded.

"The wendigo," Margaret said. "Corrupted men who feast on the souls and bodies of the innocent. The tribes here believed that when a man grew too greedy, his soul would rot and fester into something inhuman and evil—"

"No," Bill muttered. "Not these people. These people said the creatures here came from another world. They thought they might have started as men, but by the time they arrived here, they were something else. They never had a *why*. They just feared them."

"Was there any mention of a wolf?" Margaret asked.

"I don't know." Bill didn't like the nervous shift in her voice. "What does it matter, it's all just—"

"They said the wolf would summon the creatures, didn't they?" Margaret stood and stepped back, her voice dropping to a whisper. "… *raise the guardians…*"

"I mean, something like that. I don't remember," he blurted out. The worry on her face made his stomach turn.

Margaret flashed Sophie a scared look before she grasped his shirt. "Where are the keys to the truck?" she demanded with a shake.

"In my room, in the second drawer of the dresser. What the hell is going on?"

Margert released him and spun to Sophie. "We need to find Jack. I think he's done something he shouldn't have, or at least he's about to. I think… I think he's in danger."

Sophie's expression mimicked Margaret's. "Okay." She nodded and turned to the dining room. "Greg, we need you to— Greg?"

Bill looked back. Greg was no longer seated at the table.

Sophie rushed into the dining room and glanced in the bowl. The color drained from her face as she turned back to them. "The stone… it's gone."

XXX

Greg

GREG TEETERED precariously atop the old bicycle and willed his burning legs to pedal harder. The night was terrifyingly dark, and the blinding onslaught of rain cut off what little vision he had. With no illumination other the occasional flash of lightning, he struggled to keep his bearing. He gripped the bike's handle with his left hand and shielded the leathery husk of his right under his hunched torso.

He was approaching the final hill before the road bisected the forest. What had hours before been a hard-packed dirt drive was now a muddy, slimy mess that clung to the bike's tires, causing him to exhaust himself in what should have been an easy ride. As he reached the top of the hill, he pulled to a halt. Gasping desperately for air, he glanced back at distant blips of the manor's floodlights as they cut through the rain, then checked his watch.

10:06.

The Mounties. If Bill had been telling the truth, they'd be finding out his location any minute now.

The stone weighed heavy in the pocket of his jeans. He placed his hand over the soaked fabric cautiously and was rewarded with slight wave of the radiant feeling he felt first in the cave and again when he'd grasped the stone underwater in the bowl.

The mangling of his hand was only the beginning of the suffering Greg had endured over the last several hours. Since pulling the stone from the water in the cave, his mind felt like it was fractured. His thoughts had come fleeting and half coherent, strung together in random order and fighting each other tooth and nail to dominate his ever-diminishing mind's eye. It was as if his ADD had been doubled, tripled, multiplied a thousand times even, to a point that he'd been unable to fully understand events as they occurred around him in real time. Bill's words had brought him back — only for a second — with his disgusting use of Greg's real name. But even that had been difficult to hold on to. And his insides… Whatever had happened to his hand was slowly spreading through his guts and lungs. They felt rotted, scabbed, and sore. Whatever this horrible stone had done to him, it was devastating.

But then Margaret had put his hand in that water and the pain inside had subsided. While the withered appendage at his side didn't reinflate with life, his mind had slowly begun to stitch back together and regain some modicum of reasoning. Even wrapped in a dishrag, the seemingly innocuous stone terrified him enough that he was reluctant to remove the it from the water with his remaining hand. But he'd done it for a good reason

His brush with murder that morning had made a number of things incredibly clear in his mind — namely that he was far too capable of evil to ever find solace in escape. He would never be happy, even if he'd managed to begin a new life somewhere far away.

No, he had one purpose now. One chance at redemption: he needed get this cursed thing as far from these people — or any people — as possible. He would find a way to destroy it, and if he couldn't do that, then he would bury it in the deepest, darkest hole he could find to ensure it was never found again.

Greg turned back to the muddy road ahead and let his tires slide down the incline. He'd never been an athlete or the outdoorsy type, but he always loved bicycling. As the road leveled out and he pumped his legs hard, the warm feelings emanating from the stone wove together with the gliding feel of the bicycle beneath him and he felt almost like a child again. Despite his arm, despite the newfound reliance on this monstrous thing, despite those who would hunt him down, and even despite the disgust he felt for himself, Greg laughed. He laughed and laughed as he pedaled through the mud, then began to cry at the same time. As the rain washed away his tears, he felt clean for the first time in as long as he could remember.

A jagged bolt of lightning arced through the sky. Its pale blue flash illuminated the slick path ahead. Greg slammed on the brakes. There was something in the road less than a hundred yards out, right at the mouth of the forest.

The bicycle slid in the mud, but Greg managed to maintain control and stay upright. The rain beat down heavily on his shoulders, deafening him to everything besides his own panting. Even so, he could have sworn he caught the echo of an animalistic warble from somewhere in the forest ahead.

Another lightning bolt ripped through the sky, and this time Greg saw the dark silhouette of the figure in full. It hulked at the edge of the tree line, glaring back at him, a crown of jagged antlers protruding from its head. Then the lightning was gone and the tree line was black once more.

Greg straddled the bike, completely frozen. The rolling thunder snapped him back to reality with a hard flinch.

Nope.

Nope.

Nope.

As calmly as he could, he rolled the bicycle in a half circle and began pedaling back toward the mansion.

Nope.

Nope.

Nope.

His mind clung blindly to the word, and he fought to stay calm as the mud sucked at his tires.

Nope.

Nope.

Nope.

A wild howl snaked into his ears through the heavy rain.

Nope.

Nope.

Nope.

He reached the small hill and allowed some of the panic to leak out, fighting to harness it into driving his legs harder. The primal tingle on the back of his neck took over, and his legs worked so furiously that, by halfway up the hill, they began to cramp. He lost control, and after another second his legs were flailing furiously against the pedals. With only one arm to control the handlebars, he toppled over as he crested the hill.

He landed hard in the mud and tumbled ten feet down the opposite side before coming to a sliding halt. Howling in pain, he fought to his knees and scraped the mud from his eyes, then looked down at the withered stump where his forearm had broken off. The break was clean, like charred wood, and didn't bleed. He whimpered and grasped at his leg to feel the stone through his pocket.

The lump was gone.

Adrenaline spiked into his blood and he stabbed his hand deep into the pocket.

He realized his mistake too late. In his tumble, the pocket of his jeans had folded upward, getting caught in his loose belt. As he shoved his hand into the tight crevice of fabric, the pocket unfurled, and he felt the smooth stone against his fingertips.

A wave of electric pain shot up his arm. As if jolted by a live wire, his hand reflexively clenched. For the smallest fraction of a moment, the stone felt warm. Then it began to burn. Greg fought with everything he had in him to rip his hand away, but his body didn't respond. He kicked with his legs, tumbling through the mud and shrieking in agony as the burning intensified. His legs clenched tight, every fiber of muscle in them seizing in violent spasms. Unable to even writhe, Greg lay face down in the mud, curled in a knotted ball as his skin burned and shriveled.

The glow of the manor's distant lights caught in the corner of his unmoving eyes. The miniscule orbs taunted him through the rain as his jaw clenched so hard that his teeth cracked and shattered. His lungs deflated one final time as his shoulders contorted forward so violently that the bones themselves began to pop and crack.

A light erupted from the darkness beyond his vision. It was dim at first but steadily grew brighter as his body collapsed horribly inward toward death.

XXXI

Margaret

"DO YOU feel that?" Sophie asked over the whirring of the truck's wipers and the hum of its revving engine. The storm outside raged harder than ever, dumping torrents of water over the windshield as they drove.

Margaret nodded. She knew exactly what Sophie was talking about. It had started during the tail end of their interrogation of Bill as little more than a distant, warm pulse that seemed to pull her body to the west. Now, as they tore down the muddy lane away from the carriage house, it was growing stronger.

"It's like a sonar, or a radar," Sophie went on. "I don't know how to explain it, just… I feel like it's directing us toward it, you know?"

"Yeah," Margaret agreed, pressing harder on the gas pedal. The worry that perhaps this stone wasn't so much a cure-all as it was a new form of dependency had weaseled its way into her mind. Having just broken one habit, all she could do was hope desperately that she hadn't committed to another.

"I… fuck. Do you think this means we're going to become reliant on it?" Sophie asked, mirroring Margaret's concerns. "I'll be honest, as amazing as it is, I'm more than a little afraid of wha— Watch out!"

Margaret slammed on the brakes. The truck shuttered as the antilock system kicked on. They slid to a jarring halt in the mud. A toppled bicycle glinted in the headlights.

"Son of a bitch— You think he saw us coming and bailed?" Sophie wrenched open the door and leapt out into the rain, calling loudly, "Greg! Greg, we're not going to hurt you! We need you to come back! Greg!"

Margaret remained still. Something else had caught her eye: a dark, crumpled mound a few yards in front of the overturned bike. It twitched slightly in the beam of the headlights, and after a long second, she realized what it was.

"Jesus Christ…" She shoved open the door and leaned out over the road. Heavy rain pummeled the back of her head and her stomach heaved as she puked onto the road. Almost instantly, Sophie was back in the cab grabbing her shoulder.

"What is it? Are you okay?" Sophie demanded.

Margaret spit the last of the burning vomit from her mouth, then leaned back up and raised a trembling finger to point.

Sophie's eyes followed her motion. "Oh my God…"

Greg, what was left of him at least, lay half buried in the mud. His corpse was curled in the fetal position, shriveled and collapsed inward as if all of the moisture and fluid had been sucked out of his body.

They approached him together, the warm waves of radiating sonar growing stronger with each step. Margaret was able to make out the exposed skin of his arms and face which glinted blue-black in the pouring rain and was creased with a thousand horrible, cascading wrinkles. It was as if he'd been mummified, she thought, conjuring the images of thousand-year-old blackened corpses pulled from peat bogs of northern Europe.

"He must have touched it again…" Sophie's voice was distant. "Why would he… What was he…?"

"I doubt he did it on purpose," Margaret muttered. She bit her tongue and decided to accept the image before her. This wasn't the time to deal with it. She did her best to steel her mind.

Looking over his form, she saw where his shriveled arm emerged from his pocket. Doing her best to move smoothly and quickly — and to keep from once again vomiting — she pulled a small folding knife from her own pocket and cut one of her sleeves away at the shoulder. Using the sleeve like a loose glove, she approached the withered carcass and gently pulled what had been Greg's hand from its fabric encasing. It slid out easily, and she spotted the glimmer of the stone clenched in the wiry, mummified hand. Using the knife, she pried at the blackened fingers. It took a decent amount of pressure before they broke away at the joints. The sound of the snapping digits reminded Margaret of the suction pop that came from separating chicken bones, except these were loud enough to be heard over both the pouring rain and the grumble of the truck engine. A coughing gag escaped as she wrapped the stone in the sleeve and stuffed it in her pocket.

"I hope it was fast," Sophie said softly.

"I'm sure it was," Margaret lied, trying to sound reassuring. She glanced back at the younger woman and tried to form a reassuring smile, but only managed a dour grimace. Sophie stood hunched and exhausted in the pouring rain with a pained look of regret splayed across her face. She stared at what was left of Greg and made to say something, but then her eyes snapped up and went wide. Margaret followed her gaze out through the sheets of cold rain, to the crest of the hill above — to the hulking figure silhouetted against the stormy sky atop it.

"What the fuck is that?" Margaret breathed, more to herself than to Sophie.

A horrible shriek echoed from the darkness behind them. Margaret spun around and saw a blurred shape bounding across the road in the red glow of the truck's taillights. Every ounce of adrenaline dumped into her bloodstream, and her head snapped back to the hilltop.

The figure was gone.

"Run!" Her scream was hoarse and panicked. She was sprinting hard through the mud before she'd even made the conscious decision to do so. Sophie was a blur in her peripherals, and the two women simultaneously leapt into the open doors of the truck. Margaret slammed the still-running vehicle in reverse and jammed her foot down on the gas. The engine roared and the tires spun in the sucking mud, but the truck didn't move.

"Go! Fuckin' go! Go! Go! Go!" Sophie's screams came deafening and rapid fire. She spun around in the cab, searching the darkness for the figures.

"We're stuck!" Margaret screamed back.

"Go forward!"

Margaret slammed the truck in drive. Once again, the tires spun, but only for a second before they caught. With a jolt, they were swerving around Greg and the bicycle, picking up speed as they made for the forest. As they crested the hill, the high beams washed over where the road cut into the forest, clearly illuminating the two thick tree trunks that had been torn down to block it.

"No, no, no, no…" Sophie whimpered as Margaret wrenched the wheel and the truck spun in a dizzying semi-circle.

"No choice!" Margaret grunted through gritted teeth. She gunned the truck back toward the manor.

Sophie spouted off a string of hysterical curses. Margaret focused her attention on the road but couldn't help anxiously eyeing the growing porch lights. Even through the fog of adrenaline, she knew she had to make for the rifle hidden behind the door of her room. It was their best shot. She just needed to get to it.

A burst of lightning lit up the sprawling lawns.

"There! I saw one, ahead on the right!" Sophie pointed.

Margaret glanced over. Despite the darkness and the pouring rain, she caught a pale blur of movement closing quickly from the side. She swerved away from it, but the truck shuttered, and she jolted sideways in her seat as something heavy impacted their flank. There was a loud thump and the shocks bounced.

"It's in the bed!" All self-control had abandoned Sophie's screams.

The manor was still too far, but the carriage house wasn't.

"Buckle up," Margaret ordered as calmly as she could, yanking the wheel to the right. She felt Sophie's terrified eyes burn into the side of her head, then she heard the belt unraveling and the click as it was secured.

As she reached for her own belt, the cab's rear window shattered, showering Margaret with shards of glass. A searing pain stabbed through her shoulder.

But it was too late.

The headlights dilated against the carriage house doors like rapidly closing portals. There was a deafening crash, and the world exploded into darkness.

XXXII

Bill

"WHAT THE hell was that?" Bill tried to gauge the distance of the echoing roar outside. As best as he could tell, it had come from the carriage house. "Did they just wreck my goddamn truck?"

Kevin didn't so much as glance up as he was still fidgeting with the ropes that bound his hands to the armrests.

Bill glowered at him in the dull yellow lamplight. "Didn't they teach you how to escape situations like this when you were in the Navy?"

Kevin grunted and flexed harder.

Bill's mind wandered back to the traces of a documentary he'd seen years before. "SERP? SEVR? What was that stupid acronym?"

"SERE," Kevin snarled. "And it's been a really long fucking time since I went through that course, asshole."

"You know I'm not actually broke, Kevin, so maybe remember who's paying you—"

Kevin glared at him. "Don't you fuckin' lie to me, Bill. I just can't believe I didn't see it before. No, I did, I just didn't believe you'd be fucking stupid enough to try to screw *me*."

Bill started to say something bitter but held back. He was too tired to keep arguing. His back ached from the chair, his feet had fallen asleep what felt like hours ago, and now Sophie had turned on him and, together with that bitch Margaret, robbed and abandoned him.

"I'll tell you what, Kevin. Clearly you feel that you can no longer take me at my word — despite the years of loyalty and witnessing my timeliness in paying both my employees and debts — so I'll strike you a new deal."

"I don't want to fucking hear it, Bill. You owe me eight hundred grand, and I'm going to get it out of you one way or another."

"The vacation property in the Dominican," Bill offered desperately, though in reality the jungle villa had been sold off months before. "It's worth at least that, and it's yours if you help me get out of here and recover that stone."

"I don't want a fucking vacation property, Bill. I want my fucking money!" Kevin snapped, and the armrest gave a splintering creak as he flexed against it. He grunted and ripped it the other way, drawing another crunch as it contorted.

"Yes!" Bill exclaimed. "Good, break free and then cut me loose. They can't have gotten too far—"

"Shut the fuck up," Kevin growled and ripped harder until his arm broke free. He grabbed a half empty glass from the side table and shattered it on the floor. After stretching to retrieve the longest shard he could find, he began sawing away at the cords that held his other arm.

"There has to be something, some *way* for you to trust me, Kevin." Bill felt a slight tremble in his own voice. He'd watched Kevin work over an uppity Native politician in Brazil when they'd been denied a dig permit, and he had no intention of being on the receiving end of that treatment.

Kevin's other arm broke free, and he began on the long cord that held his feet to the chair legs.

"Come on, what do you want? You say it and I'll make it happen." Bill tried not to sound like he was pleading, but he knew he was doing a poor job.

"We'll split it, and anything that comes from it," Kevin grunted without looking up. "Eighty-twenty."

"The stone?"

"Obviously."

"Fine. Hell. I'll give you thirty if you throw that bitch Margaret off that cliff," Bill said.

Kevin paused his furious sawing and looked up incredulously. "No, you moron. *You* get the twenty percent."

"*What!*"

Kevin gave a mean laugh. "Fine, I'll take it all. Greedy old shit."

"You wouldn't even know what to do with it," Bill jeered. "Without my connections, you're just a regular old thug for hire. Don't think for a second that you could just cast me aside like some common—"

The front doors' latch clicked, and Kevin froze, then quickly sat back up as if he was still tied in place.

"Are you serious? The ropes are on the floor, you idiot! Just finish the damn cut!" Bill whispered. Kevin shushed him and sat completely still.

"*Fucking idiot...*" Bill muttered as the foyer's front door slowly creaked open. He cleared his throat, then called out, "Sophie, did you manage to find Greg? I shouldn't need to impress upon you that it's extremely important that we recover the stone. The young man is a *murderer*, after all. There's no saying what lengths he would go to escape with that artifact."

There was no response. Furthermore, no one crossed the threshold. The door sat ajar, and while neither man could see who had opened it, it was clear from the long shadow cast into the room that someone was standing just outside. Bill motioned for Kevin to finish the nearly severed rope at his feet. Kevin gave a short, furious headshake in response.

"Sophie, come on, are we done playing games yet? There's nothing you've done that can't be forgiven," Bill called out, continuing to urge an unwilling Kevin. "We need to work together, like professionals. Surely you remember what that means, being a professional?" The shadow shifted slightly, but still no response. Bill felt the irritation begin to leak into his voice. "Goddamnit, Sophie! I gave you my trust, I supported you, I masterminded this whole thing, and this is how you repay me? Come on, Sophie! My fuckin' back hurts! Let me out of this goddamn chair and we can talk like civilized—"

A gnarled, paper white hand two sizes too big snaked in from the darkness and grasped the door frame.

"What the fu—"

Bill's words seamlessly transformed into a high-pitched shriek as the shadow lengthened and a hulking figure slipped through the doorway. Kevin let out his own yelp before he fainted, his arms drooping over the sides of his chair and his chin flopping limply to his chest. Bill gasped at the air even after his lungs had emptied, like a fish yanked from the depths of the sea. All of his screams seemed to have left him. His jaw began to tremble violently and his eyes welled with tears.

The creature slunk into the shadows that edged the dimly lit foyer, stalking a wide circle around its perimeter. It paused in a deep crouch just outside the glow of the lamps and glared at the two bound men. Bill felt the primordial vulnerability of a prey animal as it stared at him, studying him with burning eyes that sat recessed — yet somehow still bulbous — near the center of the gaunt face. The whites weren't white at all, just inky black orbs centered by blood red pupils.

Jutting out beneath the sunken eyes and below the twin, slitted nostrils, the lipless mouth eased open in what Bill could only imagine as a horrifying smile — revealing a row of pearly human-like teeth behind a row of yellowed dog-like canines.

The skin of its body was stretched pale and paper thin over its naked figure. Its flesh was nearly transparent in the way the purplish veins and bulging maroon muscles shone through their tight wrapping. Erupting from its shoulders were a series of uneven, bony, ochre-brown growths. They jutted out of the waxen flesh of its back into horn-like points from the ridges of its shoulders all the way up its neck and to the base of its skull.

To Bill's abject horror, he realized that — despite its horrendous features — this thing still appeared to be more human than not.

"My God, who art in heaven, hallowed be Thy name…" Bill began, his voice shaking and his mind scrambling to remember the prayer. But in that moment, a large part of him already knew that the mere existence of the creature standing before him meant that there was no God.

The creature stood where it was and let out a low, hoarse grunt. Bill's stuttering prayer morphed into pleading screeches he couldn't control. An icy chill ran up his spine in waves as every bit of adrenaline flooded his veins. His fight or flight senses demanded that he run. But he couldn't run, so instead his bound limbs just flopped around outside of his control. He called Kevin's name, then Sophie's, then Jack's, then Bianchi's.

The hoarse grunt came again, then again and again in rapid succession, and as Bill began to scream for Margaret, he realized what the noise actually was. Whatever this demonic hellspawn was, it was laughing.

There was a clambering upstairs, and a string of Italian curses rang out from the stairwell. Bill's screams dropped to a whimper, but he couldn't tear his eyes away from the monstrosity before him.

"Emilio," Bill gasped between sobs. "Dr. Bianchi, help me, please…"

"*Che cazzo… che cazzo è quel rumore?*" the doctor drawled. Bill heard him stumbling at the head of the stairs, then curse again. "Where girl… *cagna…*"

The grunting laugh cut off, and the creature dropped to a crouch again. While it had entered the room with the strides of a man, it now moved like a predator, melting into the shadows below the stairwell.

"Emilio, help me," Bill begged. "It's here. Help, help please…"

The doctor grunted drunkenly then called down, his voice somewhere between a drawl and a shout. "*Fanculo!* Where is— Where is the bitch? *Dove…* Where?"

The doctor was useless, drugged or something. But the monster seemed preoccupied with him. Bill tried to tear his eyes away and focus on controlling his breathing. That was the first step. Then he needed to think. He needed to escape.

"Sophie, where is Sophie…" the doctor groaned, stumbling halfway down the stairs and into view.

The bonds that held Bill's hands were too tight to budge, but Kevin was almost free. Perhaps Kevin could kill the thing — or at least distract it and give Bill the chance to get away. Bill turned to his former valet. Kevin lay limp in his chair, eyes still pinned shut. Bill needed to wake him up. How? How do you wake someone who's fainted?

Noise?

No.

Salts?

No.

Water?

Yes!

Bill sucked at his tongue and tried to gather enough spit to launch at Kevin's face, but his mouth was dry. He thought of food. Of cake and candy, of everything sweet his mind could muster. After a moment, he gathered just enough saliva for one good shot. He sucked in a breath and took aim.

The wad of spit splattered against Kevin's eyelid and dripped down his cheek, but he didn't flinch.

"*Stupida puttana!*" The doctor moaned before tripping over the last few steps. He fell, sprawling to the foyer's floor.

"Kevin, wake up, please!" Bill begged. His eyes were blurred with tears.

"Sophie!" Bianchi groaned, rolling onto his stomach only a few yards from Bill and squirming in a pathetic attempt to stand.

Bill willed himself not to look, but he couldn't help his eyes from drifting over the doctor's prone form, and then up to the terrifying creature as it emerged from the shadows below the stairs.

XXXIII

Sophie

THE PUNGENT stench of gasoline wove through Sophie's nostrils as she stirred. She was strapped down in a cushioned seat with a repetitive dinging echoing in her ears. A lilting fog of dizziness and confusion muted her immediate memory. As her bleary eyes cracked open one at a time, they were met with dull, pulsing red lights, and she slowly began to remember what had happened.

The bit of windshield that remained was an explosion of spiderwebbed glass. A thick layer of shattered wood boards covered the truck's frame where the windshield had been. Dribbling streams of rainwater leaked between the broken pieces of the carriage house and splattered down on Sophie's trembling thighs.

We're stuck.

"Margaret," she groaned, turning to the driver's seat — but Margaret was gone. Mustering her strength, Sophie wrestled to undo the seatbelt. The buckle clicked open and the straps slithered back into place, revealing thick, painful welts where they had yanked tight against her skin in the impact. Raising her hand to massage the burning stripe across her chest resulted in a sharp pain — she was pretty sure her collarbone was broken.

She struggled to find the door handle as more and more of her senses started to flood back. Her hand grasped the latch and jerked it, but it didn't budge. She tried again, and again, a rising sense of panic driving her harder each time as the memory of the horrifying hilltop figure rematerialized.

It took her longer than it should have to realize that the door was pinned and unmovable. Looking out the driver's side window opposite her — at the shattered cross section of an old wooden wall — she understood why. The truck had smashed clean through the front doors of the old carriage house, missed the deconstructed UTV and various items within, and penetrated the thick boards of the back wall, only coming to a sudden and jarring halt when it collided with one of the several ancient boulders that lay just outside the rear of the building.

Sophie winced in pain as she made to shimmy over the center console, then froze as a flurry of broken glass cascaded from her hair. The jagged sprinkles brought with them the sudden image of the thing in the truck bed, and she spun back in terror to stare out the broken rear window. To her immediate relief, the bed was empty. In the flashing red glow of the hazard lights, she could make out the source of the stink. The five-hundred-gallon steel reservoir full of gasoline that had once sat against the carriage house's inner wall had toppled onto its side, and the dusty old floorboard around it shone dark and wet.

"Oh, shit…"

She kicked at the boards that covered her only avenue of escape. The boards themselves were thin, but there were enough of them stacked over the opening that they did not give easily. She kicked them apart until there was a small gap, but she still had to wrestle the remaining ones in order to squeeze through it. After a brief struggle, she was rolling off the crumpled steel hood, then over the edge of the short boulder it rested against.

Landing shoulder first in the soaked grass was excruciating, but she was free.

"Margaret, where are you?" she called, fighting to her feet. Her head was spinning and her entire body ached. The pounding rain left her skin clammy and frigid, and the warmth she'd felt in her core had dissipated to a dull throb. It pulled her east, toward the not-so-distant cliff.

Thunder rumbled overhead as she called for Margaret again, this time louder. No response came from beyond the shimmering wall of rain that marked the limits of the hazard lights' pulsing red glow. She fumbled with the elastic nylon strap of the headlamp that hung around her neck, pulling it up to sit snug on her forehead and flicking on the bright light. It cut a rain-stippled path through the darkness and illuminated Margaret's body. She lay on the ground ahead of Sophie in a crumpled heap, a long, pale mass clinging to her shoulder.

Looking back at the totaled truck, Sophie immediately understood; Margaret had been thrown clean in the collision.

"Margaret!" Sophie shouted, bolting toward her.

However, what had started off as a sprint ended in a sliding halt a dozen feet short, when the headlamp's beam illuminated another shadowy figure splayed out just beyond Margaret. It squirmed to life in the light, then recoiled and blocked its grotesque face with a spidery hand.

"Margaret, behind you!" Sophie screamed as loud as she could, unable to break her gaze from the creature. It struggled to rise. "Margaret!" Sophie screamed again, her hands slapping her hips and sides, searching desperately for some sort of weapon.

The creature staggered to its feet. Despite the headlamp, the darkness and rain were so thick that Sophie could scarcely make out more than the figure's shape, but its jagged movements alone struck a chord of fear in her heart. It stood to its full, hulking height like some terrifying abomination of a man. A freakshow monstrosity born of hellish nightmares. Emitting a whistling howl, it groped at the ragged mess of torn skin and exposed ligaments that hung where its arm had been. Blackish blood poured from the wound and mixed with the rain, and only then did Sophie realize what the gray-white hunk of matter hanging off Margaret's side was — the creature's dismembered arm.

The rolling grumble of thunder boomed from the distant forest behind Sophie. She tried to shout for Margaret again, but it came out only as a whimper. The creature answered back with a piercing shriek, and the dome of its head glistened in the rain as it leaned toward her, leveling the circle of antlers that capped its skull. The rumble of thunder grew louder, and then the creature charged.

Sophie stood transfixed, locked in horror as the freakishly long legs carried the beast forward in massive bounds, picking up speed as the jagged crown of spikes grew rapidly closer in the headlamp's light. She withdrew into herself, pinning her eyes shut and imagining the comfort of her bed one last time as the thunder grew to a roar.

The noise that filled her ears next was one she'd never heard before and would never hear again. At its deepest level, it was a meaty thud, like a baseball bat might make when struck against a free hanging slab of beef. Woven into the thud was another noise — the sharp crackle of a dozen bones breaking almost simultaneously. Lastly, and most horribly, was the howling scream that followed. It was guttural and rasping, and it rang with so much terror that Sophie wondered if it had come from her own mouth.

The roar of the thunder cut to a gentle idle. She stood frozen for a second, staring into the reddish black of her eyelids, and wondered if this was death. Then Jack's hoarse voice cut through the rain, "Eat that, you son of a bitch!"

Her eyes snapped open. Jack clicked on the headlights as he climbed out of the idling UTV, pistol in hand. He bore down on the wheezing pile of broken creature before it. It hissed as he leveled his gun, then flinched hard as the deafening crack of a gunshot rang out. Jack gave it a stiff kick.

"Jack..." she managed to get out.

He spun, pistol raised. Then their eyes met, and his face went slack as he lowered the gun.

"Sophie, holy shit! You… you're okay? How?" he stuttered.

She ran to him, diving into him. He wrapped her in his arms while she buried her face in his soaked shirt and gasped for the words to explain. But there were none.

She was alive.

Holy shit, she was alive.

"There might be more," she finally got out.

"Yeah. Two more," Jack confirmed, pulling away and dragging her toward the UTV. "And I've only got two bullets left. We need to get inside and mount a defense. Where the hell are the others?"

Sophie struggled to keep up with his words. "Greg's gone, and Margaret—"

"What the fuck happened to Greg?" Jack demanded.

She took a deep breath. "He's already dead, and Margaret…" she started, but rather than try to spew out the jumble of words, she just pointed.

Jack followed her gesture and muttered a curse. He pushed Sophie into the back seat and pulled the UTV around beside Margaret's limp form.

"Margaret, can you hear me?" Jack called as he climbed out of the seat. Sophie joined him and together they eased Margaret up. Her breath came shallow, but it was there.

"Fuck, come on, not again." Jack growled furiously, wiping the smeared blood from a gash across Margaret's forehead.

Sophie ran her hands over the ragged wounds that covered Margaret. The horn-like growth that extended from the palm of the creature's dismembered arm was still buried deep in Margaret's shoulder. Sophie moved to yank it free, but Jack stopped her.

"We need to get inside. We can't stop the bleeding out here," he insisted, then looked nervously around in the darkness. "We can't defend ourselves out here either. Help me load her in the UTV."

Sophie felt the rhythmic pulse emanating from the stone in Margaret's pocket as she helped haul her into the back of the small vehicle.

"Jack, we need water."

"What?"

"I know what we have to—" she started, but her words were cut off as a bloodcurdling scream echoed from the manor.

XXXIV

Bill

THE CREATURE'S foot shot down with swift precision. Doctor Emilio Bianchi's brains exploded across the grooved hardwood like thick red chunks of rotten fruit.

Bill didn't even realize he was screaming until his lungs pulled taut. The noise roused Kevin, who mumbled something and looked over lazily. His eyes widened to saucers at the sight of the creature before them. He lashed out in a panicked fit. The few unsevered strands of rope holding his legs ripped away and he was free.

"Get it, Kevin! Kill it! *Kill it!*" Bill screamed.

Kevin's horrified face tore from the creature to Bill, then back to the creature. Without a word, he grabbed Bill's chair and heaved it toward the monstrous thing. Unable to slow his fall, Bill was launched headfirst into the ground. His head slammed into the floor hard enough that his ears rang, but he could still hear Kevin's heavy footfalls sprinting away into the dining room, through the kitchen, and up the servants' stairwell. They thumped along the second-floor hallway and were punctuated by a slamming door and the grating noise of shifting furniture.

The creature loomed over Bill, rainwater and saliva dribbling down onto his back. The staccato grunting of the thing's laugh started once more.

"No!" Bill's shrieks rang higher than he'd ever known himself capable of. "No! Please, no!"

It stepped forward and reached for him, its wet arm glistening like fish scales. Tendons and purple muscles squirmed under their thin encasing as its reach bypassed Bill's face and gripped the back of his chair. With an easy movement, it hauled the chair upright, bringing the still tightly bound Bill up with it.

"Stop! Please, no! Somebody, please…" Bill's screams came weaker and weaker as the creature's hand withdrew, bony claws gently brushing his cheek as it went. It squatted, its shrunken face drawing level with Bill's. The wide slit of a mouth pulled tight and the tiny red pupils scanned over Bill's features. Finally, they came to rest on his eyes.

"*Carrnegk* …" a thin, rasping voice erupted from its throat.

"Wha… What do you want?" Bill pleaded breathlessly.

The lipless mouth sneered, exposing the row of human teeth recessed behind its fangs. It hissed the same broken word again, then slowly tilted its head downward. Bill followed the movement, too terrified not to, and saw the jagged clawed fingertip scratching an uneven oval in the floorboard.

"I don't know what— The stone! The stone, you want the stone, of course you do. It's not here; they took it! Please, I promise you it's not here!" Bill blurted out.

The skin surrounding the creature's lidless eyes tightened in what appeared to be some bastardized version of a squint. It bared its teeth and leaned closer.

"Please…" Bill begged, turning his head to avoid its hot, fetid breath.

"*Carrnegk…*" it growled again, the word barely audible.

Bill's shoulders shook as he began to sob. He was in hell, and this thing was the devil itself.

"Bill, are you okay?" Jack's voice drifted through the open front door alongside the patter of heavy rain.

The creature reared back. Suddenly Bill's chair was skittering along the floor until he sat like a shield between the creature and the front door. The points of its claws dug into the sides of his neck as it gripped his throat, and he could feel its beating pulse in the fleshy webbing between its thumb and forefinger.

"Bill?" Jack's voice came again from the darkness outside. "I, uh, I can't help but notice you're not alone in there, bud."

Bill whimpered, but when he didn't respond, the grip tightened. "Please, no!" he coughed out. As he spoke, the hand loosened. Bill understood. "I… I think it wants me to speak, to negotiate…" he called out between gasping sobs.

"Were you talking to it just now? Is that what I saw?"

"No— Yeah, no, it— it said something, something— uh, something like *cardigan?*"

"What?" Jack called back incredulously.

"*Carrnegk…*" the thing hissed.

"*Carrnegk!*" Bill repeated obediently. "It says *carrnegk.*" He let out a whimper. "Please tell me you know what the fuck that means."

"Afraid I don't, bud," Jack replied. "I don't suppose it speaks English?"

"*Carrnegk!*" the creature hissed, squeezing tight enough that Bill felt the warm trickle of blood run down the side of his neck.

"*Carrnegk,* Jack!" Bill cried out. "Fucking *carrnegk,* man! Please!"

"Okay, Bill." Jack stepped slowly into the manor, pistol raised.

The creature yanked Bill's head back against the chair with its free hand, exhibiting its clawed grip on his throat.

"Please, Jack, it's from hell. You can't… you can't just *shoot* the devil. Please, just figure out what it wants…" Bill begged.

Jack took a deep breath and eased the pistol's hammer back. "Good luck, Bill."

"No!" Bill's shout was cut off by the deafening gunshot. The hand whipped away from his neck, and he felt a stream of hot blood cascade down onto his chest. Another shot rang out. Behind him, the creature thudded against the wall and let out a bloodcurdling shriek. Jack advanced quickly, drawing the hammer back once more as he bore down on the creature.

"Shoot it again!" Bill screeched. "Finish it!"

The monster bounded across the room behind him, and Bill heard the crash of glass as it leapt through the dining room's bay windows and disappeared into the night.

Sophie piled in the door, a limp Margaret slung over her shoulder, and Jack slammed it behind her.

"Get her in the tub upstairs," Jack commanded, then crossed back, and with three quick slices of his Bowie, Bill was free. "Help her. Now!"

Bill tried to stand but his legs were wobbly. He clutched at the blood draining from under his chin and realized his injuries. Four jagged tears opened the flesh along the front of his neck. "Oh God, Jack, oh my God. My throat — my artery! I'm going to bleed to death!"

Jack grabbed Bill's face and jerked it left, then right, checking the wounds. "They're superficial," he insisted.

"You're just saying that—" Bill cried.

Jack silenced him with a hard slap. "Get the fuck upstairs. There are more of them out there."

XXXV

Jack

"WHATEVER THOSE things are, it looks like the runoff from the stone was keeping them alive," Jack called over his shoulder as he darted into his room on the second story. He paused for a moment, gathering his bearings and trying to work over all of the information he had.

Greg was dead.

Bianchi was a pile of mucky brains.

Margaret was on the brink.

His shaking fingers fumbled with the rifle case's latches. He forced himself to take a breath and slow down.

Slow is smooth.

Smooth is fast.

His father's smoky voice echoed the mantra through his head. As the trembling subsided, he managed to calmly unclasp the latches. The small box of pistol ammo was empty by the time he finished reloading the revolver, but he had enough of the massive 45-70 hollow-point to fill a soaked pocket. Jack tried to focus. There were two routes the crea- tures could take to reach them on the second floor: the main stairwell in the front, and the servants' stairwell to the rear. If Jack took up a position in the bathroom doorway, he would have a vantage on both stairwells while Margaret healed. Then they could egress to the third floor and funnel the creatures upward through the one main stairwell that led there. Blowing one of the creature's brains out across the lawn had worked well enough, so if he could get clean shots on a target, then maybe — *maybe* — between his 45-70 and the deer rifle that he'd given Margaret, they stood a chance.

Slinging the stubby lever action rifle over his shoulder, he darted back into the hall to help Sophie carry Margaret up the steps to the second floor.

A frantic Bill had already plugged the tub's drain and drawn the tap in the bathroom at the end of the hall. Now he stood stammering in front of the tarnished old mirror, nervously examining the thick scrapes on his neck.

"Move, Bill!" Jack commanded, shoving past him and helping Sophie to ease Margaret into the chipped, clawfoot bathtub.

Sophie grabbed a hand towel and carefully extracted the stone from Margaret's pocket, then placed it below the rising waterline.

The bare bulb that hung overhead illuminated the remains of the spiked arm that still clung to Margaret's shoulder. A ragged line of pale flesh and blackish tissue hung where Jack had cut it at the elbow, but the unnaturally large hand remained attached to her shoulder by the ochre-streaked growth that extended from its palm. Sophie waited patiently for the water to rise above Margaret's neck before she gently eased the bloody spike out. The wound gushed and the water swirled with pink, but the bleeding quickly slowed, and within a few seconds, it had stopped completely.

"I think it hit my artery; I can feel it," Bill stammered, clutching his neck. He was hysterical, entirely oblivious to everything occurring outside of his own reflection.

Sophie gave an annoyed grunt. She dumped out the cracked mug full of toothbrushes that sat atop the sink, scooped it in the bloody water, and splashed it in Bill's face.

He gasped and looked at her with a mix of indignance and disgust. However, when his eyes returned to the mirror, his expression quickly evolved to confusion, then a shocked delight. The shallow gashes on his throat darkened and scabbed as if in a time lapse, and the skin on his face pulled the slightest bit tighter as if he'd gained back a few years.

"Unbelievable…" Jack couldn't help but mutter as the scabs flaked off to reveal unmarred flesh.

But he only had a second to stare in awe before a heavy thud drew his attention away. He leveled the rifle down the darkened hallway. There was an unmistakable sound of shifting furniture from the room at the other end of the hall, and its closed door flexed as something slammed against it. Jack fired a round through its center.

"What the fuck!" Kevin's voice rang in a high-pitched scream from the other side. "You almost shot me!"

Jack cursed under his breath. "*Shit.* Sorry, bud. You surprised us."

A muffed boom sounded from the far room, immediately followed by the snap of a passing bullet. Jack shoved Sophie to the ground and threw himself over her like a shield.

"How do you fucking like it?!" Kevin screamed through the barricaded door. "Asshole! I've got more firepower in here than a… a… a fuckin' armory! Don't you fuck with me!"

Jack snapped the peep sight to his eye and tried to gauge which side of the door Kevin's voice was coming from, but Sophie slapped the barrel down furiously. "Are you fucking kidding me? You idiots are really going to— Jesus Christ, you two are stupid!"

Jack glared at her for a second, but he knew she was right.

"Kevin," he called, lowering his rifle. "We killed one of those things, but there are two more out there. We need to build up a defense in here until we can get word to the outside—"

"I *have* a defense!" Kevin's muffled shout interjected. "Nothing's getting in this room, nothing! Not one of those fucking monsters, and not you! You hear me?"

Jack couldn't help but roll his eyes. "Real hero you picked there, Bill," he muttered, replacing a fresh bullet into the rifle's tube.

Bill didn't respond. He stood dumbfounded, staring at himself in the mirror and massaging his healed neck. "I… Do you see what it did? I can— I can feel it in my face and my chest and it's so… so…"

"Warm," Sophie finished, using the mug to gently dribble water into an unconscious Margaret's mouth.

"Yeah…" Bill muttered. "It's magic. Real— real magic. A miracle…"

The logical part of Jack's mind fought to rebuff Bill's words, but looking at the man's pudgy, woundless neck, he realized he didn't have an argument to make. Whatever drove this thing, whether science, magic, alchemy… It didn't much matter.

It was real.

"How do you know there were three of them?" Sophie interrupted Jack's thoughts. "Those *things*, I mean."

He turned to where she crouched next to the bathtub, keeping the stairwell's wide bannister in the corner of his vision. She was marveling at the grotesque, severed hand as she turned it over in the light.

"I…" A shiver ran down his spine as he recalled the dark tomb. "The wolf I killed, it was digging at the base of one of those trees. You were hurt, and, well, we thought there was another artifact, one that could help. I was trying to find another way to get back to the cave, and I ended up finishing what the wolf had started. Dug right to them."

"They were buried?" she asked.

"Yeah." Jack grimaced. "The way they were… I think I woke them up."

"What do you mean?"

"The place they came from—" Jack's eyes snapped back to the stairs as a flash of lightning illuminated the deep maroon pattern of the flaking wallpaper. He took a deep breath and let his hammering heart slow before continuing. "It wasn't just a cave. It was a tomb. Manmade stone walls, ancient carvings, the whole shebang. There was water feeding into it — I'm guessing it was a spring from where you found the stone. I think that water was keeping them alive. It makes sense. All those giant animals and trees — they all feed from that spring. They must have gotten a taste of this thing's power. It kept them all alive far longer than they were supposed to be."

Sophie didn't reply, but raised the dismembered hand up into the glare of the bathroom's singular lightbulb. The spiderweb of black veins rippled out beneath the thin skin, but when she angled the back of the hand away from him, he saw something else.

"You see them?" she asked, tilting it back and forth.

"What are they?"

"Tattoos," Sophie said with an off-color smile. "They *were* tattoos."

"What?"

"This hand," Sophie went on, "beyond the obvious differences, it's almost entirely human. I think... I think this was a person at one time. That maybe these *things* were all people, a really long time ago at least, and that they modified themselves using the power of the stone." She flipped the hand over to reveal the spike extending from its palm. "This isn't a growth; it's a deer antler. They must have used the stone's healing powers to change themselves, to modify their bodies over time into... well, those *creatures* out there."

"So the curse was real? Those thing out there really are some Indian monsters?" Bill interrupted, still unable to tear his eyes from the mirror.

"No, these weren't *Native American* monsters," Sophie came back, tilting the hand once more in the light. "These tattoos are Celtic. Old, old, *old* Celtic. And *carrnegk* — I think it's some form of ancient Brythonic, probably the root of *careg* — modern Welsh for *stone*. Jack... I... I can't believe I'm saying this, but these things could have been related to, or even be *the* people who brought the artifact here in the first place."

"How?" Jack asked.

She paused and shook her head before continuing. "I don't know, but if I'm right about the connection to the *Mabinogi*, these things could be the three survivors of the battle between Bran and Matholwch. Remember, Maedig the druid? According to the Second Branch, he and two others took Bran's cauldron and fled to the west. What's west of the British Isles? *North America*. We already know that the stone needs water to be effective — what if that's what was *in* the cauldron? It wasn't the cauldron itself, but what it contained. It makes sense." She nodded and began to talk faster. "I'd guess they came over in the second century. I know it sounds crazy, but if these things really are human—"

Jack shook his head in disbelief. "You're grasping at straws here, Sophie. Whatever these things are, they're pretty fucking far from human."

"They aren't human anymore," Sophie agreed. "But they *were*. Think about it. Think about what you could do, what you could transform yourself into if every wound healed almost instantly. People with dwarfism undergo procedures where doctors break their femurs over and over again, all because the bones grow a fraction of an inch longer each time they heal. The *thing* outside, the way its limbs extended…"

"You're saying these things, these *people*, mutilated themselves over thousands of years—" Jack was struggling to believe what she was saying, but he couldn't deny the physical evidence that was in front of him.

"The mutilation itself probably took them a lot less time than that," Sophie explained. "They may have been this way from relatively early on — hence the local legends. I think they've been here for a *very* long time. They set themselves up in that tomb, waiting, preserved by the runoff from the stone. Feeding off of it. Margaret told me about the wolf, and it lines up that they would leave an alarm system set up to rouse them in the case that someone came too close to the stone's burial site and threatened the source of their immortality."

Jack cringed. He should have listened to his gut. He should never have returned to that goddamned pit.

"The mutilation we see here was clearly to make them more lethal." She lightly touched the sharp tip of the deer antler and shivered. She shut her eyes and took a deep breath before continuing. "Bianchi, he… did experiments on me while you were gone. The stone heals, but it can't regrow what's been lost. It's almost like it amps up your immune system, allows your body to put itself back together, to replenish its cells…" Her voice wavered as she held up her hand, exhibiting the stub of her pinky. "But it can only do so much."

"My God, Sophie, what did he—" His words were cut off as he fought to suppress the urge to vomit.

Sophie shook her head resolutely. "It doesn't matter. I think these things used it to alter their bodies. Permanently, I mean. They knew they couldn't rely on weapons to last as long as they would, so I think they took everything they could from nature to make their own weapons. This antler, they pulled it fresh from a deer. While the antler's marrow was still alive, they embedded it into this man's anatomy — fused it with his flesh knowing that as long as it stayed in regular contact with the stone's runoff, the antler's marrow would stay alive it wouldn't erode over time. These men… they knowingly transformed themselves into monsters. Armed themselves with living weapons, lengthened their limbs, trained a goddamn wolf and who knows what else to obey them — all to keep people like us from doing exactly what we did. Beyond that, it looks like they began to evolve to their situation underground. The eyes, the skin…"

Jack hated to admit it, but she was starting to make a terrifying amount of sense.

"The one that spoke to me. It had fangs *over* its teeth." Bill finally ripped himself away from the mirror. He collapsed down onto the toilet seat. "They looked like… like… like they'd just been stabbed in there, like she's saying. And those bones coming out of its back…"

"Moose antlers," Jack breathed. They'd almost looked like furled wings as the creature had bounded away, but now he realized what they were. "The bastard stuck moose antlers in its back like armor."

Margaret jerked awake with a violent cough, drawing their combined attention. She wheezed and gasped for air, then dunked her mouth under the pink water and drank. A moment later, she came back up, still coughing but looking a world better.

"What the hell happened?" she groaned.

"You drove through a goddamn building." Sophie gave a relieved laugh and squeezed Margaret's hand.

"You're right— holy shit, that hurt." Margaret tugged her hand away with an annoyed look, and gave an exasperated groan. "Why does it look like we're cornered in the bathroom?"

"Because that's our exact situation," Bill muttered.

"So, they're just humans?" Jack ignored them, turning his full attention back to Sophie. As much as he cared that Margaret was okay, he cared more about the fact that they were being hunted.

"I'm tempted to say yes," Sophie said.

"Then we go on the offensive. There're only two left, and clearly they aren't immune to bullets. I say we push our advantage, play it close, and get the UTV." Jack nodded to Margaret, who was struggling to rise from the tub. "Can you walk?"

"No, not yet." She grasped the tub's edge, but her forearms shook and she sank back down into the water. "I'd guess I broke a few things. Give me a few minutes and let this magic rock work."

"Fine," Jack said. "We hold here until she's good to move, then we—"

"Jack, we can't assume we have the upper hand," Sophie cut in. "These things, there's so much to consider… The stone, it draws you in if you've used it. That's why the box was lined with lead. Lead must muffle it, like a radiation shield. Out in the open, it's like a homing beacon. Beyond that, its powers, or whatever you want to call them, they aren't permanent, but they don't disappear right away. The effect holds in your system, keeps you going for a while before it burns out. I think that's why I survived that fall from the cave, and why Margaret survived the wreck. There's no saying what such a prolonged exposure to the stone — as these creatures have had — would do. They might be, I don't know, saturated with the stuff."

"So, you think they'll be harder to kill?" Jack asked.

"I'd bet on it."

"Then we aim for the fuckin' head," Jack said evenly. "Margaret, where did you hide that rifle I gave you?"

"It's behind the door in my room," Margaret said. "And that giant fuck-show pistol we took off Kevin should still be down on the kitchen table."

"Okay." Jack snapped his fingers in front of Bill's face to draw his attention, then addressed the group. "We move together. When Margaret is on her feet, we hit her room down the hall, get the rifle, then we roll down to the main floor and grab that pistol. We stay in the light and go for the UTV out front. I doubt they can outrun us in that, and if we get enough distance, they're gonna have to try and track us the old fashion way—"

"Jack, stop!" Sophie grabbed his arm hard. "Think for a minute! You're not the hunter here. We're the prey, all of us. The stone, it's a fucking neon sign. As long as we have it, they'll be able to find us. We could get halfway to Halifax and it wouldn't matter. These are men that mutilated themselves, sacrificed their very humanity to endure an eternity of living hell, then waited well over a thousand years in a pitch-black tomb for just this moment. They aren't dumb animals. They exist for a singular purpose, and right now that purpose is to kill us."

"Have we considered just giving them the stone?" Bill asked meekly, wringing his hands.

"It wouldn't matter," Sophie said.

"What the hell makes you so sure?" Bill gave her an annoyed side eye.

"Because I'm smarter than you, Bill," she came back snidely.

"Because if we leave here alive and knowing that the stone exists, they know we'll never stop hunting for it," Jack offered, finally coming to terms with the truth. "Sophie, you seem to know these things better than anyone. At least, you know about the world they came from originally. What do we do?"

Sophie dropped her face into her hands and let out a long breath. "If I'm right about what these things are — *who* they are — then we have to consider what they know and what they're capable of. Before the Roman conquest, the British Isles were a very different place. Warfare wasn't large scale; it was mostly carried out either in single combat between leaders or through raids focused on harassing the enemy or destroying their resources. Swords, spears, chariots, slings — none of these things would have held up in a damp tomb... unless they had bronze, but if they left Britain in the second century, then they would have already completely adapted to iron and steel. Either way, something tells me they've honed their skills with their new makeshift weapons and none of us are going to win in one-on-one combat. Assuming they're still cognizant, they probably know this too. After all, we don't exactly cut the cloth of elite premedieval warriors."

Jack nodded. "They'll try to get us one on one. We stick together and maintain the majority, and if they're smart, they'll hold back."

"I think that if they knew just how fucked we are right now," Sophie said, "they would take the time to lay siege. But we need to keep in mind that they don't know our situation. They don't know if we have reinforcements coming, or if we have the ability to fortify ourselves in here. Most of the sieges of their time took place against fortified hillforts with limited supplies. If we can assume that those forts are their only reference for buildings like this one, on top of the fact that they know the stone alone could keep us alive indefinitely... I'd guess they're most likely considering launching a full-frontal assault and hitting us before we have a chance to regroup. It's what I'd do in their shoes," she added with a shrug.

"Good." Jack pulled the pistol from his belt and handed it to Sophie. "You know how to use a gun?"

"I told you, I grew up on a farm," she said, pulling the hammer to a half cock and checking the cylinders.

Jack couldn't withhold an impressed look. "Okay. If we're going to assume they're coming at us full tilt, then we need to push our one advantage. Bill, you're gonna help support Margaret and we're going to move as a group. We follow the same plan: get the other rifle and pistol, then, once we're all armed, we form a circle in the rear of the foyer. Bill will take the back hall, Margaret will take the rear entrance, and Sophie and I will keep the front."

"Then what?" Margaret asked.

Jack shook his head. "Then we let them come at us and hope Sophie's right."

A metallic crash sounded from the back of the house. The lights flickered.

Everyone froze, and the sudden silence only amplified the sounds of the storm outside and the sloshing of water in the tub.

Then another crash came.

"Oh God," Bill moaned and drew his knees up to his chest.

"What was that?" Jack demanded.

"The generator," Bill whispered.

There was one final deafening crash, then the lights cut off.

XXXVI

Sophie

SOPHIE FIDGETED with the antique lantern until the rust-fused fuel cap finally unscrewed. "I need light," she whispered.

The beam of their only headlamp swung from the hallway down into the narrow closet she was kneeling in, illuminating the tin can of lantern fuel in her hands.

"Not in my fuckin' eyes, you twat!" she hissed.

Bill's apology came in the form of a whimper.

"Are you good?" Jack demanded in a hushed tone.

"Yeah, hold on. Give me that lighter." She held out her hand and Jack pushed the lighter into it. "Are you guys ready?"

"Just light it." Margaret's whisper was still laced with pain.

Sophie struck the flame and the small second story storage closet was illuminated in flickering yellow light.

"Are there any more of those?" Jack asked, keeping his eyes glued to the stairwell.

Sophie raised the lantern and surveyed the remaining contents of the old closet. "No," she whispered after a moment. "But there's at least one more flashlight in the kitchen. Are we still going with the same plan?"

"I don't see why not," Jack said, nudging Bill then starting forward. "Margaret, grab that rifle from your room as we pass. Then we're headed downstairs on me. Got it?"

The group gave a muttering of positive replies, and Sophie moved to help Margaret to her feet.

Margaret pushed her hand away. "No, I'm fine," she insisted, but after a wincing attempt to stand on her own, she accepted Sophie's help.

Jack took the headlamp from Bill and together the group made their way down the hall to Margaret's room. Jack entered first, rifle raised, while Sophie stood watch over the stairwell with the pistol in hand. A minute later, Margaret was armed with the old bolt action rifle. They continued, Jack leading the way down the stairs.

They entered the foyer, and Jack swept the room with the headlamp and rifle before they crossed over Bianchi's mutilated corpse to the kitchen. Bill scrambled to recover the hulking pistol from the table while Sophie darted into the kitchen and searched for the last flashlight. They then moved back into the rear of the foyer where the large room intersected with the southern wing's hallway. They formed a tiny circle, back-to-back, with Jack and Sophie facing the front doors while Bill and Margaret took the hall.

"Is everyone good with their guns?" Jack asked. "Make sure you've got a round chambered and safeties are off."

Each of them checked, and one by one muttered in affirmation.

"If Sophie's right, it means they're gonna come at us hard," Jack addressed them. "That means we need to stay alert, keep our shit together, and shoot well. Bill, Margaret, if something comes down that hall at you, you shoot center mass to slow them down. I'll roll in behind you and go for the headshots. Sophie, if they come in through the foyer, you hold off on firing unless they're charging, or unless I've rolled out to help Bill or Margaret. We don't have much ammo, but there are only two of them. I'd take those odds any day. Now flashlights off. We need to stick to lamplight and conserve battery, in case… you know."

"In case what?" Bill's voice was shaking.

"In case I was wrong," Sophie gulped, dread swelling in her chest at the thought. "In case they're smart enough to… I don't know, burn us out."

Bill squeaked, and Jack gave her a sidelong eyeroll. "Why do you have to say shit like that?"

"It's the truth," Sophie said with a shrug.

Minutes passed. Then an hour. Soon midnight had come and gone. One by one, they each dropped to a knee, nervous eyes still darting along their flickering orange quadrants.

"You know, I never imagined my life would boil down to a horror flick." Margaret leaned against the side of her designated hallway and rubbed her eyes. She looked exhausted but almost completely recovered from the wreck. "As stressful as this is, it's a lot more boring than I expected."

"I'd rather have it boring," Jack said.

Bill nodded agreement, but Sophie shook her head.

"Not me," she muttered anxiously. "This means I was wrong."

"Well, what are the alternatives to your bum rush theory?" Jack asked her.

"Maybe all that time in a tomb rotted their reasoning skills away, or perhaps they're playing chess while we're playing checkers. Either way, I don't like not knowing."

"So what now?" Margaret asked. "Do we go for the UTV?"

Jack shook his head. "No, if they figured out that they needed to destroy the generator, then they've probably disabled the UTV as well. If they haven't, then I don't doubt they're eyeing it as bait. Sunrise is in a few hours. I say we stay put and hope they get desperate enough to push on us. Worse comes to worst, we pull an all-nighter and end up with the daylight advantage."

They all agreed. Time dragged on, the only noise coming from the wind dashing rain against the old mansion and rolling thunder that seemed to rock the very walls. Every once in a while, a particularly strong gust would send a jolting creak cascading down from one of the twin turrets far above, threatening to bring the whole rotting façade crumbling down atop them.

"If do we make it through this, what do we do with the stone?" Margaret asked.

"I think that's a conversation to be had later, Margaret," Jack said.

"What?" Bill sounded indignant. "No— Why? It's *my* expedition, and *my* find. You all signed legally binding—"

"Shut the fuck up and let the grownups speak." Margaret gave him a disgusted look.

"You know what, Margaret, fuck you." Bill glared at her. "Of everyone here, you're *clearly* the least capable of making sound decisions. Almost sixty years old and couldn't even stay off the goddamn pills, and now you think you get to be the one who decides the fate of the most important find in human history?"

"Oh, Bill, look at you." Margaret smirked. "You lose that 'roided out tool-bag Kevin and you babble like a fucking baby, but you get a gun in your pudgy little hand and all of a sudden you're a tough guy again. Grow a spine."

"Enough," Jack chided. "This is exactly why we aren't gonna discuss this right now."

"We take it straight to a research museum or university," Sophie said. She gave Jack an apologetic look. "I think we need to discuss it, especially since there's a chance not all of us make it out."

Bill snorted. "A lab? What do you think what will happen if we introduce this thing to the pricks that govern academia? You think they're going to work hard to synthesize it and cure cancer for the masses? Fat fucking chance. It'll disappear on day one, then a whole bunch of the geriatric uber rich will suddenly be in their twenties again. Don't imagine for a second that those pricks are the good guys."

"Your cynicism is noted." Sophie rolled her eyes.

"As much as I absolutely abhor to admit it, he's right," Margaret cut in. "I've spent enough time with the people you look up to, Sophie, and they're all fucks just like us. Anyone we tell about this, even at that level, will try to take it for themselves."

"So we keep it," Bill said. "We — the combined *we* — share it, use it to make the world better."

"Altruism. *Right…*" Margaret snorted. "You, the man who blew a hundred-million-dollar fortune on a nonprofit that's sole purpose was bravado and personal excitement, expect us to believe that you're intending to use this power for good."

"Yes." Bill glowered at her, then under his breath said, "…snide bitch."

Margaret sighed. "What's the point in whispering, Bill? We're all right here and the rain's not that loud. I am a snide bitch. I'm actually a *royally* snide bitch, and I, along with everyone else in this room, can recognize you for what you are: an arrogant, undisciplined, poorly raised little coward. The worst part is that I can't even blame you for being the way you are. I blame your parents. You never stood a fuckin' chance."

Bill stood furiously but Margaret's rifle was already raised. They froze, glaring at each other.

"Yeah, okay, let's talk about the fucking rock, huh? Yeah, no, that sounds like a great idea," Jack muttered to himself. "If either of you shoots the other, we lose our perimeter, and the minute we lose our perimeter, those things are going to kill us. So how about you both shut the fuck—"

A bloodcurdling screech brought them all to their feet.

"It's out front." Jack kept his rifle raised as he scanned the windows. The occasional lightning bursts did little to help him make out a target.

"Why'd it do that?" Bill's voice was hushed and quavering again.

"It's communicating," Sophie said. "It was a call."

"So where's the other one?" Bill asked.

Another shriek echoed in the distance, far from the mansion, but loud enough to be heard over the pattering of rain against the windows.

"The other one's far out, in the forest from the sound of it," Jack said.

"Why?" Margaret asked.

"I don't know." Sophie's mind kicked into high gear. This was unexpected behavior; it meant these things were thinking, planning, working together and communicating. She scrambled to remember everything she could about premedieval Celtic tactics. "They… they, uh, they— they— they fought with guerilla tactics, mind games, ambushes, ummm…" She spit out ideas as they came. "Pony-driven chariots were big — they couldn't pull something like that off here though… uh…"

"Why are we assuming there are only three of them again?" Margaret cut in.

"Three sarcophagi, three guys in that old story, three figures carved into the ravine's face. It makes sense…" Jack said, now sounding unsure.

"Yeah, you're right," Sophie agreed, "It sounds ridiculous, I know, but this really could be Maedig and his two companions. That would make one of these creatures a druid. Druids were priests. They were smart. Smart as hell. They were known to engage in psychological warfare, using fear even more than violence to conquer their enemies, they would, uh—"

From far in the distance, another call pierced the night. This one was deep and low, and rolled through the windows and up Sophie's spine in a way she'd never experienced. It was a roar.

Everyone froze.

"What the fuck was that?" Margaret whispered.

"I've never heard anything like that." Jack's voice had suddenly lost a portion of its confidence. "And I've heard most things."

Without a word, Bill turned and scampered up the stairs. Jack shouted after him.

"I'm not fighting a fucking dinosaur!" Bill screamed back, and Sophie could hear him banging on Kevin's door.

"They expected us to hold up here." Margaret's voice dropped an octave. "They wanted us to, so one of them could go dig up help."

The roar came again, this time closer. Sophie's mind scrambled. "That's not a man. It's gotta be something native, maybe something else they trained like the wolf. What kind of predators are out here?"

"Sophie, get upstairs," Jack said, and she could tell he was trying to keep his voice even.

"It's not a monster, Jack. It's got to be an animal." She raised the pistol and stood beside him, her words spewing out rapid fire. "And if you can kill a wolf with a knife, we can kill whatever this it. Maybe another wolf, or a deformed moose, something they trained and locked away in hibernation just like them—"

"Margaret, get her upstairs!" Jack's voice rose to a yell and he wrapped the sling tight around his arm.

Sophie felt Margaret grab her from behind and yank her toward the stairwell. She didn't give much resistance; her mind was focused on the noise.

What the fuck could it be?

A cougar?

One of the creatures?

A ploy?

An overwhelming wave a relief hit her.

"It's nothing, Jack!" she shouted. "They play mind games! They intimidate! It's always been the crux of ancient guerilla tactics, and that's all it is — it's nothing but a scare tactic! It's just a noise! They're pushing us deeper into our defense without even having to take ground!" She wrestled against Margaret's grip. "Jack, we can't fall for it! It's just a noise!"

"No." Jack planted his feet and leveled the rifle. "It's a bear."

There was a loud thump on the porch, then the window next to the door exploded in a shower of glass. A hulking mass of sinewy muscle exploded through it. It hit the ground and bounded forward, but its momentum was stalled by Jack's barrage of gunfire. It shuddered as round after round impacted its gray, hairless flesh. Then the rifle clicked empty. A deep, horrifying roar sucked the air from the room as the bear barreled toward Jack.

XXXVII

JACK SLAMMED the lever forward and back, but the rifle clicked empty once more. The bear continued to charge him. Without any other conceivable option, Jack grabbed the rifle in a two-handed grip and slammed it into the beast's frothing mouth. It caught and cracked in the back of the bear's jaw as it crashed into him. The impact sent Jack sprawling.

As his brain recalibrated from bouncing off the hardwood, he realized that the hairless monstrosity before him wasn't bearing down on him. Instead the bear ripped its head back and forth violently and spat out the rifle. The woven paracord sling caught around its neck as it spun and charged up the stairs after Sophie and Margaret.

Jack felt a moment of stunned relief, but it was almost immediately overshadowed by a horrifying realization. "Sophie!" He shouted so hard his voice cracked. "It's coming for the stone!"

The door at the end of the hallway behind him flexed against its frame. Then the lock splintered, and it crashed open. Jack rolled over to see a shadowed figure emerge from the rain. It tromped into the flickering orange lamp light as Jack, still sprawled on the floor, scrambled backwards into the foyer. The lantern lay on its side beside the hall's entrance, its rusted oil cap leaking pungent fuel onto the wooden slats.

The monstrous figure bore down on him, moose antlers jutting from its shoulders like spiked armor. Jack rolled to the lantern and brought a fist down on it like a hammer. The bell of glass exploded across the floor. He scooped his hand under the base of the lantern and flung the steel oil reservoir just as it ignited in a ball of fire.

The result was less spectacular than Jack's panicked mind might have imagined it. The creature swatted the flaming cannister out of the air. It clacked hard against the wall, the steel container exploding open and coating a large swath of paneled wood in vibrant flames.

In the open space of the foyer, Jack managed to roll to his feet. He pulled his father's old antler-handled Bowie from his belt and squared off with the creature. It grunted out a deep, horrible laugh.

"Fuck you," Jack muttered, readying himself.

From the floors above came a cacophony of screams, gunshots, and the muted thumping of heavy pursuit, and Jack knew Sophie and Margaret needed help. But there was only one way to get to them — and it was through this *thing*.

SOPHIE HEAVED against the weight of the antique dresser in her room. It leaned slowly, then finally toppled over in front of the already barricaded door. There was a heavy thump from the hallway outside and the door flexed.

"Help me with the bed!" Margaret shouted frantically, and together they managed to shift the absurdly heavy piece of furniture across the room to reinforce the ever-growing pile of weight that pinned the door shut.

Sophie eyed the door. The bear slammed into it again, but the barricade held.

"We're trapped." Margaret looked around, then ducked over to the window. Sophie watched her, flinching as the bear slammed into the door once more.

"Where are we, I mean in relation to the house, which wall is this?" Margaret demanded, unlatching the double window and swinging the panes open.

"I don't know, toward the middle," Sophie got out. Another slam.

Margaret grasped the sill and leaned her whole upper body out into the pouring rain. When she came back in, she was soaked. "Do you work out?"

"What?"

"Are you *strong*?" Margaret gave an exasperated look.

"I don't know—" This time the impact of the bear brought with it a painfully loud splintering noise. A crack appeared along the thick oak door's center.

"The attic window is right above us," Margaret said quickly. "There aren't any stairs to get up there, just a pulldown ladder. That means no fuckin' bear," she snapped, grabbing Sophie's shirt and dragging her toward the window.

There was another loud crash, and the bear's frothing snout shattered through the center of the crack. Margaret fired her rifle from the hip, but the bullet flew wide and hit the overturned dresser. She awkwardly wrestled to work the bolt back and forward, but the rifle clicked empty. She tossed it aside. "Go!" she shouted. "I'll boost you, then you pull me up!"

Sophie shoved Jack's revolver into her belt and climbed out to perch on the windowsill. The rain was coming down hard. It slapped her face and arms and slicked her fingers as she reached precariously upward to the window. It was too far.

"Step on my shoulders!" Margaret shouted above the din, leaning out of the window beside Sophie. Sophie complied, carefully balancing one foot, then the other on Margaret's shoulders and gripping the dilapidated shingle siding for dear life.

"Hurry!" Margaret screamed against the wind.

Sophie sucked in a deep breath and stood as tall as she could, completely exposed to the elements and entirely without recourse if she were to slip. She stretched even farther than she thought possible, managing to reach the bottom of the attic window and get a fingernail under its edge.

It didn't budge.

Carefully, she pulled the revolver from her belt. Squinting against the rain, she lined it up with the latch. Despite preparing for it, the recoil almost sent her spinning away from the building. But her fingers held to the shingle siding, and a minute later, she was kicking against the side of the manor as she hauled herself up through the attic window.

"It's almost broken through! Pull me up!" Margaret's voice was muted by the storm as Sophie collapsed onto the attic floor. Her arms burned, but she ignored the pain. Taking a deep breath, she leaned back out of the window. Below, Margaret extended her hand as far as she could, but there were still several feet of cold night air between them.

"Use the rifle!" Sophie shouted.

Margaret disappeared for a second, then came back with the rifle in hand and held its barrel up for Sophie to grab. It was too slick to maintain a solid grip in the rain, but Sophie managed to lean out far enough to grab the front end of the sling.

"Are you good?" Sophie called down, bracing her legs against the window's edge and preparing her body. Margaret took several deep breaths, eyed the distant ground below, then nodded. Sophie pulled hard on the sling.

There was a loud crash and Margaret's eyes went wide with horror. She kicked off from the windowsill, launching herself in a swinging arc. The wet rifle strap yanked hard on Sophie's arms and she let out a pained gasp as her shoulders strained against the sudden weight. Directly below her, the bear erupted through the window, swatting wildly at Margaret's swinging figure. It missed wide, then, after a scrambling misstep, plummeted out of the third story window. Its bloodcurdling roar cut off with a sickening thud as it impacted the earth far below.

Margaret's eyes snapped up to meet Sophie's and she let out a victorious laugh. Then the thin metal clip that held the rifle's sling gave against her swinging weight.

The sudden release of pressure sent Sophie tumbling back into the attic.

JACK DOVE to the ground, dodging the flying end table. He barely made it back up in time to avoid the accompanying chair.

The creature was laughing still, illuminated by the flaming lamp oil and swaying back and forth as they circled each other. It was toying with him. Like a cat would a mouse.

It swatted an old ottoman, sending the heavy antique flipping out of its path with animalistic strength. Jack flipped the knife over in his hand and readied himself for its inevitable charge.

"*Carrnegk nawr.*" The creature's lips parted, and the words rasped out between offset fangs. Jack saw them for what they were: coyote canines stabbed into black gums.

"You want the *carrnegk*, right?" Jack asked as their circular dance brought his back to the dining room. "*Carrnegk?*"

The creature froze and slowly cocked its head. "*Rhoi.*"

"Yeah," Jack muttered, eyeing the creature. "*Rhoi…*" He scanned it up and down in the dull orange light of the fire.

Unlike the creature he'd executed outside, this thing's limbs were more proportional. Only its left hand bore a spiked antler extension. The right hand was normal — relatively speaking — the fingers adorned with a long, claw-like tips. Jack felt his stomach turn when he realized that the claws were actually sharpened phalanges protruding from the flesh of its fingertips.

"*Carrnegk! Nawr!*" it rasped furiously.

"I'll make you a deal," Jack said, backing slowly toward the dining room. "I'll give you the stone — *carrnegk* — but I need something from you." He waved his finger between them to signal an exchange, drawing a hiss from the creature. "Yeah, yeah, a trade. I'm gonna give you the *carrnegk*, but first, and this is really important…" He took a deep breath and readied himself. "First, you've gotta go fuck yourself."

Jack spun and sprinted through the dining room and toward the kitchen. Behind him, heavy footfalls thumped in pursuit. As he crossed through the kitchen, he knew the pursuing footsteps were already too close — he wasn't going to make it to the servants' stairwell.

He caught himself on the counter, spun back, and slammed the heavy door that joined the two rooms. It bounced back on something. Jack threw his weight against it, but once again it caught. He eyes darted up franticly in search of the obstruction, and he soon found it: the antler-laden hand had wrenched itself through the gap and now wriggled, pinned against his weight, holding the door ajar.

Jack swung the heavy knife hard. The blade cut deep into the mess of bones that made up the creature's wrist, and its shriek vibrated through the thick wood between them. Jack stabbed and ripped again and again in quick succession, and by the fourth bloody blow, the dismembered hand tumbled to the floor.

The severed arm withdrew, spurting black blood as it went, and the door slammed shut. Jack leaned on it for a second and fought against his instincts to run. *He* had the advantage now, but not for long. The wounded creature would likely heal quickly.

It was now or never.

He yanked opened the door and charged back into the dining room toward the creature. The wrinkled, bug-eyed face was far enough from human that it would normally have been impossible to read, but as Jack leapt forward, Bowie arcing in an overhead stab, he recognized the look of shock in its black eyes. It shrieked again as he barreled into it and the Bowie sank into spongey flesh. He stabbed savagely as they wrestled across the room in a violent embrace. Thick, hot blood sprayed over Jack's hand as the creature pounded wildly at his writhing body, but he didn't relent. Finally, the creature managed to fling him back, and once more Jack found himself sprawled across the foyer floor.

He made it to his feet, but a massive weight slammed him back against the wall, crushing against his chest and stealing his breath away. The Bowie's handle still protruded from the flesh over the creature's clavicle. It tried to pin Jack's hands against the wall, but his right immediately slipped free from under the creature's bloody nub. He reached desperately for the knife handle, but instead found purchase on the creature's throat.

Still gasping for breath in the smokey air, he squeezed with every ounce of strength he had, trying to rip the pulsating windpipe from its waxy encasing. Before he could free the organ from its writhing host, the creature's stump of an arm slammed into his inner elbow, collapsing his arm away. The creature reared its head and its lips curled back, exposing the lethal rows of transplanted fangs.

Jack had seen that motion a thousand times. The rear before the strike. In almost every predator, that motion meant the same thing. Jack's throat was exposed, his arms pinned, and now this thing was going for the kill, going to bury that jagged row of fangs right into his neck.

No.

Jack was the hunter.

Jack reared his head forward and sank his own teeth into the creature's exposed throat, biting hard and thrashing. He felt the cry of pain reverberate through the vocal cords clamped in his teeth, and tasted the briny, sweet blood as it filled his mouth. The creature pulled back and released its grip on him, but he wrapped it in his own tight embrace, ripping back and forth with his clenched teeth furiously. It batted at him as he groped for the knife, and only once he'd wrapped his fingers around its rough handle did he slack his jaw and let the creature kick itself free.

The two combatants fell away from each other and collapsed, the creature clutching its profusely bleeding throat. Jack clutching the blood blackened blade and spat out a mouthful of black fluid. They lay for a moment, facing each other, and this time it was Jack who was laughing.

His laugh cut short when he spotted the detached prosthetic laying between them.

"Fuck," he groaned, rising to a knee and spitting again.

The creature glared at him and snarled.

"Alright, bud." Jack readied the knife. "Let's finish this…"

MARGARET PRESSED her face against the soaked grass and moaned in pain. Her leg was broken; she didn't even have to look at it to know she'd added an extra joint to her femur. The pain was severe, but the familiar warmth had already begun its work in her core. Now it melted down her body and fused with the throbbing pain, dulling it, mending it as she drifted away…

SOMEWHERE OVER the pounding rain and rumbling thunder, Sophie was calling out to her, but it was so muffled that Margaret couldn't make out a single word. She didn't *want* to hear it. She was tired, she was fucking exhausted. This whole thing, the stone, that asshole Bill, the bear—

She slowly opened her eyes and let her head fall to the side. A dozen feet away from her, the hairless beast lay in a mottled gray heap. Its head was unnaturally canted, its eyes crimped shut. It was dead… thank fucking God, it was dead…

Margaret's eyes rolled back again, and she embraced the warmth.

"MARGARET!" SOPHIE's voice was barely audible. "Margaret, now!"

Margaret squinted and shielded her eyes from the downpour, glaring up at the distant window above. Sophie… Fucking girl had let her fall. Had she been holding onto the *strap*? Who the fuck does that?

"Just leave me alone for a second," Margaret muttered. Her own voice was distant and echoey.

"MARGARET! WAKE up!" The scream was so far away, and the world was blurry. There was the crack of a gunshot and the attic window above flashed. A bullet thudded into the wet flesh of the bear beside her. She winced against the splatter of mud and hot blood. She wiped the warm liquid from her face and cursed Sophie. She glanced over at the dead bear. It was only a foot away now, red eyes narrowed, its spittle-webbed teeth bared as its broken body inched toward her at a snail's pace.

Holy fuck, it's alive.

A shot of adrenaline reignited her mind and she scrambled to roll away. The bear growled as she did, tearing at the earth with its one working paw, pulling itself slowly toward her.

She made to stand, but her legs wouldn't respond. Clawing at the ground, she dragged her aching body forward, away from the monstrous heap and its snapping jaws. Sophie was screaming something again, and there were more gunshots and more snorting howls from the bear, but Margaret didn't care. She focused everything she had on just moving forward through the thick grass and patches of mud, away from the hellish manor. The wind howled, and the rain stung her cheeks. She had no idea what direction she was moving until a bolt of lightning illuminated the dark expanse of nothingness ahead, and she realized she was heading toward the cliff.

Fuck.

She dared a glance behind her. She'd barely made it twenty feet. The silhouette of the lumbering bear was uncomfortably close and closing in. She rolled to a new direction, toward the dull, blinking red glow that emanated between the slats of the old carriage house. It was a good distance away, but if she could outpace the bear to it, then maybe she could find something, anything, to finish off that terrifying, bald bastard.

The warmth inside of her shifted entirely to the base of her spine, and something popped hard as she twisted to pull herself forward. She groaned as her legs tingled back into her control. They were weak and wobbly, but she managed to get to her hands and knees.

"Just heal faster than that thing. That's all you've got to do, alright?" she muttered, crawling as fast as she could. Another flash of lightning, and this time an accompanying shot. The bear roared louder.

"Good girl, Sophie. Keep him bleeding, give me a chance." She fought hard to stand, but she wasn't there yet, so she worked her burning shoulders and hips to go faster. "Faster, you old shit," she goaded herself, but then she remembered that she wasn't old anymore and, despite the situation, let out a gasping laugh. "This is the price, huh?" Her mind spilled back over all the years she'd fought to reclaim exactly this: her youth. The yoga, the jogging, the diets, the facial masks, the products, the failed surgeries, the resulting dependence on the pain pills, the defeat… Now here she was. Her great cure at hand, her wonderful gift, and a pair of two-thousand-year-old monsters and their pet fucking bear trying to tear her apart. Typical.

The pulsing red outline of the carriage house grew ever closer. Finally, a few dozen feet out, she managed to stand. Behind her, the bear had made it onto three legs, wrestling to drag a limp appendage behind it and snarling at her as it tried to run. She shambled forward, stumbling through what was left of the shattered front doors and looking around desperately for something to arm herself with. The room stank of gasoline from the upturned tank, and the floorboards were grimy and soaked through. She stumbled around the bay, but everything inside had been tossed haphazardly about in the crash. Between the disorienting darkness and the blanket of broken wood siding, there were no weapons to be found.

The bear's furious roar reverberated just outside the carriage house, and she could hear its thumping stride through the wall. It was coming. She was cornered, and it was too late.

She eyed the truck. Maybe it would still start. Maybe there was something inside, a gun or even a knife, anything to help her finish off this fucking—

The bear rounded the corner as she threw herself over the side of the truck bed. Yanking her still throbbing body up and through the shattered back window, she collapsed on the seats. The truck bounced as the still half crippled bear fought to climb into the bed after her. Margaret desperately hunted through the glove box for something she could use, but there was nothing. Nor was there anything worthwhile in the center console. Under the seat, she found a roadside assistance kit, a tire iron, and a pair of old road flares. The tire iron would have to do, she decided as the truck bounced again. This time the shocks didn't spring back up; the bear was in the bed.

She pushed the door, but it didn't open. She threw her shoulder into it, then again, and realized in sudden horror that both side doors were pinned shut by the walls, and the windshield was laden with an immovable coating of debris. There was one small gap, though, she thought, testing the old boards to see how heavy they were. Maybe she could squeeze—

A stinging pain erupted from her chest as the massive bear's claws snagged her and yanked her backwards into the seat. Bright red lines opened from her sternum to her shoulder as the claw drew back and away. She gasped and dropped down to the floor, swatting wildly with the tire iron. The bear ignored the blows, thrusting itself farther through the tight fit of the rear window, each attempt with its snapping maw bringing it closer to her, inch by slow inch. The roadside kit dug into her back. She grasped at it, and her hand closed around one of the flares. She struck the bottom, and it ignited, filling the cab with blinding light. The bear winced away for a second, then clamped its eyes shut and pushed still farther in. Margaret squeezed back as far as she could under the glove box and let out a hard sob. There couldn't be a worse way to go.

The rear-view mirror glinted on the floor beside her. She looked at it. The girl who stared back at her in the bright light of the flare was young and stunning. The epitome of a terrified beauty like in the old adventure flicks, some inappropriately romantic part of her brain mused. She stared into that mirror for a long second, admiring everything she'd desired for so long. As she stared, she felt some old feeling ignite inside of her, feelings she'd sequestered away or smothered out so long ago. She let herself become that girl in the mirror, in all of her haphazard, wonderful, painless glory, and she knew what she had to do.

"You always wanted to go out a hot mess." She laughed bitterly, but she smiled approvingly at the girl in the mirror. Once more so young. Once more so full of life and love and happiness and hope. She wrenched herself up and forced her arm out of the broken window. The bear's claws dug into her side painfully as she tossed the dazzling flare into the center of the carriage house.

SOPHIE FELT the scream erupt from her lungs on its own accord. She watched in horror as the carriage house exploded in a billowing plume of white-orange flame, illuminating the night like an atomic bomb. It blinded her, and she felt the concussive pulse of heat all the way from the attic window.

Her heart pounded in her ears, and she felt dizzy. Smoke billowed from the building's burnt carcass, intertwining with steam as the rain washed down over the flames. She couldn't tear her eyes away.

No.

What if Margaret had made it out?

What if she'd managed to kill the bear? Escape the carriage house before…

Every bit of sense in Sophie's head commanded her to accept the harsh truth. But she couldn't.

Margaret was fine.

She had to be.

People don't just die. Not real people. Not people she knew. Not like that.

If Margaret could survive being throw twenty feet through a windshield, not to mention plummeting three stories, she must have survived this. The stone's residual effects, they could have preserved her, kept her safe despite… Despite being burnt away to nothing…

Sophie stepped away from the window and backed into the attic. The dim headlamp hung loose around her neck, filtering through the clutter and casting eerie shadows across the room. A distant version of her knew she should preserve what little battery was left, but that part of her was dormant. Instead she collapsed onto one of the old wooden piano stools and stared vacantly toward the window as the sooty scent of burnt wood wafted in through the rain.

Her head felt hollow. Her thoughts swam lazily around the damp, quiet attic. The heavy patter of the rain on the leaky roof above filled her ears and, in turn, her mind. It was hypnotizing, and as she hung her head in numb defeat, she found herself falling under its spell. It felt like nothing. Wonderful nothing. As long as she didn't move, didn't decide or act, then she wouldn't be forced to acknowledge the truth. She didn't *want* to acknowledge the truth. She couldn't because the second she did, she'd have to accept it. Until then, Margaret was still alive.

Sophie had no idea how long she sat there, clutching the revolver against her thigh with one hand and massaging the warm lump in her pocket with the other. It could have been minutes or even hours. It made no difference to her. The manor was quiet. There were no gunshots or screams anymore. No thumping or crashing or patter of scrambling feet…

It wasn't just Margaret. Everyone else was probably dead too…

A rasping call finally broke her trance. It came from far below and barely cut through the din of the storm. She squeezed her eyes shut and begged the universe to reveal that this was all some cruel joke, that none of it was really happening. But the call came again.

"Carrnegk!"

Steeling herself, she checked the pistol. It only had three bullets left, and the empty box of rounds Jack had given her lay discarded by the window. "Three shots," she whispered, remembering what Jack had said. "Aim for the head. They're only human."

The ladder hatch from the attic down to the third floor was jammed in place, and she had to kick it hard to open it. It came down with a loud crash. She didn't care. However many of these things were left, they knew where she was. The stone was calling them right to her. She slid down the ladder, then crossed to the stairs, pistol at the ready, and made her way down. The third story hallway was empty save for the stench of death and smoldering wood. As she continued down toward the foyer, she spotted the unmistakable shimmer of blackish blood pooled on the floor. Crouching behind the bars of the bannister, she saw the creature that had spoken to Bill. It lay face down in a sea of its own blood, one of its hands dismembered and its head marred by slashes and stab wounds. Just beyond it, illuminated only by her dull headlamp, stood a lumbering figure.

It was less monster and more man than the others. Still bearing a head of tightly knotted red hair, its face was less shrunken and its mouth wasn't filled with fangs. Its skin, while just as pale as that of the others, was still mottled with occasional splotches of freckled melanin. Kneeling before it like a hostage with his own knife pressed hard against his throat was Jack.

"Shoot it, Sophie," Jack said, then winced as the blade bit into his flesh. A trickle of fresh blood ran down the already black-encrusted blade.

The creature stared at her, stone-faced, and rasped, *"Carrnegk"*

"Carrnegk," she repeated, easing her thumb over the pistol's hammer.

The creature nodded to the pistol in her hand, then to the floor at the base of the stairs. Slowly, she eased down the stairwell, bringing herself closer to her target.

It hissed as she stepped off the last stair, then erupted in a gargling burst of words that were too hoarse and broken to understand.

"Release him— Uh— *rhyddhau.*" She tried the closest thing she knew to the old Brythonic translation.

The creature's eyes narrowed, and it shifted farther behind Jack. She needed a clean shot.

"Who are you? Uh… *Pwy wyt ti?*" She tried modern Welsh, hoping there would be some crossover. When the creature made no move to respond, she jabbed a finger into her own chest. "I am Sophie Kensington, of Ireland — *o' Iwerddon.*"

The creature hissed in clear disapproval. It tried again to speak, but its words blended together in little more than a series of animalistic grunts. It motioned again to the pistol, then pulled Jack in tighter.

Sophie had no idea what it was saying. She doubted anyone alive could understand the ancient language even if it were spoken clearly. She slowly raise the pistol. One last desperate idea popped into her mind. She drew in a deep breath, then spoke loudly, "Maedig?"

The creature froze, its head cocked ever so slightly to the side. The narrow red eyes searched her face in the darkness. There was something about them, she realized. Something painfully human. The longer Sophie looked into them, the less inhuman the features surrounding them became. What was a second before terrifying suddenly became tragic.

"Why would you do this to yourself?" she muttered, mostly to herself. "Eternity can't be worth it…"

Of course it wasn't.

Jack hissed through barred teeth. "Sophie, shoot this fuckin'—" The knife bit into his flesh again, and he strained back in pain.

Sophie felt her whole body tense at the sight and fought the urge to pull back the pistol's hammer.

The whole situation seemed so absurd, like a Faustian fever dream. Everything she'd spent her life pursuing — the years of schooling, meetings, research — was here. An untold plethora of knowledge and lore and the first-hand account of druidic mysticism stood only a few feet before her… and it had a knife to Jack's throat.

"*Carrnegk.*" It eased the knife away the smallest bit, then nodded to the pistol.

Sophie's gut told her to listen. To respect the idea that maybe — *just maybe* — this could end well. Maybe she could rectify her mistake of bringing this cursed stone back into the world. Maybe this grotesque creature before her still had some hint of humanity left in it. After all, how could it not know compassion if it were willing to endure the hell it had put itself through for the sake of its fellow man?

The feeling in her gut battled her reasoning, but after a moment, her gut won. She bent slowly and placed the gun on the floor. Only once she'd risen did the creature withdraw the knife and toss Jack to the ground before it.

"Jack, stay still," Sophie said before he could scramble away.

"What?" he snapped, eyeing her.

"Just... Do you trust me?"

Jack gritted his teeth, but he stayed where he was.

Sophie slowly withdrew the cloth-wrapped stone from her pocket and held it before her. "Jack, I think... I think it knows— *he* knows that this is a draw. If we can— if I can just talk to him, maybe we can—"

"It's a fucking monster, Sophie. What the hell do you—"

"It's really him, Jack. It's Maedig."

Jack bared his teeth and eyed the creature towering over him. "Sophie, it's gonna kill both of us if you hand that thing over."

"Maybe," Sophie muttered, steeling herself. "But I don't think so. I... We made a mistake, digging this stone up. The world's not ready for something like this."

"That doesn't matter right now," Jack insisted. He remained frozen, eyes locked on the creature, but his voice was furious. "Chuck the stone near him, make him go for it, then kick me the gun."

Maedig must have understood Jack's tone. The blood red eyes narrowed and the knife flipped deftly in his pale hand.

"No," Sophie said quickly. "Jack, I need you to not move. Please, *please* don't move." She eased forward slowly, her heart pounding so hard she thought it might crack her ribs. She felt the slick, pooled blood of the other creature beneath her feet but didn't look down. Her eyes were locked on Maedig's terrifyingly small red pupils. She passed Jack, who lay on the ground so tense he might shatter, and placed the bundled stone in Maedig's waiting hand.

He loomed over her, and as she released the weight of the stone, her instincts commanded her to brace for a strike. But it never came. The creature closed its hand around the egg-sized bundle, and he met her eyes. Up close, he really didn't look so different from a man. She could see the form of Maedig's face through the folded skin, the distant spark of sentience and humanity in his bloodshot, blackened eyes. This wasn't a monster at all, she realized. This was a man. A tortured, ancient, and profoundly loyal man.

"We're okay," she whispered to Jack. Then she let out a small, relieved laugh. "We're okay. It's—"

The near side of Maedig's head exploded, propelling wet, stinging chunks of viscera and bone into Sophie's face. She stumbled back in shock as his limp body thumped to the ground, her eyes wide despite the burn of Maedig's blood dripping into them.

"That's... That's what you get. You... you... asshole!" Bill panted from the dining room entrance, the smoking pistol still raised in front of him. He angled the pistol down toward the twitching, lifeless corpse and fired again.

The stunning boom jarred Sophie back into reality. "You idiot!" she screamed. "You colossal fuck! What have you done?"

Bill didn't seem to notice her. He fired again and again until the pistol's slide locked back. Still he stood there yanking the locked trigger, eyes unfocused and face twisted into a panicked look of desperation. "Die! Die!" he whimpered over and over.

"Bill, enough!" Jack bellowed.

Bill's head snapped over to them, staring blankly for a second before his eyes fogged with tears. "I did it," he managed to stutter out. "I... I saved the day. Oh my God, I saved both of you. I'm a hero. Guys... I'm a *hero*."

XXXVIII

Jack

"A *HERO*? You're a fucking idiot, that's what you are!" Sophie shouted.

Jack wrestled to reattach his prosthetic. It had sustained some damage, but when he slipped it over the nub of his calf, it held.

Sophie darted by him, retrieving the stone from Maedig's dead, spasming hand. She pointed an accusatory finger at Bill. "How the hell could you think that was a good idea, you fucking idiot?" she hissed, her voice furious and hoarse. "Do you realize what you've done?"

"I… I saved you…" Bill stammered.

"Saved me? *Saved me?*" Sophie scoffed, starting toward the still stricken Bill.

Jack clamored to his feet and caught her. As soon as Jack was between the two of them, Bill seemed to finally regain some confidence.

"Yeah, Sophie, I saved you! That… *thing*, it was taking the artifact from you, and I stopped it."

"He was a human being. He wasn't attacking me — we were on the verge of communication! That was our last window into a lost past, and you just shut it forever!" She snarled.

"It was a monster, and it would have killed us, you said it yourself," Bill sneered. "You just can't get over yourself and thank me, can you?"

"Enough," Jack barked. "Sophie, is the bear dead?"

Her glare shifted from Bill to the floor. "Yes."

"Where's Margaret?" Jack asked.

Sophie paused, then looked up at him and took a deep, shuddering breath. "Margaret's gone."

He opened his mouth to speak, but he had nothing to say. Instead, he drew Sophie in close and held her.

"That's terrible," Bill said, but his voice rang with disingenuity. "Truly heartbreaking, really… But right now, we need to stay on task. My knee, I believe I injured it during the combat."

"The combat?" Sophie pulled away from Jack and scoffed. "Where were you even hiding?"

"I wasn't *hiding*," Bill snapped. "I was… waiting. Waiting for the opportunity to strike, as I did."

Sophie rolled her eyes and jeered.

"I'd like to utilize the artifact," Bill went on, dramatically limping into the foyer. "Its healing properties should restore me to a hundred percent, then we can consider how exactly we're going to deal with the… well, the fallout."

"No," Jack said flatly. Bill began to protest, but Jack held up a silencing finger. Jack squinted and surveyed the dark room. The only light came from Sophie's dull headlamp and the few smoldering embers dotting the charred hallway wall. It took him a minute, but even in the dull light, he managed to make out the short rifle laying at the base of the stairs. He crossed the room and picked it up. The stock was cracked and bore deep gouges from the bear's teeth, but otherwise the gun seemed intact. He reloaded the last half dozen rounds from his pocket as he spoke. "We thought there were only three of them, but then they dug up the bear. We can't assume we're out of the woods yet. There could be more."

"More the reason for me to heal, Jack," Bill insisted. "I need all my strength too—"

"We're done using it," Sophie interrupted. "Jack, we need to find somewhere to hide it, somewhere where no one will ever find it."

"*What?*" Bill shouted, staring at her in shock. "No! You don't get to make the decisions here. You're just a… a… *girl!*"

"Really?" Sophie snapped, turning on him.

"No, not like—" Bill growled in frustration. "I didn't mean it like that! Not because you're a— a female. I meant because you're a child! How old are you? What do you know about the world? This thing, it can help people, it can save thousands, millions! We could cure cancer, we could live forever, we could have it all!"

"Have it all?" Sophie shook her head in disbelief.

"You know what I mean," Bill said. "We could *fix* everything, the world, society, we'd be unstoppable — literally! Imagine the wisdom that comes from experiencing *forever?* Imagine the imprint we could make on the world! We never say a word, the stone stays our secret, and we'd be seen as… as… as *gods!*"

"Jesus Christ," Sophie muttered.

"You know what happens when you live forever?" Jack asked, then pointed to the two inhuman corpses on the foyer floor. "You end up looking like that."

"No," Bill argued. "These things, they were prehistoric barbarians. Not us. We're intelligent. We won't lock ourselves away in some shitty little tomb and hide this gift. It'll be different for us. How can you not see that? Why the *fuck* do I have to sell you on this? You're being insane!" Bill was shaking his fists. He took a deep breath and gathered himself. When he spoke again, he was more collected. "Sophie, do you remember that story you told me? Back when you first approached me for funding for this whole dig? The Second Branch of the *Mabinogi*, right? That story, it said this thing could raise men from the dead, didn't it? If that's true, then *we could bring Margaret back.* Imagine that, imagine we—"

"Stop," Sophie commanded. "Just stop. She's gone."

"*Gone?*" Bill said in disbelief. "*Gone?* You'd be so quick to give up on her? After the way she used that same stone to bring you back from the brink of—"

Sophie's punch landed with a meaty thump and sent Bill spinning to the floor. He made to stand again but caught sight of Jack, who shook his head slowly.

"She burned away, you dumb fuck," Sophie spat. "And even if she didn't, I wouldn't tear her away from whatever comes next just to come back here and listen to your bitching."

Bill took another deep breath and nodded, signaling his defeat. "Fine. I'm sorry. But my point stands. What is it *you* propose we do next?"

"What's going to happen next." Kevin's voice filler the foyer. "Is that Jack is going to drop that old lever gun and kick it over here."

Jack spun on his heel but was immediately blinded by a dazzling light from the stairwell.

Kevin chuckled from beyond the blinding beam. "This here it a SureFire flashlight. It's attached to the barrel of a fully loaded AR-10. Safety is off, Jack, and unless you like burnt retinas, I'd avoid looking right at it — I've heard it's like staring into the sun itself."

"What the hell are you on about?" Sophie demanded.

A deafening boom filled the room as Kevin fired a warning shot into the ceiling. "Kick it away, *now*."

Jack slowly bent to place the rifle on the floor. *Fucking Kevin.* "We sure could've used that thing about fifteen minutes ago, bud."

"Yeah, yeah, blah, blah, monsters, blah. Let me guess: you think I'm a coward for leaving you to them, right?" Kevin angled the flashlight away from Jack's face and into Sophie's, then tossed a square desert-tan backpack onto the floor in front of her. It hit the hardwood with a heavy thud. "*Wrong.* I'm fuckin' smart. Now, Sophie, you're going to move real slow. Take that revolver out of your belt and slip it in the front pocket of that pack."

"This what they teach SEALs nowadays, Kevin?" Jack asked, trying to draw his attention in the hopes that it might offer Sophie a shot.

Kevin's face was invisible beyond the blinding light, but Jack could hear his sneer through his voice. "I'll be honest with you, I wouldn't know. Let's just all agree that Bill really sucks at background checks."

Jack glanced over to Bill, who fumed silently.

"The stone comes next, Sophie," Kevin went on. "Front pocket, and if I even *imagine* you're fucking around, I'll empty thirty rounds into the lot of you and just take it off your corpses. This right now is me being nice."

"Stolen valor, hiding under your bed from monsters, and stealing something you're too stupid to comprehend… Yeah, I'd say you're right about me calling you a coward, Kevin," Sophie said as she slipped the stone into the front pocket of the bulging pack.

"Oh, *shut up,* princess potato. It's not stolen valor. I did my time in the National Guard. But rich brats like Bill don't respect *that.* No, I just had to spice it up a bit. Now, back away from the bag, all of you."

They complied, easing away from the light and toward the dining room. Kevin's beam shifted as he crossed the room. Jack squinted against the blinding light, eyeing his own discarded rifle at the foot of the stairs. Through the pattering of rain, he heard Kevin wrestling to slip on the pack's straps. This was Jack's chance. But as his legs tensed to leap forward, a deafening boom froze him in place and a spattering of drywall rained down on his shoulders.

"You think I don't see you eyeing that gun, tough guy?" Kevin demanded. "Seriously? How about a little respect for the man who bested you, you fuckin' hillbilly."

"You don't know what you're dealing with, Kevin," Sophie said softly. Jack could tell she was trying to sound like she was pleading, but the hatred in her voice spilled through.

"The artifact?" Kevin's lips curled up in a thin smile. "I'll figure it out. But I like to take one thing at a time, and right now I'm dealing with you people. An uppity ginger bitch, a fat old slob, and a crippled drunk.

If I'm reading the room right, y'all are pretty pissed — not to mention driven. I get the impression that none of you have much of a reason not to follow me and try to get this back, huh?"

"Kevin, don't," Bill begged.

Jack didn't like the fear in his voice.

"'Kevin, don't' *what*? You still think you give the orders around here?"

"No, Kevin," Jack cut in. "You're in charge, and we won't follow you. We promise." He raised his hands in submission and lowered his voice. "After all of this, you're really going to kill us for a rock?"

Kevin snorted. "I'm not an executioner, Jack. I'm not gonna kill you in cold blood. I'm a good guy. I'm just — I don't know — more ambitious. And, more importantly, I'm *fucking owed*. But yeah, you're right, you won't follow me. You'll be too busy."

A tense silence filled the room.

Finally, Jack asked the looming question. "With what?"

"*Triage*," Kevin snapped.

Strobe-like flashes illuminated the manor as the air exploded in a deafening cacophony of gunshots. Jack tackled Sophie to the ground. Together they rolled into the dining room. By the time they'd reached cover, the shooting had ended.

A shrill scream cut above the ringing in Jack's ears. Bill lay at the mouth of the foyer, clutching his arm and howling like an air raid siren as blood leaked between his fingers. Beneath Jack, Sophie groaned in pain.

"Where is it, where'd he hit you?"

"My leg." Sophie gasped.

Jack pulled the headlamp from her neck and scanned her legs. The dark red entry wound was high on her thigh, just beside her groin, and squirted dark red blood in rhythm with her pounding heart.

"Fuck." Jack repeated the word again and again as he wrestled her belt off her waist and tightened it into a makeshift tourniquet. The bleeding slowed as he cinched it down, but not enough. "Bill!" he shouted. "Bill, I need a tourniquet!"

"I'm shot!" Bill cried back, squirming uselessly on the floor like an unearthed worm.

"Fuck!" Jack barked again. "Sophie, stay with me, stay awake!" He stumbled to his feet and sprinted through the foyer, up the stairs, and to the doctor's room. Several tables were upturned, and half of the instruments were scattered across the floor. He searched desperately.

The sputtering sound of the UTV engine turning over drifted through the window as he found a tourniquet. The UTV roared to life as he charged back down the stairs, then its thundering engine faded into the storm.

"Bill, you're fine!" Jack shouted as he passed. He had no idea if it was true, and for the most part, he didn't care.

"No, I'm not!" Bill shouted back.

Jack slipped the thin black strap up Sophie's leg and replaced the twisted belt, binding it tight. She looked weak by the time he finished.

"Jack, don't let him get away," she mumbled.

"Fuck him. We need to find a way to get you to a hospital — you need blood," Jack insisted, trying to sound calm, but his voice cracked.

"You need to get the stone back. Jack, please," Sophie said. "We should never have brought it up. They were protecting it from people like us, people like Kevin. Please, it's so much more important than you or me."

The rosy hue had begun to drain from her skin, and the beaded sweat on her forehead gave her face a waxy sheen. A horrifyingly familiar feeling wove its way through Jack's body. "I'm not leaving you here. We're going."

"We will," Sophie said. "We will, but you need to stop Kevin. Fuck, Jack, come on. You have to. I'll be fine. I can feel the warmth — it's left over from the stone. It's still working in me. I swear, I'll be fine. It will heal me, but you need to stop Kevin."

"Sophie…" Jack started, but he didn't know what to say or how to argue. He wasn't going to let this happen again. He wasn't leaving.

"Get the fuckin' stone back," Bill shouted. "It can heal us, you jackass!"

Sophie gave a weak laugh. "I hate him, but he's right."

"I'm not—" Jack knew they were both right and that he was wrong. "You stay here until I get back, okay? Don't fucking go anywhere."

"I don't think I'm going anywhere in this state." Sophie chuckled weakly, raising a hand and touching his cheek. "Go get it, Jack. It needs to disappear."

Jack rose and crossed to his rifle. By the time he made it to the window, the UTV's taillights were still in sight, only halfway to the forest. He braced against the windowsill and prepared his shot. To Jack's dismay, the rifle's peep sight housing had been bent almost thirty degrees in the bear's thrashing grip. Even if the sights had been intact, the UTV was pushing the extent of the rifle's range. He lined the rifle up, trying his best to compensate for the bent sight and knowing that unless he brought the vehicle to a halt, he didn't stand a chance of catching up to Kevin.

Just before he squeezed the trigger, the distant hum of the engine sputtered and fell silent.

The stupid fuck had run out of gas.

Jack slung the rifle and grabbed his knife from Maedig's cold, dead hand. He shoved it into its sheath without bothering to wipe the dried blood from its blade. He looked behind him one last time as he crossed out onto the porch. Bill squirmed on the ground, clutching his shoulder and moaning. Sophie lay still, propped up against the dining room doorway, a look of anguish displayed across her face. She met his eyes and gave him a pained smile, then nodded. He returned the nod, then stepped out into the pouring rain.

It was time to hunt.

XXXIX

Jack

JACK MOVED quickly, eyes darting around the dense wall of pines that loomed before him. The rain was coming down even heavier now. It slammed down on him, a cold shower and rendering his clothes soaked and cumbersome.

It took him too long to reach the tree line, and the storm had already eroded away most of Kevin's sparse trail, leaving almost nothing to track. From the best Jack could tell, his adversary had pushed west, in a path directly perpendicular to the jagged oceanside cliffs.

Jack pushed onward into the underbrush, only pausing in the shadow of a thick fir to recalibrate and plan his path. He had spent most of the last decade honing his skills in woodland navigation and, having spent the past two weeks doing little more than exploring and hunting these very forests, he felt comfortable conjuring up a mental map of the area. The direction Kevin was heading led to a wide brook which was bordered on the far side by nearly impenetrable underbrush. The brook ran southwest, then hooked back to the east after a good half mile. Its next bend came after another quarter mile, at the base of a small hill, overall forming a large U shape.

Kevin was lazy, and Jack doubted he was much of a navigator, so he figured Kevin would sooner follow the brook than push through the thick underbrush. There was also a good chance he wouldn't notice the waterway's gentle eastern curve in the stormy darkness.

If Jack was right, and he somehow managed to cut straight south quickly enough to beat Kevin to the hill, then he might have a chance to catch him. If he was wrong, then he'd lose at least a half hour in the wrong direction, and his chances would drop to near zero.

"He's scared, he's cold, and he's desperate, just like you," Jack muttered to himself. "But he's lazy. He'll be at the hill."

With the decision made, Jack set off in a grueling jog. The damage to the prosthetic had left it crimping hard on the stub of his calf. With every thumping stride, the searing pain grew as the nylon sleeve wore away at the wide patch of scarred flesh.

As he pushed on, the forest shifted from the sparse pines and needle-padded ground to thicker scrubs and old oaks. Finally it gave way to an overwhelmingly dense mixture of wet green and black. He took game trails where he could, but mostly fought through the foliage and rain to maintain a direct path south.

By the time he reached the hill, his heart was hammering, and he was gasping and sore. The rain was torrential. He spotted the brook through the trees. It was engorged with rainwater, and Jack worried that perhaps the wall of brambles had offered Kevin a more appealing path than skirting along the muddy, overflowing banks.

It didn't matter, Jack thought. He was here now. He'd made his bet and needed to pray that he'd made the right one. There was no going back at this point.

Laying down along the roots of a rhododendron at the crest of the hill, Jack set up his ambush. Like a deer hunter in a blind, he checked his field of fire and judged his best point of attack. The rifle's bent sight made it more difficult, but if Kevin followed the brook, then he'd cross within fifty yards. It wouldn't be a guarantee without the sights, but it would have to do.

A tense minute passed. Then another. No movement came from the dark edges of the brook. Thunder rolled overhead. Jack tried to listen past the staccato of rain on the forest's canopy, but his ears were useless against the unrelenting din of the storm. Kevin could have already passed. He could have not come this way at all. He could have been planning this since the start of the whole dig — stealing whatever came up from that cave, that is — and had a route already prepared. Kevin was in good shape, and with a series of game trails memorized and a jogging pace, he could be five miles away by now. Jack pushed the thoughts from his mind. None of that mattered. All he could do now was wait.

Another five minutes passed, and the cold started to seep in. As his heart rate slowed and the earth sucked the heat from his torso, Jack felt the first chill. It ran along his spine and up his neck, knocking on the backdoor of his mind like an unwanted visitor. He pushed it out. This wasn't cold. He'd felt cold before. This was nothing.

Ten more minutes. The soaking clothes clung to his numb flesh. The hurricane had brought with it a cold wind that whipped through the trees violently and sprayed his face with stinging droplets. His fingers had begun to grow numb. He ignored it all, focusing everything on the dark brook below.

Fifteen minutes. The shivering had begun. It was minor at first — uncontrollable little spasms that ran up and down his back. They grew stronger as his body fought to raise its core temperature. They were familiar. Agonizingly so. The colder he got, the closer to the mountain he came.

No. He wasn't anywhere near the mountain.

Sam's frozen, dead-eyed face flashed in his mind. It stared at him, damning him. He pushed the image away, focusing instead on Sophie. On that afternoon in the forest. He needed to keep it together. For her. She needed him. She needed the stone. Her face flashed in his mind again, this time bearing the pained smile and pale sheen. It looked… waxy.

No.

Something splashed in the darkness ahead. Jack tensed, driving all thoughts from his mind and peering through the broken sights.

Kevin's hushed curses drifted in with the wind, and Jack made out his figure as he approached. He was wading along the edge of the brook, pack secured to his back and rifle held in a loose grip. He swore continuously, swatting at the claw-like branches that clung to his clothes as he tromped loudly through the water.

As Kevin's silhouette crossed fully into sight. Jack lined up his shot. He aimed center mass, knowing the lack of sights cut his accuracy down to damn near luck. As he flipped the safety off, he considered his target. He'd never killed a man. He'd always imagined it as some sort of heinous taboo. An unredeemable action, his father had called it. Maybe that's why the old vet drank.

But as Jack pulled the trigger, he felt nothing.

The rain did little to muffle the rifle's *crack*. The massive bullet sent Kevin spinning. Jack remained completely still, not so much as recycling the rifle's action. Kevin let out a small yelp at first, then, after a second, came the wounded howl. A furious barrage of .308 spattered the side of the hill. A few bullets snapped harmlessly over Jack's head, but for the most part, the wild volley went wide. Just like a deer, the surprised Kevin struggled to orient himself and hadn't been able to place the shot.

Jack could hear Kevin reloading as he stumbled back behind a thick maple. "I thought you could fucking shoot, asshole!" Kevin screamed. "You… You fuckin' gutshotted me, you fuck!"

Ever so slowly, Jack edged back from the crest of the hill, dropping down its back side and moving cautiously to flank.

Kevin's rifle barked again, releasing another aimless burst into the hillside. "Come on, fuck-o! Let's do it old school! You're the cowboy — how about you come and face me like a man?"

Jack eased around the edge of the hill, eyes glued to the earth immediately before him. Beneath the cover of the rain, he was silent, invisible as he moved in a wide circle around his prey.

Kevin let out another pained grunt as he reloaded once more. "How'd you catch up to me? Huh? Is that even you, Jack?"

Jack rounded the far edge of the brook and spotted his quarry. Kevin kneeled at the base of the tree, nursing a large wound just above his hip. His pack sat open and half submerged in a shallow, motionless pool of the brook's overflow. Kevin took several panting breaths then rolled halfway out from cover, blasting the rifle into the opposing hill until it clicked empty.

"Fuck!" he shouted, fishing through the pack for another magazine.

Jack crept to a shrouded bend in the brook and discreetly eased across it. He needed to be closer. He'd have to rack the next round before firing, which meant he'd likely only have time for one shot. It needed to count.

Kevin rooted through the pack and swore, apparently out of ammo. "Uh, Jack, how about a draw? I mean, you're like me, you're not a killer." Kevin's voice was still too confident for a defeated man. "Look, I'm tossing my rifle out!"

Kevin unclipped the empty rifle from the one-point sling attached to his combat vest and threw it aside, out into clear view of the hill. He kept one hand clamped to the pistol holstered on his leg as he bent and yanked a thick black mass from the pack. Jack watched as Kevin extended the stock of a stubby MP5K submachine gun and clipped it into the sling, then plugged a thin magazine into its underside.

"Come on, Jack! Look!" Kevin grimaced in pain as he raised his empty hands up to either side of the tree, letting the submachine gun hang loose from his chest. "I'm unarmed, guy! I give up. Let's talk!"

Ever so slowly, Jack raised his rifle. The broken sight taunted him as he keyed in on Kevin's heart; he was still too far away. He needed it to be a guarantee.

"Jack!" Kevin was getting frustrated. He grimaced in pain and pressed against the massive wound in his side. "What was it your old man said? 'Only true scum leave an animal to suffer.' Right?"

Jack froze.

"I read the police reports when we recruited you!" Kevin went on. "That is what you said to them, right? About why you led your buddy to his death?" He bent forward and rifled through the front the pack. A second later, his hand emerged holding the bundled stone. "How does this fucking thing work?" Jack barely heard Kevin murmur before his voice shifted back to a shout. "I'm not like Bill. I do my homework! If you *are* a killer, why the fuck would you let me suffer like this! I'm giving myself up, Jack. Either accept my surrender or come out here and end it!"

Kevin paused in his shuffling. He leaned out and eyed the hill behind him to see if Jack would answer. When a rolling cacophony of thunder came as his only response, Kevin turned his attention back to the stone. "Water," Jack saw him mouth. Kevin winced again as he touched the wound at his side. He shook his head and took a deep breath before dropping the hand clutching the cloth-bound stone into the shallow pool. There was a moment of confusion, then his eyes went wide and his lips pulled back into a stunned grin.

Jack stepped out from the bushes twenty feet away, directly facing him. Kevin barely seemed to notice, looking up with a disoriented laugh only as Jack racked the lever of his rifle.

"Jack," he gasped. "It's amazing."

The tree trunk directly over Kevin's head spattered with red. Kevin's head snapped back, and his limp body toppled forward and splashed into the shallow, stagnant pool. Jack racked the rifle again and lowered it to the prostrate corpse. Seeing the canyon of brains and broken skull his bullet had carved along the top of Kevin's head, Jack knew he wouldn't need another bullet.

"You were wrong, old man," Jack muttered, conjuring the image of his father. "That didn't feel like a damn thing."

He slung his rifle and crossed the brook to Kevin's corpse. Flipping on the dull headlamp, Jack reached down to retrieve the stone. As his hand entered the water, he felt its warm, creeping embrace. He had to fight to not allow himself to fall under its hypnotizing spell. Moving quickly, he pocketed the wrapped stone and fished his revolver from Kevin's pack. The pistol was soaked through, and the three cartridges within were probably useless, he mused, shoving it into its holster. It didn't matter, though. The fight was over.

As he tossed the pack aside and made to leave, a horrifying gasp cut the air behind him. He spun as Kevin's body snapped upright. The dark divot of exposed brains glinted in the rain and the yellow beam of the headlamp shone on his horrified features. His eyes bugged out of his head in shock. They darted around the forest for a split second, then focused on Jack as an earsplitting scream broke free from his lips.

Jack stared in stunned silence.

Kevin was dead. His brains were…

The stone.

Jack grasped for his slung rifle, but Kevin's hands were already on the pistol strapped to his leg. He fired several rounds through the holster and into the earth before ripping it free and firing wildly in Jack's direction. The booming gunshots sounded hollow beside the hellish screams.

XL

Jack

"JACK! WHY did you do this to me?"

The words pursued Jack just as they had for the past seven years, only now they were howled in anguish and accompanied by gunfire.

He sprinted through the trees, Kevin's throaty, tortured screams echoing all around. He had no idea what direction he was heading — it didn't even matter at this point. The only thing he could do was try to outpace the moaning abomination that was crashing through the underbrush behind him with complete abandon.

"Jack!" Kevin's words were hoarse and slurred, and his cadence was broken as if he'd forgotten half the language. They pursued Jack, hot on his tail. "Jack, where you go?"

He didn't respond. His lungs burned almost as bad as his legs. Another peppering of bullets snapped through the forest around him, whacking into trees and hissing through shrubs.

"Jack, there… there's nothing else! Nothing!" Kevin's screams had turned into wails amid the sporadic shooting.

Jack's prosthetic caught on a root and he fell, tumbling down a shallow ravine and almost losing his rifle. He pulled it up in both hands and fired three rounds in rapid succession toward the sound of his pursuer.

Kevin's moaning shifted once again, this time to an enraged, wet screech. "No! No! No! Not going back!"

Jack clambered to his feet and ran harder. The trees quickly began to thin, and despite the darkness and the rain, he recognized the area around him. His path had brought him straight east toward the cliffs. To a small, mostly forested offshoot peninsula along the ocean's edge.

Fuck.

He'd be cornered here if he pushed too much farther, trapped between the Kevin and a plummeting death.

Another barrage of automatic gunfire snapped through the thinning trees. Jack dove for cover behind a thin birch.

"Jack! Give me! Give me rock!" Kevin's words were heavy and sounded like his mouth was overflowing with saliva. "I won't… I won't kill, just give me!"

Jack tried to key in on the noise. Between the crashing of the nearby waves, the wind, the rain, and the relentless sound of his own ragged breathing, he only had a rough idea of where Kevin was. He took a guess and fired.

Kevin's enraged scream echoed back. "No! Jack, stop it! I won't go back!"

Jack shook the horrifying voice from his head and stumbled to his feet once more. With no other choice and no feasible cover in sight, he sprinted onward through the ever-thinning forest, toward the boom of crashing waves.

"Jack, come back!" Kevin moaned, his voice growing louder. "Come back!"

The forest ended in a wavy, overgrown field a good thirty yards before the cliff's edge. Near the tip of the peninsula, a narrow, rocky outcropping stood as the only cover from the sporadic 9mm rounds that hissed through the air at Jack's back. He waded through the sea of wind-turned, waist-high grass and managed to dive behind the handful of boulders just as Kevin let loose another long burst. He pulled his body in as close as he could as the bullets clacked off the stone at his back.

"Come get me, Kevin!" Jack shouted over the wind and thunderous waves below.

Another spattering of 9mm came as a response. Kevin might have been missing a good chunk of his brain, but even so, he apparently wasn't stupid enough to cross into the open.

"Jack," the heavy voice sobbed from the tree line. "Jack, it hurts!"

"Just give up then!" Jack screamed back, focusing on the direction of the noise. "Let go!"

"No, Jack, no! I can't go back! I'll never go back! Please, don't make me…"

Jack checked the rifle's tube — it was empty. He had one bullet in the chamber and that was it. "I won't make you, bud. Just… just stop trying to shoot me. We'll figure it out, okay?"

Kevin's sobbing moans lessened, but his slur had worsened. "You help me, Jack?"

"Yeah," Jack called, flicking the safety off. "Just… I need you to come out, okay? We'll both come out — into the open. Okay, bud?"

There was a pause, then Kevin shouted, "Yeah, yeah, Jack. You'll help me. Please, you have to help me, Jack."

"I will. Just… come out real slow, and I will too. Okay, Kevin?" Jack called, slowly rising with the rifle held over his head. As he emerged, he spotted Kevin's hunched silhouette stumble out from behind the cover of trees. His gait was canted, and the submachine gun hung limp from his chest.

"Kevin," Jack called. "I want you to come over here, alright?"

"It hurts… it hurts to move." Kevin motioned a limp wrist toward the center of the field. The second his hand raised away from the sub-machine gun, Jack swung his own rifle down to his shoulder, lined it up, and fired. The bullet missed entirely, and after a moment of shock,

Kevin stumbled back into the trees. Jack dropped back into cover just in time to avoid Kevin's returned fire.

"Fuck!" Jack screamed as bullets ricocheted off the outcropping. He had nothing, no recourse outside of what, the knife? Three soggy revolver rounds? Kevin's vest had been covered in several thin 9mm magazines. Kevin could wait him out, and the minute he realized Jack was out of ammo…

But Kevin wouldn't have to wait long.

Sophie was still bleeding out. It had already been too long. If Jack didn't get to her soon—

Another burst of incoming bullets derailed his train of thought.

He needed to end this.

Jack's mind raced for a solution. He had the knife, the pistol, an empty rifle, and an almost dead headlamp. What the fuck good were any of those in this situation? If he couldn't kill Kevin — again — then maybe he could escape, beat him back to the manor and… and what? Even if Jack somehow managed to make it past him, how long until the maniacal invalid stumbled his way back there and killed the lot of them?

No. Escape wasn't an option.

Jack's eyes wandered over the cliffside, then down to his hands. They were shaking and pruned and felt creaky as he tightened his grip on the rifle.

"Jaaaaack!" Kevin was crying even harder now. "Jack, I don't want to send you there!"

"Shut the fuck up!" Jack yelled back. He turned the rifle over in his hands and considered its weight as a club.

"Jack, listen!" Kevin drawled. "It's nothing. Just… I went there, Jack, to the Nothing, and I'm not going back. I don't want to send you there either. Just give me the stone!"

The sling tangled around Jack's arm as he gave the rifle a test swing. He unclipped the woven paracord strap and dropped it into the mud at his feet, then stopped and stared at it.

It won't work. It's stupid, Jack thought, leaning the rifle back on the stones and picking up the sling.

"Jaaack, please!" Kevin screamed and let loose another burst.

"Fuck it," Jack muttered. He pulled the knife from its sheath and sliced the end of the woven sling. The paracord slid loose and unraveled from its tight weaves, growing longer with each rushed tug. Only once it was entirely unraveled did he tie one end tight around the center of the rifle. He then slid the rifle between two of the outcropping's large boulders, the paracord extending from between the two boulders like an anchor line. He scrambled to tie a wide slipknot on the opposite end of the cord, then stepped into it.

The cliff's jutting edge was only ten feet away, and by his estimates he had maybe twice that length in slacked paracord. Pulling the slipknot tight around his chest, he took a long breath and considered what he was about to do.

"Kevin!" he shouted. "I'm taking the stone, and I'm going to jump now!"

"What? No!" Kevin screamed. "You're a liar!"

"I wish," Jack said to himself.

He took a deep breath, then sprinted forward to the cliff's edge. Rapid gunshots erupted behind him and the air was filled with the snap of passing bullets. Then he was airborne, plummeting into the rainy void. For a moment, he was weightless, then the paracord slipknot wrenched tight around his chest like a hangman's noose, the thin cord digging painfully into his armpits. The swinging momentum of the jump brough him crashing back into the cliff face, dazing him and drawing a hint of déjà vu. The iron taste of blood was thick in his mouth as he wrenched his body to face the rough rock wall, then struggled to walk his legs up and plant his feet against the vertical façade. There he stood, suspended horizontally three hundred feet over the crashing ocean, the cord biting so hard into his spine that he thought it might break.

"Jack! No!" Kevin's prolonged scream grew louder as Jack fought to steady himself and draw the revolver. Then Kevin's head darted into sight, leaning out over the cliff edge a dozen feet above. He was barely a silhouette against the dark, rolling clouds above. Jack yanked the hammer back, lined up the barrel, and pulled the trigger. The gun gave a wet click.

"Jack!" Kevin sounded surprised. Far out over the ocean, a chain of lightning flashed, illuminating his face. The canyon that cut through the top of his head had stopped bleeding, and the exposed portion of his brain was gray and dead-looking. One of his eyes bulged out, staring into nothingness, and thick lines of rabid drool hung from his gaping mouth, whipping away in the wind. Jack yanked back the hammer again.

"Why'd you do this to me?" Kevin moaned.

The pistol kicked, and the dark silhouette jerked back. Hot blood rained down on Jack alongside the cold raindrops, and Kevin's body toppled forward over the cliff.

DAY 10

*"Why should not my cheeks be starved and my face drawn?
Despair is in my heart, and my face is the face
of one who has made a long journey."*
    — *Epic of Gilgamesh*

XLI

Jack

JACK PUSHED open the manor's front door. Bill lay propped up against the foyer wall. His head snapped up and he leveled a small pistol at Jack's chest. Jack stared at him for a second in return, almost wishing the pudgy old shit would pull the trigger. But once Bill realized who it was, his arm went slack and dropped back to his side.

"Jack..." he started weakly.

Jack ignored him, instead whisking by and crossing to Sophie. The storm had slowed on his trek back, and the horizon glowed just enough with dawn to cast the room in a dark blue hue.

Sophie lay unmoving just where he had left her. She looked peaceful, almost as if she'd simply drifted off to sleep waiting for him to return. Only her eyes lay half open.

"I'm sorry..." Bill went on, shutting his eyes and beginning to cry. "I tried, but... there was nothing I could..."

Jack sank down beside her. Her hands were cold, but he held them regardless.

"How long ago?" he asked.

Bill wiped his face and drew in a shuddered breath. "Maybe five, ten minutes after you left."

She had lied about feeling the remnant warmth from the stone. She knew there was nothing left in her system. She must have known she would bleed out.

"Did you catch Kevin?" The tiniest bit of hopefulness leaked into Bill's voice.

"No," Jack lied.

"There's still hope though, I mean, if you do manage to. Maybe we could try to bring her back like last time—"

"No," Jack said again, this time harsher.

Sophie's face was smooth and full, unmarred by frostbite. She looked at rest, as if she could wake right up if he were to just ignite the spark of life in her beautiful, vacant blue eyes.

He thought of the stone in his pocket. How bad could it be? She'd only just gone, and there was no canyon carved through her head... Maybe it would be different. Maybe she'd just come back, like waking up from a cold, hollow sleep. How many times had he wished he could have brought Sam back? A thousand? A million? Now here he was, once again beside someone he'd failed. Only this time, he *could* bring her back.

Kevin's face, the disfigured features twisted in a horrified, pleading glare, haunted his mind. He pulled his hand away from where it had subconsciously come to rest on the lump in his pocket. "No," he repeated softy. "Some things you have to just... accept."

"But Jack—"

"Where'd you get the gun?" Jack asked, gently pushing her eyes shut and forcing himself to turn away.

Bill looked down on the small pistol. "It was in Kevin's room. I thought, well, I thought there might be something else out there, just like you said there could be. I needed to be prepared."

"Was there anything else useful up there?"

"No," Bill said, nursing his wounded arm like a baby. "Not really, just computer stuff. Jack, I think he turned off the satellite when we uncovered the stone. Maybe we could get it working—"

"You think that, huh? You sure you didn't tell him to so no one would get away with your precious artifact?" Jack shook his head.

"*Excuse me*—" Bill started with an angry look, but he caught himself. "Look, I'm sorry about what happened, but I didn't know about him. How *could* I have known—"

"It doesn't matter now." Jack rose and crossed to Bill, who grimaced as Jack hoisted him to his feet. "We need to go. Those things — Maedig and his men — they had two thousand years to prepare this place for people like us. I'm not about to sit around and wait for the next surprise."

"Yeah," Bill agreed. "You're right. What do we about…" He looked from Sophie to the creatures' bodies, and then to the mound of Bianchi that had been kicked into a corner during the scuffle.

"What does the stove run on?" Jack making for the kitchen.

"A propane tank just out the back of the house. Why?"

Jack dropped to his hands and knees in front of the stove, rooting under it until he found the line, then ripped it free. "Go wait outside."

Bill gave a worried look, then hustled out onto the porch. Jack crossed back to the dining room. He gave Sophie's hand one last squeeze, then grabbed one of the wax logs from beside the fireplace, placed it at the center of the dining room table, and lit it.

IT WAS ten minutes before the explosion, and another fifteen before the flames fully engulfed the rain-soaked manor. It heaved and groaned as the windows spewed long, dark clouds of smoke. Jack stood at the edge of the cliffs, facing the ocean, and listened to the distant, raging flames as they battled the ebbing rain to consume the old Victorian mansion. He didn't turn back as the decrepit corpse finally gave in, the turrets each collapsing inward with a final, echoing wail.

"We should go," Bill said nervously. "Someone might see the smoke from the ocean. I'm not sure… you know, how we would explain all of this."

Jack knew he was right. Still, he had a hard time tearing his eyes away from the sea.

It's nothing.

Kevin's slurred plea echoed in his ears.

It's nothing…

Was nothing so bad?

"Jack?" Bill's voice prodded him.

"What?" Jack asked.

"We need to go," Bill said softy.

"Fine."

THE SUN rose, glinting off the ocean and driving the rain back into fat, random sprinkles. Gulls called in the distance, and the howling wind had retreated, replaced by a gentle breeze.

They walked south along the cliffs. Bill had claimed they would make it to a seaside town eventually if they pushed on in that direction, and that once they found it, he could call an elite travel service that would take them wherever they needed to go. Jack had no intention of traveling with the pudgy millionaire at length, but for now his mind was full — he didn't see another obvious path.

"I didn't think I'd live to see this," Bill stammered, a little breathless from their pace.

Jack ignored him, walking a bit faster in the hopes that it would discourage his unwelcomed companion from wasting air.

"It's just, you know, I— uh… When that thing had me, when it slashed my throat… I really did think that was it." Bill gave a weak laugh. "You think we'll ever catch Kevin?"

"No."

"Oh, well, I hope you're wrong…" Bill muttered, failing to make pace and falling behind. "Do you think, you know, he'll use it for good?"

"I don't know." Jack refused to look back.

"What would you do with it?" Bill asked. "I know Sophie said we should hide it, but do you believe that? That something like that should be hidden away? Stolen from the people?"

"I don't know, Bill."

"It's just that," Bill stammered. "I… I think of my mother, when she was sick. I think of all those hospital wards full of dying children, needlessly suffering. I think of cancer, AIDS, Ebola, all those terrible—"

"Enough," Jack commanded. "It doesn't matter. Kevin's gone, and so is the stone."

"I spoke to Sophie about it before she passed."

Jack sucked his teeth as anger welled deep in his belly.

"She changed her mind. She thought we could harness it for good. She said if she died, she wanted you to—"

"Shut the fuck up, Bill," Jack muttered, picking up the pace even more.

"Jack, come on," Bill pleaded, falling farther behind. "Just think about all the good we could do."

"Why does it matter? It's gone."

Bill's footsteps came to a halt. "Jack, I know you're lying. I know you have it. I can *feel* it coming off you."

Jack stopped walking. He slowly turned. Bill stood panting a dozen feet away.

"So what if I do?"

"We need to *use* it," Bill insisted. "Not hide it away like some selfish fools. Share it with me. Think of all that we can do with it! You and I, Jack, with my resources and your, uh… well, you know, we could accomplish *so much*."

"It'll never see the light of day again," Jack said flatly.

"What, you're going to do the same thing those monsters did? Keep it for yourself in some dingy cave while the world around you suffers?" Bill spat the words out desperately. "How can you be so selfish?"

Jack sighed. "Did Sophie ever tell you the one about the Accursed Huntsman?"

"No. I don't know, maybe? What the hell does that have to do with anything?"

Jack couldn't help but smile at the memory of enjoying the warm summer night with Sophie on the porch. It felt like ages ago. "I can't stop thinking about it this morning. It's the story of this guy way back in the olden days. All he wants to do is hunt his fucking deer. But he gets old and he's gonna eat shit just like the rest of us, so he strikes a deal with gods that lets him hunt forever. The thing is that this deal ends up being a monkey's paw. You know, a King Midas type deal. Just another trope of a guy who gets greedy and the powers that be fuck him for it."

Jack scanned Bill like he would a wild animal. The fat little man's shoulders were slumped forward. His right foot was placed just a half step behind the left, and his hands open and tense at his sides. Whether intentional or not, it was a stance of aggression. Jack couldn't help but notice the handle of the small pistol protruding from within Bill's pocket, and he thought of his own revolver holstered at his side, and the single waterlogged bullet chambered within.

"At least that's what I thought when she first told it to me," Jack went on. "Now, I'm not so sure. I'm thinking it never really had much to do with greed. It doesn't matter why he wanted what he wanted. It could have been greed or lust or honor or love, it all still would have turned out the same. Eternity… it's a curse. Regardless of circumstances."

"It's not a curse, it's a gift. You just need to use it right—" Bill insisted.

"You're just proving my point, bud. Too much of *anything* is a curse. I mean, look at *you*. You were born with the whole world just sitting right in the palm of your hand. Now look what you turned out as— just a completely worthless, volatile, selfish piece of shit."

Bill's face convulsed in surprise. "Excuse me? Who the hell do you think—"

"You're the worst of us all, Bill." Jack could hear the apathy in his own voice. "But eternity is a curse I wouldn't even wish on you."

Bill stood there, stunned, as Jack turned away and resumed walking.

"Fuck you…" Bill's muttered voice carried on the wind alongside another noise.

Jack wasn't sure if he heard it right. A light click, like the hammer being drawn back on a small pistol. He took a deep, steadying breath then drew his revolver and spun.

A single gunshot rang out over the cliffs.

EPILOGUE

A COOL fall breeze penetrated the rural cabin. It whistled in through the broken window above the sink and wound around the disheveled chaos of old furniture and weather-beaten appliances.

While the frame of the old structure still stood strong months after its abandonment, its soul had already begun to meld together with the vast Maine wilderness that surrounded it. The door hung loosely from its hinges, bearing the claw marks of a hungry black bear that had come exploring for food weeks before. Orange and yellow leaves lay strewn atop the derelict floors and counters. A fine film of pollen coated nearly everything, revealing countless zigzagging trails of scurrying mice and rats. A chickadee's nest balanced in the rafters, and a single chipmunk had taken up residence in a cabinet bearing a scotch tape label reading *Chewie Snacks*. Now the dog biscuits were little more than a pile of crumbs beneath a mound of stored acorns.

The air was alive with the murmur of life. The scratch of tiny paws on wood intermingled with the whistling of distant birds. The shuffling gait of a possum wading through the sea of leaves outside broke through the cicada's high-pitched drone, and somewhere far away a doe snorted at an unknown threat. What was once a home for a man and his dog had now become a place of solace for all the wild things that scurried and scampered and fluttered.

The phone in the corner rang. In an instant, the symphony of the woodland creatures cut silent. It rang again and again until finally a voice sounded from the machine.

"This is Jack, leave a message."

There was a sharp tone, then an older woman's voice filled the room.

"Hey, Jack. It's Catherine, again. I know this is, well, it must be the sixth or seventh message I've left, and I guess I should probably take the hint, huh?" There was a short, pained laugh. "I just… I just want to know you're okay. We missed you at the fundraiser. It was small, but we managed to get enough to— Well, the real reason I'm calling is because I thought you'd want to know that Olivia is doing better. A lot better, actually. The doctors weren't very optimistic at first… No, that's not right. They were pretty certain that she was terminal, but… well, you know her, she's a fighter. Just like her brother. They're still running some tests, but they're saying now that she's likely to make a full recovery. I know it sounds silly, but it still feels like a miracle. Hell, even one of the doctors called it that." Her voice cracked then drifted away for a moment, silence once again enveloping the cabin. "That's all. I just wanted to let you know and tell you that we love you and hope you're doing okay up there. I'll, uh… I'll try you again later, I guess. I hope you're well. Goodbye, Jack."

For a long moment the cabin remained dead silent. Then, slowly, the birds began to sing. The scratching began again as the cicadas resumed their drone, and the possum ambled on.

ACKNOWLEDGEMENTS

First, I must give thanks to everyone at Emerson College who helped me to enhance both this story and my skills as a writer. More specifically, I would like to thank Professors Edwin Hill and Jon Papernick for their invaluable insights. I would also like to thank Professor George Baroud for his eye-opening seminars in mythology. Many thanks to student editors Kime and Ellie for their many hours spent grinding and polishing the roughness away. I owe a debt of gratitude to my trusted beta readers: Peter DiFilippo, Tim Lyons, Suzanne Piecuch, Robin Kerber, and all those who took time to sift through the relative nonsense that made up the early versions of this manuscript. Special thanks to the workers at the Glenlivet distillery, without whom this book likely never would have been completed. An overwhelming thanks goes out to my family, who have always gone above and beyond in supporting my endeavors, no matter how foolhardy. Most of all I have to thank my editor and beloved wife, Patience, for her countless hours of hard work and her neverending supply of… patience.

Also by Douglass Hoover

THE HOMESTEAD

Centered deep in the Alaskan bush, the Homestead offers a primal refuge for young men and women disenchanted by the modern era. Only accessible via helicopter or a series of rugged, treacherous trails, this Thoreauvian utopia stands as a testament to humanity's ability to thrive in its natural state.

But when a bear attack kicks off an increasingly violent chain of events, the secrets of the Homestead's founder, Augustin Stark, risk being brought into the light. As he grapples to keep the family he's created together, a malevolent outside force joins the fray. One that threatens to destroy not only the community, but the people themselves.

Praise for The Homestead

"This is a thriller with a capital T. Intrigue, action, adventure and mystery all combine to make this an unforgettable novel in every respect. Superbly written with a breath-taking pace, the story sprints into action from the very beginning... An excellent and exciting read."
—Readers' Favorite

"It's one that refuses to be disregarded or easily forgotten, particularly given its jaw-dropping ending. A passionate, sometimes-brutal tale of violence begetting violence."
—Kirkus Reviews

"Hoover pulls no punches—there is blood, language, and violence comparable to reality, and that is a big part of what makes this book so damned good... If you appreciate verisimilitude in what you read or watch on film... this is a book for you. I loved it."
—Lex Allen, Author

"High-quality, highly violent fiction... The Homestead is a book about survival, about love for your brothers, about sacrificing for the people you care about. But, it is also a cautionary tale of the vainglorious nature of violence... I rate this stirring piece of soul-searching a solid four spades and recommend that any of you looking to get lost while also finding something out about yourself scoop this thing up and give it a go."
—OAF Nation

About the Author

Douglass Hoover is the author of *The Homestead* and *The Accursed Huntsman*. He is a Marine Corps veteran and holds an MFA from Emerson College. His days are spent writing and blacksmithing on his small farm in rural Maine with his wife, Patience, and their three mutts, Bug, Furiosa, and Skootcha Nunchuck Monsterface.

Follow their adventures on Instagram @StripedDogForge or at www.stripeddogforge.com